**Don't miss these terrific thrillers
by William Bernhardt!**

PRIMARY JUSTICE
BLIND JUSTICE
DEADLY JUSTICE
PERFECT JUSTICE
NAKED JUSTICE
DOUBLE JEOPARDY

BB
Ballantine / Del Rey /
Fawcett / Ivy

S0-BBB-015

ISBN 0-345-41807-7

U.S. $3.50/Canada $4.50

9 780345 418074

50350

EAN

WILLIAM
BERNHARDT

CRUEL
JUSTICE

CRUEL JUSTICE

William Bernhardt

BALLANTINE BOOKS • NEW YORK

This book contains an excerpt from the hardcover edition of *Naked Justice* by William Bernhardt. This excerpt has been set for this edition only and may not reflect the final content of the hardcover edition.

Copyright © 1996 by William Bernhardt
Excerpt from *Naked Justice* copyright © 1997 by William Bernhardt

All rights reserved under International and Pan-American Copyright Conventions. Published in the United States by Ballantine Books, a division of Random House, Inc., New York, and simultaneously in Canada by Random House of Canada Limited, Toronto.

http://www.randomhouse.com

ISBN 0-345-41807-7

Manufactured in the United States of America

First Edition: November 1997

10 9 8 7 6 5 4 3 2 1

*For
my father
and
my son*

Yet in my lineaments they trace
Some features of my father's face.
—LORD BYRON (1788–1824), "PARISINA"

* *

Prologue

ONE

*   *

Twenty-five Years
Before

"It's dark in here, Daddy."

The boy doesn't know how long he has been in the closet, tied to this chair. He doesn't know what time it is, or even what day it is. He knows he is hungry. And thirsty. And scared.

Very, very scared.

"Please, Daddy. I don't like it in the dark."

The ropes chafe against his wrists and burn his skin. His legs and groin are sore and sticky. He doesn't know how many times he has wet himself. He's been in here so long.

"Daddy? Mommy? Please help me."

He knows they are out there. Daddy is listening, laughing maybe. Mommy is out there, too. She won't laugh, but she won't do anything. She never does. She pretends she doesn't hear, pretends she doesn't know what's happening. But she knows.

He rocks back and forth, straining against the ropes. "Please, Daddy! I can't stand it in here. I'll do anything you want. I'll—"

The door opens. The sudden brightness is blinding. The boy scrunches his eyes closed, then slowly opens them as he adjusts to the light.

His father towers over him. He can't see his father's face, just the outline of his immense body silhouetted in the closet door. He is everywhere and endless, like an enormous shadow, a real-life bogeyman.

Suddenly the boy is far more frightened than he had been when he was alone.

"You're a dirty boy," his father growls. Even in the darkness, the child knows his father's fists are balled up—two tremendous battering rams. The boy wants to escape, but the ropes hold him fast to the chair.

"Are you ready for your punishment?" His father's voice booms and echoes in the tiny closet.

"But I didn't do anything, Daddy. Honest I didn't!"

"Shut up." One of the huge fists strikes the boy across the face. "I've had enough of your lies. Lying is a sin against God. Don't you know that, you ignorant boy?"

The child wants to answer, but his whole body is trembling and he can't control his voice.

"I checked your sheets. They were wet. Again." His father leans in closer, his huge head swallowing the light. "What did I tell you would happen if you did that again?"

The boy forces words from his throat. "I—I didn't mean to, Daddy. I tried to hold it, but—"

"Shut up." Another fist batters the boy, this time on the other cheek. He begins to cry.

"Pansy. Weak, dirty pansy. Don't think I don't know what you do when I'm not around. I've seen you. Touching yourself. I've seen the way you look at your mother, too, when she parades around in her underwear and her high-heeled shoes like some—"

He leans in even closer, till his nose is barely an inch from his son's face and the boy can smell his hot, whiskey-soaked breath. "You're a dirty boy. And you won't be clean till you've taken your punishment."

"Please don't," the boy cries, his voice quivering. "Please, please don't."

"You have to be punished."

"I don't want to hurt, Daddy. Please!"

His father draws back. His voice becomes oddly calm. "I brought someone to see you." He holds up a small stuffed animal.

"Oliver!" It's the boy's teddy bear. "Thank you, Daddy. I missed—"

His father jerks the bear away. "Since you won't take your punishment, Oliver will have to take it for you."

"No!" The boy's eyes are impossibly wide. He realizes what his father is about to do. "Please, Daddy! *No!*"

His father's huge hands clutch the bear's head and rip it off. The foam stuffing spills out from the neck onto the boy's head.

"Noooo!" he cries, choking as the foam falls into his mouth. "You're killing him!"

"Oliver isn't dead yet," his father replies. "But he will be. Because you betrayed him." The father withdraws a lighter from his pocket. The flame casts an eerie glow on his face. It makes his eyes seem red, evil, like the pictures of the devil the boy has seen in his mother's Bible.

"Don't do it, Daddy! *Please!*"

The father ignites the teddy bear. When it is nothing more than a ball of flame and embers, the father tosses it into a trash barrel.

"You killed him!" the boy wails, tears streaking his face. "You killed Oliver!"

"No, I didn't," his father replies. "You did. You were a dirty bad boy and you wouldn't take your punishment, so Oliver had to take it for you. It's your fault. You killed him." The father folds his mighty arms across his chest. "Are you ready to take your punishment now?"

The boy finds he cannot answer. He is crying, choking, gasping for air.

"I said, *are you ready?*" his father bellows.

"I guess so," the boy whispers.

The father pulls himself erect. "Well, then. That's more like it. Good boys always take their punishment. You make Daddy very happy when you take your punishment."

He says more, but the boy doesn't hear it. He's already distancing himself, relocating to that faraway place he goes to when his father punishes him. It's the only way he can endure the hurt, the humiliation. The only way he can survive.

In that distant place, he dreams about a better world. A world without closets, without pain. A world free of his father. A world where he will be the punisher, instead of the victim.

TWO

* *

Ten Years Before

Sergeant Sandstrom steered the patrol car down the curving road that wound around Philbrook. The lights inside the museum were off; no one would notice if he drove a bit faster than he should. Anything to drown out that damned harmonica.

"Hey! Watch it!" Sandstrom's partner, a young, baby-faced punk with thick curly black hair, slammed sideways against the door. The impact knocked the harmonica out of his hands. "You spoiled my song."

"Sorry," Sandstrom lied. "Wasn't watching the road." Morelli was okay, as far as kids fresh out of the academy went, but Sandstrom could stand those Bob Dylan songs only so long. Morelli sang worse than Dylan himself, if such a thing was possible. "Did you say you used to play in nightclubs?"

"Yeah. Pizza parlors, campus bars, dives. With a friend of mine."

"And you gave that up for the glamorous world of law enforcement?"

"What can I say? Every night it was the same old same-old. Thunderous applause. Babes throwing themselves at my feet and begging to bear my children. You get tired of that after a while."

"Yeah. I'll bet your wife did, too."

"You got that right." He pulled a wallet-sized photo out of his shirt pocket.

"Oh, jeez," Sandstrom said. "You're not going to start mooning over her picture again, are you?"

11

His partner grinned. "I can't help myself." He sighed. "She's beautiful, isn't she?"

Sandstrom turned the steering wheel hard to the left. "Look, how many times I gotta tell you? This sucker stuff is strictly for newlyweds. You gotta get over it."

Morelli continued gazing at her picture. "Why?"

" 'Cause a cop can't afford to be distracted, that's why. You gotta be . . . focused." Of course, that wasn't the real reason. The real reason Sandstrom hated to see new cops get entangled in whirlwind romances was because they never lasted. History kept repeating itself. Another year, maybe two, and that gorgeous gal Morelli was making goo-goo eyes at would be the biggest liability in his life. But there was no telling him.

Sandstrom had been on the force for over thirteen years, but his partner tonight was an APO (Apprentice Police Officer). Just getting started. Michelangelo A. Morelli—Mike to his friends—was an English major who for some perverse reason had gone to the police academy. Go figure. Mike had all the attributes of a new recruit. A fresh face, not yet worn down by the grind and menace of the patrol. Preposterous idealism and naïveté that bordered on the comical. And an annoying habit of quoting Shakespeare to perps.

"I must be the luckiest guy in the world," Mike said, still gazing fondly at the photo.

"Yeah."

"You wouldn't believe what she did the other day. I came home and she'd bought me a brand-new car. A Corvette. Can you believe that?"

"A Corvette? Christ, kid, can you afford it?"

"That's what I asked her." Mike beamed. "And she said, 'Honey, where you're concerned, money is no object.' "

Sweet sentiment, Sandstrom thought, but the bank might have a different opinion. "So this morning why did I see you parking that beat-up Dodge Omni?"

"Well, Julia had a lot of shopping to do, so she took the new car."

"Ah," Sandstrom said. "I see." He was beginning to, anyway.

They were cruising—gliding, really—down the residential streets of Utica Hills, Tulsa's poshest neighborhood. The exclusive enclave of the old rich. Sandstrom hated this beat. There was rarely any street crime around here at this time of night, but it gratified the well-heeled citizens to know that the boys in blue (brown, actually) were keeping an eye on their swimming pools and Ferraris. Since their bank accounts largely determined who the mayor and city council members were, and thus determined who ran the police department, they tended to get whatever they wanted.

"So how's your lovely bride adjusting to life as a cop's wife?" Sandstrom ventured.

Mike tucked the photo back into his breast pocket. "Oh, Julia's very understanding. All she cares about is my happiness. She doesn't complain at all when I come in late. Just as long as I'm not too tired to . . ." He flushed, suddenly embarrassed. "Well, you know."

"Kid, I truly do not want to hear about this."

"We've been trying to have a baby—"

"Aw, jeez . . ."

"Julia wants a girl, but I want a boy. A little curly-haired Morelli. A chip off the old block. I just hope I can be half the dad to him that mine was to me." His head lowered, and his smile faded somewhat. "We've been going at it every chance we get for a solid six months, but so far, no luck."

"Six months is nothin'. My sister Amelia and her husband tried for eight years before they got their first bundle of joy. Now they have five."

"Really? Julia thought maybe we should see a doctor. Of course, her father's a doctor, so she thinks they're the solution to everything."

Sandstrom winced. "Her father's a doctor?"

"Cardiologist."

"Rich?"

"Like you wouldn't believe."

And you're going to keep her happy on a cop's salary? For the first time Sandstrom's heart went out to the poor schmuck. This marriage was even more doomed than he had realized.

"Julia keeps buying all those home pregnancy test kits. She does about three a night, just to be sure. So far, no luck."

Sandstrom tried to sound reassuring. "Don't worry, pal. You've still got lots of time."

Mike shrugged. "I suppose." He sank down into his seat. "I sure would like to have a kid, though. Our kid."

The police radio crackled. Sandstrom picked up the handset and exchanged a few words with the dispatcher. To Mike's inexperienced ears, it all sounded like unintelligible squawks and static.

"We're on our way." Sandstrom snapped the handset back into place, then bore down on the accelerator.

"What's up?" Mike asked.

"Sounds like a one-eighty-seven."

That meant homicide. "Seriously? Who took out who?"

Sandstrom whipped around a corner, almost taking the car up on two wheels. "No one seems to know yet. On both counts."

"Where did it happen?"

"Utica Greens Country Club."

"Really!" Mike's eyes glistened. "What was the weapon, a polo mallet?"

"You're close. A golf club."

"A golf club? How—"

Mike didn't have a chance to complete his inquiry. Sandstrom soared through the main gates, parked in the front lot beside another patrol car, then jumped out of the car. "Ever seen a murder before, Morelli?"

Mike hedged. "Well, I've seen pictures."

Sandstrom clapped him on the back. "Brace yourself. It isn't the same."

They were greeted by another police officer, a man only slightly older than Mike. He pointed toward a small building at the crest of a hill near the first tee of the golf course. "It's a caddyshack," Patrolman Tompkins explained. "The victim is still inside. I haven't moved her. I was the first to arrive. Homicide hasn't made the scene yet."

As they mounted the hill Mike saw something move about

fifty feet away, on the pillared porch behind the main country-club building. The moonlight glinted, and he had a fleeting impression of blonde hair.

"Look over there," Mike said, pointing. "See? A woman, I think. Moving away from us. Fast. I think she's wearing a white dress."

Tompkins squinted. "I don't see anyone."

Sandstrom grinned. "He's been fantasizing about his gorgeous wife all night. Now he's having visions."

"I saw someone," Mike insisted. He ran into the shadows, trying to find a trace of the figure he had briefly glimpsed. But by the time he arrived, there was no one there. After running all over the general area, he returned to the other officers just outside the caddyshack.

"No gorgeous woman in white?" Sandstrom asked.

"No," Mike replied. "A phantom of delight."

"More literary lingo—la-di-da."

"Don't sweat it," Tompkins told Mike. "We've already got a suspect."

Sandstrom and Mike followed Tompkins into the caddyshack. A black teenage boy cowered near the front door. His face was streaked with tears. He seemed terrified.

"That's the suspect," Tompkins explained.

Mike's eyes crisscrossed the room. "Yeah, so where's the—"

The question caught in his throat. The north corner of the room held all the answers.

Blood was everywhere.

Sandstrom was right. It wasn't like the pictures. Not in the least.

"Oh, my God," Mike mouthed. His words seemed to evaporate before they were spoken. He felt his gorge rising. "Oh, my God. Oh, my God."

He stood there, transfixed, repeating himself until Sandstrom finally led him away to a bathroom where he could be sick.

"Hey, take it easy," Sandstrom said gently. "Try to forget about it."

Even as he hunched there over the porcelain throne, Mike knew he would never forget what he had seen in that caddy-shack. No matter how long he lived, no matter how many corpses he saw.

Never.

Gnats swarmed around her head and the thick clotted blood on her neck. Even in death, she stood erect, pinioned against the wall, as if crucified for unimaginable sins.

THREE

* *

Now

Harold Rutherford met his wife, Rachel, at the front door of the elegant main foyer of the Utica Greens Country Club. Sweat dripped from his brow, and a golf club was cocked over his shoulder.

"Where's Abie?" he asked.

"I sent him in to have his picture taken," Rachel said. "Isn't that why we're here?"

Rutherford pressed his lips together in that subtle and thoroughly annoying way he had of expressing irritation. "I wanted us to have our picture taken together."

"The group portrait was scheduled for ten. You're fifteen minutes late," Rachel said sharply. "And you're a mess." She had a few ways of expressing irritation herself.

Rutherford checked his watch. "I was in a board meeting."

Rachel's eyes conveyed her disbelief. "You've been outside."

"We decided to take in nine holes while we talked."

"That doesn't explain why you're late."

He stared at her uncomprehendingly. "Well, I couldn't just leave."

"Why not?"

He cast his eyes skyward. "You don't understand."

"Hal, Western civilization wouldn't crumble because you left a country-club board meeting a few minutes early."

"I have responsibilities. . . ."

"You have a responsibility to your son! Your family! You talk a good talk, babbling to your buddies about what a devoted

19

father you are, and you insist that we come in for these family portraits, so you can have something showy to hang on your wall, but when it comes right down to it, you put everything else before your family."

"That isn't true."

"It is. Sometimes I think you never wanted—"

He cut her off with a harsh glare. "I can't believe you would say that. I love my son."

"Does he know that?"

The question took him aback. "Well . . . what a stupid question. Of course he does."

"Are you sure?"

"Yes," Rutherford answered her. "He knows. I'm sure."

Royce waited patiently for the boy to enter the country-club ballroom. He passed the time by thumbing through the Polaroids he'd snapped so far that morning. No. No. Definitely not. Too old. Too fair. Just not right.

The sound of the heavy wooden door closing reverberated through the cavernous room. Quickly, Royce put the Polaroids back in his satchel and stepped behind his portrait camera.

"You must be Abie," Royce said, glancing at his master list. "Abie Rutherford."

"Yeah." Royce judged the boy to be about nine or ten. He had dark hair, dark features. His locks swooped wildly across his head and dangled down onto his forehead. He was wearing a loose Polo T-shirt and a Drillers baseball cap.

He was lovely.

Royce pressed his hand over his mouth, concealing his smile.

This was the one.

"I thought we were going to have a family portrait," Royce said as the boy positioned himself on the stool.

"We were s'posed to," the boy said sullenly. "My dad didn't show up."

"That's a shame." Royce fidgeted with the camera settings. "Will your father be wanting the economy ten-pic pack, the standard-size twenty-five assorted pack, or the super-deluxe combo sixty-pic pack?"

The boy shrugged. "My dad prob'ly won't buy any of them."

Royce huddled down over the lens and focused. "Looks like you're a Drillers fan."

"So?"

"Does your dad take you to the ball games?"

Abie's fake camera smile disappeared. "No."

"Why not?"

Abie didn't answer.

"Come on, you can tell me. Who am I going to tell? I'm just a photographer."

Abie considered. "My dad never takes me anywhere. He says ball games are for ordinary people. Drones, he calls them." He folded his arms unhappily. "I think he hates me."

Royce nodded sympathetically. "And your mom?"

"She doesn't hate me. She's always arguing with my dad. I hate it when they argue."

"Poor thing." Royce walked around the camera, smiled, then pressed his hand against Abie's cheek. "All right now, tilt your head to the side. A little more. That's it."

Royce reached down and adjusted Abie's clothes, running his hands down the boy's arms and legs. "There you are. What a perfect child. A photographer's dream."

Royce pressed his eye to the viewfinder and started clicking. He took twice as many pictures as normal. He couldn't be too careful; he wanted to make sure he had a flattering photo for his friend's scrutiny.

"You really are a delightful subject," Royce remarked. "Have you ever thought about becoming a professional model?"

"A model?" Abie's face wrinkled. "What kind of dumb job is that? I'm going to be a baseball player."

"Of course." Royce finished the roll of film in the camera, then surreptitiously took a shot with each of his two Polaroids. "There now. That'll do it."

The boy hopped off the stool. "Can I go now?"

"Of course you can." Royce reached out and patted Abie on the head. "Have a nice day, sweet boy."

As soon as he finished for the day, Royce packed up his equipment and drove directly to his friend's apartment, a separate room behind a house on the North Side.

"What are you doing here?" his friend asked, anything but friendly. "Haven't I told you never to come here?"

"I couldn't wait," Royce said enthusiastically. "And I knew you wouldn't want me to, either. I have something you're going to love."

"I'll be surprised. You haven't come up with anything suitable for weeks."

"How quickly you forget. I found the kid that—" Royce stopped, immediately realizing his mistake.

"Yes, you were responsible for that, weren't you?" His friend's eyes became two small beads buried deeply beneath a heavy brow. "Believe me, I haven't forgotten."

Royce reached for his satchel. He was so nervous he dropped it while fumbling with the buckle. "Wasn't my fault," he mumbled. "I always do the best I can for you. Fat lot I get in return."

"I got you this gig for the country-club photo directory, didn't I?"

"Right, right." Royce pulled out one of the Polaroids. "Take a look at this."

His friend snatched the photo from Royce's hands. There was a sudden intake of breath. "You took this picture at the country club?"

"Yes. This morning."

His friend frowned. That was a bit close to home. "Who is it?"

"You don't know?"

"You think I have time to keep up with everyone's kids? What's his name?"

"On the flip side."

His friend turned over the photo and reacted first with

surprise, then, gradually, with delight. "Perfect. Absolutely perfect."

Royce was relieved. "Then . . . he's the one?"

"Oh, yes," his friend said breathlessly. "He's the one. He's the one I want."

ONE

*   *

Don't Be Such a Sucker

* 1 *

The instant Ben pushed open his office door, three men with briefcases sprang to their feet.

"Mr. Kincaid!" they shouted in unison.

Bill collectors, Ben thought unhappily. He could spot 'em anywhere. Why did everyone expect Ben to pay his bills on time? None of his clients did. "Sorry, gents, I'm on my way to an important meeting."

The three men flung invoices in his path, but Ben side-stepped them and rushed to Jones's desk in the center of the lobby.

"Jones," he said sotto voce, "please tell me I have an important meeting this morning."

Jones, Ben's office assistant, pushed a thick expanding file across his desk. "Even better. You're due in court. The Johnson case, remember? Continued from last week. Judge Hart awaits."

"Right, right. Of course I remember," Ben bluffed. "This is the public inebriation case, right?"

"Close. Solicitation."

Ben thumbed hurriedly through the file. "Well, that's what I meant. Where's Christina?"

"Excuse me, sir. I must insist." One member of the briefcase brigade tapped Ben on the shoulder. "My name is Scott Scofield, and I represent the Arctic Breath Air Company. I'm concerned—"

"You're the one who installed the air conditioner."

"Well, my company did. Certainly I was not personally involved in the installation of your unit." Scofield adjusted his tie. "At any rate, your payments are woefully behind schedule."

Ben pointed toward the machine in question. "This pathetic bucket of bolts you sold me hasn't worked since day one!"

"Perhaps you should consider our extended care package for your unit. Of course, I'm not at liberty to offer it to you while your account is in arrears, but once everything is in order, and assuming you have not made any unauthorized alterations to the unit or attempted to repair it yourself, you could take advantage of our long-term maintenance service. This particular unit . . ."

Scofield droned on. Ben waited patiently for the man to take a breath. He wasn't going to permit him to slide by with the standard salesman snappy patter. This was serious business. The temperature in Tulsa was over a hundred, and had been for almost a month. August in Tulsa was never a picnic, but this summer had been a record-breaking sweatfest. As a rule, Ben was not fond of summer, and he liked it even less when the air conditioner in his apartment worked only sporadically and the clunker in his office didn't work at all.

Ben detected a momentary break in Scofield's spiel and seized the opportunity. "Look, at the moment I don't have a penny, and even if I did, *this unit* is a flat-out dud—"

"The debt must be paid, sir."

"Look around, pal. You're in a closet of an office on a block full of pawnshops and bars in the worst part of downtown Tulsa. My staff is on half-salary and my assistant is typing on the back of old pleadings because he can't afford typing paper! Do you think I have money to throw at faulty air conditioners?"

"Your financial status is no concern of mine, I'm sure."

"Thanks for your compassion."

"If you do not remedy this deficit immediately, we will be forced to turn your account over to a collection agency—"

"No you won't. I've filed a formal complaint pursuant to the warranty clause in our sales contract."

Scofield shook his head despairingly. "Lawyers." He sighed.

"And if you mess up my credit," Ben continued, "I'll haul you into court for defamation and abuse of process!"

Scofield drew himself up. "Are you threatening me, sir?"

"I'll do a heck of a lot more than threaten if—"

"Boss," Jones interrupted. "You're due in court, remember? The Johnson case."

Ben stopped in midoutburst. "Right. I don't have time for this, Scofield. Work it out with my assistant."

"Oh, thank you very much," Jones said.

"I'll be at the courthouse if—" Jones grabbed Ben's arm and yanked him back. "What do you want now?"

Jones pointed through the street-front windows. "Psst. New client alert."

Ben looked through the front windows and saw a middle-aged black man carrying a large shopping bag. "Well, if he is, make an appointment. I gotta vamoose."

He started to leave again, but Jones jerked him back. "Boss, *look* at him."

"I'm looking, Jones, but I don't see anything that inspires me to incur Judge Hart's wrath by being late."

"Some detective you are," Jones snorted. "You see, but you do not observe."

"Okay, Sherlock. Give me the lowdown."

"Take a look at his car, Boss. What do you see?"

"Nothing in particular, except that it's a cheap old Ford Pinto with the front end smashed in."

Scofield tried to cut back into the conversation. "Mr. Kincaid, I really must insist—"

"Butt out, Scofield. We're doing important detective work here. Okay, Jones, his car is a wreck. So what?"

"Note the loose flecks of paint near the impact area. This was caused by a recent accident. Now notice how the man limps. Put it together and what have you got?"

"Traffic accident," Ben murmured. "Personal injury case."

"Contingency fee agreement," Jones added. "Quick settlement. Easy money. Staff gets paid. Bill collectors go home. Take the case, Boss."

"You've certainly become a venal so-and-so, Jones."

"I like to eat regularly, if that's what you mean. And I've been on half-salary since June. Which of course is more than the air conditioner manufacturer is getting, but still . . ."

"All right already. I'll take the case."

Jones batted his eyelashes. "My hero."

Ben made a break for the north door, but the way was blocked by the other two briefcase men. He pivoted quickly and made his way toward the other door, only to find himself standing face-to-face with . . .

"Julia!" Ben said awkwardly. "It's been . . . well, it's been . . . well, at least . . . I mean . . ." He inhaled. "What are you doing here?"

"I came to see you, of course." Julia Kincaid Morelli Collins, Ben's sister, was cradling her baby son, one arm expertly curled beneath his body. Her long brown hair fell over her shoulders and tickled his chubby little face. "Is this a good time?"

"Well, to tell you the truth—"

"This is your nephew, Joey." Julia propped the baby up in her arms. "Joey, say hello to your uncle Ben."

"Please don't call me that. I feel like I should be cooking Minute rice."

Julia ignored him. "Can you say hi to your uncle Ben?" She looked up. "He's seven months old. He can only say a few words." She wiggled her fingers and spoke in high-pitched baby talk. "Say, 'Hi there, Uncle Ben. Hi there!' "

Joey did not follow her lead, which Ben thought showed great presence of mind on his part. Ben took the moment to give his sister a quick once-over. She'd changed since he'd last seen her. Not surprising, really—it had been more than two years.

She had slimmed down considerably. Working as an emergency room nurse in Glasgow, Montana, had undoubtedly played a part in that. Not to mention her second divorce, just after the baby was born, and the stress of caring for a newborn on her own. Something about the new improved Julia bothered him, though.

"So what have you been up to?" he asked.

"Oh, you wouldn't believe it." Joey was getting restless—squirming and scrunching up his face. Julia plopped him over her shoulder, burped him, then switched him to her other arm. "I finished my contract term at the hospital in Glasgow and got offered a seat in a graduate program in Connecticut. It's very exclusive."

"So you'll be accepting?"

"I hope to, but there are a few problems." She smiled at Joey, then wiped a bit of drool from his face. "I can't believe how long it's been since we last saw each other, Ben. Why is that?"

"Well," Ben said hesitantly, "I thought it was because you didn't like me very much."

"Don't be silly. Where would you get that idea?"

"Because you always said I was a jerk."

"Did I? Sorry about that."

"Because you said I don't care about anyone other than myself."

"I'm sure I didn't mean it."

"Because you told Mother I tried to drown you in the swimming pool when you were eight."

"Well, you did do that, but let's let bygones be bygones." She wriggled the diaper bag down off her shoulder, wrested free a wet-wipe, and cleaned up Joey's face. "It didn't help family relations, you know, when you took Mike's side during our divorce."

Mike Morelli was her first husband—and Ben's old college buddy, currently a homicide detective with the Tulsa PD. "Did I? He thinks I took your side."

"Well, he's wrong. As usual."

Ben diverted his attention to the infant. "He's a cute little guy, isn't he?"

"Oh yeah. And very advanced for his age. He can already pull himself up in his crib. He'll be walking in another month or two. Here, why don't you hold him?"

"Oh, no," Ben said quickly. "That's all right."

"Come on, Ben. He's your nephew. He won't break. Hold him a second."

Ben reluctantly extended his arms. It wasn't anything personal against Joey. Ben just didn't know the slightest thing about babies. He didn't even know where to place his hands.

"No, no," Julia said, "like this. He can hold up his head now, but you still need to brace his body."

Ben contorted in accordance with her directions. Joey gazed up at his uncle and made a strange gurgling noise.

"See?" Julia said. "He likes you."

"If you say so."

"Tickle his lower lip. He loves that."

Ben did as instructed. The baby did seem to smile a bit.

" 'Scuse me, sir."

Ben turned. It was the black man he and Jones had spotted outside. He stood unevenly, leaning heavily on his right leg. "My name's Ernest Hayes. Friends call me Ernie. Sorry to interrupt, but I'm wantin' to talk with you 'bout handlin' a case—"

"Right," Ben said. "I'd be happy to do it."

The man blinked. "Jus' like that?"

"Sure. My pleasure."

Ernie hesitated. "I gotta be honest with you, Mr. Kincaid. I ain't got much money."

"Not a problem. I'll do it on a contingency fee. My assistant will give you some forms to fill out—terms, provisions, and so on. There are standard percentages for cases of this sort. Here, I'll sign now." Ben scrawled his name on the bottom of one of the forms. "We'll talk about the details when I get back from court."

"Land sakes. This was even easier than I thought it would be."

Ben winked at Jones. "Happy now?"

"Ecstatic."

"I'm sorry, Mr. Kincaid. I'm attempting to be patient, but this is truly the limit."

It was Scofield again. "You know," Ben said, "if your air conditioner was half as resilient as you are, I wouldn't be standing here worrying about the baby sniffing my sweaty pits."

Scofield appeared shocked. "Really! If this is your idea of humor—"

"Can't you leave me alone for a minute? I'm bonding with my nephew."

"I hate to interrupt any familial bonding," Jones said, "but you seem to keep forgetting about your trial."

"Yikes! What time does it start?"

"Nine A.M." Jones glanced at his Mickey Mouse watch. "That would be exactly five minutes ago."

"Jiminy Christmas!" Ben shouldered Scofield aside, using the baby to run interference. "Julia, I hate to make goo-goo faces and run, but—"

He froze in his tracks. *"Julia?"*

Ben whirled around, but Julia was gone. Without a trace.

And he was left holding the baby.

* 2 *

"Where'd she go?" Ben screeched.

One of the briefcase brigadiers guarding the front door offered an explanation. "She left. Got in a green convertible and drove away."

"Drove away? You're kidding!"

"Why would I kid? Looked like she was going somewhere in a hurry."

Ben cast his eyes upward. "This is so like Julia. Only she could leave and forget to take her baby. I don't believe this!"

Jones rose from his desk. "Stay calm, Boss."

"Stay calm? How can I stay calm? I'm due in court. And my sister disappears and leaves me with this—this—" He looked down at the bundle in his arms.

Joey's tiny blue eyes suddenly widened. After gazing up at his uncle's face for a second or two, he began to wail.

"Omigosh." Ben pulled the baby up to his face. "I didn't mean anything—I mean—don't take it personal, but I have this court date, see. . . ."

"He's seven months old, Boss. I don't think he understands about court dates."

"Oh, jeez." Ben swung the baby back and forth in a herky-jerky manner. The wailing attained an all-time-high decibel level. Ben awkwardly cradled Joey in his arms and tried to prop him against his chest. The bawling continued, but went into decrescendo.

"Jones, he's crying!"

"I noticed, Boss. We all did."

"Did I hurt his feelings somehow?"

"More likely he has a wet diaper."

Ben held the baby out at arm's length. "Really?"

"Or maybe he's hungry. Beats me."

"Well, you're the would-be detective. Detect already."

Jones rummaged through the red diaper bag Julia had left on the floor. "Here's some toys. Lots, actually. Say, this is nifty stuff."

"Jones, stop playing with the baby toys!"

"Oh, right." He continued searching. "Several outfits of clothes." He frowned. "And diapers. Dozens of diapers. Hmmm."

"What do you mean, *hmmm*?"

"What I mean is," Jones said slowly, "I don't think Julia left him behind by mistake."

"What are you saying?"

"Remember? Julia said she wanted to start that graduate program in Connecticut, but there was a problem? The problem was, she had a seven-month-old baby." Jones clasped Ben on the shoulder. "So she left the baby with Uncle Ben."

"With *me*?" Ben's face flushed. "But—I can't have a baby. I'm a lawyer!" He looked down at Joey. His cheeks were puffy and red and streaked with tears. "I'm sorry, little guy. If I knew why you were crying, I'd do something about it. But I don't." Ben looked up abruptly. "Here, Jones. Take him."

"*Me*? I don't know nothin' 'bout holdin' babies."

"Well, learn. I have to get to court!"

"What am I going to do with him? This is a law office—sort of. Not a day-care center."

Ben pressed the baby against Jones's chest. Joey's sporadic sobs reverted to a full-throttled wail. "You're a resourceful guy, Jones. You'll think of something. I've got to get to the courthouse before Judge Hart holds me in contempt."

Jones cautiously took the infant into his arms. "Boy, Boss . . . if I do this . . ."

"I know. I'll owe you."

"You already owe me. We're now talking about a debt the magnitude of which most men have never contemplated."

* * *

After a five-minute sprint in the sweltering downtown heat, Ben made it to the Tulsa County Courthouse at Fifth and Denver. The courthouse elevators were the oldest and slowest in all creation, and Ben couldn't afford to wait around, so he panted up the stairs to the sixth floor. Breathing heavily, he slid through the doors to the Honorable Sarah Hart's courtroom, hoping he could enter unnoticed.

No such luck. "Mr. Kincaid," the judge said, the instant he stepped through the door. "How kind of you to grace us with your presence."

"Sorry, Judge. I was unavoidably delayed."

Judge Hart nodded. "Creditor problems again?"

"Uh, no." Well, not entirely, anyway. "Someone brought me a baby."

"A baby?" Hart lowered the glasses on her nose. "Does this relate to some previously undisclosed episode in your past?"

Ben smiled. Hart could be a tough judge, but at least she had a sense of humor. "No, ma'am. It relates to the dangers of being a member of a family."

"You'll forgive me if I fail to follow up on this intriguing dialogue, but the assistant district attorney is anxious to continue the trial. I believe you know Mr. Bullock. So you know how insistent he can be."

Ben glanced over at Jack Bullock, who was sitting at the prosecution table. He did indeed know Mr. Bullock. Before Ben moved to Tulsa, they both had worked at the district attorney's office in Oklahoma City. Jack Bullock had been his boss. More than his boss, really. His mentor. His idol. His hero.

Bullock and Ben had spent a long summer working on several incredibly complicated white-collar crime cases, Bullock as lead trial counsel, Ben as lead research grunt. And Ben had loved every minute of it. Not because Bullock was such an excellent attorney, although he was, but because he believed in what he did. When you worked with Jack Bullock, you were on a holy crusade, a battle of right versus wrong. All summer long, they worked shoulder to shoulder, upholding the letter of the law, putting the bad guys behind bars. Their work—indeed, their lives—were imbued with a sense of purposefulness, of optimism, of idealism, that Ben had seldom glimpsed since.

At the time Ben had thought he'd stay at the DA's office forever. Till unforeseen circumstances proved him wrong. Till unforeseen circumstances turned his life upside down.

Like the man said, chance makes fools of us all.

"If you'll give me two minutes to confer with my legal assistant and client," Ben said, "I'll be ready to proceed, your honor."

"Another delay, counsel?"

Ben held his thumb and finger barely apart. "Just a teensy-weensy one, Judge."

She removed her glasses and laid them on the bench. "I really should find you in contempt and toss you in jail, but I'm so anxious to hear your examination of the next witness that I'm going to hold off. At least for the moment. You have two minutes, Mr. Kincaid. Teensy-weensy ones."

Ben tossed his briefcase on the defendant's table, nodded politely at Bullock, and exchanged a cursory greeting with his client, a nineteen-year-old bleached blonde named Jessie (short for Jezebel) Johnson. She had run away from home a few months before and somehow ended up in Tulsa, totally broke. According to her, she was wandering the streets a few days after she arrived, aimless and destitute, when the prosecution's star witness approached her and suggested an interesting way she could make some fast money.

Ben scanned the courtroom for his legal assistant, Christina McCall. She wasn't hard to find. Her vivid strawberry-blonde hair billowed out, adding several inches to her five-foot, one-inch height. But the glaring clash of unmatched colors below was the real eye-catcher. Today she was decked out in a sleeveless white blouse, a bell-shaped blue skirt with large yellow polka dots, green ankle socks, and black-and-white oxfords.

"What are you wearing?" Ben asked as he approached. "This is a courtroom, not a sock hop."

"It's part of my new summer wardrobe." She twirled around

in a small pirouette, letting her skirt and hair swirl around her. "I told you I hit some flea markets last weekend, remember?"

"Yes. The prospect of your obtaining a new wardrobe was very exciting. Now I'm having second thoughts."

"I'm not wearing some stuffy business suit in this heat," Christina said emphatically. "Take me or leave me."

While Ben considered, Judge Hart spoke up. "One minute left, Mr. Kincaid."

"Great. Listen, Christina, have you got any ideas for my cross?"

"Of course. Am I not your faithful aide-de-camp? I stayed up all night rereading the preliminary hearing transcript, and I think I've detected a critical discrepancy. A major faux pas. Problem is, it involves some rather, um, outré elements. . . . It's . . . somewhat risqué. . . ."

Ben's eyes rolled at the barrage of bad French. "Christina, what are you saying?"

"You won't be able to get near it without discussing certain delicate matters relating to human sexuality, a subject with which I know you are pitifully uncomfortable."

"Not true."

"*Is* true. I'll never forget your expression when you were channel-surfing at my place and stumbled across the Playboy Channel. And I thought you were going to die that time we went to the zoo."

Ben noticed the judge alternating between impatient glances at her watch and hostile glares at Ben. "No time for modesty, Christina. Tell me what you've got."

* 3 *

After the break, Bullock recalled the complainant to the stand. He was a middle-aged balding man named Harvey Applebee. According to his direct examination testimony, Jezebel propositioned Applebee just off the corner of Eleventh and Cincinnati. She took him back to a "health facility" she was sharing with five other working girls, removed her clothes, removed his clothes, and placed him in a hot tub. The complainant didn't actually do any complaining until after the vice squad burst through the front door. Applebee traded his testimony for personal immunity from prosecution.

"What exactly did the defendant say to you when she approached you on the street?" Bullock asked.

Applebee cleared his throat. "She said I looked as if I could use some exercise and she invited me over to her facility to, er, firm up."

Sitting beside Ben at counsel table, Jezebel giggled. Ben jabbed his elbow in her side.

Bullock continued. "Did she indicate that she had any specialized training as a . . . personal fitness trainer?"

"She did demonstrate a great deal of . . . flexibility, and she suggested some positions—I mean, exercises—that she thought I might find beneficial."

Bullock was becoming annoyed. "Mr. Applebee, let's stop beating around the bush." A gruff laugh emerged from the gallery. Ben's face turned bright crimson. "I mean, let's get to the point. Did Ms. Johnson offer to engage in sexual intercourse with you?"

"I don't recall that she ever used those words, no."

"Well . . . did she touch you?"

"You mean, emotionally?"

Bullock ground his teeth. "No, sir. I mean did any part of her body come into contact with any part of your body?"

"At what time?"

"Before you got into the hot tub."

"She called it a relaxation temple."

"What*ever*."

"I don't think so. She touched my clothes, of course, but I don't think she ever touched me."

Bullock's frustration mounted. "Mr. Applebee, are you changing your testimony from . . . earlier?" Bullock was attempting to remind the witness his immunity could be revoked without reminding the jury that his testimony had been bought and paid for.

"Not at all. The touching came later."

"Fine. Where were you when it occurred?"

"In the relaxation temple."

Bullock's eyes looked skyward. "What were you wearing?"

"I was in my shorts and she had, um, removed all her clothing."

"Were you sitting or standing?"

"Sitting."

"And where were you sitting?"

"On the bottom of the tub. Temple, I mean."

"And where did she touch you?"

"Well . . ." He looked down at his hands. "That's kind of personal."

Judge Hart intervened on Bullock's behalf. "I'm afraid you'll have to answer the question."

Applebee squirmed uncomfortably. "All right, ma'am. If you say so. I just hate to—you know. Especially with ladies present."

"Answer the question," Bullock growled.

"She touched me on—" He stretched his neck and loosened his collar. "Well, she touched Little Elvis."

Ben stared down at his legal pad. What a classy practice he had. No wonder he'd endured three years of law school.

Bullock continued. "And with what part of . . . *her* anatomy did she touch you?"

"Please, Mr. Prosecutor," Judge Hart said. "Can't we leave a few things to the jurors' imaginations?"

"If you wish, your honor. Mr. Applebee, did this . . . touching appear to occur by accident?"

"Uh, no."

"And did Ms. Johnson appear . . . awkward about it?"

"Oh, no. On the contrary, she handled herself very adroitly."

"What happened after she . . . touched you, Mr. Applebee?"

"That's when the police broke in." He sighed heavily.

"Indeed." Bullock's face became stern. "But you weren't disappointed about that, *were* you?"

"Oh, no. Of course not," Applebee said. "I was relieved. I had begun to suspect that she . . . wasn't a trained health-care professional."

Ben and Christina exchanged a look.

"That's all I have," Bullock said, stepping away from the podium.

"Very well," Judge Hart replied. "Care to cross, Mr. Kincaid?"

"Yes, your honor," Ben said, springing to his feet.

"You may inquire. If you dare."

Ben positioned himself between the prosecution table and the witness. "Tell me, Mr. Applebee, had you ever been in a hot tub before?"

"No."

"Did you find it . . . unpleasant?"

"Well, no. I found it . . . quite stimulating."

"How deep was the water?"

Applebee frowned. This was obviously not the line of questioning he'd been prepped for. "I'd say about three feet, from the bottom to the top. Maybe more."

"I see." Ben moved in closer. "And I believe you testified that you were sitting on the bottom of the tub."

"That's correct."

"Did you move later?"

A line formed between Applebee's eyes. "No."

Bullock rose to his feet. "Your honor, I'm not following Mr. Kincaid's line of questioning."

That's the general idea, Ben thought. "I'll tie it up, your honor."

"Please do, counselor. We're all waiting breathlessly."

Ben turned back to the witness. "Then you were still sitting on the bottom of the tub when Ms. Johnson allegedly touched"—he pressed his fingers against his forehead—"Little Elvis."

"That's correct."

Ben paused. "Mr. Applebee, let's be honest with the jury. You've been granted immunity by the prosecution, right?"

"Well . . ." He glanced uncertainly at Bullock. "Yes . . ."

"The only reason you're testifying today is because you made a deal with the prosecutors exonerating you if you testify against Jessie."

"Well . . . that isn't the only reason. . . ."

"Tell us the truth, Mr. Applebee. When you got into that hot tub, you weren't trying to get fit. You were trying to get laid."

"That isn't so!" He began to fluster. "I thought it was a health spa!"

Ben put on his best disbelieving sneer. "Give us a break."

"I did!" Applebee said indignantly. "That's what I thought."

"Well, what did you think when she took off her clothes?"

Applebee twined his fingers nervously. "I thought that was . . . very therapeutic. . . ."

"Come on, now. A naked woman snuggles up to you in a hot tub and you think it's time for calisthenics?"

Applebee began to stammer. "But—but it wasn't like that!"

"It wasn't?"

"No. She didn't snuggle up to me in the tub. Temple, I mean."

"She didn't?"

"No!" Applebee insisted. "She never even got wet."

"I see." Ben faced the jury and smiled. "That's what you said at the preliminary hearing, too. She never even got wet."

"It's true. Amazing woman."

Ben leaned in for the kill. "Sir, would you please explain

how it would be possible for her to touch you, um, there, when you're sitting on the bottom of three feet of water—without getting wet?"

Applebee's mouth opened, then closed.

Ben continued. "If the water was three feet deep, even subtracting a few inches for your, um, buttocks, that would leave your lap over two and a half feet underwater. It would be impossible for Ms. Johnson to touch you without getting wet—unless Little Elvis is over two and a half feet long."

Amused expressions crossed the faces of a few of the jurors. One older woman covered her eyes.

"Well," Ben asked insistently. "Is it?"

Applebee's eyebrows met in the center of his face. "Is it what?"

"Is Little Elvis over two and a half feet long?"

"You mean now?"

"Or at any other time, sir. I'm not particular."

"Your honor," Bullock said, "I must protest."

"Indeed you must," Judge Hart replied. "Have you got any grounds?"

"Well . . . Mr. Kincaid is ridiculing the witness."

"Is that forbidden in cross-examination now? Procedures must've changed since I went to law school."

"But it doesn't have anything to do with the case!"

"I disagree," Ben interjected. "It goes directly to the credibility of the witness's testimony."

"I'm afraid I have to agree," the judge said. "Proceed, Mr. Kincaid."

"Thank you, your honor. So, Mr. Applebee, I repeat: Is Little Elvis over two and a half feet long?"

"Well . . . I don't exactly know."

"How long is it? Or should I say, how long is *he*?"

"I haven't the slightest idea."

"Well, there's an easy way to find out, isn't there?" Ben whipped a tape measure out of his coat pocket.

Applebee looked horrified. "What the hell!"

Ben addressed the judge. "Your honor, I move that the

evidence in question be produced by the witness and published to the jury."

"Wh-what?" Applebee yammered.

Judge Hart rubbed the place where her glasses had rested on her nose, a faint smile playing on her lips. "Any response, Mr. Bullock?"

Bullock waved his arms in the air. "Judge, surely he doesn't need to . . . to do this to . . . to prove this to the jurors."

She glanced back at the prosecutor. "Well, they can hardly be expected to take it on faith."

"But there must be another way. Perhaps some sort of medical examination . . ."

"I don't think so," Ben said. "Under the best-evidence rule, hearsay testimony is not an acceptable substitute for a . . . hands-on inspection."

"You never told me I'd have to do anything like this," Applebee protested. He was speaking directly to Bullock. "I won't do it. Wouldn't be accurate, anyway," he added, sniffing. "Circumstances are different now than they were at the temple."

"I'm sure we can simulate the circumstances at the temple," Ben suggested.

"I'm not simulating myself right here in the middle of the courtroom!" Applebee shouted.

"Your honor!" Bullock protested. "I can't have my witness . . . *expose* himself to the jury."

"Mr. Bullock," the judge said sternly, "you put this man on the stand and elicited the testimony that began this entire line of questioning. I have to give Mr. Kincaid a fair opportunity to impeach the credibility—"

"Well, I ain't doin' it," Applebee said, folding his arms across his chest. "And no judge on earth can make me. No way, no how."

Judge Hart covered her mouth. "Mr. Bullock, perhaps you should reconsider your decision to use this particular witness."

"But your honor! Without this witness, I don't have a case!"

"I'm glad to hear you admit that, counsel. It appears that

way to the court as well. Perhaps a brief conference with your co-counsel is in order."

Grumbling, Bullock whispered a few words to the female attorney sitting beside him at counsel table. A minute or so later he announced, "Your honor, all things considered, we move to dismiss the charges."

Jezebel sat up straight and clapped her hands.

Judge Hart looked at Ben. "I take it you have no objection?"

"None at all, your honor. We'll even pay our own costs."

"Smart move, counsel." She apologized to the jurors and formally discharged them. "This case is dismissed. Court is adjourned."

Ben ran forward to intercept the judge before she retreated into chambers. "Your honor, I want to apologize again for being late. And I'm also sorry about, well, the disruption in the courtroom. I know it's not the first time—and I'm truly sorry."

"Not at all, Mr. Kincaid," she replied, smiling. "Your cases do tend to be a bit irregular. But my goodness, they're always entertaining."

* 4 *

Jessie thanked Ben profusely. "I just don't know what I would have done if you hadn't agreed to help me. Dixie was absolutely right. 'You can trust our Ben,' she told me." Jessie leaned forward and kissed Ben on the cheek. "She was right."

"Well, thanks . . ." Ben mumbled awkwardly.

"Now, don't think I've forgotten your fee." She reached for a wad of cash tucked strategically inside her blouse. By Ben's reckoning, it was a hundred dollars, tops. "I know it's not much, but I want you—"

"Jessie," Ben said, "is that all the money you have in the world?"

"Well, yes . . ."

He frowned. "Keep it."

"But—"

"And buy a bus ticket home."

"Home! You think—"

"Yeah. I do. At the least, put it toward getting a new place to live. And a new occupation."

"Well . . . if you're sure . . ."

"I'm sure."

She leaned forward and kissed him again, square on the lips. "Dixie was right. You're the best!"

Or the cheapest, anyway, Ben thought as he watched her leave.

Jack Bullock intercepted Ben on his way back to counsel table.

Ben stretched out his hand and smiled. "It's great to see you again, Jack. Even if it had to be—"

46

Bullock cut him off. "So this is what's become of you, Ben?"

Ben's brow knitted. "What's become . . . ? I'm not sure what you're talking about."

"I'm talking about your wasting your talents putting prostitutes back on the street."

Ben shrugged his shoulders. "Jack . . . Jessie is just a teenager. She ran away from home and didn't know what to do—"

"Don't give me your closing argument. This is Jack, remember? Jack Bullock. I know the way of the world."

"I guess I don't understand. . . ."

"I'm the one who doesn't understand, Ben. I don't understand how you ended up representing the same sleazebags we used to bust our guts trying to put behind bars."

Ben felt a catch in his throat. "Jack, everyone is entitled to a defense. . . ."

"Don't try to squirm away with some civics class lecture. I know perfectly well that every hairball is entitled to a defense. I also know there'll always be some ambulance chaser ready to give it to them. I just can't believe it's you."

"Jack . . . this is just one case. . . ."

"One case of many. Since I moved to the Tulsa office, I've been asking around about you. You seem to have made a career out of setting free creeps the police have sweated blood to catch."

"A lot of those people were wrongly accused, Jack. Some of them were as innocent as—"

"Don't be such a sucker. Most of the people the police arrest *are* guilty—if not of the crime charged, then of something else. And you know it."

"Still, the Bill of Rights ensures—"

"And don't behave like a stupid schoolboy. We all have to grow up sometime, Ben. We all have to face reality."

"Everyone is entitled to a fair trial. That's the law."

"Don't 'fair trial' me. What you did here today had nothing to do with law. You performed a bit of sleight of hand to subvert the law."

"But—"

"The law should be the law. For everyone. Period. No exceptions."

"But you can't treat everyone like interchangeable ciphers, Jack. Some people are not well educated and they can't afford—"

Bullock shook his head in disgust. "Listen to you, rattling off trite liberal homilies. You're defensive, because you know I'm right." He lowered his eyes. "I'm so disappointed, Ben. How could you let this happen to you?"

Ben felt a sharp stinging in his eyes. "Jack, I don't know what to say. . . ."

"When you and I were colleagues, our work meant something. What we did was significant. We went shoulder to shoulder against the enemy, striking important blows for the good and the right."

"You don't have to remind me, Jack. The time we spent together was perhaps the most meaningful—"

"Stow the flattery, okay? I invested a lot of time in you, Ben. I taught you everything I knew. I can't believe you're now using that knowledge to thwart justice. I can't believe you sold out to the other side."

"Sold out? I can't even pay my bills."

"I expected you to have a positive impact in this world. I thought you were going to make a difference. Instead, I find you resorting to pathetic courtroom high jinks to set the guilty free. Are you going to spend the rest of your life representing every petty felon and hard-luck story that slithers into your office?"

"I had an obligation to represent my client zealously."

Bullock's upper lip curled. "I'm trying to clean up the streets, to make this state a decent place to live, to raise a family. And frankly, I'm tired of seeing my work short-circuited by two-bit shysters willing to sell their souls for a quick buck!"

"Jack . . ." Ben's voice suddenly became quiet. "You were like a father to me. More so . . . than my own father."

"And you were like a son. That's why I can't stand to see what's happened to you." He turned his back to Ben and returned to his table. "Someone needs to remind you what it's all about," he muttered. "Someone needs to teach you a lesson."

Ben's face contorted. "What is that, some kind of threat?"

Bullock began packing his briefcase. "I've got a lot of friends here at the courthouse. In fact, I've got a lot of friends everywhere."

"What's your point, Jack?"

"How long can you go on representing the scum of the earth?" His eyes met Ben's. "Someone needs to straighten you out, Ben. Before it's too late." And with that, Bullock marched out of the courtroom.

Christina inched forward and filled the space vacated by Bullock. "So," she said, "what was that about?"

Ben's head turned slowly. "That was about the most depressing conversation I've had in my entire life."

"I heard what he said vis-à-vis straightening you out. Jeez, you'd think he'd never lost a case."

"It isn't that," Ben said. "He just . . . believes strongly in what he does."

"Just the same, you'd better steer clear of criminal work for a while, Ben. Sounds to me like Bullock may be gunning for you."

"Bullock doesn't control the whole judicial system."

"Maybe not, but he could do some major damage."

Ben had learned long ago to trust Christina's instincts. He'd been working with her in one capacity or another since he moved to Tulsa, and he'd never known those instincts to be wrong yet. They were her greatest asset—even greater than her legal-assistant skills, which were considerable.

"Christina, you've been with me for some time now. Am I doing a disservice?"

"A disservice? What do you mean?"

"Oh . . . you know. Contributing to the crime rate. Putting pond scum back on the street."

"Like who? Me?" Ben had represented Christina a few years before when she found herself accused of murder.

"That was an exceptional case. Most of the time—"

"Enough of this grimness," Christina said, cutting him off. "You should be celebrating, not castigating yourself. Congrats on the slick cross-ex. *Formidable*."

"It wasn't that big a deal."

"Says you. You've come a long way, kiddo. When I first met you, you couldn't say *conjugal relations* without turning beet red."

"We all have to grow up sometime," Ben said. The words rang in his ears. "Thanks for burning the midnight oil and catching the discrepancy in Applebee's testimony."

"I'm just glad you made it to the courtroom. For a while there, I was afraid I was going to have to do the cross-ex myself."

"And you'd have been great, too. Seriously, Christina." She acknowledged his compliment with a beatific smile. "Meanwhile, back at the office, I had a morning like you wouldn't believe."

"What happened?"

"Well . . ." In the corner of his eye, Ben saw his new client—the middle-aged black man with the pronounced limp—hobbling into the courtroom. "It's too complicated to explain. But tell me. Do you know how to change a diaper?"

"What?"

Ben moved toward the door. "I need to talk to my new client. Why don't you sit in?"

Ben greeted the man and introduced him to Christina. "Mr. Hayes, you didn't need to come to the courthouse. I would've returned to the office."

"It's no problem. 'Sides—I thought I might jus' get a chance to see you in action."

"I'm afraid you missed it. The case has already been dismissed."

"Hoo-ee! You *are* good, ain'tcha?"

Ben looked embarrassed. "It was nothing, really. Christina did—"

"I been readin' about you, Mr. Kincaid. In that magazine they give out in restaurants and stuff." A few months before, an article about Ben's efforts against an Arkansas white supremacy group had appeared in *Tulsa People*, a classy biweekly distributed in Tulsa retail outlets. "You really fight for the reg'lar folks, don'tcha? That's what the magazine said. Said you had to get right down in the mud and wrestle with those Klan boys. But you did it. That's when I knew who I wanted. See, I been talkin' to lawyers all over town, and no one wants to help me. They say it's hopeless. But after I read that article and saw your picture, I knew. I knew you were the one who was finally going to help my boy."

"Your . . . boy?"

"My little Leeman. 'Course he's twenty-eight now, not really a boy, but still. You wouldn't believe what they're accusin' him of. Lord, but he's had a hard life. And it's about to get a sight worse." He reached out and shook Ben's hand vigorously. "It's so good of you to take on his case like you did. 'Specially since I barely got two pennies to rub together."

Christina stared at Ben as if, once again, he'd lost his mind.

"Wait a minute," Ben said. "I thought you wanted me to represent you regarding an automobile accident."

He cocked his head. "Cain't say as I do. What made you think that?"

"Well—my assistant—the front of your car—"

" 'Fraid one of my boys drove it into a lamppost on Riverside Drive. I think he'd had one too many at Orpha's Lounge. Prob'ly more than one too many. Can we sue somebody over that?"

"I wouldn't recommend it." Ben inhaled sharply. "You'll forgive me for pointing this out . . . but you do appear to be having some trouble walking."

"Well, son, I am sixty-three years old."

"Sixty-three?" He didn't look a day over forty-five.

"That's right. I been gettin' the arthritis in this leg for five years now. It's especially bad when it's hot outside. And Lordie, is it ever hot outside."

"Then . . . there's no personal-injury case?"

"Nope. My only problem is gettin' my boy out of trouble. That's why I was so happy when you agreed to take him on."

"About that," Ben said. "You know, I've been very busy lately—"

"I know. That's why I went ahead and filled out all these forms like your secretary told me. He said I was all taken care of. Done deal."

Ben glanced pleadingly at Christina, whose sole response was an unhelpful shrug. He took the forms and scanned them. Fully executed employment agreements, signed by both parties. Great.

"So what is it your son is accused of?"

Ernie Hayes hung his head down low, his face cradled in knobby, veined hands. "Murder, Mr. Kincaid. Murder in the first degree."

* 5 *

"Murder?" Ben's brain reeled. Not only a criminal case, but of the most serious variety. "Who is he accused of killing?"

"This foreign woman. I cain't rightly pronounce her name. Killed at the country club where my boy usta caddy. And the police think he did it. Fact is, everyone does."

A cold-blooded murder, Ben thought. What timing. *How long can you go on representing the scum of the earth?* "What does your son say happened?"

"Well, now, he ain't all that easy to talk to."

"He won't tell you what happened?"

"It ain't that he won't tell. It's that he cain't. Not really. He ain't quite right in the head."

"I'm sorry. You mean—"

"Ment'lly retarded. Been that way since he was born, poor boy. I know there's different words for it now that we're supposed to use to make everyone feel better, but that's what it is. He's retarded."

"So, actually, you don't know if your son killed the woman or not."

Ernie Hayes raised his chin. "That's where you're wrong. I know my boy. And I know he wouldn't kill no one. No, sir. He wouldn't hurt a fly."

Don't be such a sucker. Bullock's voice was ringing in Ben's head. *Most of the people the police arrest are guilty. And you know it.* "I haven't heard anything about this murder. When did it occur?"

" 'Bout ten years ago."

"Ten years ago!" Ben stared at the man wide-eyed. "And it's just now coming to trial? How can that be?"

"Don't be askin' me to explain that legal mumbo jumbo. All I know is he was arrested, then he hadta go away to some kinda hospital, and now they've sent him back for trial."

That didn't make sense at all. If what Hayes said was correct, this would be the all-time violation of the defendant's right to a speedy trial. Ben made a mental note to check some more reliable sources to unravel the background of the case. "When is he scheduled to go to trial?"

"Next week."

"Next week!" The nightmare just got worse and worse. "On a capital offense? What about the arraignment? What about the probable-cause hearing?"

"Thass all been handled by some other fella."

"Some other fella?" Ben could measure the depth of his consternation by the fact that his responses had been reduced to parrotlike repetitions. "You mean another attorney?"

"Yeah. Some old dude the judge assigned. I don't like him. I want you to try the case, Mr. Kincaid. You're the only one who can help him now."

Ben didn't share Hayes's sentiment, flattering though it might be. In his experience, most public defenders did first-class work despite a backbreaking caseload. Nonetheless, there was the troubling matter of the signed employment agreement. "I don't want to handle your son's case unless I'm sure I can do the best job possible. And I don't see how I can get up to speed by next week."

"You can. I know you can. You've done it before."

"I have?"

"Yup. In Arkansas. I read about it in that magazine."

"Well, yes, but there were some extenuating circumstances." Ben gazed deeply into the man's eyes. "Look, that employment agreement we signed isn't binding. I misunderstood the circumstances. The Rules of Professional Conduct don't even permit contingency-fee agreements in criminal cases."

"Are you sayin' you're backin' out on my Leeman?"

"I'm not—I'm just—" *How long can you go on representing the scum of the earth?* "You have to understand—"

Ernie Hayes continued to stare at Ben with his deep black eyes.

"Seriously, it—" Ben stopped. "Look, I'll go out and meet your son. I'll talk to him. But that's all I'm promising."

To his surprise, Hayes sprang forward and shook his hand vigorously. "Oh, thank you, Mr. Kincaid. Praise the Lord. I knew you'd understand." Ernie shook his hand a few more times, then walked out of the courtroom.

Ben couldn't help but notice that his limp did not seem nearly as pronounced as it had before.

6

The man strode down the sidewalk, a Polaroid photo clenched in one hand. The fingers of his other hand brushed against the wrought-iron fence surrounding the playground. He felt like a fool, wearing a red fright wig and fake glasses. But it was necessary.

He would need time with his new little sweetheart. He would need to become his trusted friend. And that would take a while. He had to make sure that, in the meantime, the boy wasn't able to describe him accurately.

He spotted the boy almost immediately, standing by himself between the swing set and the slides. Abie Rutherford. He wasn't playing with anyone. He was just hanging out—a frown on his face, one hand on his hip—in an adorable pose of preadolescent aloofness.

What a lovely child. His photograph did not do justice to his true beauty. But then, what reproduction could do justice to such an immaculate creature? How he ached to take that child into his arms, to press him against his breast. To take care of him. To smother him with affection.

He continued strolling down the sidewalk, past the playground, then around the corner. It wouldn't do for him to be spotted, even in disguise. Not so soon. Not before he had a chance to make contact.

He glanced at his watch. Three more hours, and then the private school would let out for the day. The boy's home was nearby; the kid probably walked. Cross Twenty-first, cut through Woodward Park, and he'd be home. Good.

He crossed the street and looked for a place he could quietly pass the next three hours. As he reached the opposite side, however, he couldn't resist turning back for one last look at his new golden child.

His heart swooned. "You're all mine, Abie Rutherford," he whispered under his breath. "All mine."

* 7 *

Ben stopped by the public defenders' office and checked out the Leeman Hayes file, telling them he had been asked to represent the defendant and was in the process of deciding whether to do it. Assuming Leeman consented, they didn't object to a substitution of counsel. Not that they didn't think the case was important. But when a staff of four lawyers has to handle over a thousand criminal cases a year, they tend to take all the help they can get.

Before he left for the treatment facility where Leeman was being held, Ben thumbed through the file. The mystery of the ten-year trial delay soon became clear. Leeman had been arrested almost immediately after the murder occurred. His lawyer, since deceased, ordered a battery of physical and mental tests. After being presented with the results, the trial judge ruled that Leeman was not capable of assisting in his own defense and therefore constitutionally could not be tried.

Leeman was committed to a series of institutions and therapy centers. The reports received were of a kind; only the words changed. Leeman Hayes was born with a genetic condition that resulted in profound retardation. The neurological disorder affected his perceptions of and reactions to the world around him. It was like a thick sheet, a gauzy veil between Leeman and everyone else.

According to the file, Leeman was generally good-natured, but he had a temper that sometimes flared up with little provocation. During these aggravated seizures, especially given his limited ability to comprehend outside stimuli, his behavior was utterly unpredictable.

Leeman had been shuffled from one center to another for years, until last spring, when a treating psychiatrist—a Dr. Herbert Fischer—suddenly declared that Leeman was mentally capable of assisting in his own defense and remanded the case to the district court for trial. The minute orders in the file suggested to Ben that the judge had little enthusiasm for this case, but he had no choice. He set the matter down for trial.

To Ben's dismay, the file did not suggest any exculpatory evidence to support Leeman's not-guilty plea. Despite the recent determination of Dr. Fischer, file memos of client interviews indicated that Leeman was virtually no help whatsoever. The concept of the passage of time was beyond him. Trying to get him to focus on what happened ten years ago was almost impossible. Ben would be starting from square one.

If he took the case.

Don't be such a sucker.

Given the circumstances, only a crazy man would do it.

Ben arrived at the clinic near Shadow Mountain just off Sixty-first in south Tulsa. After a brief conversation with the physician in charge, Dr. Montague, Ben was permitted to see Leeman Hayes. The doctor asked the woman who sat at a desk outside his office—a tall, black woman whose name tag identified her as VERA—to escort Ben to Leeman's room.

Ben wanted to ask Vera about Leeman, but he wasn't sure whether Vera was a nurse, or secretary, or what, and he didn't want to offend her by asking. He decided to try to work it out for himself.

"So . . . you work with Dr. Montague?"

"Oh yes. Every day."

"I see." Ben followed her down a long antiseptic corridor. "He probably depends on you quite a bit. On a day-to-day basis."

"That's true."

"You probably . . . check on the patients every so often. Make sure they're okay."

"Actually, we usually let the nurses do that."

Aha. Not a nurse. "Do you ... prepare Dr. Montague's reports?"

"Oh yes. I do all his reports now."

Bingo. "So you must be his personal secretary."

Vera peered down at him. "Close. I'm a doctor."

If there had been an available closet, Ben would've crawled into it. "I'm sorry. I just assumed . . ."

"You assumed that since I'm a woman, I must be a nurse or a secretary."

"Not at all," Ben said, although in truth, of all the possibilities he had considered, somehow *doctor* never came to mind. "I just—I assumed that since you did his paperwork, you must be his secretary. Goodness knows my secretary does all my paperwork."

"I do his paperwork because I have to. I'm a GP—a family physician. He's the specialist—a clinical psychiatrist with specialized training in intellectual disorders. Since I'm a mere generalist, I do the paperwork, and the dictation, and all the other grunt work. Soon I'll probably be washing his Jaguar."

Ben thought this might be an opportune moment to change the subject. "How well is Leeman Hayes able to communicate?"

"Only in the most rudimentary way. His verbal skills are keenly lower than even most developmentally disabled persons."

"Developmentally disabled—"

"That's the current politically correct euphemism for mental retardation. I know, it's hard to stay on top of them all. If people spent half as much time developing remedies as they spent trying to tell other people what words to use, we'd probably have a cure for the common cold."

"And, because Leeman is ... developmentally disabled ... he can't communicate?" Somehow, that didn't seem right. Ben had met mentally retarded persons before, and he'd always been able to talk to them. "Why is that?"

"How much do you know about mental retardation?"

"Not much," Ben admitted.

"Then you'll pardon me if I go into my lecture mode.

Mental retardation affects about three percent of the American population. Supposedly it's caused by genetics. Biological abnormalities."

"Supposedly?"

Vera pressed her glasses higher on her nose. "Well, statistics have shown that a vastly disproportionate number of retarded persons come from underprivileged families." She paused. "That's yuppie talk for *po' folk*. Now, if it's all genetics, why is retardation visited so often on the poor? Doesn't make any sense."

"What do you think causes it?" Ben asked.

"I think, at least in many cases, that it's caused by poverty in combination with negative social and cultural conditions and a lack of stimulation during the child's early developmental years. Early training is critical—sensory, verbal, and emotional stimulation, along with training in certain fundamental skills. Problem is, many po' folk don't have the time or the opportunity to provide it. Or they may not be well enough educated themselves to know what to do."

"How retarded is Leeman?"

"Eighty-seven percent of all retarded persons are what we call mildly retarded. They can be educated to about a sixth-grade level and can usually support themselves. Ten percent are moderately retarded. They can be educated to about the second-grade level and develop only minimal speech and communication skills. Three percent are severely or profoundly retarded. The severely retarded will require care throughout their lives but may be able to do some things for themselves. The profoundly retarded will never be able to do anything for themselves."

"I read in the file that Leeman is moderately retarded."

"True, although he's at the low end of the moderate scale, and he has virtually no communication skills. In fact, when he was first institutionalized, he had none at all. Since then, he's learned a few words. Not many. Mind you, he does understand some of what goes on in the world around him. He's able to learn simple tasks and repeat them. He's able to work with his hands and has good motor skills. He just has no way to communicate."

"I saw a reference in the file to PKU."

"Right. Leeman has been diagnosed as suffering from phenylketonuria, a metabolic abnormality believed to be caused by genetic errors. Not unlike Down's syndrome. PKU is characterized by eczema, attention deficiencies, and a musty body odor."

"And there's no cure?"

"Actually, there is. In at least some cases, PKU can be prevented in infants who have the metabolic defect if their diet is changed before permanent brain damage occurs. Unfortunately, Leeman's parents couldn't afford fancy doctors and high-class hospitals. They didn't even have health insurance. So the condition wasn't detected. And Leeman spends the rest of his life as a retard."

A long time passed before either of them spoke again.

"From what you've told me," Ben said finally, "I'm surprised Leeman was able to caddy."

"Oh, he was a splendid caddy," Vera replied. "Mind you, he wouldn't be advising people on what club to use, but he was perfectly able to schlep a bag of clubs around the course. He was strong, uncomplaining, and he knew the course like it was his backyard. In most instances, no communication was required."

Ben nodded. "Is Leeman being guarded?"

"Only in the most superficial way," Vera answered. "After all, he's been in institutions of one sort or another for the last ten years. He's not going to escape. I don't think he'd know where to go if he did."

"Is Dr. Montague the psychiatrist who's been treating Leeman?"

"He's not the one who certified him competent to stand trial, if that's what you're asking. That learned scholar lives in Ponca City. Met with Leeman for two hours, then rendered his expert opinion. An opinion we all find mystifying."

"Then . . . you disagree that Leeman is competent to stand trial?"

"I disagree that anything has changed. Leeman is mentally retarded. His condition can't be treated. We can try to improve his communication skills, or to train him for an occupation. But that's it. Able to assist in a murder trial? Absurd. If he was unable to assist in his own defense ten years ago, then he still is."

They stopped in the corridor outside a closed door. "Then how do you explain this new ruling?"

"Politics."

"What?"

"You heard me. Politics. And the inexactitude of the psychiatric sciences."

"I don't follow. . . ."

"Despite what some doctors may tell you, psychiatry is still an inexact science. And our knowledge about mental retardation is woefully incomplete. Two different doctors, both competent, can still give wildly varying evaluations. And if one of those doctors is an arch-conservative who believes that murderers should be punished for their crimes—"

"Then you're much more likely to get an evaluation that the accused is competent to stand trial. Is that what happened to Leeman Hayes?"

Vera smiled thinly. "Don't ask me. I'm just a family doctor. What do I know?"

* 8 *

Leeman Hayes sat on the floor on the far side of the room assembling small white plastic model parts. Ben knew virtually nothing about automobiles, but he could tell it was a slick sports car. As he looked around the room Ben saw a vast array of assembled and painted models. Leeman's specialty appeared to be transportation; Ben spotted models of everything from the *Titanic* to the starship *Enterprise*.

Leeman was big, even for a man in his late twenties. He had a broad, moon-shaped face. His skin was flaky and he reeked of some unidentifiable odor. Rolls of fat spilled over his belt. Somehow calling them love handles seemed woefully inappropriate. Despite the flab, Ben sensed real power residing in that bulky frame.

Leeman's eyes were fixed and his tongue curled up toward his nose; Ben could almost feel the strain to focus attention as Leeman carefully glued a tail fin into place.

Ben spoke quietly so as not to startle him. "Excuse me."

Leeman was not startled; in fact, he didn't react at all. Ben sensed that he knew Ben had entered the room; he just wasn't particularly interested.

"My name is Ben Kincaid. I'm a lawyer."

Leeman looked up, not because of anything Ben had said but because he had completed adhering the tail fin and he needed another piece of the model. His cheeks and chin were covered with pimples. The extra fat made his face seem dough-like and his expression perpetually uncertain. He peered at Ben as if he were not simply meeting a new person but contemplating a previously unknown life-form.

64

Ben peered back. It was not so much Leeman's appearance as it was his manner that signaled that something was not quite right. He held his head at an odd, unnatural angle, and it moved not fluidly but in brief, spasmodic bursts. His eyes seemed to move independently of his face.

"Al . . . *read-y*." He overpronounced and protracted each syllable, as if every sound required special effort.

"I know you already have a lawyer. But your lawyer is very busy, and your father thought it might help if I took over your case."

Leeman's face brightened the instant he heard the word *father*. "Papa." His eyes raced around the room. "Papa?"

"I'm afraid he isn't here right now. He came to my office and asked me to represent you. I haven't decided yet. I wanted to talk with you first. Since he's been appointed to serve as your guardian, technically, his okay is all I need. But I wanted to make sure it was all right with you. After all, you're the one who's going to be on trial."

Leeman made no response. He shoved his hands into his pockets, a particularly difficult task because his corduroy pants (in August?) were small and ill-fitting. The front of his un-tucked shirt showed the spillage of many meals past.

The truth struck Ben like a baseball bat to the head. When Leeman's first trial was canceled, and he was committed to his first institution, some poor liberal soul probably thought it was the humane thing to do.

That person had been horribly wrong. Instead of giving Leeman a fair trial, they gave him a life sentence.

"Do you have any objection to my becoming your attorney?" Ben had no inkling how much, if any, of what he had said to Leeman was understood.

Leeman twisted his head one way, then the other. "Papa?"

"Your father wants me here. As I said, it was his idea."

"Okay." Leeman flashed a quick smile, then turned back to his model.

"That's a great car you're making," Ben said. He had to remind himself not to talk baby talk. This was a mentally retarded adult, not his nephew. "Did you make all these?"

Leeman's eyes brightened. "All."

"I tried to make a model once, when I was a kid. An Aurora model of Superman crashing through a brick wall. I totally screwed it up. Came out looking like the Bride of Frankenstein."

Leeman hunkered down on the carpet and picked up a saucer-shaped piece. A hubcap or something.

"I read that you like music, Leeman. Is that right?"

Leeman's head tilted on the word *music*. Without comment, he walked to a cabinet against the wall and opened it.

Inside, Ben saw a stereo system—receiver, turntable, and two speakers. Not the best system in the world, but not garbage, either. And beneath the stereo were two shelves filled with albums. Hundreds of them. Most of them in covers well-worn and tattered.

Ben scanned the titles. "Are all these albums yours?"

Leeman nodded his head enthusiastically. "You?"

Ben nodded. "Yeah, I like music. I majored in music. I still play the piano, when there's time." Ben pulled out a blue album cover. "I have this one. Leonard Bernstein conducts Beethoven's Fifth with the New York Philharmonic. What do you think of it?"

Leeman waggled his shoulders in an indifferent manner.

"Yeah, same here. Great musician, but not his best recording. I think he was trying too hard to be innovative."

Leeman pointed to a group of albums on the same shelf.

Ben scanned the spines. "Wow. Are all of these recordings of Beethoven's Fifth? You've got good taste, Leeman."

Leeman moved in closer and pulled out one of the albums.

Ben read the label. "Roger Norrington. Yeah, I've got that one, too. Darn good recording. All period instruments. Fascinating interpretation. Is it your favorite?"

Leeman shook his head and placed his finger on another album.

Ben drew in his breath. "Hans Schmidt-Isserstedt. Vienna Philharmonic, 1966. A first-pressing analog recording." He pulled out the album and clutched it to his chest. "I've been looking for this album all my life. The experts say it's the greatest, most authentic recording of the Fifth ever made, but it's been out of print for years. I've haunted every used record store in Tulsa, but I've never found it. Where did you get it?"

"Papa," he replied simply.

Somehow, Ben wasn't surprised. "Leeman, you're a lucky man. I'd give almost anything for this record." He glanced at his watch. Enough pleasantries. Time to get to work. "Leeman. I'd like to ask you a few questions. Do you understand the charges that have been brought against you?"

Leeman's expression changed almost immediately—from one of utter tranquillity to one of haunted despair.

"Leeman, a doctor has said that you're capable of assisting in your own defense. Let's prove him right, okay? Help me out here."

Leeman looked back at Ben, his eyes wide and helpless. One of two possibilities was true. Leeman didn't want to help—he didn't even want to talk about it. Or, the doctor in Ponca City was out of his mind and Leeman was not capable of assisting in his own defense.

"Leeman, did you know the woman who was killed?"

Leeman turned away from the stereo and closed the cabinet.

"Did you see anything at the country club that night?"

Still no answer. Leeman was acting as he had when Ben first came in—as if he wasn't there.

"Leeman, you're going to have to tell me what you know about the murder."

"Hon . . . da," Leeman said abruptly.

"Honda?"

"Honda." Leeman held up his hands as if steering a car. "Honda."

"Oh—right. I drive a Honda. An eighty-two Honda Accord. How did you know?"

Leeman twisted around and faced the window. He held his right hand over his eyes, as if to block out the nonexistent sun. "See?"

Ben did see. Leeman's window overlooked the front parking lot. Leeman must've seen Ben park.

"You know your cars, don't you?" Ben refused to be so

easily distracted. "But getting back to the murder. Can you tell me what happened?"

Leeman turned away.

"Or what you saw? Whatever you know. Anything could help."

Leeman did not respond, did not turn around.

Ben grabbed Leeman by the shoulders and whirled him around. To his astonishment, he found that Leeman was crying.

Tears spilled out of his eyes and streamed down his bloated cheeks, dripping off his chin and onto his stained shirt. His lips trembled; the tears continued to flow.

Ben took a step back. "I'm sorry, Leeman. I didn't mean to—I didn't think."

He decided against any further questions. It was pointless. All the doctors in the Southwest couldn't convince Ben that Leeman was capable of assisting in his defense. Leeman might have some limited capacity for understanding, but he couldn't communicate. Whatever information he possessed in his head was locked up tight.

"I'm going to go now, Leeman."

"Honda?"

"Right. I'm going to drive away in my Honda. But I'll be back. Whether I take your case or not."

Leeman looked at him pensively.

"And next time I'll ask you to play me that Isserstedt recording. No excuses."

Leeman grinned. " 'Scuses," he echoed. He began humming the intro to the second movement of the Fifth while he carefully glued a left rear hubcap into place.

* 9 *

Ben walked briskly through the downtown office of the Tulsa Police Department Central Division and turned the corner around the gray office partition bearing the nameplate of LT. M. MORELLI, HOMICIDE. He was pleased to find the detective was in.

"How goes it, shamus?"

Mike looked up from his desk. A toothpick was cocked in the side of his mouth. "Surviving. Yourself?"

"I had a morning like you wouldn't—" Ben stopped short. "Wait a minute. Something's different."

"I beg your pardon?"

"Something's not right." Ben snapped his fingers. "Your pipe! Where is it?"

Mike shifted the toothpick to the other side of his mouth. "In my safe. Locked."

"And you're sucking on a sliver of wood?" The light dawned in Ben's eyes. "You're trying to quit."

"Yeah, well, all my friends were doing it."

"Is it hard? I always assumed that tobacco inhalation was just part of your macho two-fisted facade."

"That, plus a major nicotine addiction."

"So you're having trouble quitting?"

Mike grunted. "Gained ten pounds last week. That's when I switched to toothpicks."

"Well, I'm proud of you, pal." He laughed. "One of the boys at the desk told me you were kind of grumpy today. This explains why."

"This has nothing to do with it. Got a sicko chickenhawk who's costing me a lot of sleep."

"A what?"

"Chickenhawk. A pedophile. And, in this case, a pornographer."

Ben's face crinkled. "Do I want to hear about this?"

"Probably not. This perverted bastard has already snatched four little boys and he's still at large, like a nightmare haunting every child in the city. You wouldn't believe the disgusting things he does to these kids. It'd tear your heart out. This goes way beyond your run-of-the-mill pedophilia. We're talking about a major-league pervert with a taste for violence. And torture."

"Do you have a description?"

"Not yet. None of the kids was alive after this creep was done with them."

Ben's throat suddenly felt dry. "How does he . . . get them?"

"We don't know how he picks his victims, but once he does, he grabs them, molests them, and makes them pose for dirty pictures. We found some photos in some homegrown magazines."

Mike opened his top desk drawer, then thought better of it. "Never mind. They'd make you sick. I guarantee it."

"Can't you go after the publishers?"

"Not anymore. Pornography's become a cottage industry. Anyone with a computer and a desktop publishing program, or even a typewriter and a photocopier, can print pornographic magazines. They distribute the stuff through the mail, or fax machines. Even computer bulletin boards. Makes it damn near impossible to trace."

"How can you be sure the dirty pictures are connected to the child molestation and murders?"

"I'm sure. Every single kid snatched to date has ended up in a magazine spread. That can't be a coincidence. And even if it was, we'd still hunt these kiddie-porn creeps. The line between child-porn fan and child molester is thin and quickly crossed. Show me a guy who's obsessed with these pictures, and I'll show you a guy who's probably going to act out his dreams someday with some poor little kid. He may be fantasizing, working up his courage, but mark my words, it will happen. These pictures feed it. They whet the appetite. They make it impossible to put these ideas out of their sick little minds."

Mike pressed a hand against his forehead. "This slime killed his first three playthings. His last victim ran out into the street and got creamed by a car on Memorial. We looked all around, but never found the pervert. We don't know where the kid was running from. We think he might've jumped out of a car while it was stopped at a light. Probably trying to escape." Mike shook his head. "He's been in a deep coma since the accident. He's not expected to—" Mike looked up suddenly.

Ben gripped Mike's shoulder. "Hang in there, pal."

Mike's face twisted. "Yeah."

"Do you have any leads?"

"Not to speak of. The last boy was wearing a red baseball cap when he disappeared. Wasn't wearing it when the car hit him. What I wouldn't give to find that cap in the trunk of some schmuck's car." He bit down on his toothpick. "And the odds of that are probably only about a hundred million to one."

"I'm sure you'll catch him in time," Ben said. "No one works harder than you."

"Yeah. But I want to get him before he ruins another little kid's life. Or ends it." He slapped the top of his desk. "But enough about my problems. How's my favorite piano player turned pettifogger?"

"Managing. As best I can, under the circumstances."

Ben had known Mike since their college days at the University of Oklahoma. They had been the best of friends—even roommates one year. In those days they played music gigs— Ben on piano, Mike on guitar and vocals—in some of the Norman beer joints and pizza parlors. Everything was fine— until Mike fell in love with Julia, Ben's younger sister.

Once married, Mike canceled his plans for graduate school and began concocting one plan after another for earning enough money to accommodate Julia in the manner to which she had become accustomed. It didn't work. The marriage disintegrated shortly after Mike graduated from the police academy. It all culminated in a nasty, protracted divorce—with Ben caught in the middle.

"I've been asked to take over the Leeman Hayes case," Ben explained.

Mike winced. "Boy, you know how to pick 'em, don't you? You must've been sitting around thinking: What could possibly be grimmer than representing a white supremacist? I know! The Leeman Hayes trial!"

"So you remember the case?"

Mike's eyes became hooded. "That, my friend, is a killing I will never forget. Never. It happened one of my first nights on patrol. First murder victim I ever saw."

"Really? You were the investigating officer?"

"No. I was the third man on the scene. Still—" His voice dropped. "If you had seen that victim, seen her blood-soaked body skewered up—" He looked away. "Well, it's a sight you'd never forget, I can guarantee you that. God knows I never have."

"Sounds like this case really left its mark."

"Changed my life, if you want to know the truth. That was the night I decided I wanted to work homicides."

"So you could prevent more horrible murders like that?"

"No. I knew murder would always be with us. I wanted to be in a position to guarantee the inhuman scum who did these hideous things didn't go unpunished." Mike gradually raised his head. "Lots of luck, pal. You're looking at a case I wouldn't wish on my worst enemy."

"Who's handling it at the district attorney's office?"

"Last I heard Myrna Adams was prosecuting."

Ben heaved a sigh of relief. "I was afraid Bullock might get it."

Mike switched his toothpick to the other side of his mouth. "I heard about your little run-in with him this morning."

"Already?"

"Gossip travels fast. After all, Ben, we're government employees. We don't do any real work."

"Right. So what evidence does the state have?"

"Don't you think you should ask Myrna?"

"I will. And I know what she'll tell me, too. As little as possible."

Mike stood up and stretched. "Well, I suppose I could help a bit. After all, the state is duty bound to come forth with exculpatory evidence."

"That's what the books say. But I usually have to file a ton of motions to get anything, and frankly, I don't have time for that rigmarole."

Mike ran his finger through his curly black hair. "Fair enough. Do you know how this crime was committed?"

"I know the victim was a woman. And—she was killed at a country club?"

"Correct. Utica Greens. Near the golf course, in the caddy-shack."

"And the victim was . . . ?"

"Maria Escondita Alvarez."

"Where was she from?"

"Peru. About six months before she had applied for a visa to the United States. I guess red tape in Peru is even thicker than it is here. She didn't get it until about a week before the murder. Then she flew to Tulsa."

"But why?"

"We never found out. We investigated, both here and in Peru, but it all came a cropper. She had no family to speak of, and few friends. She spent almost every cent she had just to get here. And as soon as she did, she got axed."

"Speculation?"

"You're asking me to guess?"

Ben nodded.

"Well, a lot of illegal drugs come to the United States via the Peru connection. Especially cocaine. She might've been involved. They say the average life span of a drug trafficker after he—or she—starts running drugs is less than ten years. God knows those country-club types are probably the only ones who can afford to be addicted to cocaine anymore."

"How was she killed?"

Mike stared at him. "You really don't know *anything* about this case, do you? You haven't heard?"

"Not the details."

"I keep forgetting you've only lived in Tulsa a few years. Anyone who was around ten years ago would remember. Maria got beat over the head with a golf club. A nine iron, as I recall."

Ben's eyebrows rose. "And that killed her?"

"No. She died when the broken shaft was driven through her neck."

Ben's hand reached tentatively for the nearest chair.

"Nailed her to the wall," Mike continued. "Like she'd been crucified in some grisly satanic ritual. She was still hanging upright—clothes torn, blood splashed all over her sagging body—when I arrived. The location and the weapon suggested that the crime wasn't premeditated. A spur-of-the-moment murder by an angry assailant with a deadly violent temper."

The words in Leeman's psychiatric report came back unbidden to Ben. A sudden, explosive temper. Hmm.

How long can you go on representing the scum of the earth?

"Why did the police arrest Leeman Hayes?" Ben asked.

"Leeman worked as a caddy at the country club. He'd been there for a couple of months. He wasn't the most brilliant caddy in the world—mentally retarded, you know—but by all accounts, he tried hard and managed the essentials. Everyone liked him. Until he turned up at the scene of the crime, in the middle of the night, and they found his fingerprints all over the murder victim. And the murder weapon."

"But if he was a caddy—"

"That wouldn't explain why he was there after midnight."

"But surely the fingerprints—"

"Granted, Leeman might have held the club before the murder occurred. But if so, where were the murderer's prints? If he had wiped the club clean, he would've wiped away Leeman's prints as well. And why would his prints be all over the victim? No, it just doesn't make sense. And there was more evidence—I forget the details. I think they found some of the woman's possessions in Leeman's locker."

"So that's the prosecution's case?"

"That—plus the confession."

Ben felt a sudden heaviness on his shoulders. "He *confessed*?"

"In a manner of speaking. We brought him in for questioning, but he wasn't capable of answering the questions. Not verbally, anyway. But then one of the officers asked him to *show* us what happened. He did that— pantomimed the whole scene."

"And?"

"You can see for yourself. It's on videotape—one of the first our department ever made. But I can tell you what you'll see. You'll see a reenactment of Leeman Hayes clubbing Maria Alvarez to death."

Ben decided to get that tape as soon as possible. "Thanks for the inside scoop, Mike. I won't forget it."

"No problem. Put in a good word for me next time you see your sis."

Ben raised a finger. "Speaking of whom—" He briefly told Mike what had happened that morning in his office.

Mike listened to Ben with astonishment. "I can't believe it!"

"Yeah. Hard to believe she'd leave her baby behind like that."

"Oh, I can believe that," Mike replied. "That part is pure Julia. I just can't believe she'd leave him with you."

Ben lowered his chin. "And what, may I ask, is wrong with me?"

Mike slapped him reassuringly on the shoulder. "Oh, you're nice enough, in your own stiff, mildly neurotic way. But you're hardly what I'd call a family man."

"I resent that."

"Come on, Ben. You've never gotten along with anyone in your family. Certainly not your sister. And when was the last time you visited your mother? Most guys would trip over themselves kissing up to a mommy with as much moolah as yours. But you see her, what? Maybe once a year. If there's no snow on the turnpike on Christmas Day."

"My mother and I have an understanding."

"And what about your dad? You upset him so badly he wrote you right out of his will!"

All traces of good humor disappeared from Ben's face. "You really don't know what the hell you're talking about, Mike."

Mike held his hands out. "Did I hit a sensitive spot? Sorry, chum. I was just attempting to explain my mystification that Julia would choose you to be her indentured baby-sitter when you've alienated every member of your family. Is there some family member I've omitted?"

Well, Ben thought, there was someone I thought of like a father, but that was hardly worth bringing up now. *I'm so disappointed, Ben. How could you let this happen to you?*

"Julia will be back soon," Ben said. "I'm sure she will. I bet she'll be back before nightfall."

"You're deluding yourself, *kemo sabe*."

Ben fidgeted with his briefcase. "I remember you told me you saw Julia not too long ago. Did she seem . . . distraught? Stressed out?"

Mike shrugged. "No more so than usual. But that was over a year ago. Becoming a mother changes women."

"If you say so." Ben started to leave, then stopped. "If worse comes to worst, I don't suppose you'd care to do some baby-sitting?"

"For my ex-wife's new baby?" Mike's look of amazement slowly faded into a soft smile. "There was a time when I would've done anything in the world for Julia. Anything. If she just would've stayed with me one more night."

He took a deep breath, then slowly released it. "Sure thing, pal. I can help look after the little booger. Just tell me when to show up. I'll bring the pizza and beer."

* 10 *

Carlee Crane watched as her husband, Dave, introduced their two sons to the joys of whittling.

"It's like this," Dave said, carefully demonstrating how to open and close their pocketknives. "Put your knife in your right hand, and hold the block of wood in your left. Always stroke away from you, not toward you. Understand, Ethan?"

Ethan, who had just turned six, peered up at his father with his usual inquisitive, somewhat skeptical expression. "Why?"

Dave's eyes soared toward the heavens. It was an inquiry Ethan had made with increasing frequency during the past year.

"Because you don't want to hurt yourself."

Their other son, Gavin, an elder sage of eight, volunteered an answer. "If you stroke toward yourself, Ethan, you'll end up cutting off your hand or poking a hole in your stomach. Knowing you, you'd probably kill all four of us with a single blow."

"Gavin," Carlee said, "don't talk to your brother like that."

"I'm just trying to keep him from slaughtering us, Mom, like that guy who kills all the campers in those *Friday the 13th* movies."

"Gavin," Dave interjected, "your brother is not Jason."

"I don't know," Gavin said. "He looks pretty scary in a hockey mask."

Carlee smiled. This was her family, God help her. It was too late to trade them in now.

She reached over and turned on the portable radio they had brought with them. It was tuned to the NPR station. Terry

Gross was finishing an interview with yet another jazz musician.

"Let's continue the whittling lesson," Dave said.

"Aw, gee, Dad," Ethan said. "Do we have to?"

"Yes, you have to," Dave said emphatically. "You don't want to hurt yourself, do you?"

There was no immediate answer forthcoming.

"Of course you don't," Dave answered for him. "Smart campers don't hurt themselves."

Here we go again, Carlee thought. Since they had arrived at their Turner Falls campsite in the Arbuckle Mountains two days before, Carlee had heard Dave indoctrinate his children on his own personal code of forbidden camp conduct, which could be titled *What Smart Campers Don't Do*. Don't swim for an hour after eating. Don't build a campfire without a protective ring of rocks. Don't pitch your tent on a slope. All these lessons and more were reinforced with the injunction "Only stupid campers do that." Presumably, Dave believed that nothing would mortify the boys more than being thought stupid campers. In truth, Gavin and Ethan would probably be more attentive if he threatened to take away their Game Boys.

Fresh Air ended, and a local news update began. Carlee turned up the volume. ". . . commenting on the impending trial of Leeman Hayes ten years after the heinous killing occurred. Hayes is accused of murdering a Peruvian woman in the caddyshack at the Utica Greens Country Club."

"Hear that?" Carlee said. "That's where I used to work."

No one heard her. The menfolk were all focusing their full attention on their knives and blocks.

"A murder at Utica Greens," she murmured. "I'm surprised I don't remember it." Even as she said it to herself, though, something struck her as not quite right.

She glanced at her watch. It was almost time to fix supper, which meant deciding which of several cans she was going to open. Dave had made some noise about "roughing it" and learning to cook such campfire delicacies as steak Diane and foil taters. When all was said and done, however, she was the cook, and the cook was on vacation. There was a reason God made canned food, the cook announced, and this was it.

She knew she should get started, but somehow, she couldn't quite work up the energy. It was so peaceful here, watching her family, feeling the wind toss about her long hair, seeing the sun slowly dip behind the Arbuckle Mountains.

Nah. The cans would keep.

"Now, first," Dave continued, "you need to decide what you're going to make. What are you going to make, Gavin?"

Gavin blinked several times. "Gosh, I dunno."

"Well, what does your block of wood look like to you?"

"Well . . ." Gavin stared at it intently. "It looks like a square."

"It is a square, but—" Dave's face tightened. "Don't you have an imagination?"

"I guess not," Gavin replied. "Least not when it comes to blocks of wood."

"It's Nintendo that's done it," Dave said, glancing at his wife. "Nintendo and MTV. Pollutes their minds. Feeds them everything. Before long, they've forgotten how to use their imaginations and they can't tolerate anything that takes longer than three and a half minutes."

"Maybe you could teach them by example," Carlee suggested.

"Wow, what a concept," Dave murmured. "I see now how you got that degree in secondary education." He picked up his knife and block. "Okay, craft lovers, watch this."

"Will it take long?" Ethan whined.

"Why, have you got a date or something?"

"No . . . but I am getting kinda hungry. . . ."

Dave bit down on his lower lip. "Just watch for a minute, okay? Good. Now, I think my block of wood looks like"— his eyes wandered about, then lighted on Carlee—". . . your mother."

"Mother!" Both Gavin and Ethan cackled with laughter. "Dad thinks you look like a square block of wood!"

"How flattering," Carlee said.

"It's not that it looks like her *now*," Dave said. "But see what happens when I do . . . this." He sliced his knife through the block, curling off a sliver of wood.

"Hey," Gavin observed, "shouldn't you be stroking away from—"

"Shush and watch," Dave said. He continued cutting. "And then I do this . . . and this . . . and—*ow!*"

Dave shouted, then dropped the knife and block. Both boys jumped into the air, startled.

"What happened?" Carlee asked. "What did you—"

The answer was evident before she finished the question. Violating his own code, Dave had stroked toward himself and cut his hand.

"How bad is it?" Carlee blanched. Blood was spurting from the wound. Dave squeezed down on it with his other hand, but the blood spilled out through his fingers.

"Get the first-aid kit!" Dave shouted.

Carlee continued staring at the blood streaming from his wound. It smeared his arms and dripped onto the ground, making gruesome dark puddles. A sickly sweet odor permeated the air.

Carlee felt a wave of nausea sweeping over her. She put down a hand to steady herself, but was unable to take her eyes away from him. She saw her husband clutching his hand, covered with blood, and—

And then she saw something else. Some . . . *where* else. She was still outside, but she was . . . looking through an open window. She was looking into a building. No, a room. She was looking into the corner where a woman stood against the wall. The woman was covered with blood, blood was spurting everywhere, blood was soaking her clothes and the walls and the floor. . . .

"Carlee, are you going to help me or not?"

Carlee heard his voice, but it seemed far away, distant. Unreal. What was real was what she was . . . *seeing*. That poor woman, backed into the corner. The woman was crying, screaming, and . . . and . . .

Something struck the woman again, this time in the neck. A bloodcurdling howl was choked off and replaced by a death rattle. Blood spurted again and splashed throughout the room and the color and the smell and the sticky wetness was all over everything and . . .

Carlee screamed.

"Carlee, what is wrong with you? You're scaring the kids!"

Carlee clenched her eyes shut. The woman in the corner faded away. Carlee reopened her eyes slowly and saw her husband hovering over her. Somehow she had ended up on the ground, flat on her back.

Dave was still gripping his hand, but the flow of blood had subsided. "Are you all right?"

"I—I think so." She licked her lips. Her throat was dry. "I don't know what happened."

Dave's forehead creased. "I'll get the first-aid kit myself."

"Oh, but—"

Too late. He was gone.

When Dave returned, about a minute later, his hand was wrapped in white gauze. "It isn't serious," he informed his family. "It bled like crazy, but it was just a superficial cut." He sat down beside his wife. "What about you? Are you all right?"

It's not superficial, Carlee thought. Her eyes were closed. It's everywhere. The blood is everywhere.

"Carlee, did you hear me?"

"She needs help," Carlee said aloud. "That poor woman needs help."

"Carlee?" Dave took her by the shoulders, favoring his injured hand. "What are you talking about?"

Carlee shook her head, then brought her eyes around to face him. "I—I—" She didn't know where to begin.

"What happened to you?"

"I—I guess it was the sight of all that blood. . . ."

"You were acting like—I don't know—like you were in a trance or something."

Carlee was suddenly aware that their two boys were standing around her with very concerned expressions on their faces. "I'm fine, everyone. Really I am. I was just . . . I don't know. But I'm fine." She took Dave's hand and examined his wound. "Looks like you'll live."

"Yeah." Neither Dave nor the boys moved away from her. "We're more concerned about you. You said something about blood, and—a woman?"

Had she? She didn't remember saying that. She didn't remember speaking at all. And yet, she knew Dave wouldn't lie. And she had seen something.

She closed her eyes and tried to remember, but nothing came to her. It was gone.

"I was just . . . daydreaming," she said, doing her level best to sound convincing. "Probably induced by hunger." She slapped her boys on the back. "I think it's time for dinner. Any takers?"

"I dunno," Gavin said meekly. "Is it Beenie Weenies again?"

Carlee laughed and guided them back to the designated mess tent. She tried to remain chipper while she fixed dinner, and tried to avoid doing anything that would alarm the children. She could tell Dave was watching her, though. He knew something had happened to her. Something serious. And it bothered him.

Which was only natural, she supposed, because it bothered her, too. What had happened was incredibly strange. In fact, it was unlike anything she could—

Remember.

* 11 *

The blazing sun was setting and the Bank of Oklahoma Tower, Tulsa's tallest office building, cast a long shadow across downtown. Ben tried to walk in its shade, but that didn't diminish the heat in the least. As soon as he stepped off the sidewalk, the humidity enveloped him. Like stepping into an oven, Ben thought.

He heard the screaming while he was still on the opposite sidewalk. He broke into a sprint, raced across the street, and threw open the front door.

Joey was on top of Jones's desk, wailing at what had to be the top capacity of his tiny lungs. His face was red and blotchy; his nose was running. Jones hovered over the infant, his hands pressed against his head in abject frustration.

"I don't know what to do!" Jones screamed, easily matching Joey for high-pitched audibility. "I've tried everything I can think of. I hold him; I don't hold him. I talk to him; I don't talk to him. I rock him; I throw him up in the air. Nothing makes any difference. I'm pulling my hair out, but he just keeps on crying!"

Jones gripped Ben by the lapels. "I even tried *singing* to him, for God's sake, and I don't sing! I think that's in my employment contract. But here I was, singing every dumb little ditty that came to mind—and it *still* didn't help! I don't know what to do!"

"So . . ." Ben ventured. "How's the baby-sitting going?"

Jones's face bore a crazed expression. "This nephew of yours is pushing me over the edge, Boss."

"Sorry to hear that." Ben had to shout to be heard over the bawling. "What's wrong with him?"

"I wish I knew. I've been asking for over an hour, but he never says anything." Jones's left eye twitched; by all appearances, he was just shy of a nervous breakdown.

"He's only seven months old, Jones. He doesn't talk."

"Couldn't he at least nod?"

To their mutual relief, Christina entered the office, her arms loaded down with files. "Good Lord, what a brouhaha! What have you two done to that poor baby?"

"I suspect it's more a matter of what we haven't done," Ben murmured.

She threw the files down on her desk. "Well, don't just stand there. Pick him up."

Ben looked at her blank-faced. "Who? Me?"

"Yes! He's your nephew. Pick him up."

Ben stared down at the squirming infant. "To tell the truth . . . I don't really know how."

"Haven't you ever held him before?"

"Well, once, but Julia put him in my arms . . ."

"Criminy. Didn't you ever baby-sit for spare change when you were a kid? Never mind, don't answer. You probably just had your banker wire some funds." She wedged herself in front of Jones's desk. "Look, he's seven months old. He's not that fragile." She lifted the baby up and plopped him into Ben's arms. "See? Just put your hand behind his little neck. That's right."

Ben wrapped his arms around the baby. The volume of the screeching seemed to diminish.

"Now, that wasn't so hard, was it?" Christina asked.

"No," Ben said, "but I notice the baby is still crying."

"Good point. What did you feed him?"

Jones and Ben looked blankly at one another. "Feed him?"

"Yes, feed him." She pressed two fingers against her temples. "Regular Mr. Moms, you guys are."

"What do you think he eats?"

"I'm not sure." Christina foraged in Joey's red diaper bag. "He may still be breast-feeding."

"Now wait just a minute," Ben said. "There's no way I'm going to—"

"Keep your masculinity in check." She pulled a quart can of Isomil out of the bag. "Formula."

"Thank God," Ben said. "Can opener's on top of the mini-fridge."

Christina pulled an empty bottle out of the diaper bag and poured in the Isomil. "He'd probably prefer to have his formula warmed, but this will have to do for the moment." She passed the bottle to Ben. "Here, give him this."

"Here? Now?"

"Yes! *Tout de suite!*"

Ben shifted the baby around in his arms, took the bottle, and tried to hand it to Joey. "Here you go, chum. Eat up."

Christina shook her head sadly. "I don't think so." She took the bottle and aimed the nipple in the general direction of Joey's mouth. Joey eagerly began to suck. The crying stopped immediately.

"Success," Ben said softly.

"Hurray," Christina echoed. "And see how he's looking at you? You're his hero now."

"Well, gosh," Ben said. "That's swell. Now all we need to do is get Julia back here as soon as possible."

"About that . . ." Christina held a slip of paper between her fingers. "I found this in the diaper bag."

Christina held up the note and Ben read it aloud while he fed the baby: " 'Dear Ben: I'm sorry to do this to you, but I don't know who else to turn to. You know how screwed up I've been. This graduate-school program in Connecticut is a chance to get my life back in order. Maybe my last chance. But they'll never take me if I have a baby. I'll be pulling emergency-room duty for days at a time—day care won't cut it. A single mother simply cannot do this. Terry hasn't spoken to me since the divorce. He never visits Joey. Claims he doesn't think the baby is his, which is just a stupid excuse to justify not paying child support. I don't even know where he is now. I couldn't get hold of Mother. You were my last chance.

" 'Take care of my little baby.

" 'Ninny-poo.' "

Christina folded the note and put it back in the diaper bag. "Ninny-poo?"

Ben's eyes seemed to turn inward. "That's . . . just a silly nickname. What I used to call Julia when we played together as little kids. You know, just three or four years old." He shook his head. "Haven't thought about that in years."

"I thought you and your sister never got along."

"We—" Ben paused. "Well, we didn't. I mean—" He frowned. "Never mind. We have urgent business to address. I can't possibly keep Julia's baby for her, especially if I decide to handle this trial next week. Jones, call my mother."

Jones's eyebrow arched. "Is it Christmas already?"

"Ha-ha." As everyone in the office knew, Ben's mother was a wealthy matron who lived in Nichols Hills, one of the most upscale neighborhoods in Oklahoma City. None of them had ever met her, but Ben usually described her as "frosty" or "disapproving." She had repeatedly offered to help Ben out of his financially strapped circumstances, particularly after his father died and left Ben zippo, but Ben steadfastly refused to take her money.

"See if you can track Mother down. Maybe she can help. After all, the kid's her only grandchild."

"I'll do it."

"Good. Then start trying to find Julia."

"Aye-aye, Boss."

"Where's Loving?" Loving was their nails-for-knuckles private investigator. "I haven't seen him around today."

"He's working on a case of his own."

"Know what he's doing?"

"Not exactly. But today's entry on his desk calendar says, 'Make Guntharp's life a misery.' "

"I pity poor Guntharp."

"Yeah. Me, too."

"Well, ask Loving to come into the office first thing tomorrow morning. We'll have a team meeting. By then I should know whether we're taking this murder case."

"Should I be here, too?" Christina asked.

"Actually . . . I'd appreciate it if you would come by my apartment tomorrow morning before work."

Christina beamed. "Because you think I'm so *magnifique* it will brighten your whole day?"

"Actually . . . I'm concerned that Joey may need to be fed again. . . ."

Christina's smile collapsed. "And I'm sure he'll wait patiently until morning before he brings that to your attention. Boy, have you got a lot to learn. By the way, gentlemen— when was the last time you changed the baby's diaper?"

Ben and Jones exchanged another look.

Christina groaned. "Maybe you two had better start taking notes."

12

The man in the red wig wasn't entirely sure how the fight began. He had been following Abie since he left school, waiting for an opportunity to make his first move. While he watched and waited two boys approached Abie from the other side of the street. Both looked as if they were a year or two older than Abie. One was eating a hot dog; the more menacing one was swinging a baseball bat.

"Look at the rich kid, Seth," the older boy said. "He thinks he's a baseball player." He knocked the Drillers cap off Abie's head. "I think he's a weenie."

"I think you're right, Jeremy." He began to chant in a singsong voice, "Weenie boy, weenie boy. Abie is a weenie boy."

"Am not!" Abie shouted. He bent over to scoop up his hat. The older boy knocked him down.

"What's the matter, Abie? Lost your balance? Maybe you could get the butler to help you up."

Both boys laughed heartily. The older one snatched the cap away before Abie could retrieve it.

"You know, Seth, I kinda like this cap. I think I'm gonna keep it."

"Are not!" Abie said. The side of his face was scraped from his fall onto the concrete. "It's mine! Give it back!"

"Oh yeah?" Jeremy said, swinging his bat in the air. "Who's gonna make me, *weenie*?"

The man in the wig knew he'd never get a better entrance cue than that. He ran in between them and pushed the bullies away from Abie.

"What's going on here?" he demanded.

The boys' eyes ballooned. Jeremy raised his baseball bat, but the man took it away with no trouble.

"Well, now," the man said, swinging the bat through the air, "maybe I should just treat you two like you've been treating this boy. How would you like that?"

The two bullies turned to run away. Reaching out quickly, the man grabbed the shorter of the two, Seth, by the back of his collar. He whirled the boy around.

"Your name is Abie, right?" the man asked.

Abie nodded.

"That's what I heard them say." He pushed Seth closer to him. "What do you think I should do with him, Abie?"

"Gosh. I dunno."

"It's up to you. His fate is in your hands. Personally, I think he should be punished."

"Well, gee . . ." Abie mumbled.

"Punishment is very important, Abie. Especially for bad boys like this one. So I'm putting you in charge. You choose his punishment." He peered down at the now-terrified boy he held tight. "Makes you wish you'd been a bit nicer to my friend Abie, doesn't it?"

"Don't hurt me, mister. My dad is home and—"

"Be quiet. Abie, what's it going to be?"

"Well," Abie said, tentatively reaching forward, "how about . . . *this*?" He grabbed Seth's hot dog and mashed it into his face. Bits of frankfurter and mustard clung to his cheeks. "Now who's a weenie, huh?"

The man released Seth's collar and he bolted away. "Nice job, Abie."

Abie shrugged. "I didn't do nothin'. You did it all."

The man held out his hand. "My name's . . . Sam."

Abie hesitantly shook the man's hand.

"Why were they teasing you, Abie?"

"I dunno. I didn't do nothin' to them."

"It's because your father is rich, isn't it? I heard what they said."

Abie kicked a rock down the sidewalk. "I guess. It's so unfair."

"Of course it is. It's not your fault your father has all that money, is it?"

"No. I never wanted any money. I just—" He looked at the man, frowned, fell silent.

"That's all right, Abie," the man said. His smile was smooth and warm. "I won't tell. You'd rather your father spent time with you than at his job, right?"

"It isn't his job," Abie blurted out, as if an emotional dam had suddenly burst. "He doesn't really have a job. It's all his friends down at that stupid country club. All those stupid fat rich guys. And those ladies—"

"You don't like those ladies, do you?"

Abie shrugged. "I dunno. Mom doesn't."

The man nodded. "Do you mind if I walk you home? Um . . . those boys might come back."

"Sure."

They began to stroll down the sidewalk together, side by side. Abie cleared his throat. "I guess I forgot to say thank you for, you know. Back there."

"Not necessary. I'm sure you could've handled them."

Abie hung his head low. "I woulda gotten creamed."

The man smiled. "If you'd like, I could teach you how to defend yourself."

"Really?" In his excitement, Abie grabbed the man's arm. A frisson of pleasure tingled through the man's body. "You know how to fight?"

"I know enough to take care of those two. You'd pick it up easily. You look like a natural athlete to me."

"That's not what my father says."

They rounded the corner onto Twenty-first Street and strolled through Woodward Park. A few minutes later they were in front of Abie's home.

"Thanks for letting me walk you home, Abie. I hope I see you again sometime."

"Sure. Me, too." Abie bit down on his lip. "Mister—I mean,

Sam. You won't tell my father about those two kids pushing me around, will you?"

"Of course not," he replied. "I already told you, you can trust me. I'll keep your secrets. And in return, I know I can trust you not to tell anyone about me."

"Gee. Sure. Um . . . you're not in any kind of . . . trouble, are you?"

The man grinned. "No. I just thought your father might not approve if he knew I walked you home."

"Yeah. Prob'ly right. He'd say I should fight my own battles or somethin' like that. And he never likes any of my friends." He glanced at his huge Tudor-style mansion home. "I guess I'd better go inside now."

Abie started to leave, then hesitated. "Um . . . Sam?"

"Yes?"

Abie peered up at him. "Why did you do that?"

"Do what?"

"You know. Help me."

The man was genuinely surprised at the question. "No particular reason, Abie. I just want to be your friend. Your very special friend."

Abie smiled, then scampered up the front lawn and ran into his house.

* 13 *

Lieutenant Mike Morelli spat the soggy toothpick out of his mouth. Goddamn those tasteless little slivers of wood, anyway, he thought. I think I got a splinter in my tongue.

When did smokers become the modern-day Typhoid Marys? It was only a pipe, after all. The flavor barely mattered. He enjoyed messing around with the tobacco, the tamper, the pipe cleaners. It was relaxing. It gave him something to do during all-night stakeouts or interminable departmental meetings. He liked the feel of the warm pipe bowl in his hands. Hell, sometimes he forgot to puff the thing. He probably sent more nicotine into the ozone layer than he did into his lungs. How much harm could it do?

Oh, what's the use? He'd been over all this before. It was a dangerous affectation, one he could live without. If Jane Fonda could quit smoking, then by God, he could, too. He reopened his economy-size box of five hundred toothpicks and shoved another one into his mouth.

Truth of the matter was, this entire exercise in angst was just a stalling device. He was sick of this research and he didn't want to do it anymore. He'd read a dozen profiles of pedophilic offenders, each one worse than the one before. The words, and worse, the pictures, branded themselves on his memory. Nude pictures of eight-year-olds. Anal assaults. Forced fellatio. His stomach ached and his brain yearned to be diverted to a different subject.

It just wasn't fair. He'd worked hard to get himself into Homicide, making painstaking efforts to avoid any contact with the Sex Crimes Division. And now he was confronted by child homicides that doubled as sex crimes. And a bloodthirsty pedophile. The worst kind.

Not that there were any good kinds. Mike had been up all night researching, trying to educate himself on topics he had intentionally avoided when he was at the academy. He found the whole subject revolting—and incomprehensible. Some crimes, after all, anyone could understand. Anyone could be driven to murder, Mike firmly believed, given the right circumstances. Anyone could be driven to steal; Victor Hugo had taught him that. But pedophilia—that was too foreign, too sickening.

As he was learning, pedophiles were not all the slavering, skid-row monsters that he thought they would be—indeed, that he wanted them to be. Pedophiles came from all walks of life—all income brackets, all occupations. According to the shrinks, they know they're different at an early age.

Since they know what they're interested in early on, they can plan accordingly. It wasn't an accident that so many of these perverts turned up as teachers or camp counselors or scout leaders. If you know what you want, you figure out a way to get it. So pedophiles intentionally choose professions that put them in contact with children, preferably in some sort of trusted-adviser role.

Mike generally thought psychological profiles were a lot of useless mumbo jumbo and scrupulously avoided them. In this case, however, it was unavoidable; anyone who would do this stuff obviously had serious mental problems. The shrinks, he learned, divided pedophiles into two categories. The more common were *situational* child molesters—the ones the boys in Sex Crimes called *try-sexuals*. They were experimenters. They'd try anything—homosexuality, animals, children. The other class were the *preferential* pedophiles—the hard-core cases. They went after children because that's what they liked. Period.

The vicious, repetitive cycle of so many domestic crimes was also evident in child molestation, Mike learned. Pedophiles almost always were sexually abused when they were young. When they grew up, they shifted from being victims to being abusers. According to the experts, this was why most pedophiles have a preference for children of a particular age. Turns out, pedophiles fixate on children of the same age they were when they were first sexually abused.

Sometimes, Mike read, pedophiles will start grooming a child, cozying up to him, before he reaches the target age, so that when he does arrive, the stage will be set. And the victims covered the full range of ages, too. Mike read about cases of sexual abuse of infants—less than one-year-olds. He found a case where the pedophile insisted that the kid had "asked for it," led him on, exposed himself in a provocative manner. The kid was barely two and still in diapers.

When he first tried to trace the kiddie porn back to the killer, Mike learned that the stereotype of pedophile-as-sicko-loner was often false. Many pedophiles worked in teams. Networks, in the modern jargon. They had mailing lists, fax machines, computer bulletin boards, even Internet Web pages, for exchanging names and circulating photos. Most of the slick foreign magazines—like *Kinderlieb, Ballbusters*—had been driven out of the country by a concerted federal law-enforcement effort. So the creeps began to grow their own.

Perhaps the most amazing fact Mike learned was that pedophiles often seemed to have a genuine affection for children, including their young lovers. They were concerned about their welfare. Almost uniformly, the child molesters studied didn't think they'd done anything wrong. They didn't understand what all the fuss was about. After all, all they'd done was share a little love. What could be wrong with that?

This was an important piece of information, Mike realized, because once you understood what made molesters tick, you could figure out how to catch them. Unlike rapists and serial killers, he learned, pedophiles rarely grab kids and force themselves on them immediately. Pedophiles try to seduce their victims. They try to win them over. They try to earn the kid's trust. They seek out children from dysfunctional families, children who are unhappy at home. Children who are vulnerable. The pedophile finds an opening and tries to fill it. If Mom and Dad can't afford to give the kid a bicycle, he'll give the kid a bicycle. If the kid needs to be treated with respect, he treats him with respect. If the kid doesn't get enough attention, he'll give him attention. Warm fuzzies. Trust. Whatever it takes.

And so the seduction goes.

Sometimes, even after the creeps are caught, the kids won't rat on them. After all, they don't want to hurt their best friend.

That's what the pedophile counts on.

Mike found the crime statistics inconsistent and unreliable. No one really knew how prevalent this crime was. It was pitifully underreported, even more so than rape. There were a million reasons for a kid not to tell. He might be financially dependent on the molester, or the molester might be in a position of authority over him. The kid might have genuine affection for him, or think he does, anyway. Worse, sometimes parents encourage their kids to remain quiet. They don't want the stigma, the horrible publicity. They don't want their kid dragged through the police, the newspapers, the courts. Who would want their neighbors to hear a report on the six o'clock news about their little boy being molested?

Mike pushed away his notes and pressed his hands against his face. He knew this research was changing him, changing the way he viewed the world. Now every time he saw a stranger at a bus stop talking to a little boy, or a Little League coach swatting one of his players on the backside, he'd wonder: *Is he the one?* It wasn't fair—there were many good-hearted, upright people working with kids. But nowadays parents couldn't help but be suspicious. They *had* to be suspicious.

"Christ," Mike whispered. "What a nightmare. Just as well we never had any kids."

Mike thought about calling it quits for the night and heading home, but what was the point? There was nothing waiting for him there. Nothing but a half-empty bottle of Mogen-David and the *Complete Works of William Shakespeare*. Hip, hip, hooray. What was it Mark Twain said? Be good, and you will be lonesome.

Very true. Except Mike wasn't sure he had been all that good.

On a sudden whim, Mike pulled his wallet out of his back pocket, removed his Citibank credit card, and looked at the small photo hidden behind it.

There she was, in all her glory. Beautiful long chestnut-brown hair. Silly turned-up nose. Freckles. All those years ago.

The picture had been taken the day he and Julia were married.

When he'd seen her last, more than a year ago, she was not in great shape. Her new marriage was on the skids, and she'd regained a lot of weight. But she was still beautiful. Just seeing her again made him forget all the pain, all the emptiness, all the disillusionment. After the divorce, he swore that commitment was for suckers, that nothing lasted, nothing remained. That it was all hopeless.

Hopeless. Nothing remained.

If he knew what he had done wrong, he could fantasize about going back in time and changing things, doing it right. But the fact was, he had no idea what he would do differently. He had done everything he could think of to keep her—hadn't he? But in the end, it hadn't made any difference.

He should get rid of this picture. He should tear it up, forget about her, and get on with his life. But somehow . . .

He carefully slid the picture back under his credit card and shoved the wallet into his pocket. Nothing had changed—not really. Not about the way he felt. No matter what he tried to tell himself, through all the heartache, all the misery, all the tears . . .

Some things remained.

* 14 *

Ben punched the remote and sent the videotape back to the beginning, trying to be as quiet as possible. He didn't normally think of operating the VCR as a noisy chore, but tonight he was taking no chances. It had taken him hours to get Joey to sleep. He hadn't gone down until well after midnight, and Ben suspected that the slightest sound could bring him back to life at full roar.

Ben's first night at home alone with his nephew had been an unmitigated nightmare. His ignorance of the world of child care knew no bounds. He didn't know the first thing about babies. How do you get the nipple to go inside that plastic ring? Why do women squirt milk on their wrist? How can you tell which side of the diaper goes up? Does it matter?

And this was a good one—where do you put them down to sleep if you don't happen to have a crib in your bachelor pad? He'd made do with an oversized plastic laundry basket. All right—it looked stupid, but it was the best he could come up with on the spur of the moment. Joey didn't seem to mind; he just didn't want Uncle Ben to leave him there alone. So he cried. Loudly. After striking out with every lullaby he knew, Ben tried all the poetry he could recite from memory, which wasn't all that much. Only "Annabel Lee" seemed to calm Joey. Somewhat. Ben hoped it was the rhythm and rhyme that turned the trick, not the melancholy ruminations on premature death. *It was many and many a year ago, in a kingdom by the sea . . .*

Joey quieted, but he still wasn't asleep. Ben tried several quiet songs he knew, a few half-remembered Disney tunes, but nothing seemed to work. Finally, for no reason he could fathom, he began singing the theme from *The Flintstones*. Hardly a nursery standard. It was a wacky idea, but . . .

It worked. A sweet contented smile emerged the instant Joey heard "Flintstones . . . meet the Flintstones . . ." Halfway through the song, his eyelids fluttered closed.

At long last, he had drifted to sleep. Of course, once he was asleep, Ben worried about whether he was breathing. Ben pressed his ear up to Joey's mouth until he heard the soft intake of baby breath. He couldn't remember what the latest was—were babies supposed to sleep on their backs or their tummies? Or maybe their sides? Were they allowed to have pillows? Why did Joey keep kicking off the blankets?

Ben finally tore himself away from baby watching and plopped down, thoroughly exhausted, on the sofa in the front room of his apartment. As soon as he was situated, Giselle, Ben's cat, pounced into his lap. Giselle was obviously not pleased about this interloper who had invaded their apartment and occupied Ben's attention, not to mention his lap, all night long.

Christina had given Giselle to Ben as a present a few birthdays back, and the cat seemed to have been eating continuously ever since. Of course, she would eat nothing but the most expensive gourmet cat food. Ben had never had a pet before and never particularly wanted one either, but since Christina was a dear friend and tended to drop by his apartment fairly frequently, the animal shelter was out of the question. He had never quite determined what breed of cat Giselle was; all he knew was that she was black and she was large. Huge, really. The dinosaur of cats.

Giselle rubbed her wet nose into Ben's face. Charming. Her nuzzle felt scratchier than usual, though. Ben glanced down casually, then shot off the sofa.

Giselle had a dead bird clutched in her teeth.

"Giselle!" He started to shout, then remembered the sleeping babe in the next room. "What have I told you about dragging carcasses into the living room?"

Ben paused, breathing rapidly, almost as if he expected

Giselle to answer. Instead, she clenched the tattered remains of the unfortunate blue jay in her mouth and purred.

"If you must act upon your biological imperative and kill living creatures, at least don't drag them inside!" Ben tried to keep Giselle indoors, but about two weeks earlier she had discovered the trapdoor in the ceiling of his bedroom closet. The trapdoor permitted access to the roof. Ben crawled up there sometimes to gaze at the stars and remind himself that he wasn't afraid of heights anymore.

Giselle went up there to hunt.

Ben continued scolding to no avail. Finally, he ran into the kitchen and opened a can of Feline's Fancy. As soon as Giselle heard the motor of the can opener, she dropped her treasure and bolted toward her food dish. Ben then circled back to the living room, scooped up the lifeless remains, and dropped them out his bedroom window into the open trash bins in the back alley.

Once his domestic chores were completed, he sat down to review the videotape of the Leeman Hayes confession. He watched it three times, front to back, without intermission.

And each time he got more depressed.

Small wonder they were going forward with the prosecution of Leeman Hayes. The effect of that videotape on an Oklahoma jury would be devastating.

The first half hour was an exercise in sheer frustration. Leeman was represented by his first attorney, an old-school lawyer now deceased. The DA was present, as was a physician who had been assigned to the case. Ben also recognized Ernie Hayes—a ten-years-younger version of the one he had met.

The DA began asking questions, trying to get Leeman to tell what he knew about the murder of Maria Alvarez.

They got absolutely nowhere. Leeman was not uncooperative; on the contrary, he seemed willing to do anything for these nice men in white shirts and ties. He just couldn't. He didn't possess even the most rudimentary communication skills that would allow him to answer their questions.

The interrogators tried using different approaches, simpler terms. They spoke loud; they spoke soft. They acted friendly;

they acted angry. Friend, foe; good cop, bad cop. It made no difference.

Finally, someone had the brilliant idea of showing Leeman a picture. They gave him the only known premortem photo of Maria Alvarez, taken about three years before.

Leeman recognized her. That much was clear. Even Leeman's stoutest defender could no longer doubt that he had seen her before.

Next, over Ernie's vigorous objection, the interrogating officer showed Leeman a photo of Maria taken at the crime scene. Her face and chest were soaked with blood; the shaft of the broken golf club still protruded from her neck.

Leeman turned away almost instantly. But again there was little doubt—he had seen this before.

The lead interrogating officer asked Leeman to tell him what had happened that night, and when that didn't work, he pantomimed the act of clubbing someone over the head. That turned the trick. Leeman began not to talk, but to *act out* the murder.

Leeman's face was transformed. The eager, friendly, puppy-dog expression disappeared. He stood on his tiptoes and crept across the expanse of the room, then made a shoving gesture.

"That's how he got the woman's attention," one of the detectives on the tape said.

Amazingly enough, Leeman then switched characters. He became Maria, and enacted her reaction. She was startled, then angry. It was impossible to discern why she was upset, as Leeman used no words. But something was definitely the matter.

In the next few moments Leeman shifted back and forth between characters so many times it was difficult to tell who did what to whom. Somehow, a fight broke out, and Maria got the worst of it.

Then, in what was by far the most horrifying part of the performance, Leeman's face contorted with rage. Hatred boiled forth from every pore. This was more than mere mortal anger; this was the fury of the gods. His body trembled; his hands shook. Ben had read about Leeman's supposed violent temper, but had never truly believed it possible.

Until now.

Ben saw Leeman mime picking up a golf club and swinging it down onto Maria's head. The club apparently broke upon impact. Leeman picked up the broken shaft and rammed it through Maria's neck.

His face still transfixed with rage, Leeman withdrew slowly, wiping his hands and face. He looked all around, then bolted away.

When he reached the far wall, he stopped. The reenactment was over. Leeman closed his eyes and, like some primitive Method actor, stepped out of character.

Leeman returned to his chair. Everyone else in the room was staring at him with blank faces, with wide eyes. It was a long time before anyone spoke.

Finally the DA said, "I don't believe any more questions will be necessary. Thank you for your time." He stepped out of the room and closed the door behind him.

Twenty minutes later Leeman Hayes was charged with murder in the first degree.

After Ben had watched the tape three times, he became convinced that Leeman's case was hopeless. He saw no opening, or ambiguity, or anything else he could use to convince a jury this was anything other than what it appeared to be—a pantomimic confession of guilt.

Ben hit the rewind button and watched Leeman run through the performance backward. Giselle jumped back into his lap. Sweet kitty—and no dead bird in her mouth, he was relieved to see. He stroked the back of her neck. She purred and looked up at him, peering intently with those big green cat eyes. . . .

Wait a minute. Ben grabbed the remote and stopped the tape just as Leeman was beginning his performance.

It was so quick he almost missed it. In fact, he had missed it during each previous viewing. Leeman did not move directly from unresponsiveness to the performance. First, in a gesture that took less than a second, he held his right hand over his eyes, as if shading off an imaginary sun.

See.

It was the same gesture he had used to tell Ben he had seen him getting out of his Honda. There were no words attached— Leeman was still preverbal—but the gesture was absolutely the same.

See.

Leeman wasn't telling the police officers what he did. He was telling them what he *saw*.

See.

It wasn't a confession. It was an eyewitness account. Ben was certain of it.

But how would he convince a jury? Regardless of what he told them, Ben knew most jurors, most *anybody*, would view that taped performance as a confession. Ben's explanation about the gesture would be written off as a desperate ploy by a desperate defense attorney.

And Leeman Hayes would be convicted of a crime he didn't commit. And sentenced. In addition to the ten years of institutionalization to which he had already been condemned, even though he had never been convicted of a crime, he would spend the rest of his life a prisoner.

Or he would be sentenced to death.

It would be hard to say which penalty would be worse for Leeman.

Ben pushed the stop button on the remote. He couldn't let that happen. Could he?

Are you going to spend the rest of your life representing every petty felon and hard-luck story that slithers into your office?

The words thundered in Ben's brain. He would never be able to convince the jury Leeman's taped performance wasn't a confession, and Leeman himself would be absolutely worthless at trial. The file had virtually no exculpatory evidence in Leeman's favor. Ben would have to start his investigation from scratch. He would have to unearth witnesses and evidence on a ten-year-old crime.

An extremely difficult task.

Difficult? Try impossible.

Don't be such a sucker.

One thing was certain. If Ben took this case, he could kiss goodbye any chance of regaining Jack Bullock's respect.

I'm so disappointed, Ben. You were like a son to me.

But other images from the day flashed through Ben's mind. Leeman's face on the videotape—scared, helpless, alone. Leeman Hayes ten years later—bloated, locked away in dirty, ill-fitting clothes, his whole life passing him by. The eager, desperate look in Ernie Hayes's eyes. What was it he had said? *I knew you were the one who was finally going to help my boy.*

I knew it.

At least one thing Ernie had said was true. If Ben didn't take the case, who would?

Ten years. Ten long years.

Ben turned off the television. His deliberation was over. Despite all the dangers, all the difficulties, and all common sense, he was representing Leeman Hayes.

He had no choice.

They didn't have much of a chance. But that was better than no chance at all. That was better than condemning Leeman to more wasted days. More isolation and fear. And suffering.

Even more than he had already suffered.

At the hands of justice.

TWO

*   *

Tales of Two Cities

* 15 *

"But you promised!"

"I did nothing of the sort."

"Did so. You said you'd come home early and we'd go to the ball game."

"I said I would try. That's all."

"I shoulda known better. You never wanna do anything with me. You hate me."

"I do not. Now listen to me, son."

The man in the red wig listened carefully to Abie and his father's argument. Nice of them to squabble on the front porch. He was safely tucked away behind the eight-foot-high hedge surrounding the Rutherford estate, but he could hear every word. He could see them, too, but they would never notice him. The estates were spaced so generously that none of the neighbors were likely to see him either.

"Listen to me, son," Rutherford continued. He was much fairer than his son; it heightened the contrast between them. Family relations in chiaroscuro. "Your father has many important business affairs that have to be managed. I wish I could spend all day playing with you, but I can't."

Abie folded his arms across his chest. "You could if you wanted to."

Rutherford's lips tightened. "Abie, sometimes I have to work. Look around you. Look at this house. Look at those cars in the garage. Not everybody lives like you do. Who do you think paid for that? Where do you think all that money came from?"

"Mommy says you got it all from your daddy."

"That's—beside the point. Someone has to manage the money. Protect our investments. That's what your daddy does—"

"Mommy says you spend all day at that stupid country club."

"Your mother—" He muttered something under his breath. "That isn't true, and it isn't—"

Abie pushed away. "You play all the time. You just don't wanna play with me!"

"Abie. *Abie!*" Rutherford reached for his son, but Abie slipped out of his grasp. "I go to the country club to maintain business relationships. Those club members are my partners. They're movers and shakers. Some of the wealthiest men in the state. I know you're only ten, but try to understand."

"I understand. You'd rather swing a stupid golf club than take me to a baseball game."

The man in the red wig grinned. The dysfunctional family was a beautiful thing, at least from his point of view. If it weren't for fathers who couldn't find time for their sons, or who treated their sons badly when they were around, he'd never find an opening. But rich, pompous asses like Rutherford made his job almost too easy.

"Look, son." Rutherford's face was flushed with exasperation. "I have some meetings tomorrow, but . . . what time is the game?"

"Two o'clock. Like always."

"All right. Let me see what I can do. . . ."

"Is that a promise?"

Rutherford laid his hands on his son's shoulders. "All right, then. It's a promise."

"We'll have to leave by one-thirty to be there for the opening pitch."

"All right. To save time, why don't I pick you up on the corner of Peoria and Twenty-sixth, all right? At one-thirty."

"You won't forget?"

"Of course not." He hesitated. "I promise."

The man behind the hedge could see the change in Rutherford's expression, could see his arms tentatively extended. He had undoubtedly hoped his son might give him a hug. The first step on the road to reconciliation. But it was not to be. Having extracted his promise, Abie turned away and ran inside the house.

It would take more than a stupid half-baked promise to fix problems that ran so deep.

Quietly, the man moved away from the hedge, back to the street. What a splendid idea this impromptu visit had been. What a gold mine of information. Now he knew everything he needed to make his dream a reality. To claim another conquest.

He took a ballpoint pen and wrote himself a note on his wrist. Peoria and Twenty-sixth. One-thirty.

He'd be there.

* 16 *

Just about the time Ben had finally managed to fall asleep, he was awakened by the bristly sensation of whiskers on stubbled cheek.

Giselle, natch.

"Giselle," he mumbled, eyelids closed, "do me a favor and . . . *go away*." Nothing personal, Ben thought, but that kid of Julia's kept me up almost all night. Whoever invented the phrase *slept like a baby* obviously never had one.

He rolled over and pulled the pillow on top of his head. It was no use. Giselle was insistent. It was breakfast time, and she would not take *go away* for an answer. She insinuated her wet nose between the pillow and Ben's face.

She's awfully scratchy this morning, Ben thought. And then it hit him.

He shot bolt upright, bug-eyed. *"Giselle!"*

Her mouth was empty. He ripped the covers off his bed and searched.

Thankfully, there did not appear to be any mangled remains of wildlife foolish enough to come near Giselle's piece of the roof. Giselle wasn't bringing him another victim. She was just hungry.

Relieved, Ben stumbled to his closet and threw on a robe. He opened his back window and inhaled the fresh morning air. Well, he inhaled the air, anyway. It was a pity they kept those trash bins just below his window.

Out the window, pressed up against the building, Ben saw Joni Singleton in a romantic clinch with a tall black teenager about her age. Joni and her twin sister, Jami, lived with their parents, and their two-year-old brothers, also twins, in one of the other apartments in the building. How they all managed to coexist in a space barely bigger than Ben's he did not understand.

Overcoming a mild pang of guilt, he watched the two smooch for a while. They talked and kissed, talked and kissed. Mostly kissed. They appeared very comfortable with one another. Probably not a first date.

Ben closed the window and left them alone. He hadn't heard anything about this new boyfriend; he suspected it was a closely guarded secret. An interracial romance—bet Joni's parents will be thrilled about that.

He made a quick stop in the bathroom, humming his way down the hallway. "A country dance was being held in a garden...." "Polka Dots and Moonbeams" was an old tune from the 1920s. Ben couldn't remember where he had learned it, but somewhere along the line it had become his favorite song. "Suddenly I saw ... polka dots and moonbeams ... all around a pug-nosed dream...."

He wandered into the kitchen and opened a can of Feline's Fancy. He was just reaching for the Cap'n Crunch when he heard the door buzzer.

He checked the clock over the oven. It was barely seven. This could only be Mrs. Marmelstein.

Mrs. Marmelstein owned the boardinghouse. She and her husband had moved to Tulsa decades ago and made a fortune in the oil business. They traveled the world, bought and sold ritzy Utica Hills real estate, and generally lived high off the hog. A little too high, as it turned out. In the mid-Seventies, Mr. Marmelstein passed away, and in the early Eighties, the oil business imploded. When the dust had settled, Mrs. Marmelstein had almost no money left, and her only remaining property was this third-rate house in one of the least desirable neighborhoods in Tulsa.

Ben opened the front door. Mrs. Marmelstein was wearing a green print dress with a lace collar. Her silver-gray hair was tied back in a bun.

She looked at him sternly. "Benjamin Kincaid."

"That's me," Ben said amiably.

She wagged her head back and forth. "Ben-ja-min Kin-caid."

"Is there going to be more to this conversation? You know, it is rather early. . . ."

She made a tsking noise. "Did you think I wouldn't hear?"

"Ah . . . hear what?"

"Benjamin, I'm sixty-nine years old. I know what a baby sounds like."

"Oh, the baby!" His voice dropped to a whisper. "That reminds me, could you talk a little softer?"

"And what may I ask would you be doing with a baby?"

"Well, that's kind of complicated. . . ."

"No doubt." She folded her arms disapprovingly. "You know, Ben, I've been very liberal with you. I think we both know I've . . . shall we say . . . relaxed my standards where you're concerned. I've allowed your police friends to tromp through my house on several occasions. And I've permitted unchaperoned visitation by that . . . redhead."

Ben suppressed a smile. He wasn't sure if Mrs. Marmelstein disapproved of Christina because she was a single working woman, because she dropped by Ben's place at all hours of the day and night, or simply because she was a redhead. "You've been very generous to me, Mrs. Marmelstein. No two ways about it."

"Well, of course, you've helped me here and there as well." Here and there wasn't the half of it. Since he had moved in, Ben had taken over the management of her beleaguered finances, which typically involved cooling off creditors (a task with which Ben was singularly familiar), juggling bills, and occasionally slipping a few bucks of his own money into her petty-cash envelope. Unfortunately, even though Ben knew Mrs. Marmelstein wasn't rich anymore, Mrs. Marmelstein hadn't quite figured it out yet. "And I have always been grateful for your assistance. But now I simply must draw the line."

"At what?"

"At . . ." Her head trembled. "Babies."

"You don't allow babies? The Singletons have two!"

"Yes, but that's different, isn't it?" She leaned forward. "Benjamin Kincaid, we both know that you are not married!"

The corners of Ben's mouth slowly turned up. "Mrs. Marmelstein, allow me to explain—"

She raised a hand. "That's hardly necessary. I know how babies come into the world. And I know boys will be boys. But I expected a bit more discretion from you."

"Really, Mrs. Marmelstein, it isn't at all—"

"Even if such an . . . accident had to occur, you should have done the decent thing and married the poor girl. It was that red-head, wasn't it?"

"Mrs. Marmelstein, Christina and I are just good friends and coworkers. The baby belongs to my sister, Julia. Joey's my nephew."

"He's—" Her expression could not have been much different if she'd been hit by a truck. "Oh. Well, that changes things, doesn't it?" She shuffled her hands awkwardly. "Why are you keeping the baby?"

"I'm not entirely clear on that myself. . . ."

"How long will he be staying?"

"I'm not sure. It may be a while."

Mrs. Marmelstein frowned. "Well, if he'll be here longer than a week, let me know. There'll have to be a rent adjustment, you know."

"Naturally."

Her expression seemed to soften. "If you have time, you might stop by my room later. After you get dressed, of course. I've made a new fruitcake."

"Ah, well, I'm actually very busy today—"

"Speaking of that baby, I think I hear him."

Ben held his breath in suspense. Sure enough, the plaintive wail with which he had become so familiar during the night was rattling the walls. "Right you are." He sighed. "By the way, Mrs. Marmelstein, I don't suppose you know how to change a diaper. . . ."

* * *

Mere seconds after Christina pushed the door buzzer, Ben flung it open, his face marked by panic and desperation.

"Do you know what *butt* is?" he asked urgently.

Christina blinked. "I beg your pardon."

"Butt. *Butt!*" Ben waved his arms wildly in the air.

"I'm afraid I don't quite follow. . . ."

"He keeps saying *butt*."

"Who does?"

"Joey! Who else? I think it's the only word he knows!"

"That seems unlikely. . . ."

"He keeps looking at me like I'm supposed to do something, like I'm the stupidest uncle on earth because I don't know what *butt* is. He wants something, but I don't know what it is. You wouldn't believe some of the things I tried."

"I don't want to hear about it."

Christina looked past Ben into the front room. Joey was trying to pull himself up on the side of the laundry basket. He was indeed chirping the same word over and over again. "It does sound like *butt*," she admitted, "but unless Julia has an unusually perverse sense of humor, it must be something else."

She began rummaging through Joey's enormous diaper bag. "Aha!" she cried a moment later. *"Bert!"*

"Bert?"

She withdrew a small stuffed doll from the bag. It was a longish, yellow, vaguely humanoid creature.

"What is that?" Ben asked.

"It's Bert, you ninny."

"And what is Bert, some sort of mutant?"

"He's a Muppet, you ding-a-ling." She put the doll in Joey's little hands. He hugged the doll under his chin and quietly sat down in the basket.

Christina reached back into the diaper bag and pulled out a shorter, rounder, orange-faced doll. "This is Ernie."

"How can you tell?"

"How can I tell? He just . . . *is*. I can't believe you don't know them. These characters are world-famous. Didn't you ever watch *Sesame Street*?"

"No."

Christina stared at him. "How did you learn the alphabet?"

"Actually, I had a private tutor."

She slapped her forehead. "God save me from rich kids."

With Christina's assistance, Ben changed Joey's diaper (after being instructed that the end with the *Sesame Street* characters goes on top), filled a bottle, warmed it so it was not too hot and not too cold, and gave Joey his morning feeding. For such a tiny slip of a thing, he could pack away a lot of formula.

While Joey chowed down, Ben told Christina about the videotape.

"Sounds like we'd best get started *tout de suite,*" she said. That was Christina—always ready to take on the least desirable chore and to do whatever was required. Ben only hoped that continued to prove true today. "Have you got assignments ready?"

"Well ... I'll have Loving start investigating the country club. All the members, all the staff. And Jones should dig up all the written accounts of the murder from ten years ago. Any additional information would be welcome, especially any information he can find about the victim. I'm going to check out the scene of the crime. But don't tell Jones that. He'll want to come."

Christina nodded. "What should I do?"

"Well ... to tell you the truth ... I need you to look after the baby."

"What?" Christina rose to her feet. "How dare you!"

"Christina, someone has to—"

"Someone, yes. Do I look like an au pair? This is so sexist."

"You know me better than that. But you're the only person in the office who knows anything about babies."

"I still don't see why—"

"What else can I do? Leave the baby with Jones?"

Christina frowned.

"Loving?"

Christina blanched. "All right already. I'll look after the baby. But not forever."

"Understood. Just until I can make other arrangements. I'll call some child-care centers. Maybe they can rent me a nanny."

"You can't afford them," Christina replied succinctly.

"I'll see what I can do, anyway." He pulled out a chair. "Make yourself at home. Do anything, eat anything. Pretend it's your place."

"I may take you up on that. I overslept and didn't get a chance to shower." She ran her fingers through her tangled red hair. "But tell your concierge to stop giving me those looks every time I come up the stairs."

"Mrs. Marmelstein gives you looks?" Ben asked innocently.

"Yes, she does. I feel like a tainted woman."

"I'll talk to her. Thanks, Christina. I really appreciate this."

"Like I had any choice," she muttered. "Either I spend all day with the baby, or I leave him in the clutches of someone who doesn't know Bert from Ernie." She pulled out a clean diaper. "Such a life I lead."

17

The Utica Greens Country Club was without question Tulsa's oldest, most famous, most prestigious, and most exclusive playground for the rich and pampered. Built on land formerly owned by the Phillips family, it occupied two city blocks. It was conveniently located in the ritziest part of town, less than a mile from the Utica Square shopping emporium and Philbrook, the former Phillips mansion, now converted to a sprawling museum and cultural center.

As soon as he drove up to the front guardhouse in his beat-up Accord, Ben knew he was going to have problems. The paint had chipped and rusted in so many places he had long since stopped worrying about it, and the engine made a loud churning noise all the time. Well, not all the time. Only when the wheels moved. Despite several repair attempts, the muffler still hung low and tended to scrape the pavement every time he hit a bump. To be fair, the Accord had been a great car in its day, but its day had ended roughly about a hundred and fifty thousand miles ago.

The security man in the guardhouse stared at Ben as if he might have dynamite strapped to his chest. Eventually, after giving the guard everything from his Tulsa County Bar number to his Book-of-the-Month Club membership card, he was grudgingly admitted onto the club grounds.

The road wove its way through the gentle hills separating the thirteenth and eighteenth greens. Ben couldn't believe anyone would be playing golf in this sweltering heat, but there they were, in their pastel cotton shirts and spiffy checkered caps. He watched an all-male foursome play through; they looked hot. Once again, Ben was grateful that he had never taken the game up, despite the fact that one is never really taken seriously as a Tulsa lawyer until one has played Utica Greens with a one-digit handicap.

Ben was not looking forward to this visit. All this privileged, exclusionary, keep-them-away-from-us stuff struck a little too close to home. He'd grown up, after all, in the ultrarich Nichols Hills, which some people considered an overgrown residential country club. When he was young, Ben's father used to drag him to a place not unlike this on a regular basis so he could "get out in the sun and get some exercise." As Ben drove through the club grounds a cascade of unpleasant memories returned to him. The golf shoes with the stupid floppy ties, the afternoon martinis, the chatter about "keeping the country pure."

Like it or not, though, this was the scene of the crime. Moreover, according to the file, only four men, the four members of the country club's controlling board, had keys to the caddyshack where Maria Alvarez was murdered. The shack should have been locked that late at night. Therefore, once you eliminated Leeman as a suspect, the question of who could have killed Maria Alvarez necessarily led to the question of access—who could've gotten in there?

Inside the main building, Ben found the office of the club's chairman of the board, Ronald Pearson. As he learned from the sign on the man's desk, Pearson worked under the title of CAPTAIN PEARSON, although somehow Ben doubted this represented a military rank.

Ben was lucky enough to find the man in his office. He was a large burly sort, mildly overweight, with a deep ruddy complexion and a large speckled nose. He was on the phone when Ben arrived.

Pearson covered the receiver with his hand and whispered, "Just a moment. I'm on the line with the employment agency. Trying to get new help for the dining room."

Ben nodded, then took the nearest chair.

"Yeah," he heard Pearson say, "let me talk to Mary. No, not Maria. Not Rochelle. That's right. Thanks."

Ben scanned the office. The walls had a rich mahogany finish and were ornamented with fishing and golf trophies.

"That's fine," Pearson continued. "Let me have suites fifteen through twenty-five. Yes, that would be very attractive." Pearson mumbled a few more words, then hung up the phone. "Damn. It's getting harder to run a country club every goddamn day."

"Really. Why is that?"

"Oh, ever since Southern Hills had the PGA tournament, everybody acts like it's the only country club in town. Hell, any lowlife with thirty thousand dollars to burn can get in Southern Hills. You call that exclusive?"

He looked up and seemed to notice Ben for the first time. "'I don't recognize you," he said to Ben, frowning. "Are you a member?"

"Uh, no. My name is Ben Kincaid. I called ahead and made an appointment with your secretary."

"I don't recall being told. . . ."

"I'm a lawyer. I'm representing Leeman Hayes."

Pearson continued to look at him uncomprehendingly.

"He's the man who's been accused of killing Maria Alvarez. In your caddyshack."

Pearson removed his wire-rim shades and rubbed the bridge of his nose. "Christ. Won't we ever hear the end of that? One lousy murder of one wetback, and we've got cops and cameras crawling all over us for the next ten years."

"All I want to do is tour the grounds and view the place where the murder occurred. And maybe have a chance to talk to a few people who were here way back then."

Pearson threw himself back in his chair. He was wearing a captain's cap and a blue blazer with an anchor embroidered over the pocket. He looked like Dick Cavett gone to seed. "Do you have a court order?"

"No," Ben answered.

"Well, then I can't allow you on the course."

"Sir, if I may—"

"Let me tell you something, son. We have people calling in days in advance to schedule a game. These are members who pay sixty thousand smackers down and five thousand more every year to have a nice place to play a round of golf. I'm not going to let you prance around and screw up everyone's tee times."

"Sir, it's just a game. This is a murder—"

"What do you mean, it's just a game?" Pearson's temper appeared to be on full boil. "Let me tell you something, sonny. The members of this club run this town. This state, really. Important deals are made out on that course. Decisions that affect the economy. Decisions that affect the well-being of everyone. To my mind, that's about a million times more important than your pointless little investigation."

Ben tried to remain cool. "If you want me to get a court order, I will. It won't be hard. This is a capital murder charge, sir."

"Damn it all to hell." Pearson slammed his hand down on his desk. "As if I didn't already have enough to do." Ben surveyed the man's barren desk and wondered what it was exactly that he did. "I guess Mitch might be able to show you around. He's the operations manager."

Operations manager, Ben thought. Read: the one who actually does the work around here.

"Of course, he's not a member, you understand. But he can give you a tour of the toilets or whatever the hell it is you want." He picked up the phone on his desk and pushed a single direct-dial button. "Mitch? Captain Pearson. Get your butt down here. I need you to give the grand tour."

A short pause. "Prospect?" he chuckled. "Not hardly. Some kind of lawyer. Yeah. You and me both. Well, you can give him the short version, anyway. See you in a minute."

He hung up the phone. "You'll excuse me if I don't take you around myself. We've got a board meeting in less than an hour. I have to prepare." His oversized chest rose and fell heavily. "I don't know why I let the board stick me with this captaincy, year after year. I barely have time left over to manage my business."

"What business is that?"

"I'm an oilman, natch. One of the last of the true believers. One of the men who put this cowtown on the map."

"And you're still working? I thought the oil-and-gas business had all but dried up."

"Maybe for the schmucks. Not for me. I drilled thirty-five gas wells last year."

"And you found someone to buy the gas?"

"Hell, yeah. I got Dick Crenshaw to make me a sweet deal. I had the gas companies over the barrel with a lot of long-term, take-or-pay contracts when the price went bad. After we beat them over the head with lawyers for a few years, they agreed to my terms. I'll have a buyer for my gas for the next ten years. Even the sour gas. Even the foreign stuff. Canadian, Peruvian. I can sell anything."

The office door opened and a tall, dark-haired man entered. "The tour bus is leaving," he said.

"This is Mitch Dryer," Pearson said. "Mitch, this is . . . the lawyer." He had obviously forgotten Ben's name. "Show him around."

"Anything he wants to see?" Mitch asked tentatively.

Pearson peered back at him. "Within reason. But make it quick. Because . . . I need you at the board meeting. Don't be late."

Right, Ben thought. And that gives Mitch the perfect excuse for rushing through the tour, and maybe omitting a few key locations. So he can hold Pearson's hand at the board meeting.

Ben followed Mitch out of Pearson's office. He might just have to drop in at that board meeting himself.

* 18 *

Ben was amazed at how Mitch's demeanor relaxed the instant they were away from Pearson. He had previously been stiff and obedient—the perfect flunky. A few minutes out of Pearson's office, however, and he was casual, lighthearted— almost impish. Ben wondered if he just put on an act for his boss, or if he put on an act for whomever he was with at any given moment.

Mitch started the tour in the main dining room. The word *impressive* did not do justice to the immense majesty of this room. The walls were oak, on all sides. Huge bay windows with burnished drapes provided a breathtaking view of the course. The raised ceiling gave the room a feeling of almost infinite size. The enormous bricked-in fireplace was taller than Ben.

Mitch waltzed Ben through a series of smaller areas— offices and conference rooms. A music room with a grand piano Ben would die for. A stereo system he would die twice for. And the obligatory pro shop overlooking the putting green. Ben quickly surveyed the leisurewear, all sporting the Utica Greens crest. Not a price tag under seventy-five bucks. Not even the sun visors.

They descended a staircase to the main locker room, which Ben was informed was referred to as "Chambers." Huge bathing areas, rows of spacious showers, a Jacuzzi, implacable attendants, sky-high mirrors, wall-attached hair dryers, and forty different bottles of cologne and aftershave. The faucets and handles were made of brass; the countertops were solid black marble.

Not someplace you'd drop by just to clip your toenails.

It occurred to Ben that this might be an appropriate time to milk Mitch for whatever information he could provide. "So how long have you been working for Pearson? Uh, Captain Pearson, I mean."

"Now there's a captain who never sailed the stormy seas. I don't think he could pilot a paddleboat." Mitch laughed. "It's an honorary title, I guess. To answer your question, I came onboard fresh out of business school, a little less than ten years ago, not long after that murder. All the bad publicity that incident generated convinced the board members they needed someone to manage the grounds on a full-time basis. So they hired me. As you may have guessed, I do the work that keeps this Disneyland-for-dilettantes afloat."

"Does the job pay well?"

"Not as well as having rich parents does."

Mitch spun Ben through the locker room. The lockers were of carved pine. None of them had locks; Ben surmised that would be considered bad taste. Such a measure would suggest it was possible that one of the esteemed members might actually commit theft, perish the thought.

"Not a bad place to take a leak, huh?" Mitch said dryly.

"It'd do in a pinch," Ben concurred.

They left the building and walked outside to survey the perfectly trimmed greens. The sun was still blazing; Ben found himself feeling nostalgic for the air-conditioned paradise of the locker room.

At Ben's request, Mitch showed him the caddyshack. The scene of the ancient crime. After a short walk, Mitch removed a key and opened the door.

"Who has keys to this place?" Ben asked.

"Ten years ago all the board members. Today, just me. After the murder, when the keys turned them into suspects, the board didn't want anything to do with it anymore. They turned in their keys and put me in charge of the shack. Actually, I requested the assignment. I figured I couldn't do any worse than those guys had."

Together, they entered. The *shack* was a well-constructed

building more spacious than Ben's apartment. Benches and chairs lined the walls; golf magazines cluttered every table.

"I don't see many caddies around today," Ben observed.

"Right. Welcome to the post–golf cart era. Caddies are not essential anymore to ensuring that you can play eighteen holes without the least bit of physical exertion. It's mostly just the old codgers who use caddies these days."

Well, thank goodness someone is preserving those grand old traditions, Ben thought. "You know, I'm kind of surprised that this club would hire Leeman Hayes as a caddy. Or anything else."

"What's wrong with this picture, huh? Well, I think I can explain that mystery. You read the papers much?"

"Almost never."

"Then you wouldn't know. About every five years or so, some crusading-journalist type decides to rail against the gross inequities represented by the old boys' country-club system. 'How dare they live in such grand opulence, when less than ten miles away you can find the poorest, most impoverished families of north Tulsa?' Or: 'Why are all the board members men?' Or: 'Why are the employees all the same color?' "

"So the board indulges in a little equal-opportunity sham," Ben murmured.

"Right the first time." Mitch picked up some golf shoes and slid them under a bench. "Leeman was a perfect face-saving hire. Not only was he black, not only was he from a bitterly poor family—he was retarded as well. Now how could anyone say Utica Greens was heartless after they made a magnanimous gesture like hiring him?"

"No comment," Ben said.

"Hey, don't spare my feelings. I've been living with it for a good long time."

"And it doesn't bother you?"

"What, you mean like, do I have a conscience?" He grinned. "Naaaaah. I checked that in my locker my first day here and I haven't seen it since."

Ben walked to the far north corner of the shack. "This is where it happened, isn't it?"

"Yup. That's where they found her, slammed against the wall, the club shaft rammed through her throat."

Ben stared at the empty corner. "I suppose all traces have been long since eliminated."

"Obviously. In fact, that was a major source of controversy. The board wanted her removed and the room repainted immediately after she was found. They were having a big tournament the next day, and the last thing they wanted was a murder scene. The police, however, insisted on roping off the shack, taking pictures, and scouring the room for evidence. Put the board members' noses extremely out of joint."

"And the four members of the board back then . . ."

"Are the same four who compose the board today."

"Did they ever try to find out who committed the murder?"

"Who? The board?" Mitch laughed. "You must be joking. Leeman was arrested at the scene. That was good enough for them. Once they cleaned up the mess and got their tournament back on schedule, I doubt if any of them ever thought about it again."

"Didn't they try to protect Leeman? He was their employee, after all."

"Protect him? Hardly. I think they were glad to feed him to the wolves, to resolve the mystery before it attracted any more attention. He was the perfect scapegoat, for the board and the police. Ever since then, the board has used Leeman as an object lesson in what happens when you bring 'one of them' into the hallowed halls of Utica Greens."

"Mitch," Ben said, his teeth clenched, "would you get me the hell out of here?"

"My pleasure." He opened the door and together they walked back into the blinding sunlight.

* 19 *

After the feeding and the changing and the burping, Christina spent the remainder of the morning trying to convince Joey it really wouldn't be such a horrible idea to take a nap. Or even just to close his eyes and pretend he was taking a nap. She wasn't particular. Just so he wasn't screaming anymore.

Christina had done a considerable amount of baby-sitting during her teen years and thought she was fairly competent, but Joey was proving particularly fussy. She began to have a bit more sympathy for Ben, who had been dealing with the kid all night without any of her experience to fall back on. She wasn't sure what Joey's problem was; he was just unhappy. Poor babe was going through a lot of trauma—separated from his mommy and dumped with a bunch of weirdos he'd never seen before.

Eventually she resorted to singing. He seemed interested, but didn't care for any of her tunes. Everyone's a critic. She tried "Annie Laurie," a tune her mother used to sing to her when she was a little girl. Not interested. She tried "Ave Maria." She tried "A Tisket, a Tasket." "The Noble Duke of York." "Polly Wolly Doodle." She tried twenty other songs. No luck.

Ben had made a suggestion before he left, but Christina had disregarded it. Totally lame. What did he know about babies, anyway? But finally, in sheer desperation, she gave in and began singing, "Flintstones . . . meet the Flintstones . . ."

The caterwauling ceased, and by the time she got to the part about "courtesy of Fred's two feet," Joey was making a soft chortling noise. He giggled when she said, "Yabba-dabba-doo." And after a few quiet repetitions, he was asleep.

Praise the Lord. She rocked him a bit longer, then set him down in his laundry-basket-cum-crib. What an ordeal. A few more experiences like that and she could almost stop regretting her decision to—

No. Even just thinking to herself, Christina couldn't make herself believe that lie. She would regret that decision for the rest of her life.

She went to the bathroom and splashed some revitalizing cold water on her face. She was burning up. The temperature was dancing around a hundred and five, and no big surprise, the air-conditioning in Ben's apartment was on the fritz. She cranked the thermostat down to sixty-five, but it didn't help.

She suddenly realized she had never gotten that shower and shampoo she had wanted. When better than now? She decided to take a quick, quiet soak before the tyrannical tyke returned to the world of the waking.

She peeled off her clothes and stepped into the shower. The cool beads of water flowed down her body, providing almost instant relief from the heat and stress of the morning. What a splendid invention showers were. What did people do before? She sang a quiet chorus of "Annie Laurie," just for her own benefit, then borrowed some of Ben's Pert Plus and washed her hair.

When she was finished, she dried off and wrapped a white towel around her body and another one around her wet hair. Just as she twisted the towel into place she heard the front door buzzer.

Isn't this always the way it goes? she thought. Just great. Mrs. Marmelstein, no doubt. She probably heard me singing and ran up to make sure I wasn't holding an orgy or anything.

Christina trudged into the front parlor, wearing only her two towels, and opened the front door.

The woman on the other side of the door was in her mid-sixties, although she was quite well preserved and almost wrinkle free. She was dressed in an elegant, obviously expensive pant suit. She clutched a Gucci purse and wore a diamond ring the size of a quarter.

Christina pressed her hand against the towel covering her torso. "Oh, my gosh. You must be Mrs. Kincaid. Ben's mother."

The older woman nodded slightly.

"Omigosh. Oh my *gosh*." She tugged desperately at her towel, trying to make sure she was amply covered. To her dismay, the knot came apart and the towel started to fall. She clutched it desperately to her chest. The back flopped open, exposing her pink wet backside.

"I bet you're wondering who I am," Christina said, trying to pull the towel closed in back with her free hand.

Mrs. Kincaid nodded again, even more imperceptibly than before. "I must admit to a soupçon of curiosity. . . ."

"I . . . well, gosh . . ." As Christina spoke, the towel around her hair began to slip down her forehead, covering her forehead, then her eyes. She wanted to push the towel back up, but she couldn't take her hands off the lower towel without exposing herself. She tried to blow the towel back up, but it didn't work. The towel drooped down farther, over her nose.

"I'm Christina McCall," she said, trying to ignore the towel obscuring her vision. "I'm . . . well, I'm Ben's friend. His . . . good friend."

"But of course you are, my dear." Mrs. Kincaid brushed past Christina and entered the apartment.

"No—I mean—you don't understand." Christina suddenly realized she was standing in front of the open door half-naked. She pushed it closed with her foot. "I work for Ben."

Mrs. Kincaid positioned herself on the natty sofa in the center of Ben's living room. "You mean he *pays* you?"

"Yes. Exactly. That's it."

Mrs. Kincaid shook her head and made a tsking noise. "It's come to that, then. What a pity."

Christina realized she couldn't go on conversing with this towel hanging over her eyes, so she shook the towel off her head. Her damp red hair cascaded around her shoulders. "I still don't think you've quite got it. I'm a legal assistant. I work for

Ben. In his office. I help him with his legal practice." She looked at Mrs. Kincaid pleadingly. "I'm a *professional*!"

Beads of water flew from Christina's wet head into Mrs. Kincaid's face. The older woman raised a hand and pointedly wiped away the drops. "And precisely what professional services are you rendering today?" she asked, scrutinizing Christina.

"I was taking a shower," Christina said, totally exasperated. "I was hot and sticky because, as you'll soon realize, Ben's air conditioner doesn't work, and I wanted to wash off while the baby was still asleep—"

"The baby!" Mrs. Kincaid's face suddenly became animated. "Then he's here?"

"Yes," Christina said. "That's why *I'm* here. I'm baby-sitting."

Mrs. Kincaid rose to her feet. "May I see him?"

"Of course. He's in Ben's bedroom in his, er, crib." Christina showed Mrs. Kincaid to the back room.

There, Mrs. Kincaid cracked open the door and peeked in at the slumbering child. He was lying on his back; a soft whistle streamed out of his mouth with each breath.

Mrs. Kincaid did not actually smile, but her eyes crinkled and glowed. "That's my grandchild, you know," she whispered. They tiptoed back to the front room. "My only one."

"Yeah." Christina laughed. "Unless there's something Ben hasn't gotten around to telling you yet."

Mrs. Kincaid whirled on her. "What do you mean? Do you know something?"

Christina flustered. "No, no. It was just a joke. Really. I don't know why I said that. What a stupid thing to say." Stupid, stupid, stupid.

"Oh." With a quick, almost invisible gesture, Mrs. Kincaid smoothed the crease of her slacks, whisking away several cat hairs she had acquired on the sofa, and reseated herself. "Pardon me if I overreacted."

The two women sat in silence. Christina knew Mrs. Kincaid was eyeing her, like a scientist analyzing a strange new specimen. She felt extremely uncomfortable. "Well, perhaps I should get dressed—"

"So this is Ben's apartment," Mrs. Kincaid said.

"Yup." Christina knotted her fingers awkwardly. "Chez Kincaid. Have you never been here before?"

"No. Never." Her eyes drank in the room. "I'm beginning to understand why he hasn't invited me to visit." She pulled out a sofa cushion and stared at the considerable accretion of cookie crumbs, change, and chewed-up ballpoint pens. Wordlessly, she dropped the cushion back into place.

"Ben's been pretty short on cash these past few years," Christina said in his defense.

"I've offered him money a dozen times," Mrs. Kincaid replied. "But he refuses to take it."

"Yeah. I know."

Mrs. Kincaid entered the kitchen, opened the refrigerator, and inventoried the contents. Two cases of Coke Classic, two large cartons of chocolate milk, a half-empty bottle of white milk that had expired three weeks before, and a stick of butter covered with toast crumbs.

"Some things never change." She pushed the fridge closed. "And so nutritious. I assume the white milk is for the cat?"

"Cap'n Crunch cereal," Christina said. "Although sometimes he eats it straight out of the box."

Mrs. Kincaid's eyelashes fluttered. "His diet hasn't altered in twenty-five years."

"Yeah, well, he gets takeout a lot."

Mrs. Kincaid noticed a spot of unidentified grunge on the kitchen counter and wiped it away with a quick and precise sweep of her hand. While she was at it she rolled up the paper towels and rearranged the canisters.

"Uh, ma'am, I'm sure Ben wouldn't want you to—"

Mrs. Kincaid brushed past Christina and looked into the sink. She gasped. The sink was filled with plates, glasses, and silverware, all encrusted with dried food (takeout, probably) and unrecognizable goop. On the bottom layer of plates, a gray fungus was growing.

Mrs. Kincaid pressed her hand to her throat. "Do you suppose he has any . . . rubber gloves?"

"Oh, look, I'm sure he wouldn't want you to—"

"I don't *want* to, my dear." She drew herself erect. "Frankly, I haven't done dishes in years. But this is an emergency."

Christina showed her the place under the sink where Ben kept his cleaning supplies (but no rubber gloves). After inhaling deeply to fortify herself, Mrs. Kincaid poured a half bottle of dishwashing liquid into the sink and turned on the tap. She held her breath and tried not to look at what she was doing. " 'Once more unto the breach . . .' "

"Well," Christina said, "now that you're here, I guess I can bid adieu. . . ."

"No, please." To Christina's surprise, Mrs. Kincaid reached out and placed a wet hand on her arm. "Please don't."

Christina blinked. "You want me to stay?"

"Please. If you can."

"I suppose. But . . . why?"

Mrs. Kincaid picked up a plate and began to scrub. "I thought perhaps . . . we could talk."

Christina smiled nervously. "I can't imagine anything we could discuss."

"That won't be hard," Mrs. Kincaid said reassuringly. "We'll discuss my son."

"What about him?"

"Anything would be of interest, when it comes to Benjamin. He's an absolute mystery to me. I've never understood him."

"Aw, Ben's not so tough," Christina said. She was beginning to relax, despite the fact that she was still standing around practically starkers. "He's a good guy. Goodhearted, you know?"

"Tilting at windmills? Trying to save the world from itself?"

"Well . . . sometimes."

"Always taking on projects he shouldn't?"

"True."

Mrs. Kincaid nodded. "He got that from his father."

"But he can be very persistent. When he starts something, he sees it through to the bitter end."

Mrs. Kincaid's eyes glistened. "He got that from me."

"Ben really has done some outstanding work." Christina had the odd sensation that she was pleading the worth of the son to the mother. "He's resolved cases the police couldn't. He's won trials everyone said couldn't be won. I can't tell you how many times I've told him not to take some impossible case, only to see him do it anyway—and win. He never turns down a client who needs help. He takes any case he thinks worthwhile, even when he knows he'll never make any money off it. I keep telling him, 'Ben, *il faut de l'argent*'—that means 'one must have money.' "

"I know, dear."

"But he never listens." She paused. "He doesn't always have a lot of common sense, but—"

"But that's where you come in?" Mrs. Kincaid said abruptly.

"What?"

"I'm sorry. I don't mean to be presumptuous. I've only known you for a few minutes. But I tend to form early impressions and stick with them. And you strike me as a very . . . practical person. A good match for Benjamin."

"Really." Christina tilted her head. "Huh. I guess I never thought about it like that."

Mrs. Kincaid continued her industrial-strength scrubbing.

"Look," Christina said tentatively, "do you like Earl Grey tea?"

"Mmm. I adore it."

"I thought you might." Christina glanced toward the back room. Joey was still sleeping peacefully. "Why don't I get dressed, then I'll put on the tea." To her own surprise, she found herself looking forward to it. "We might have something to discuss after all."

* 20 *

"Do you think they'll mind if I sit in?" Ben asked as he took
a seat in the back of the country club's main conference room.

"I doubt if they'll even notice," Mitch replied. "They're usually pretty mellow in the early afternoon. Until they've had a
chance to shake off those three-martini lunches."

Mitch left Ben and unlocked a cabinet at the north end of the
room. As soon as Mitch turned the key, the lid popped up,
revealing an extensive liquor cabinet. Ben saw countless
bottles with more varied and expensive labels than he could
find in most Tulsa liquor stores.

Like Giselle at the sound of a can opener, as soon as the
cabinet was open the board members began to flow into the
conference room. The first was a short, round man with a
bushy red beard and not a single hair on his head. He had
apparently just come in from outside; he wiped sweat off his
forehead and temples with the sleeve of his monogrammed
shirt.

"Some enchanted evening . . ." The man crooned to no one
in particular as he swaggered over to the liquor cabinet. He
poured himself a Scotch and soda, then held it aloft in one hand
and serenaded the glass. "You will meet a stran-ger . . ."

So, Ben thought, the first board member is an out-of-work
lounge singer.

The red-bearded man downed half his Scotch, then shifted
songs. "A foggy day, in London town . . ."

He stopped when he noticed the club secretary, already
seated at the conference table. She was young, probably in her
early twenties. Her well-coiffed hair was almost as short as her

skirt. Ben had the immediate impression that her shorthand skills were probably slight and her salary enormous.

"How about a hug, baby doll?" the man said as he approached. The young woman smiled, stood, and stretched out her arms to receive him.

"Are they sweethearts?" Ben whispered.

"No. Dick Crenshaw is a strong believer in hug therapy."

"I beg your pardon?"

"Hug therapy. It's supposed to be very healthy. Relieves the stress of the workplace."

"I'll bet."

"It's entirely platonic, or so Dick keeps telling us. Good for the staff. Good for everybody."

Ben watched the man's hands rove and squeeze. "So he's actually providing a community service. And here I thought he was just trying to get a cheap thrill."

Over the secretary's shoulder, Crenshaw saw another man in the hallway. "Rutherford! Stop talking about your god-damned rutabagas and get in here!"

This man, Rutherford, was taller and thicker and older. He walked with a slow, slightly hunched gait. "Jesus H. Christ. It was hot as hell out there today. I had to shower off."

"Shower off? I bet you had to jerk off." Crenshaw passed his friend the bottle of Scotch.

"That's really more your specialty, isn't it?"

"Me? My dick's so short I can't even find it. Hell, my wife's been looking for it for years."

"Ah." Rutherford swirled his drink around in his mouth, then swallowed. "That would explain why Emily bought that magnifying glass last Christmas."

"Magnifying glass? She'd need a microscope." Crenshaw poured himself another Scotch. "Dick Dickless, that's what they used to call me back in school."

Rutherford contemplated the refraction of light in his glass. "Dick, why is it every time I see you we end up talking about your genitals?"

"I don't know, Rutherford." He batted his eyelids. "Maybe you're thweet on me."

Ben leaned over and whispered to Mitch. "The short guy has a real, uh, rich sense of humor."

Mitch nodded. "He fancies himself quite the humorist. Problem is, all his jokes are about his—"

"I get the general idea."

"I'm sure," Mitch reflected, "that his mother had no idea, when she decided to call him Dick, that she was determining the course of his life and setting the stage for a thousand variations on the same tasteless joke."

"Pearson told me Crenshaw bought some of his foreign import gas. So he must be loaded."

"You know it. Beaucoup bucks. 'Course, he's a lawyer."

"Oh, right," Ben said. "All us lawyers are swimming in moolah."

"Crenshaw was born rich and managed to stay that way by protecting his country-club buddies from the IRS and keeping their kids out of jail. He's handled a bunch of big-bucks divorce cases, too. D'you hear about the Finney breakup?"

"How could I not? It was all over the TV and radio."

"Exactly. I'm told that Crenshaw isn't really that good a lawyer, but he's well enough known now that he can get on all the talk shows. They don't hire him for his courtroom prowess. They hire him because he can win the case before it gets to the courtroom, by trying it in the media."

"Why would anyone want him on a talk show?"

"See for yourself."

Ben looked. Crenshaw, third drink in hand, was grabbing his crotch and singing "In the Mood."

"He's a character," Mitch said.

"And works pretty hard at it," Ben added.

"Doesn't matter. Most lawyers are so boring. Tailored suits and long complicated words. TV people love characters."

Ben frowned. This presumably explained why he wasn't on the talk-show circuit. "Who's the other man?"

"Harold Rutherford. Hal to his friends. Old money. His job is managing the family fortune. His hobby is organic gardening. He's nuts about it. Has a garden just a short stroll from the eighteenth hole. Insists that the club dining room use his vegetables."

"Is he popular?"

"As popular as anyone can be who habitually babbles on about high-grade manure and compost heaps."

Ben scrutinized the man's ruddy, weather-worn face. "For a guy born to privilege, he looks like he's had a hard life."

"He has. Hard drinking, hard gambling, and hard womanizing."

"I take it you don't like him."

"You got that right. Son of a bitch almost got me fired."

"Why?"

"Oh, nothing really. Typical case of upper-class snobs holding the peons to standards they never come close to meeting themselves. He caught me in the men's room sleeping it off one New Year's Eve after I'd had a few too many."

"And he was mad?"

"Kicked up a real fuss. In front of half the party. I wouldn't be here now if his wife hadn't intervened. She's the one with the heart in the family. Her and the little boy."

"Rutherford has a little boy? He's got to be in his fifties, at least."

"Yeah. Adopted the kid the same year he hit the big five-oh."

"Wow. Never too late."

"Especially if your wife wants a kid in the worst way. That's her, sitting on the far left." He pointed to a slender, attractive woman with short blonde hair. She was significantly younger than her husband. "I wonder what she's doing here."

"Looks like she takes care of herself," Ben commented.

"She does. And the kid, too. I've been told that several years back she was miserable—drunk, bitchy. Everyone avoided her whenever possible. Their marriage was on the skids. Finally, to everyone's relief, they managed to adopt that boy."

Ben saw Captain Pearson enter the room and, a few paces behind him, a well-built man with wavy brown hair. His skin was golden-tanned, his hair was brushed back and immaculately styled.

"Bentley!" Crenshaw waddled up to the newcomer, who

was about a foot and a half taller. "What are you doing here? We keep the hair spray in the locker room."

Bentley spoke with a distinct Southern accent. "Always the clown, Dick?"

"Better than always being a dick, you clown!"

Bentley grinned. "Still stinging from yesterday's golf game? I only beat you by eighteen strokes."

"Yeah? Well, stroke my dick."

"Thanks, I'll pass. Didn't bring my bifocals." Pearson and Rutherford laughed. "Face it, Crenshaw. As a golfer, you suck."

"Spare me your ego. You're so fond of yourself you'd probably like to use your dick for a five iron."

"Ten iron," Bentley corrected. "We're talking about me, not you." All four men laughed.

Ben tried to process the information he was receiving. "So, basically, these four all hate each other, right?"

"Actually," Mitch replied, "I think they're best friends. This is just their idea of convivial male interaction."

"What do you know about the new guy? The one who looks like an underwear model."

"Chris Bentley. Pretty Boy Bentley, we call him."

"Judging by his unblemished good looks, I assume he was also born wealthy?"

"Actually, no. He's the only one of the bunch who has to work for it, although it isn't work as you and I understand it."

"What's he do?"

"He marries."

"I don't quite follow you."

"Sure you do. He marries rich women, preferably widows, usually older than himself. He's done it three times. Marries, divorces, then enjoys himself until the money runs out. His last divorce was two years ago. I understand he's searching for a fourth."

"Surely no one would fall for—"

"You might be amazed what you can get away with when you're monstrously good-looking. Especially with a woman who thinks she's past her prime. She may not care whether it's true and eternal love. A couple of good years in the sack may be sufficient. Particularly with his reputation."

"His reputation?"

"Yeah." Mitch's voice dropped. "Club gossip has it that he likes to engage in . . . deviant sexual practices."

"What exactly does that mean?"

"I don't know," Mitch replied. "But it's gotten him three very wealthy wives."

Pearson waved his hands in the air. "All right, you knuckle-heads. Let's get this meeting started. If we hurry, we can still get in nine more holes before the sun sets."

"Yes, and I need to water my turnips," Rutherford added. "Do hurry."

Pearson rolled his eyes and took a seat at the head of the table. The other three sat nearby. Pearson removed a gavel from a walnut box and pounded it a few times on the tabletop. "The meeting is hereby called to order. The Honorable Ronald Pearson hereby comes—"

"Pearson is going to come?" Crenshaw squealed. "I want to see this!"

Rutherford pressed his hand against his forehead and sighed. "Is it time for Crenshaw's nap?"

"Evidently." Pearson cleared his throat. "Let's all calm down and see if we can have one of those classy Robert's Rules of Order–type meetings, okay? After all, we have spec-tators today."

As one body, all four men turned and stared at Ben. The three who had not met him frowned; Ben wasn't sure if their expressions spoke of curiosity or irritation. On the other hand, the one man who did know him—Pearson—seemed outright hostile.

Pearson briskly moved through the meeting's agenda. They discussed green fees and dress codes and reported scandalous incidents of nude badminton and golf-cart drag races. A lot of talking occurred, but no decisions were reached. Ben felt his head nodding; this meeting was giving new meaning to the word *bored*room.

"How do these people ever accomplish anything?" Ben whispered.

"They don't," Mitch replied. "They hire flunkies like me and write checks. Real work is beyond them and has been for generations."

"I need to talk to these guys," Ben said, glancing at his watch. "Someplace I can get each of them alone, if possible."

"They'll never agree to an interview."

"Maybe we could arrange something less intimidating."

"Well," Mitch said. "They play golf together almost every day."

"Great. Can you get me in on a game?"

"I don't know. Can you play golf?"

"Well enough," Ben bluffed. "I don't have to win."

"No. On the contrary, it's better if you don't. I'll see what I can do."

"Thanks." Crouching, Ben tiptoed out of the conference room. On his way, he had a chance to observe Rachel Rutherford's face at closer range. Despite what Mitch had said, there was something disturbing in her face, some almost invisible stress, some unspoken tension. She wasn't paying the least bit of attention to the meeting. There was something else on her mind.

Ben didn't know what that could possibly be. But he had a suspicion that he should find out.

* 21 *

Carlee rummaged through the cardboard box she had stuffed with canned food before they left Tulsa. Unfortunately, nothing miraculously appeared that hadn't been there the day before. Their dinner options were still severely limited. Baked beans, chili beans, and everyone's favorite: lima beans.

Carlee juggled the three cans. Eeeny, meeny, miney, moe . . .

Dave crawled into the tent on all fours. "How's my favorite cook?" He pinched her on the rear.

She tried to feign irritation. "Likely to be replaced, if we don't drive into town for more supplies soon."

Dave wrapped his arms around her and kissed her on the back of the neck. "Aw, we'd never replace you. Who'd make the s'mores?" He squeezed her tightly, then rolled her over onto her back. "So . . . how are you feeling?"

She knew what he meant, what he really wanted to know. Neither of them had mentioned the incident, but he'd been watching her carefully. He'd been scrupulously courteous and accommodating—more so than she cared for. He was obviously worried. Worried that his beloved wife of nine years was losing her marbles.

"What are the kids doing?" she asked as she ran her fingertips down his shirt.

"Gavin is looking for fossils. There's some species of dinosaur with a name far too long for me to remember that he says lived in the Arbuckles sixty-five million years ago. He wants to find a fossil."

"I didn't know there were any dinosaurs in Oklahoma."

"Me neither, but if Gavin says there were, it must be so."

"What about Ethan?" She put down the bean cans and began massaging Dave's neck.

"Ethan is looking for lizards."

"Lizards? What on earth would he want with lizards?"

"I'm not certain, but given his perverse sense of humor, which I maintain he inherited from your side of the family, I rather suspect an elaborate prank is being contemplated."

"I hope I'm not the intended victim." She rolled over until she was lying almost directly on top of him. "So whaddaya say, lover boy? Wanna quickie?"

"Tempting, tempting. But I'm well aware of the fact that the second we decide to go for it Gavin will be in here asking if rattlesnakes are poisonous. Besides, before it gets too dark, I need to chop some wood so we can have a campfire tonight. Rain check, okay?"

He gently lifted her up and rolled out from under her. She marveled once more at his strength, both inner and outer, and his eternal good nature. She was so lucky to have him. That she, a poor girl from the sticks, should end up with a guy who makes a decent living and was pretty nice to boot—well, it was more than she had ever expected out of life. She was one of the lucky ones, and she knew it.

If there was to be no romantic rendezvous, she might as well get supper on. Lima beans it was. If they complained, she'd bribe them with the prospect of toasted marshmallows. It was a mother's prerogative.

She clambered out of the tent and pushed herself quickly to her feet. Too quickly. The blood rushed to her head. She felt woozy; her vision blurred.

Trying to regain her balance, she looked out toward the center of their camp. She could see the hazy outline of her husband, standing, facing away from her. He was doing . . . something. Raising something over his head, bringing it down hard. Raising it, bringing it down. Raising it, bringing it down. Hard. It thumped upon impact like . . . like . . .

Her vision blurred even more, and then she wasn't looking at her husband anymore. She was looking through the window—*that* window—and she was seeing it all acted out once again. The person facing away from her was holding something, something thin and metallic, raising it overhead, and then—

The club came down with the force of a sledgehammer and thudded onto the woman's head. Once more the club went into the sky, and once more it came down, even harder than before.

The woman screamed. Her voice was thick and foreign. Her words were incomprehensible, but her voice was etched with pain. The club went down again, this time with such force that it snapped in two.

Carlee was horrified; she didn't want to watch, but found she couldn't look away. The assailant picked up the broken shaft, reared back like a twisted javelin thrower, and thrust the shaft through the woman's neck.

And then it happened—the blood. Dark blood spurted from the carotid artery, splashing the walls, the floor, her clothes, her face. Everything. The sticky black mess coated the room and the sickly sweet smell drifted out the window to Carlee and the woman screamed and screamed and screamed. . . .

Carlee crumpled into a heap on the ground, facedown in the dirt. She wept in great heaving waves, her entire body trembling. She felt as if she would never stop crying, never could stop crying.

"Carlee! What is it? My God, what's wrong with you?"

She heard Dave's voice, but it was so far away, so distant, not even real, not even real. . . .

"Carlee, answer me. *Answer me!*"

"Dave?" she answered, in the barest of whispers.

"Are you all right?"

She looked up, and there he was, bending over her, his voice insistent. He was obviously terrified.

"I'll be all right," she said. She tried to be reassuring. "I'm fine."

"You said that before." His concern gave his voice an unnatural edge. "What's wrong with you?"

"I—" She shook her head back and forth. "I just don't

know." She rose up on one knee and crawled into his arms. "Hold me, Dave. Please."

He took hold of her and squeezed tightly. "I was just cutting the firewood and all of a sudden I heard you scream and I turned around and you were lying on the ground and—and—" His voice broke off as if it had nowhere to go. "What's happening to you?"

"I—" Carlee closed her eyes. Yes, it was still there. The blood-soaked corner. The screaming woman. The golf club.

It was all still there.

She could remember this time.

"I saw something," she said simply.

"Saw something? You mean—like a vision?"

"No." Her voice choked. "Like a memory."

"A memory? Of what?"

"Of something horrible." Her eyes darkened. "Something I saw a long time ago, then forgot. Until now."

* 22 *

After taking care of a few pressing matters, Ben headed back to his boardinghouse. The oldies station, 106.1 FM, was playing "Summer in the City," as if it were necessary to remind its listeners of the sizzling heat. Tulsa has one of the highest average humidity counts in the country, and that combined with triple-digit temperatures was more than enough to keep everyone frazzled.

Ben made a sharp left turn off Twenty-first onto Yale. In Tulsa, all the east-west streets were numbered consecutively (Eleventh, Twelfth, Thirteenth, with major intersections ten numbers apart) and all the north-south streets were named after cities, in alphabetical order (Boston, Cincinnati, Denver). Even Ben had a hard time getting lost.

He arrived at his boardinghouse, parked on the street, and grabbed the takeout food he had picked up at Ri Le's. Although the sun had long since set, it was still hot enough for Ben to work up a sweat as he walked from his parking place to the house. He tried to brighten his beleaguered spirits by singing to himself. "And I'll always see polka dots and moonbeams . . . when I kiss that pug-nosed dream. . . ."

Inside, he found Joni Singleton sitting on the stairs. She was curled up lengthwise on a middle step, her hands wrapped under her long legs. She had the headphones of a Sony Discman plugged into her ears. Her eyes were closed; she was grooving. She was wearing a red baseball cap—backward—a T-shirt advertising Sam Adams beer (I'M REVOLTING AGAINST BEER DRINKERS!), and ten-hole utility Docs (boots). She was seventeen, and she looked it.

Her black hair was tucked behind her ears. It wasn't until she turned her head slightly that Ben noticed—she'd cut her hair. For as long as Ben had known Joni and her twin sister, Jami, they had prided themselves on their long lustrous hair. Now Joni's had been sliced off above the shoulder.

"You cut your hair," he remarked. There was no response.

Ben gently removed one of the Discman plugs from her ears. An orchestral arrangement with a strong piano lead streamed out. She was listening to R.E.M., her favorite group. Joni had tried to educate Ben on contemporary music; consequently, Ben knew the tune—"Night Swimming." A brilliant song.

But hardly conducive to conversation. He removed the earphones from her head.

She looked up. "Welcome back to the maxipad, Ben."

He smiled. "You cut your hair."

"Yeah. Does it look skanky?"

"Not at all," Ben assured her. "I like it. I was just surprised. You won't look just like your sister anymore."

"That was the idea."

Ben sat down on the step below her. "You and Jami have a falling-out?"

"Of course not. But we can't go through our entire lives wearing the same chokers and halter tops."

"I see."

"I was smothering. I couldn't evolve!"

"That sounds dreadful."

"I'm seven*teen*," Joni said, as if it were an eternity. "It's time I found my own identity."

Ben nodded. "And here I thought the haircut might have something to do with your new boyfriend."

Her eyes widened perceptibly. "What are you talking about? I dumped Creamo months ago."

"Sorry, Joni. I didn't mean to spy, but I saw you smooching with some tall, dark handsome boy this morning."

Joni grabbed Ben's hand. "Have you told anyone?"

"No. Why?"

"Please don't tell my parents. Seriously. This is life or death!"

"Why?"

"Just take my word for it. They wouldn't understand."

"Mom and Pop aren't into interracial romance?"

"That isn't the half of it. Take my word for it. They wouldn't approve."

"Hmm. Well, they won't find out from me. Mum's the word."

"Thanks." Considerably relieved, she retrieved her earphones. "He's a really nice guy. Promise. He's great."

"He looked like a handsome dude."

"Yeah, but he's more than that. He's deep, you know? Philosophical. He's seen every episode of *Star Trek*."

"Wow."

"Kinda like a black Brad Pitt, you know?"

"Don't sell him too hard, Joni. I may become jealous." Ben stood, then had a second thought. "By the way, Joni . . . do you ever do any baby-sitting?"

A sly smile crept over her face. "You mean for that kid I heard screaming all night and day in your room? No way, compadre." She stuck the plugs back in her ears and fell into the rhapsodic embrace of Michael Stipe and the rest of R.E.M.

Ben stepped over her and walked up the stairs. Sounded as if Christina might have been having a spot of trouble with Joey. He'd best relieve her as soon as possible.

Ben pushed open the door to his apartment. "I'm home! If you're not decent, get that way!"

He stopped in his tracks. There was something in the air, an unaccustomed odor. It wasn't unpleasant, but it was definitely unusual. What was it?

Cooking.

Ben did a sensory double take. *Cooking?* How could that be? He heard the sizzling of the stove inside the kitchen. Problem was, he knew the only meals Christina could prepare were hot dogs and macaroni and cheese. And neither one required a sizzling stove.

Cautiously, he stepped into the kitchen.

"Mother!"

She was standing by the stove, stirring chicken in a fryer. Batter was splattering all over her zillion-dollar pant suit. "Nice to see you, Benjamin. Am I decent enough?"

Ben flushed a sudden and vivid crimson. "That . . . was really meant for . . . never mind. What are you doing?"

"Making your favorite food."

Ben blinked. "Cap'n Crunch?"

"No, silly. Your favorite *meal*."

"I didn't know I had a favorite meal."

"Of course you do. Have you got any more flour? I couldn't find any. Or much of anything else. I had to send Christina for supplies."

"Uh, sorry."

"Well, I'll just have to make do with what I have."

Ben edged closer to the frying pan. "So . . . what are you making?"

"Don't you know? Every Sunday, when we came back from St. Paul's, back when you were just a little tyke, you used to demand that I make my fried chicken."

"I did?"

"Of course. Don't you remember?"

A deep furrow crossed Ben's brow. "I don't remember ever seeing you cook anything before now."

"Well, it has been a while," she said as she stirred the gravy. "Rhiana does such a good job in the kitchen that I haven't had much cause to interfere. But I'm sure it will come back to me. It's like riding a bicycle. I hope."

Ben leaned over the frying pan. It did smell appetizing. And somehow—reminiscent. Could she be right? He didn't recall any of this.

"What brings you here, Mother?"

"Your secretary called me. Said you desperately needed help with the baby."

Ben nodded. No lie there. "Where is Joey?"

"In your bedroom. Asleep, naturally. Babies do that, you know. It's what they do best."

"He's already down? Great. Maybe he'll sleep through the night."

Mrs. Kincaid chuckled. "I wouldn't count on it."

"Well . . . thanks for coming down. I really appreciate it. I've got this big trial coming up—"

"Christina told me. It was my pleasure. I always knew you'd invite me to visit. Someday," she added pointedly.

"I'm sorry this place is such a mess. If I'd known you were coming, I would've tidied up. . . ."

"Oh, don't worry about it. You never cleaned your room, either."

Ben undid his top button and loosened his tie. For some reason, this conversation was making him uncomfortable. "I hope this isn't too much of an imposition. . . ."

"Not at all. I'm sure Julia planned to leave Joey with me, but I was still in Scandinavia when she came by. It was the least I could do."

Ben fidgeted absently with his hands. "When did you get here?"

"This morning."

"You've been here all day? What have you been doing?"

"Oh, this and that. Looking around. Tidying up. And tending to the baby, of course." She paused. "Christina and I had a nice long chat."

Oh, God. "What did you talk about?"

"You, mostly."

"Me?" He laughed nervously. "Sounds pretty boring."

"On the contrary, I found it fascinating. I learned more about you in one afternoon than you've told me in the last twelve years."

"What kinds of things did you—"

"I was quite impressed with some of your accomplishments. As she described them, anyway."

"Christina probably exaggerated."

Mrs. Kincaid smiled. "That's possible. She's a great cheerleader for you. All in all, it was a very pleasant afternoon. I enjoyed her company."

"You—*liked* Christina?"

"But of course. Don't you?"

"Well, yes, but—"

"I thought she was charming. Why wouldn't I?"

"Well . . . she is somewhat eccentric. . . ."

"So what if she is? Benjamin, I'm not quite as banal as you seem to think. I liked her very much. What's more"—she looked up at him and smiled—"I approve."

Ben covered his face with his hand. "Mo-*ther* . . . Christina and I are just friends."

Mrs. Kincaid returned her attention to the cooking. "Yes, that's what she kept insisting also."

"Where is Christina, anyway?"

"I believe she's on the roof. Said she wanted to meditate. Something about staying in touch with her past selves."

"I think I'll go interrupt her meditation, since you seem to have everything here under control."

"That's fine. But don't be late for dinner."

"And miss my favorite meal? Of course not."

Ben tiptoed into his bedroom, careful not to wake the baby, set down his briefcase, and opened the closet. Inside the closet, he popped out the panel that opened onto the roof. The architect probably included the access passage for repair purposes, little knowing it would be used by Giselle for hunting, Ben for stargazing, and Christina for past-life regressions.

Christina was sitting between two gables on a relatively flat section of the roof. Her legs were crisscrossed in the lotus position and she was murmuring under her breath.

"Contemplating the mysteries of the universe?" Ben asked.

She continued to stare straight ahead, eyes closed. "Focusing on my third eye."

Ben sat down beside her. "Focusing on your third eye? Is that like using the Force?"

"No. The third eye is for real. It's the one we lost in antiquity. You close your eyes, shut out the world of temporal intrusions, and turn your third eye in on yourself."

"Sounds very mystical."

"It's a time-tested meditation technique. Everyone does it. Kathie Lee Gifford. Suzanne Somers. Ally Sheedy. The giants." She squinted. "Too late. I've lost it now."

"Sorry. Didn't mean to interrupt your flow."

"Maybe not, but you did." She raised her left eyelid. "Don't sweat it. *Comme ci, comme ça.* I'm out of practice. I was trying to get back in shape. The Tulsa Past Lives Society's annual banquet is coming soon, you know."

"Really? And me without a tuxedo."

"Ha-ha." She manually unlocked her legs and stretched. "It's a gala event. A lot of important people come. You might enjoy it."

"It sounds splendid, spending an evening swilling cocktails and listening to people talk about the good old days back at the Tigris and Euphrates."

"Come on. If you go, I'll buy you a brick at the zoo."

"A what?"

"A brick. You know, inscribed. It's a fund-raiser."

"Gee, you really make it tough to say no."

Christina scowled. "Fret not. Jones already said he'd take me."

"Jones? Why on earth would he want to go?"

"Because he's a nice guy, Ben. Hint, hint." She stretched out on the roof. "So how goes the investigation?"

Ben sat down carefully on the old, knotholed wooden shingles. "Not well. I haven't learned anything that's likely to bust that videotaped confession. I visited the scene of the crime, but ten years after the fact, there's not much to learn. I did see the bigwigs who run that country club."

"Did you talk to them?"

"Only the Captain. And he wasn't very interested in chatting."

"Probably doesn't like scandal and intrigue tainting the club."

"I thought it was more than that."

"What then?"

Ben shook his head. "I don't know. But I'm going to see them again. And now that you've got a relief baby-sitter, you can help. Let's all meet in my office tomorrow morning and plot a course of action."

"Will do."

Ben stretched out and tried to make himself comfortable. "Sorry you had to spend the day with Mother."

"Not at all. We got along famously."

Ben looked concerned. "That's what she said, too."

"In fact, we're going shopping together."

"You're going shopping—*with my mother*?"

"I didn't think you'd mind. You're always complaining about my attire."

"Well, yes, but—"

"Your mother obviously has impeccable fashion sense."

"Granted, but—"

"I'll cancel if you don't want me to go."

"No, no, no. I'm sure it'll be fine." He folded his arms. The idea definitely bothered him, although it was hard to explain why. "I don't want to disappoint Mother. She was telling me how much she likes you."

"Good." Christina beamed. "I'm glad she liked me as much as I liked her."

"You did?"

"Oh, yeah. She's great. After all I've heard you say about her, I was expecting some monstrous grande dame. She isn't."

"Well," Ben said carefully, "of course, you're only seeing her on her best behavior—"

"Your mother is an amazing woman. Do you know—she doesn't sweat."

"Uh, what?"

"Sweat. She doesn't sweat. You know what the temperature is, and your air conditioner doesn't work worth a flip. I've been dripping like a faucet, but she stays cool as a cucumber."

"In more ways than one."

"Oh, Ben, give her some credit. Any mom who drives all the way to Tulsa to baby-sit her grandson and fix her son—who almost never visits her—his favorite meal can't be the cold fish you've always described."

"It's not that she's cold, exactly," Ben said defensively. "It's that she's—" He thought for a long moment, then shook his head. "I don't know. That woman downstairs stirring gravy isn't the mother I remember."

"Memories are tricky things."

"You're not going to start talking about past lives now, are you?"

"No. But I'm beginning to wonder about the accuracy of your past life."

"The only life I've had is the one I'm still living."

She nodded. "That's the one I'm talking about."

* 23 *

"You're trying to poison him against me, that's what you're doing!"

"You're a paranoid fool!"

"I know what I know. What I can see!"

"You're four martinis past being able to see anything clearly."

"Stupid ungrateful cow."

"Pig."

Harold Rutherford pressed his hand against his throbbing temples. He could feel his pulse quickening, his blood pressure rising. Why did he allow himself to be drawn into these shameless displays? All he'd done was ask Rachel to stop telling their son that his father didn't like him. Was that so very much to ask?

"It's hard enough to keep this family together without you telling Abie I hate him."

"I never said any such thing." Rachel folded herself into a furry white overstuffed couch. "He figured it out for himself."

"See?" Rutherford shouted, pointing a finger at her. "That's exactly what I'm talking about. That kind of smart remark is doing Abie a lot of harm. And it doesn't do anyone any good."

"It does me a world of good," Rachel said. She walked to the wet bar and poured herself a drink. "I always feel better for having spoken the truth."

"You're destroying this family, that's what you're doing!"

"Spare me the *Father Knows Best* routine, Hal. You never wanted a family, as we both well know. Family is something you condescended to for me."

Rutherford's neck stiffened. "Maybe I didn't particularly want children, in the abstract. But once I saw that precious little bundle of—"

Her drink spurted out from between her lips. "Give me a break. You? Sentimental about Abie? You've spent more time holding a golf club than you ever spent holding our child."

Rutherford checked his watch. "I don't have time for this. I'm late."

"For what? Tee time?"

"For an appointment with our son, for your information. You remember, the one I never spend any time with!"

Rutherford stomped out the front door, slamming it behind him with gusto. He just didn't understand Rachel anymore. After all the agony they had gone through to adopt, all the false hopes and disappointments, he would have thought that when they finally did get a child, and a beautiful one at that, they would never again have another problem. He had staked so much on this. He had assumed that once they had a baby, their marriage would cure itself.

He should have known better. Nothing cures itself. Nothing ever improves unless you take it into your hands and force it to do what you want.

He slid into the front seat of his cream-colored Mercedes and turned the key. To his surprise, nothing happened.

Now that was strange. The car drove just fine this morning.

He tried the ignition again. Still no response. No impotent revving, no sputtering noises under the hood. Nothing.

Damn these foreign cars, anyway. He should've bought a Saturn, and to hell with what the neighbors would think.

He checked his watch again. He was already running late, and now he was going to be a good deal later.

Abie would never forgive him.

Rutherford slumped down in the car seat. Everything seemed to hit him all at once, like a wall. He loved his son, he really did. But he didn't know how to . . . show it. Everything was so different now. Jesus, his own father never once said "I love you" in his entire life. Did that mean he didn't? Of course not. People understood those things back then. But not anymore. Now everyone was expected to babble on about their feelings all the time. Fathers were supposed to be mothers. Everything was different. And not particularly better.

He tried the ignition again, but there was still no response. Abie would be so upset. The rift between them would be even deeper than before. Perhaps irreparable.

Rutherford pressed his hand against his face and, to his surprise, wiped away a tear.

Abie sat on the corner of Twenty-sixth Street, his arms wrapped around his knees, hugging them tightly. It was one-forty, and no Dad.

It would take his father only a few minutes to get here from home or the country club. Abie had to face facts. He wasn't coming.

He had broken his promise.

Abie pushed himself to his feet. So what, anyway? He didn't really want to go to some stupid ball game, at least not with his dad. He jerked the Drillers cap off his head and threw it to the ground.

He looked at it there, lying in the mud, and then, with a sudden burst of energy, smashed it down with his foot till the colors were entirely obliterated.

A gray sedan with smoked-glass windows eased up to the corner. The window rolled down and inside, Abie saw—that man. Sam. The one who had fought off the bullies and then walked him home.

"How's it going, Abie?"

Abie thrust his hands into his pockets. "I dunno." He realized suddenly that his face was streaked with tears. He wiped them away furiously. "I'm fine. How'd you find me?"

"Well, it was pure accident. I just happened to be driving by when I saw you standing there on the corner. I'm on my way to the Drillers game."

Abie's eyes widened. "Really?"

"Oh yeah. I go to all the games." The man smiled warmly. "What about you?"

Abie shrugged. "I was supposed to go, but . . . well, it didn't work out."

"Oh, that's a shame. Today's game is supposed to be the best all year. They're playing Shreveport for a place in the playoffs."

"I know."

"Look, I don't want to push my luck or anything, but—" The man stopped abruptly. "Oh, never mind."

"What?"

"Oh, nothing. It isn't right. You barely know me."

Abie looked at the man and his kind, friendly face. It was true he had just met the man, but he felt as though he had known him for years. He liked him. What's more, he trusted him.

"My dad was supposed to take me to the game," Abie said quietly. He could feel tears welling up again inside. "But he didn't show up." Abie paused. "He forgot about me."

"Aw, I can't believe that." The man leaned out the car window. "You know, if you were my kid, I'd never leave you standing around on a street corner all by yourself. And we'd go to all the games."

"Really?"

"Oh yeah. Heck, I've got season tickets." He hesitated. "You know, Abie, I probably shouldn't say this, but I like you so much I'm going to do it anyway. If you want, I'll take you to the game."

Abie swallowed. "You will?"

"I'd consider it an honor. Just hop in, and away we'll go."

Abie pondered. His brain was a mishmash of confusion and indecision. "I'm not supposed to get into cars with—you know. People I don't know so well."

The man smiled. "Of course not. That's a smart rule. I understand entirely. Well, say hi to your father for me, if he ever shows up." The man began rolling up the window.

"Wait!" Abie bit down on his lower lip. What could it hurt, anyway? He'd be a lot safer with Sam than he'd ever be with his stupid father. And this *was* the biggest game of the season—

"Okay. I'll come." He tossed his blue book bag into the backseat.

A broad smile spread across the man's face. He popped open the passenger-side door. "That's great, Abie. I can't tell you how happy that makes me."

Abie reached for the door and, at just that moment, noticed a green sports car pulling up behind Sam. "That's Mom's car!"

The tall man glanced into his rearview mirror. "What?"

"It's my mom's Jaguar—and Dad is driving it!" Abie beamed. "I guess he didn't forget after all. I wonder why he's driving her car?"

"Yes," the man said evenly. "I wonder why."

Abie stepped away from the man's car. "Gosh, Sam, I'm sorry, but—"

"It's all right. You run along." His disappointment was evident, but he was being nice about it. What a good sport he is, Abie thought. A really good guy. "We'll go some other day."

"Sure. See ya." Abie scampered to the green Jaguar and crawled into the front seat beside his father. As he buckled his seat belt he saw Sam pull away from the corner and drive on toward Twenty-first. He was going awfully fast, like he was in a big hurry to get away. Well, he probably didn't want to miss the first pitch.

"Are you up for a hot dog?" Abie's father asked.

"That sounds great. Can I?"

"Of course. It's not really a ball game unless you get a few stale hot dogs."

Abie looked up at his father, eyes bright. "And . . . if it's not too much, could I maybe get a new ball cap, too?"

✳ 24 ✳

When Ben entered his office, Jones was huddling with Loving, the office investigator.

"Haven't seen much of you lately, Loving," Ben said. "What have you been doing?"

Loving shrugged his immense shoulders. "Nothin' special, Skipper. Stalkin' a wayward wife."

"I see. You're probably supposed to take some pictures the husband can use in divorce court."

Loving shook his head. "Nah. I'm supposed to make the boyfriend wish he'd never been born."

He would be good at that. Loving was a huge, barrel-chested two-hundred-and-fifty-pounder. His idea of going easy on a suspect was to leave all his body parts intact.

"Did Christina give you the details on the Leeman Hayes case?"

"I think I got the general picture. Whaddaya need me to do?"

"Well, for starters, see if you can find any potential witnesses. Anyone who knows anything about the murder. I'd start with the members of the country club and the staff. Ten years ago."

Loving frowned. "That ain't exactly gonna be easy."

"I know. But I need a witness in the worst way. You'll do it, won't you?"

Loving half smiled. "Only for you, Skipper. Only for you."

A few years before, Ben had won a nasty divorce case—*Loving* v. *Loving*. Afterward, the disgruntled and estranged husband showed up at Ben's office with a gun. Ben managed to survive, and Loving was so grateful to Ben for not pressing charges that he insisted on helping Ben with his caseload. In a matter of months Loving had become a full-fledged, licensed private investigator. He did all Ben's litigation investigations and handled some clients of his own when he had time.

"I'll do my best, Skipper. But I know the police have been looking for the same info, and they totally flushed out."

"I may have a helpful piece of data the police didn't." He told Loving and Jones about his meeting with Captain Pearson, and Pearson's oil-and-gas operations in Peru. "Gas prices aren't that high, but Pearson appears to be rolling in dough. Mike told me there's a lot of illegal narcotics coming this way from Peru. I just wonder if there might be a connection."

"Someone should fly to Peru and check it out," Jones said. "As it happens, I'm available."

"No doubt. Unfortunately, that's not in the Kincaid office budget. I was hoping you could do some database research. Like without leaving your chair."

"Right," Jones said. "Booting up now." He turned on his desktop computer and keyed up the modem. "But you know, Peru isn't going to have as many computerized records as the United States does. Plus, access will be much harder. I haven't read Spanish since high school."

"Do the best you can," Ben said. "And come up with something I can use."

Christina came through the front office door with a large file folder under her arm. She was wearing a billowing purple sequined skirt with gold frill. It made Ben wonder if the national square-dancing convention was in town.

"Here I am," she announced. "This had better be good. Your mom wanted to take me to Utica Square."

"Did you stop by to see her this morning?"

"Oh, yes. She has your little pigpen completely under control. Joey was happily downing his formula and she was doing a little housecleaning."

"Housecleaning?" Ben groaned. "Like what?"

"Well, when I arrived, she was tossing out some maggot-infested food. Under the sink she found a bag of potatoes that the entire Tulsa pest population has been munching on for months. Later she was planning to alphabetize your record albums."

"*Aaargh!* Why can't she leave things alone?"

"Because she's your mother, Ben." Christina giggled. "I mean Benjamin. I'm afraid she thinks your apartment is pretty shabby."

"She thinks every place on earth should look like a Nichols Hills mansion."

"Ben, I've been poor all my life, but I still think your apartment is pretty shabby. Let the woman do what she can."

Ben decided to change the subject. "Let's get on with the team meeting. You should probably go to the courthouse and—"

"I'm way ahead of you." Christina thunked the large file down on Jones's desk.

Ben lifted an eyebrow. "Good news or bad?"

"A little of both. Which do you want first?"

"The good news. Definitely the good."

"Myrna Adams is the assistant DA who's going to try the case. You remember Myrna."

"Sure. Tall, attractive. Great legs."

Christina drummed her fingers. "Legal skills, Ben. Focus on the legal skills."

"Right. She's pretty good. A straight shooter. She won't try to pull any sleazy prosecutorial tricks."

"Women never do. It's you testosterone types who try to turn the courtroom into a macho meter."

"Facts, Christina, not feminism."

"Right. I talked to Myrna for a few minutes. She was getting ready for the pretrial conference today at ten. She's not crazy about this case and she knows you're in a tough spot. I think we'll be able to work something out. Like a plea bargain. Maybe even for time served, if the judge okays it."

"Well, it's worth pursuing. It always helps when the prosecutor is rational. What's the bad news?"

"Judge Hawkins."

"Not again!" Ben threw his head down against the desk. "I've already had three cases before him this year. And I lost every single one."

"Well, here's your chance to go for oh-and-four."

"Are you certain about this?"

"Positive. And there's no chance of a transfer."

"What's wrong with Hawkins?" Loving asked. "Does he hate your guts as much as that federal judge?"

"It isn't anything to do with me," Ben explained. "It's all him. Hang 'em High Hawkins. He's the closest thing to a hanging judge we have in Tulsa County. As far as he's concerned, anyone the police arrest is guilty until proven innocent. And he always gives the maximum sentence. He doesn't have any sympathy for anyone."

"Well, maybe if you talk to him . . ."

"Forget it. Hawkins is the most inattentive, indifferent, indolent judge on the bench. As far as he's concerned, trials are just rigmarole he's forced to endure before he can toss the defendants in the hoosegow. He never takes charge of his cases. Lets the prosecutors get away with anything."

"I'm sorry I asked."

Ben pointed at the file folder on the desk. "What's in there?"

"My pièce de résistance. Trial exhibits. Everything the prosecution is planning to use. Mike got them for you."

"Great. That'll cut through the red tape. Have you got time to review them?"

"I live to serve." Christina pulled a chair up to the desk. "I may check in on your mother at lunchtime, though. Just to make sure she's doing all right with Joey."

"She'll be fine," Ben said. "She's done kids before. I don't want you to impugn your professional reputation."

"I don't mind." Christina opened the folder and began poring over the documents. "To tell the truth, I kind of miss the little squirt."

"There seems to be some magic memory-erasure effect that makes people remember how cute babies are and forget everything else about them."

"Just as well. If it were the other way 'round, the species would have gone extinct aeons ago."

* 25 *

Ben couldn't find a parking space in the underground lot
between the state courthouse and the library, so he ended up
having to park at the Convention Center and hoof it. The heat
was still blistering—over a hundred and eight now, according
to KWGS—and he wasn't the only one feeling it. The homeless people occupying the bus stop on Denver looked singularly miserable. The air conditioner in his apartment might not
work, Ben noted, but at least he had an apartment.

Knowing as he did that riding the elevator always entailed at
least a fifteen-minute wait, Ben took to the stairs. He was doing
some significant huffing and puffing by the time he reached the
seventh floor. Judge Hawkins's clerk waved him into the
judge's chambers. Ben pushed open the door and found Judge
Hawkins reclining in the chair behind his desk . . .

. . . and Jack Bullock sitting in the chair on the opposite side.

"Ben," Bullock said. His hands were folded steeple-style
before his face. "We were just talking about you."

What a delight to find the notorious hanging judge was
talking about him with the man who had recently sworn to
"teach you a lesson." "About the case, or me?"

"You," Bullock said. "And your . . . tactics."

Ben took the available chair opposite the judge's desk. "You
know, Jack, some people might consider an ex parte conversation with the judge mildly improper."

Ben glanced at Judge Hawkins, assuming he would inter-
vene and assure Ben that nothing untoward had occurred. Ben
was sorely disappointed. Hawkins just leaned back in his chair
with the usual indifferent expression plastered across his face.

If anything, he appeared amused and content to enjoy the banter.

"Like I said," Bullock growled, "we talked about you, not your case. As long as we don't specifically discuss the case, there's no ethical impropriety."

"Why are you here, anyway? I thought Myrna Adams was handling this case."

"Not anymore. As of one hour ago the case was transferred to me."

Ben felt a clutching in his throat. This was all he needed. In addition to a client who couldn't communicate, a hanging judge, and a smoking-gun videotape, now he had Bullock for a prosecutor. "What happened to Myrna?"

"Myrna decided she was too busy to be lead counsel on this case."

"Too busy? Why?"

"Because I dumped sixteen new felony cases and two grand-jury investigations on her this morning. She had little choice."

Ben was confused and amazed. "You *wanted* this case? Why on earth would you want this case?"

Bullock's eyes focused on Ben. "So I can ram it down your throat."

For the longest time Ben didn't seem to be able to make his mouth work.

"You need a lesson in the difference between right and wrong," Bullock continued. "So we're going to give it to you."

Ben whirled to face Judge Hawkins. "Are you in on this with him?"

The judge spread his hands. "I don't know what he's talking about. Don't let it worry you, son. You know how over-wrought prosecutors get."

Somehow, Ben didn't find the judge's reassurances the least bit comforting. "I heard the prosecution was interested in a plea bargain."

"All offers are hereby withdrawn," Bullock announced. "I wouldn't cut you a deal if you were representing the pope, and your clients are considerably less saintly."

"Who's being immature now? You're trying to turn a murder trial into a revenge play. Or a referendum on my personal ethics."

"Call it what you will. This is one murderer we're not going to let you put back on the street."

"Leeman Hayes hasn't hurt anyone."

"Maybe not lately, because he's been locked up for the past ten years. 'Course, if his case had gone to trial when it was supposed to, he'd probably be dead now. Instead, a few fancy-lawyer tricks from your ilk got him a ten-year lease on life. At the taxpayers' expense."

"That isn't even accurate—"

"I'm tired of seeing our taxpayer dollars wasted on day care for unexecuted murderers. We have an obligation to the people of this state—"

"Are you sure you're not running for office?" Ben asked. "You sure sound like it."

"Gentlemen." Judge Hawkins eased forward. "Let's not bicker. I'll note for the record that counsel for both parties are present and ready to proceed. Anything else we need to discuss?" He held out his hands for the briefest of moments, then slapped them down on his desk. "So, if there's nothing else—"

Ben couldn't leave without trying to accomplish something. "I asked for the prosecution's witness list. And I haven't got it yet."

"Well, let me say a word on that," Bullock said, leaning across the judge's desk. "The first day he took this case, we got all these discovery requests from Kincaid. From his secretary, actually. We haven't had time to put together all the exhibits—"

"I've already got the exhibits," Ben interrupted. "So you can forget that wheeze."

Bullock was taken by surprise. "I gave strict instructions—"

"To stonewall? Figures." Ben turned his attention to the judge. "Your honor, I'm entitled to know who he plans to call to the stand."

Judge Hawkins sighed wearily. "Any reason why you can't get him a list today, Jack?"

"Well, of course, I just took this case this morning. I'm still feeling my way around."

"Jack." The judge looked at him sternly. "We don't want Mr. Kincaid to have any excuses later on for the appeal court, do we?" He cleared his throat. "Just in case his client is convicted."

Uh-huh, Ben thought. Just in case.

"I'll do my best, your honor," Bullock said.

"I'd appreciate it." Hawkins glanced at his watch. "Now, if there's nothing else—"

"One more matter," Ben said. He knew he was pushing his luck, but he felt obligated to give it the old college try. "I'm bringing a motion in limine to suppress the use of a certain videotape by the prosecution at trial."

"Videotape?" Hawkins frowned. "What is this, some Rodney King deal?"

"Even better," Bullock said. "Hayes actually confessed on tape."

"That's a question of fact," Ben said firmly. "Leeman Hayes doesn't say a word on the tape. It's all pantomime, and extremely ambiguous. I believe it will confuse the jury and prove more prejudicial than probative. Especially after Mr. Bullock gives it his slanted spin-doctor routine—"

Bullock looked wounded. "I wouldn't do that."

"—just like he did a few seconds ago."

Hawkins frowned. "Is this a . . . lengthy videotape?"

"Not too long, your honor," Bullock replied. "About an hour."

"But the jury will probably have to watch it several times," Ben interjected.

Hawkins sighed again. "Is this absolutely necessary, Mr. Prosecutor?"

"It's the crux of my case," Bullock insisted. "This kid is guilty, and the tape proves it."

He'd said the magic words. When all was said and done, in Hawkins's eyes, Bullock worked for the forces of good, and

Ben was trying to interfere with Hawkins's summary imposition of the maximum sentence. "Well, I hate to make a decision in advance of trial. . . ."

Ben tried not to snicker. Hawkins hated to make a decision, period.

"So why don't we just overrule the motion for now. You can renew your motion at trial, Mr. Kincaid. In the event that I sustain it, I'll instruct the jury to disregard the taped evidence."

And a fat lot of good that will do, Ben thought. Despite this fiction judges liked to employ, there was no way the jurors could disregard evidence once they had seen it. On the contrary, most jurors tended to give particular consideration to anything they'd been told to forget.

Hawkins pushed himself out of his chair. "If there's nothing more, gentlemen, I do have a golf game this afternoon. . . ."

"What a coincidence," Ben said. "I'm playing golf this afternoon, too. At Utica Greens."

The judge did a double take. "*You're* playing at Utica Greens?"

"Oh, sure," Ben bluffed. "I play there all the time. Don't you?"

Hawkins's eyes moved closer together. "I applied for membership three years ago. I was turned down."

"Well, perhaps you can come out with me sometime."

Hawkins's eyes lit up. "Really? How about next Friday?"

Ben tried to simulate Hawkins's most indifferent expression. "I'll see what I can do."

"Thanks. I'll look forward to it." Hawkins shook Ben's hand energetically, disregarded Bullock's, and scurried out of chambers.

"Now wait a minute," Bullock said. "You two are going to play golf together? As in ex parte? I'm not sure I approve of this."

"Don't get excited," Ben said. "As long as we don't specifically discuss this case, it's okay, remember?" He strolled out of the judge's chambers. "Actually, we'll probably spend the whole time talking about you."

* 26 *

It took Ben almost half an hour to find the address Ernie had given Jones. Not that Ben was any whiz with directions, but the North Side always seemed particularly labyrinthine to him. Not the shallow North Side, close to downtown, or the yuppie North Side in Gilcrease Hills, but the real thing. The other side of the tracks. The poor part of town. Poor and black.

At the turn of the century, over eighty thousand African Americans poured into Oklahoma (Indian Territory, until 1906). In Oklahoma, they hoped to find, or make, a society free of bigotry and prejudice. By 1907, blacks outnumbered both Native Americans and those of European descent; Oklahoma had more all-black towns than all the other states combined. Even in mixed cities like Tulsa, blacks had more success and more clout than anywhere else.

In Tulsa, African Americans settled in a segregated community on the North Side known as Greenwood. Oil dollars made the city, both white and black, prosperous. During the first two decades of the twentieth century, Greenwood was the most successful black community on the map. It boasted black lawyers, doctors, and tailors; it contained forty-one grocers, nine billiard halls, and thirty restaurants.

Despite the city's overall financial strength, racial tensions between the two segregated communities, long-held prejudices, and economic competition eventually led to conflict. Mob violence, and even lynchings, began to plague Greenwood. Then, in 1921, a white female elevator operator in the downtown Drexel Building accused a black teenager of trying to rape her while he rode the elevator from his shoeshine stand

168

to the rest rooms, a trip he made several times a day. According to the most reliable account, the boy lost his balance and accidentally stepped on her foot, causing her to lurch backward. He reflexively grabbed her arm to keep her from falling, and she screamed.

There was never any real evidence of an attempted assault. Everyone who knew the boy said he would never commit such an act, especially not in as unlikely a place as a crowded office building. Despite the dubiousness of the claim, the *Tulsa Tribune*, which customarily referred to Greenwood as "Little Africa," ran an inflammatory front-page feature on the affair headlined TO LYNCH NEGRO TONIGHT. White citizens took up arms.

Approximately two thousand white men surrounded the courthouse, hoping to hang the arrested teenage boy. Later about seventy-five armed black men arrived to help the sheriff defend the prisoner. Shots broke out, and in minutes the race riot was in full force. Pistol-packing white mobs surged into Greenwood, burning and looting businesses, destroying homes, and shooting residents. The rioters particularly targeted the homes of wealthy and prosperous black families. An elderly black couple was killed while walking home from church. Another black man was killed after surrendering peacefully to a gang of looters. Less than twenty-four hours after the riot began, all of black Tulsa was in flames, and hundreds were dead. It was the worst race riot in American history, not excepting the more recent Los Angeles riots.

Greenwood was eventually rebuilt, and became known in the 1930s as the Black Wall Street. But it was never the same. The sense of optimism that once permeated Greenwood never returned, and the black community never recovered the autonomy, mobility, and economic and political power it once had. As time passed, north Tulsa became another inner-city slum—poor, shoddy, ruined. Although recent urban-renewal efforts had restored some historical landmarks, most North Side residences were still poor, the businesses were still struggling, and the streets were still dangerous. If you didn't live there, you didn't go there.

Ben turned onto the street where the Hayes family resided. The street was lined with small white houses—shacks, really—with thin plywood walls, warped and swollen, and peeling paint, where there was any paint at all. Torn screen doors, chipped steps, cracked sidewalks. Trash littering the street, the lawns. Everything spoke of poverty of the worst, most debilitating sort.

Ben carefully mounted the stone steps to Ernie's house. Actually, they weren't steps; they were cinder blocks. The house appeared to have once been red, but age and weather had turned it an ugly rust orange. He noted two cars parked on the street outside—the smashed Ford Pinto and a Chevy station wagon, about fifteen years old by Ben's guess. While it was no prize, it was certainly more presentable than the Pinto. He wondered why Ernie had driven the clunkier car to Ben's office.

Through the screen, Ben saw Ernie hurry to the door. Was it his imagination, or was his limp not nearly as pronounced as it had been before?

Ernie Hayes had intentionally driven his worst, most beat-up-looking car, and limped like an accident victim as he approached Ben's office, which of course had resulted in Ben's taking this case.

Hmmm.

"Mr. Kincaid," Ernie said. "Ain't this a nice su'prise." He showed Ben into the tiny living room of his home.

Ben was appalled. The room was cluttered with food containers, potato-chip bags, empty beer bottles. There was no central air, and in this unrelenting heat, the room was a sweatbox. Every window was open as wide as it would go. Ben's own apartment was small and cheap, but in comparison with the Hayes residence, it was a mansion. In fact, their so-called living room could probably have fit in his bathroom. And at the moment there were six people in it.

"This must be your family," Ben commented.

"This's my brood." He pointed at the kids on the floor. "What's left of it, anyhow. Monique and Kevin and Julius and

Corey and Bartholemew. That's my family, not counting the three that done already left home. And Leeman, of course."

Ben's lips parted. "You have nine children?"

"That I do. My wife and I, we got along real good, you know? She was a honey, God rest her soul." He took Ben's arm. "Let's go into the kitchen."

They walked into the small kitchenette and sat at a wobbly plastic table. "This here's where Leeman grew up," he explained. "I know it ain't much, but I've done the best I can with what little we've had. It ain't been easy. 'Specially since I lost my job at the glass factory."

"What happened?"

"Got laid off. I'd been there eighteen years, and I got nine kids and all that, but I was still one of the first let go. I complained to that big white supervisor they put over me, even though he's half my age, and you know what he said? He said, 'Aw, don't go cryin' them crocodile tears to me, Ernie. You'll probably be a lot happier drawin' welfare anyway, won't you?' "

"What about the children?" Ben asked. "Some of them look old enough to work, at least part-time."

"I've been trying to get Julius—he's my oldest at home—to get a job. But he won't listen. Says I'm just a stupid old man. Been hanging around with one of them street gangs that's crawlin' all over this neighborhood scarin' everybody. And they're always goin' out to that damn country club where Leeman usta work. As if that cursed place hasn't caused this family enough misery."

Gang members at the country club? How could that be? Ben couldn't imagine what gang members would be doing at the country club, but whatever it was, it probably wasn't legal.

"Now, Corey, he's a good boy," Ernie said, his face brightening slightly. "He sells papers."

"He has a paper route?"

"No, not 'zactly. He tried to get him one of those, but they wouldn't give it to him. Said someone else already had all of 'em. He goes through people's trash, see, finds old newspapers, goes into eating places, and sells them. Till he gets chased out."

They heard a knock on the door. "Papa!"

If Ben remembered properly, the shouting offspring was Julius. "I'm goin' out with Booker."

"I don't want you hangin' out with that boy! He's trouble!"

Through the passageway, Ben saw Julius smirk. Ignoring his father, he slapped a high five with his friend and went outside.

Just before the door closed, Ben caught a fleeting glimpse of the visitor. The face was familiar.

It took Ben a moment, but he finally pulled the memory out of deep storage. It was Joni's boyfriend. The one he had seen her smooching with out his bedroom window.

If Ernie was right about Julius's connection to youth gangs, Joni's new romance was going to be even more controversial—and dangerous—than he had imagined. No wonder she hadn't mentioned it to her parents.

Ben ran to the front window and watched them depart. They both wore matching jackets with a bloodred emblem on the back—a swastika with a heart around it. Ben made a mental note to ask Mike about that later.

Ben returned to the kitchen and tried to ask Ernie a few questions about the case.

"Mr. Hayes, I understand that the murder ten years ago took place late at night—after midnight. Do you have any idea what Leeman would have been doing out there at that hour?"

" 'Course I do. It was the middle of the week, Mr. Kincaid. He was out there late every night."

"Surely there was no caddying after dark."

Ernie laughed. "Well, 'course not. Naw, he slept out there."

"He slept at the caddyshack?"

"Sure. Why not? That shack is a nice lil ol' place. Leeman had a lot more room out there than he did here, and he didn't have to share it with all these brothers and sisters, neitherwise. He'd sleep out there during the workweek, then come home on the weekends."

"Did the management approve of his sleeping in the caddyshack?"

Ernie tilted his head to one side. "Well . . . to tell you the truth, I'm not entirely sure they ever knew. We figgered, what they don't know cain't hurt them, right?"

It might not have hurt them, Ben thought, but he wondered if it hadn't hurt Leeman. To the tune of about ten years. "Did you hire an attorney to represent Leeman when he was arrested?"

"With what? My good looks?" He laughed again. "Naw. We got one of them freebie lawyers appointed to us."

"How was he?"

"I think he did the best he could under the circumstances. Didn't think he was the brightest man I'd ever met, but he seemed earnest. Problem was, he had about twenty other cases he was juggling, all at the same time. He'd run in real quick like and expect Leeman to tell him his whole life story in ten minutes, which for Leeman was absolutely impossible. He never had no time to do any real checkin' around."

"Did you ever . . . talk with Leeman about the murder?"

"Talk with *Leeman*?"

"In pantomime. Or however you used to communicate."

"Not as I recall."

"Weren't you . . . curious?"

" 'Bout what?"

"Well, about whether he killed Maria Alvarez."

"Didn't have to ask no fool questions to know he didn't commit no murder. 'Specially not like that, what with the golf club and bein' so mean and all. Not my Leeman. A boy's papa knows these things."

"Mmmm." Not an answer that was likely to carry much weight in court, unfortunately. No matter. There was little point in calling Ernie to the stand, anyway. The jury would assume a father would be willing to lie to prevent his son from being executed. "You were present when Leeman was questioned by the district attorney, weren't you? I saw you on the videotape."

"Oh, yes," he said wearily. "Lord, yes. I was there."

"You know the prosecution considers that performance by Leeman to be a confession. That's probably going to be the most damning evidence brought against him."

"Yes," he repeated. "Yes, I 'spect so."

"Did you ever talk to Leeman about that? Or did you understand what he was trying to do?"

He shook his head sadly. "No, Mr. Kincaid. Cain't say as I did."

Ben had hoped Ernie might have some insight that made it all make sense. No such luck. If anything, he appeared to consider the evidence even more damaging than Ben did. It made Ben wonder if he was as certain of Leeman's innocence as he claimed.

Or if he knew something more he wasn't telling Ben.

"Mr. Hayes, can you recall anything else you haven't told me that relates to this case?"

Was there just the slightest hesitation, or was it all in Ben's imagination? "No, sir. Nothing."

"Well, then I'll be going."

Ernie grabbed Ben's arm and held him down. "Do you think you'll be able to help my boy?"

"I'll make every possible effort—"

"That ain't enough." Ernie drew himself up slowly, his eyes dark and clouded. "You know, Leeman was my favorite, ever since he was a little tyke. I wouldn't tell none of the other kids that, you understand, but it's true. I usta work out at that country club myself. Part-time, in the evenings, to make a little extra to spread around the family. I was a waiter at that fancy restaurant. In fact, I got Leeman his job there. It was all my idea."

He shook his head sadly. "When Leeman got arrested and taken away—I felt responsible, you know? Felt jus' awful. Like someone ripped my heart out and sealed it in a box for ten years. I felt so powerless. I kept thinkin', if I was some rich white dude like them country-club boys, my Leeman would be a free man. I felt so bad. So guilty." He looked up suddenly. "It's hard to go on livin', thinkin' like that. You know?"

Ben nodded sympathetically. "I'll be in touch before the trial."

Ernie walked Ben to the screen door. "I couldn't help but notice," Ben remarked. "Your arthritic limp seems to be considerably better than it was when you came to my office."

A quick grin snuck across Ernie's face but was immediately suppressed. "Comes and goes, don't you know. Comes and goes."

Right, Ben thought as he walked through the doorway. You're a sly old dog, Ernie Hayes.

"I know what people think," Ernie said abruptly. "They don't say nothin', but they think, Well, you're probably better off now with that dumb retarded kid off your hands. But he's my *boy*, Mr. Kincaid, you know?"

He took Ben's hand and pressed it between his. "I couldn't bear to see nothin' more happen to my Leeman than what already has. I jus' couldn't bear it."

Ben swallowed, didn't say anything.

"Take care of my boy, Mr. Kincaid."

"I'll do my best," Ben replied, his voice cracking.

Ben walked back to his car. As he left the house he surveyed the landscape—the dirt lawns, the cracked and ruined houses, the filthy streets. And just over the top of the Hayes home, just over the horizon, he could see the upper stories of the elegant Utica mansions, not ten miles away from this abject poverty.

It was like two cities, really. Two cities in one.

What a thing to be reminded of, day after day. Bad enough to live in these horrible conditions. But then, as if to add insult to injury, every time you cast your eyes upward, you see the tall gables, the blue swimming pools, the fancy cars of millionaires who spend more on their stereo systems than you make all year long. And then you go to work at their country club, and have constant firsthand exposure to the lifestyles of the pampered and privileged. The people who have everything you don't.

That, Ben speculated, could drive a person to do almost anything.

* 27 *

Ben experienced a profound sensation of culture shock as he drove across town to the Edward Woltz Spa for his meeting with Rachel Rutherford. In less than ten minutes, he had left the poverty and degradation of the North Side for safe south Tulsa—upscale, clean, trendy. Caffe latte bars, children's bookstores, gourmet groceries.

A world of difference.

Ben parked his Honda and entered the austere white front lobby of the spa. The cosmic tinkling of piped-in New Age music drifted through the walls. Rock crystals were artfully arranged on the countertops. A prim, dark-haired woman greeted him at the front desk. She was wearing something that was not quite a doctor's or a nurse's uniform, but it had a certain sense of officialdom to it, just the same.

"Can I help you?" the woman asked.

"I'm Ben Kincaid. I'm here to see Rachel Rutherford."

"Right. She told me to show you on back. Follow me."

The woman pushed open a swinging door. Ben followed her down a long white corridor with doors on either side. Through the windows in the doors, he saw people, mostly women, engaged in various therapeutic exercises, lying on massage tables, or soaking in tubs.

He peered through a large window into the room on his immediate right. A green face popped up suddenly on the other side.

"Yikes!" Ben said, jerking his head back. "What was that?"

"That was Mrs. Buckner."

176

Ben glanced nervously back at the door. "But she was . . . *green*."

The woman smiled. "Mrs. Buckner is having the seaweed facial."

Ben grimaced. "You mean that gunk smeared all over her face is seaweed?"

"Uh-huh."

"I assume this is punishment for some egregious crime against nature."

"Silly boy! It's a thick green paste made from a special Mediterranean seaweed. We apply it to her face, bake it, cool it, then scrape it off. Makes your pores feel wonderful."

"I'll bet," Ben said. "Especially when it's off."

The woman laughed. "Believe me, it's exhilarating. Women pay as much as three hundred dollars for a single treatment. Makes them feel relaxed. All our treatments are extremely relaxing."

"What other treatments do you offer?" Ben asked, not entirely sure he wanted to know. "I have a friend who keeps telling me I need to learn how to unwind."

"We provide a full range of relaxation therapies. Body scrub, shiatsu, or vibration massages. Mud baths, with a special mud imported from the Dead Sea. You name it. We'll do whatever it takes to unknot those kinks and ease those tensions. I'd be happy to sign you up for a trial membership."

"Thanks just the same," Ben said. "I can't afford it."

"Oh, but that's the best part," the woman explained. "We're very economical. A bargain, really. If you go to a first-class luxury spa in Florida or Hawaii, you can expect to pay thirty-five hundred bucks a week. Here, you don't have to leave home, and we don't have a single treatment that costs more than five hundred."

"Is that all?" Ben mumbled.

"Many are less than two. And you can be in and out of here in an hour."

Ben nodded. "Therapy in a bottle."

"Hey, that's pretty good. I'll pass it along to Mr. Woltz. It would make a fine advertising slogan. Do you mind?"

"Feel free."

The woman pushed open a door at the end of the corridor. "Mrs. Rutherford is in the tub."

The woman escorted Ben into a small tiled room, then excused herself. The main feature of the small room was the even smaller Jacuzzi in the center. It was a circular tub, barely big enough to hold one person. Water flowed and bubbled through jets on the sides; steam rose from the rippling surface of the water.

Rachel Rutherford was immersed in the tub, hands on her knees, eyes closed. Her short blonde hair fell gracefully above her bare shoulders. The bubbles lapped at her cleavage. Ben knew she had to be in her forties, but she looked ten years younger. Maybe this seaweed stuff works after all, he mused. She was very attractive.

She was also, Ben suddenly realized, nude. If not for the bubbling foam on the surface, this would become an extremely revealing interview.

Ben suddenly felt rather warm under the collar. "Why don't I wait outside while you . . ."

Rachel opened her eyes. "Didn't you want to talk to me?"

"Well, yesss . . ."

"Your secretary said it was urgent."

"Well, yesss . . ."

"After I get out, I have a mixed-doubles match I can't miss, and tonight I'm going to Chris Bentley's charity ball. If you want conversation, it had better be now."

Ben wiped his damp palms on his slacks. "I don't want to make you uncomfortable. . . ."

She laughed. Her bosom vibrated in an amazingly enticing manner. Ben found it very difficult to avert his eyes. "Don't worry about me. At the moment I'm at peace with the universe. What can I do for you?"

"Well, ma'am, I'm a lawyer—"

"I'm sorry."

"I represent Leeman Hayes."

"Don't believe I know him." Her eyelids fluttered closed.

"He used to be a caddy at the country club, ma'am. About ten years ago."

Her eyes reopened. "He's the one who killed that poor foreign woman, isn't he?"

Ben frowned. "That's the accusation, ma'am. I don't think he did it."

"I remember my husband telling me the . . . details of the murder. Horrible." She shuddered. "But what can I do for you?"

"I understand you spent a great deal of time at the country club around the time of the murder."

"I'm sure I did. So?"

Ben wasn't certain how to begin. He didn't really know why he wanted to talk to her. It was just a hunch. Or desperation. "Well . . . did you see anything suspicious? Anything that might bear on the murder?"

"I wasn't loitering around the caddyshack much in those days."

"Yes, but still—"

"Mr. Kincaid, I was interviewed by the police at the time, as you must know, and I told them I didn't possess any information about the murder, which I don't."

"What can you tell me about Ronald Pearson?"

"You think Ronnie killed that woman?"

"Not necessarily. But the woman was from Peru, and I know he has business ties to Peru. The woman came to this country and immediately went to the country club, where he happened to be chairman of the board—"

"That doesn't make him a murderer."

"No. But it gives me cause to ask questions."

She gently splashed water on her shoulders. "Then go ask Ronnie."

Ben tried a different tack. "I understand your little boy comes to the country club sometimes, too."

"Abie? Occasionally. Not often."

"Forgive me for prying, ma'am, but I've seen a picture and . . . Abie doesn't much resemble his father."

"He doesn't resemble either of us. He's adopted."

"So I've been told. Why did you—"

"It's a long story, Mr. Kincaid." She stretched back in the tub, revealing ever-increasing portions of hot pink skin. "Are you sure you want to hear it? It has nothing to do with your case."

"Still—"

"All right. You asked for it. First, you have to understand—I've always wanted children. A baby of my own. Practically since I was a baby myself, that was my driving goal. Truth to tell, that was the main reason I got married. I didn't need Hal's money. I had plenty of my own. What I needed was a husband. So I could get my baby."

"I'm not sure I see . . ."

"Of course, I've learned since that what you want most in life, what you can't live without, is the very thing most often denied. We tried for seven years to conceive. Time and time again I had sex with that man." Her face scrunched up in disgust.

Ben felt himself flushing. He couldn't believe she was saying this to someone she barely knew. Of course, he couldn't believe she was sitting there naked in front of someone she barely knew either.

"Hal was much older than me, of course. He would grunt and thrust and strain. I just lay there every night, enduring it, thinking, maybe this will be the magic one. Maybe this will be the time I get my little baby." She pressed her wet polished fingertips against her lips. "But it never was."

"Was there . . . a problem?"

"So I wondered. To tell you the truth, that's why I had the affair."

"The—the—"

"Yes, that. To find out the cause of the problem. Was it Hal or was it me? Well, it was me." She paused. "Don't worry, I've confessed to Hal. I'm sure it seems odd to have this woman blabbing her innermost secrets, but let me tell you, I was in therapy for twelve years, and my shrink recommended that I stop keeping my feelings locked inside, that I try to be honest.

So I do. I was honest with Hal, and I'll be honest with you, too."

She paused again, then returned to her narrative. "I thought perhaps Hal was sterile, so I tried to get pregnant with someone else. Didn't enjoy him much, either. He's a bit of a pig, when you get right down to it. I just thought, please, God, *please*, let this be the time. Let me have my baby."

She splashed hot water on her face. "But that didn't take, either. I had to face facts. I was the problem."

"You saw a doctor?"

"Several. Turns out my insides are all screwed up. Ovaries are a mess. My body doesn't release eggs the way it's supposed to. I wasn't going to be having any children. At least not the natural way."

She folded up her legs and sank lower into the tub, as if to hide herself in the foamy bubbles. "I was devastated. Ruined. I—well, I tried to kill myself. Sat in the garage with the car running. If Hal hadn't come home early, it might have worked. That's when I went into therapy. But nothing made me feel any better. Nothing made me feel I had any reason to live."

She looked up abruptly. "Until someone suggested the possibility of adoption. Hal was against it at first, but eventually he agreed to try."

"That must have made your life better."

"That," she said emphatically, "turned my life into a fucking nightmare."

"I—I don't understand."

"How much do you know about the adoption business?"

"Not much," Ben admitted.

"Well, it's a seller's market. Been that way for years. What with the pill and all manner of contraceptives and legal abortion, birthrates are declining. And single motherhood is no longer the unbearable social stigma it once was. Bottom line, there aren't that many babies around."

"Surely, given your husband's . . . influence . . ."

Her chin raised. "You mean his affluence? Wrong. Adoptions in America are tightly regulated. Hal couldn't pay enough bribes to get around all the sycophants and supernumeraries with their rules and guidelines. As it turned out, Hal was the biggest strike against us. He was fifty; the adoption agencies considered him too old to become a father for the first time. Ironic, huh? The man I had married just to get a baby was now my main obstacle."

She stretched out her legs and floated to the surface of the tub. Her buoyant breasts rose to the surface, nipples bobbing in the foam. She didn't seem to notice. Or if she did, she didn't care. "This was not a good time for our marriage," she continued. "After a while I gave up all hope. I knew I was going to kill myself. It was just a matter of time.

"Finally, Hal contacted a lawyer who supposedly specialized in arranging difficult adoptions. Paid him twenty-five thousand bucks up front. He found us a pregnant woman. So he said. Single. Fifteen. Wanted to put her child up for adoption. So we were told.

"I was ecstatic. We were waiting at home the day she was supposed to deliver, with our new crib and baby monitors and car seats and baby clothes and all those other child-care essentials. I even redecorated a room."

Her eyes darkened. "About six o'clock that night, the lawyer calls and says the baby died. He's real sorry. Maybe next time." She inhaled deeply, sending concentric ripples across the surface of the tub. "I cried for weeks. And I tried to kill myself again. This time with a knife. In a pool not unlike this one." She held out her left wrist. "Wanna see the scars?"

"No, thanks," Ben said quietly.

"Obviously, I didn't die. I just hurt like hell. For months. Then the lawyer announced that he had found us another pregnant woman. So I held on. Maybe this time, I kept saying. Maybe this time. I got excited again, all ready to go. One of my girlfriends at the club even threw me a shower. Then we got the call." Another deep, purging breath. " 'The mother changed her mind,' he said. He was so sorry. His voice even trembled a bit as he gave us the news."

"What a horrible coincidence," Ben said.

"I don't believe in coincidence. Neither does Hal. He had the lawyer investigated. Turns out the whole operation was a charade. A scam. The lawyer took the money and fabricated the stuff about mothers and babies. What's worse, we found out he'd pulled the same scam on fourteen other couples. Got them excited, absconded with their money. He never gave anyone a baby because he didn't have a baby to give." She looked up at Ben. "So you'll have to excuse me if I'm not all that fond of lawyers."

"Not at all."

"That lawyer is in the pen now, which was certainly gratifying, but it didn't get me a baby."

"You must have been horribly depressed."

She tilted her head to one side. "Not so much that time, actually. I don't know why. By then I had somehow . . . hardened. I didn't expect anything. It was as if some chunk of my soul, some capacity for caring . . . disappeared. Even now, I think there's a part of me I lost that I'll never get back."

"You gave up?"

"No. I . . . toughened up. I stopped depending on Hal. I took matters into my own hands."

"What did you do?"

"I went to see my friend. The one I had the affair with. The man who could get anything. I didn't need any more sensitive males. I needed a broker. So I went to him and I said, 'Buddy, you owe me.' He said, 'Okay, what do you want?' And I told him. 'I want a baby,' I said. 'Get me a baby.' "

"And?"

For the first time a vibrant smile crossed her face. "And he did. I got my little Abie. Our beautiful boy."

"But—how? Where did the boy come from?"

"I don't know," she said flatly. "And I don't care. I don't even want to know."

"But—"

"He saved my life. He really did. I would've gone on trying to kill myself. Eventually I would've succeeded. But Abie changed everything."

"You haven't adopted any other children?"

"After all that? No. I wanted a baby. I got him. That's

enough. No need to be selfish. So you see, Mr. Kincaid, that's my adoption story. Are you happy now?"

She glanced at her watch. "Oh, wow. It's two o'clock already. I'll be late for my tennis game." She rose from the tub.

"Oh—wait!" Ben grabbed a towel for her.

Too late. There she stood, in all her glory. And it was pretty glorious, too.

"Is something wrong?" she asked innocently.

Embarrassed as he was, Ben couldn't seem to avert his eyes. "You're—"

"Don't fall for me," Rachel said as she stepped out of the tub and took her white terrycloth robe off its hook. "I'm much too old for you. Besides, I'm a mother."

And with that, she bounced out of the room.

* 28 *

Carlee felt a surge of relief as they pulled up to their home in the Richmond Hills section of south Tulsa near St. Francis's Hospital. It wasn't that their camping vacation had been unpleasant—at least, not most of it. She was just glad to be home. Glad and happy and . . . comforted.

Gavin and Ethan poured out of the car and scrambled toward the front door.

"Don't forget your bags!" Dave shouted behind them. "If you think I'm carrying in everyone's luggage, you've got—" He stopped, recognizing the utter futility of it. They were already well out of earshot.

Carlee turned to him and smiled. "But you will carry in my luggage, won't you, lover boy?"

"But—"

She quickly scurried out of the car and beyond the point of protest. She scooped the morning paper off the driveway; the Bloms must not have been by yet to collect the mail.

Inside the house, she found few surprises. All the major appliances and electronic devices appeared to be where they had been left. Ethan was already perched in front of the television set. Gavin was on the phone.

"Let me know if she still loves you, Gavin," Carlee shouted merrily.

Gavin frowned, covered his free ear, and pressed the receiver closer to his head.

Carlee entered the kitchen. She poured herself a Dr Pepper—the real thing—with honest-to-God crushed ice from the refrigerator. Heaven on earth. The door slammed, and she heard Dave struggle to haul in all the luggage at once, grunting and groaning up the stairs. She felt a little sorry for him, though not sorry enough to help.

He'd survive. What Carlee wanted desperately were a few minutes alone, a little quiet time, a chance to think. Camp-outs were great for familial bonding, but they were lousy for private meditation. And she needed to pull herself together.

She still didn't know what had happened to her at Turner Falls. Dave had tried to take care of her as best he could. He even ended up fixing the beans. But he never mentioned what had happened. He wasn't being inconsiderate; it was just his way. Misbehaving kids he could deal with. A wife needing some TLC he could deal with. But something so . . . foreign to their experience . . . He just couldn't handle it. He didn't know what to do. So he pretended it hadn't happened.

Unfortunately, Carlee knew it had happened. Twice. And more and more she became convinced that it was not just a dream, not just a hallucination. Every time she thought about it, she saw a little more. It was like a movie unspooling reel by reel. New details came to light.

Like, for instance, that window she was looking through, when she saw the woman. She knew now that the window was open; that's how she smelled the blood and heard the screams. And the room . . .

It was the caddyshack at the Utica Greens Country Club. She was certain of it.

But how could that be? She hadn't been to that country club for almost ten years, since she quit her job in the kitchen. She hadn't been anywhere near the place; she and Dave certainly couldn't afford to be members. And yet, she knew that was what she was seeing.

A sudden pounding upstairs brought her back to the present. It was Dave, stomping around with the luggage. Well, perhaps she could give him a teeny bit of help. In a minute. She pulled the rubber band off the paper and dropped it flat on the kitchen table. Her eyes drifted across the front-page stories.

The air flowed from her lungs as if sucked out by a vacuum.

Her lips moved wordlessly; her eyes were transfixed, locked onto the photograph on the front page of the *Tulsa World*.

It was her.

The woman.

Carlee stumbled backward, caught herself, then slowly sank into a chair. She suddenly became aware that she was making a sharp high-pitched noise, something like a cross between a cry for help and an aching moan. She put her hand over her mouth and willed herself to stop.

"Is somethin' wrong, Mom?"

It was Ethan. He was staring up at her with worried eyes, for the second time in recent memory. Kids never miss anything.

"Get your father," she said breathlessly. "Then go back to your television program. I'm fine."

A few moments later Dave came barreling much too fast down the stairs and into the kitchen. He put his hands on her shoulders. "What is it, honey? What's wrong?"

Carlee lifted a shaking hand and pointed at the newspaper on the table. "That's her," she said.

"That's who?" Dave glanced at the paper and the black-and-white photo on the front page. The accompanying article explained that the woman had been murdered about ten years before; a Tulsa man was accused of the crime. The trial was scheduled to start soon. "Did you know this woman?"

Carlee shook her head from side to side.

"Then—*what*?" His face was a combination of sympathy and helplessness.

"That's the woman I saw," Carlee said. She wrapped her arms around herself. "The woman I saw covered with blood."

"At Turner Falls? At the campground? But she's been dead for ten years." His voice evidenced his utter lack of comprehension. "What are you saying? That you had some kind of . . . psychic vision or something?"

"No," she said, still trembling. "I saw her murdered. With my own eyes."

"But—if you saw it, why didn't you mention it before now?"

She looked up at the ceiling, as if hoping for some assistance, some answer, some salvation. She looked in vain. "Because I didn't remember."

"You didn't remember?" Deep wrinkles furrowed Dave's brow. "You're saying you saw this woman get killed and then . . . *forgot about it?*"

Carlee placed her head against his chest. "I know it sounds insane. I don't understand it either. But that's what happened. I saw that woman die. I know I did."

"And you forgot about it. And now, just as the case is about to go to trial, you remember again. Isn't that an incredible coincidence?"

"It isn't a coincidence," she said softly. "I heard a report about the trial on the radio. I didn't even think about it consciously, but afterward—that's when I remembered."

"This still doesn't make any sense to me. How could you see a murder and forget about it?"

"I don't know," she said. Tears streaked her suntanned face. "I don't know. But I did."

* 29 *

Ben signed the chit in the pro shop and threw a bag of rented golf clubs over his shoulder. The bag knocked him forward, almost across the counter. Man, they were heavy. And people do this for fun?

Gritting his teeth, Ben schlepped the clubs to the first tee, where he was supposed to meet the rest of the group. He didn't actually remember where the first tee was, but he headed in the general direction of the course and hoped for the best.

Ben stumbled across the driving range, irritating several serious golfers who were mastering their slices, but he still couldn't find the tee. The sun was hot and the bag was heavy, and getting heavier by the step. He realized he was dripping with sweat, and he hadn't even started playing yet. He was about to give up when he heard strains of fractured Frankie wafting over the next hill.

"That's why the lady . . . is a traaaamp. Ka-boom boom."

That would be Dick Crenshaw. Like a hound tracking a scent, Ben followed the semimelodic rendition of the second verse to the first tee.

The course was beautiful; rolling hills undulated down the fairway. The grass was immaculately trimmed and the greens well watered.

Ben found Crenshaw pacing in a circle, with Chris Bentley and Captain Pearson nearby. And—*yes!* They had a golf cart.

Ben approached the group and, with a great grunting noise, heaved his golf bag into the back of the cart with the others. Pearson's bag, with his initials embroidered on the side, had each of his clubs neatly separated inside plastic tubes.

Crenshaw's clubs were hooded with soft leather gloves bearing the images of various Warner Brothers cartoon characters—Bugs Bunny, Wile E. Coyote, and Pepe Le Pew.

"Are you the fourth?" Crenshaw asked, interrupting his song.

Pearson frowned. "Mitch didn't tell me anything about this."

"It was my idea," Ben said hurriedly. He introduced himself to Crenshaw and Bentley. "I'd been wanting to chat with you. I heard you were playing golf today and lost your fourth player when Hal Rutherford begged out. It seemed like a perfect fit."

"I hope you won't be asking a lot of distressing questions," Bentley said in his soft Southern accent. "We came here to play golf. We don't want anybody disturbing our equilibrium with a lot of fool questions."

"I'll try to keep myself in line," Ben replied.

"Are you sure you know how to play golf?" Pearson asked, eyeing Ben's clumsy grip on his wood.

"Of course I do," Ben replied. "I'm a lawyer, aren't I? It's required." In fact, Ben's last visit to a golf course had been in law school when a professor took him out one morning to play nine holes. He hadn't been any good then and he hadn't played since. But how hard could it be? he reasoned. All you do is swing a club at a little ball and knock it down the fairway, for Pete's sake. Piece of cake.

"Fine," Pearson said. "You go first."

This was not particularly encouraging. Ben had hoped to pick up a few pointers by watching the other men play. But he couldn't back down now.

He rammed a little orange tee into the soft earth and placed his ball on top. It fell off. He did it again. It fell off again. After two more repetitions, Pearson bent down, huffing and puffing, and fixed Ben's tee for him.

"Thanks a million," Ben said. All right, he told himself. Concentrate. First impressions are everything. If I can just hit a good one first off, they'll assume I can play and won't notice if I fumble a bit later on.

He held the club next to the ball, closed his eyes, concentrated, and inhaled deeply. What was it Christina was always talking about? Focusing on your third eye? All right, third eye. Come through for me.

He reared back and swung the club as hard as he could.

And missed. The ball wobbled a bit from the rush of wind as the club passed over it, then settled back onto the tee.

"That was my practice shot," Ben said hurriedly. "We all get practice shots, right? Okay, this one is for real."

Bentley, Pearson, and Crenshaw all exchanged silent looks.

"Here I go." This time, for a change in approach, Ben decided to keep his eyes open. He swung the club around and actually managed to make contact with the ball. Barely. The tiny white sphere dribbled off the tee and rolled pathetically down the fairway at an extreme left angle. The golf equivalent of a gutter ball.

"Huh," Ben said, looking away. "Wrist's a little stiff. Must've spent too long on the driving range. Who's next?"

After they all took their tee shot, Bentley walked with Ben to his ball. Given the distance involved, or lack thereof, the golf cart seemed rather unnecessary.

"Now look here, Kincaid," Bentley said. "If you're going to play the entire nine holes with us, you're going to have to know something about the game."

"Well, I suppose I could use a few pointers. . . ."

"I can boil the whole thing down to four rules for you. Hell, I taught my third ex-wife to play in half an hour. Now first, you need to loosen your grip. Club head speed generates power, not your grip. So there's no point in swinging the club like you're trying to kill someone."

A noteworthy choice of phrase, Ben thought.

"Swing like this." Bentley demonstrated his smooth, easy approach. "Hold the club like it's a tube of toothpaste, not a battle-ax."

"Okay, I can do that," Ben said, practicing the swing.

"Second, be generous with yourself when you're picking

out a club. Pick a club that's one size longer than you think you need."

Ben was confident he could do that, too. Especially since he didn't understand the differences between the clubs, anyway.

"Third, check your club."

"For what?"

"The fidelity of the club is critical. Golf clubs take a real pounding over time, especially cheap rented ones like you're using."

They arrived at the spot where Ben's ball now rested. "If your club is off, your ball will veer to the side, even if your stroke is perfect. Have the golf pro check your clubs before you start."

"I'll remember that," Ben said, positioning himself behind his ball. "What's the fourth rule?"

"Whenever possible, cheat." Bentley looked all around, made sure no one else was watching, then picked up Ben's ball and hurled it toward the green. It landed maybe a hundred feet from the hole.

"But . . . that's cheating," Ben said.

"Only if you get caught."

By the fifth hole, Ben had begun to kinda sorta get the hang of it. His scores still came in at roughly three times par, but at least his balls rose off the ground.

"So how's the investigation coming?" Bentley asked with unexpected interest.

"Slowly. It's hard to dig up evidence on a ten-year-old crime. The floors have all been scrubbed, if you know what I mean."

"I can imagine."

"I'm getting a subpoena to search the country-club offices and lockers and all, but I don't have high hopes."

"Sounds like a huge waste of time to me."

"You're probably right. But I have to try. I heard you're throwing a charity ball tonight," Ben said as they left the fifth green.

"That's my business," Bentley replied cheerily. "I spend most of my working time on charity assignments these days."

"Really?" Perhaps he had misjudged the man. "What charity are you working for?"

"Several. I think tonight's shindig is about providing meals for homeless children. Or vaccinations. Something like that. I run an umbrella organization that provides services to a variety of charities."

"You . . . provide services? To charity? What does that mean?"

"Whatever they need, I try to provide. Volunteers, parties, fund-raisers, whatever."

"Interesting." Ben washed his ball in the cute plastic washer stand beside the tee. "How did you get involved with that?"

"Well, it's something I started about ten years ago."

Ben looked up. "Oh?"

"Yeah. I was . . . well, lemme see. How can I phrase it? Between wives. Flat busted is what I was. And the bar bill was getting pretty damn high. So I started this line of work."

"But how can you make money working for charity?"

"I didn't say I was working for charity. I said I was providing services to charities. There's a big difference. See, when national charitable organizations want to raise some money in a particular locality, say, Tulsa, they need a local who knows who's got the big money and knows how to pry it out of their tight little wallets. That's what I do. If they need a hundred well-heeled socialites for a black-tie fund-raiser, I round them up. If they need a hundred volunteers to staff phone lines, I enlist some rich housewives who feel guilty because their lives don't amount to a hill of beans."

"And this is profitable?"

"Extremely. I typically charge a twenty-five-thousand-dollar retainer up front per job, and keep twenty-five percent of the ultimate take. And I have almost no expenses! After all, the charity pays the expenses for the fund-raisers and I don't have to pay any of those women to make phone calls. They're volunteers! They do it for nothing, because they think they're helping a worthy cause. I get a percentage of what they collect, the charity gets the rest. And the volunteers get to sleep easy with the knowledge that they're making a difference." He chortled softly. "It's a perfect arrangement."

"I don't suppose any of those volunteers knows that you're running a for-profit business."

"Why kill the goose that lays the golden eggs?"

"But think how many meals for homeless children your cut could provide. If you didn't carve out your piece of the action, that money might actually do some good in the world instead of being frittered away on green fees and martinis."

Bentley gave Ben a long look. "As I mentioned, Kincaid, I got into this business because I needed money. Big money. Back then, I would've done almost anything to make a few bucks. But the glory of it was, I turned out to be good at this. I see nothing wrong with being adequately compensated for a job well done. Charities seek me out and gladly pay my fee, because they know I can make their fund-raising drive a success."

"But still—"

"Look, Kincaid, it's easy to be sanctimonious in the abstract. But I have practical considerations. My pot of gold isn't as infinite as the rest of these jokers'. I had to seek a balance. I had to merge my living with my charitable works. Is that a crime?"

"It's not a crime, but—"

"I'm sure you're a paragon of compassion, Kincaid, but are all your cases pro bono cases?"

"Well, no, of course not . . ."

"Of course not. Neither are mine. I make money for myself, and I make money for the other guy. What's wrong with that?"

Ben shrugged. Perhaps he had been too hasty to condemn these people. He was letting the experiences of his childhood, the stereotype of the wealthy Ugly American, taint his perceptions. Maybe. "Well, I hope your charity ball is a success."

"Me, too. You'd be welcome to come, Kincaid, if you've got a tux and you promise not to spend the whole night talking about the damn murder."

Not a bad idea, Ben thought, but I really can't spare the time. "I'm afraid I have to prepare for trial. Maybe I could send my legal assistant."

Bentley's head turned. "A woman?"

"Ye-es."

"Good-looking?"

"Well . . . it's a matter of opinion, I suppose. I think so."

"You know, Kincaid, I don't have a date for the ball. You may have heard that I'm . . ."

"Between wives?"

"Right."

Ben cleared his throat. "I don't think Christina is your type."

"Why not?"

"Well . . . she's, um, she's . . ."

"Yes?"

Ben swallowed. "She's poor. Well, not rich, anyway. After all, she works for me."

All of a sudden Bentley burst into laughter. "Kincaid, where did you get the idea that all I care about is how much money a woman has?"

"Then . . . it isn't true?"

Bentley bent down and checked the slope of the hill. "I didn't say that. I just want to know who's been talking about me."

Bentley took his shot, a beautiful drive right down the fairway and just a bit short of the green.

"I'm surprised the police have time for this ten-year-old murder," Bentley commented as they walked toward their balls. "I would've thought they'd have all hands out looking for the man who's killing those little boys."

"They're trying," Ben said. "Believe me."

"That's such a disgusting crime. I don't understand these kiddie perverts. I think they should all be castrated and hanged."

"The police are scouring the area where the last boy was killed."

"Would they know him if they found him? He's not likely to walk up and say, 'Yes, sir, I'm the pedophile. Why do you ask?' "

"There are certain pieces of physical evidence they hope to find. The last little boy disappeared wearing a red baseball cap, for instance. It's never been found. If it turns up—"

"Someone's going to have the police descending upon him like flies. Got it." Bentley pulled back his club. The ball descended onto the green just inches from the hole. "Excellent. You're next, Kincaid."

"Oh. Well, if you insist." He squared himself in front of his ball. "Here goes nothing."

Bentley grinned. "Truer words were never spoken."

By the seventh hole, Ben was really feeling the heat. He seemed to be sweating more than anyone else. Of course, he was swinging about three times as often as anyone else.

Just when he thought he was going to have to call for an oxygen mask, he saw Mitch tootling over the hill in a golf cart. "Refreshments, anyone?"

Mitch unpacked a chest filled with drinks, both soft and hard, then unwrapped an elaborate food spread. He had pâté and chips, caviar and crackers, and several other exotic treats Ben couldn't identify. Mitch passed Pearson and Crenshaw ice-cold beers; Bentley got a martini poured out of a thermos.

"What about for you, Ben?" Mitch asked.

"I don't suppose by any wild chance you'd be carrying chocolate milk?"

"Uh, no. I could go back to the clubhouse. . . ."

"Never mind." Ben took a can of Coke Classic. "Thanks anyway, Mitch. You're a lifesaver."

"That's why they pay me the big money. Not."

After everyone was done munching and imbibing, Mitch cleared away the spread and packed up the cart. "How's it going, anyway?" he whispered to Ben.

"Not too bad."

"Are they talking?"

"Some. Mostly about Rutherford, since he's not here today. Bentley says at dinner last night Rutherford droned on for an hour about soil composition and bagworm infestation. And he tried to make everyone eat his radishes. Sounded unpleasant."

Mitch laughed. "Humorous, but not very helpful."

"True. Still, I'm probably getting a lot more than I would've if we were sitting around in some office. Thanks for getting me in on this game."

"No problem." Mitch climbed behind the wheel of the cart and turned the key. "Anything else I can bring you?"

"Yeah. Arnold Palmer. Hey, let me ask you a question before you go." He glanced over his shoulder to make sure none of his golf partners was listening. "How does Pearson make so much money?"

"Like he says. Oil and gas. Foreign investments."

"So as far as you know, he doesn't have . . . anything going on the side?"

Mitch laughed. "Oh, you found out about the green fees."

Ben didn't know what Mitch was talking about, but he saw no reason to admit it. "Then it's true?"

"It's true. Pearson skims a healthy percentage off the top of the green fees. Hell, he makes back twice what he contributes in dues each year."

"Why don't the other board members stop him?"

"Because they've each got a little fiddle of their own. Crenshaw takes his from the pro shop. Bentley takes his from the dining room. I could make you a list."

In due time, Ben thought. "Do they know that you know about this?"

"I'd have to be a blind man, or seriously mathematically challenged, to miss it. What do they care? What could I do? As Pearson has repeatedly pointed out, I'm an employee, not a member. And how they decide to divvy up the money in their own private club is their own business."

"The dues-paying members who aren't on the board might have a different view."

"Probably," Mitch agreed. "But they'll never know."

By the time the golfing party reached the ninth hole, Crenshaw was looking seriously winded. Although they had a cart, and Crenshaw spent more time in it than anyone, he still looked beat. His eyes were lined and hollow; sweat dripped from every pore. Of course, it was an abominably hot day. And, Ben reasoned, being a short fat bald man, Crenshaw was probably more subject to heat prostration.

"Looks to me like Dick needs a shower," Ben whispered to Bentley.

"Looks to me like Dick needs a hit," Bentley replied.

"A hit?"

"You know." Bentley mimed an exaggerated snorting through his nose.

"Crenshaw? You're kidding."

"How do you think that man keeps going all day long at that energy level? He's more high-strung than Robin Williams."

Ben watched carefully as Crenshaw approached the tee. Ten minutes ago he'd been loud, animated, and boisterous. Now he looked as if he'd gone six days without sleep. Ben was no expert on substance abusers, but he supposed it was possible.

Crenshaw took a swing and totally missed his golf ball. Wasn't even close. Privately, Ben was pleased to see he wasn't the only one who had ever committed that humiliating gaffe, although, of course, Crenshaw did it when he was exhausted, and Ben did it on his first swing of the day.

"Damn, damn, damn!" Crenshaw shouted. He hurled his golf club across the fairway at a tree with sudden and startling force. The club hit a tree and splintered, just as the club that killed Maria Alvarez must have done.

"Now don't get your dick in a twist," Pearson grumbled.

"I can't get it in a twist!" Crenshaw shouted back. "It isn't big enough!"

Ah, Ben thought. Here we go again.

"I hate this game. I don't know why I play it. I quit."

"Calm down, Dick," Bentley said. He glanced at the score-card. "You're only . . . twenty strokes over par. You're still beating Kincaid, though!" Bentley and Pearson laughed heartily.

Crenshaw ripped off the Porky Pig cover and grabbed a new club. "Sure, laugh. I know you guys just make fun of me because my dick's so small. Sons of bitches."

Eventually Crenshaw managed to get off his shot. After all four had teed off, Ben managed to pair himself in the cart with Crenshaw for the drive down the fairway.

"Mitch told me you knew Leeman Hayes back when he was caddying here ten years ago."

"Oh, damn it all to hell. You're not going to hassle me about that, are you? I've already told the police everything I know about a thousand times."

"The police questioned you?"

"Damn straight. Just because I had the kid over to my house a few times."

Ben's head turned. "You had Leeman at your home?"

"Sure. Why not? I didn't know he was going to kill someone."

"I don't believe he did—"

"Man, it's blazing today! I'm pooped." He stopped the cart, bent over, and placed his hands on his knees. "Look, Leeman caddied for me a few times. He was okay. Quiet, but I like that in a caddy. You could tell he wasn't quite right in the head, but what did it matter? Caddying doesn't require rocket scientists. I needed some work done at my house, laying bricks around the garden and such. Simple stuff, but tiring. I didn't want to do it. I figured he would." Crenshaw winked. "I also figured I wouldn't have to pay him too much, since he couldn't tell a nickel from a hundred-dollar bill."

"You mean you—"

"It was just a few times. I got some work done; he made some pin money. It was a perfect arrangement."

Where have I heard that before? Ben reflected.

"But after the kid got arrested, the cops started acting like we were best friends or something."

"You didn't know anything about the murder?"

"Absolutely nothing. How would I know why he killed that woman? He was probably trying to get into her pants. You know how those retards are."

Ben felt his neck stiffening. "Mr. Crenshaw—"

"Quiet. I'm taking my shot." Crenshaw positioned himself, then swung. The ball flew about a hundred feet, still a good ways from the hole. "Damn! Rack up another one to Dick Crenshaw, the dickless wonder."

"Mr. Crenshaw—"

He grinned. "Sorry, kid. Guess I'm embarrassing you with my ribald sense of humor. You're probably not used to public discussions about genitalia."

"You should've been at my last trial."

That slowed Crenshaw down—for a moment, anyway. "What kind of work do you do, Kincaid, when you're not representing underprivileged killers?"

Ben gave Crenshaw a brief description of his keenly unglamorous practice. *How long can you go on representing the scum of the earth?*

"Sounds like you stay pretty, uh, diverse," Crenshaw said. "Is that by choice, or do you have to take whatever walks in the door?"

"I don't—"

"Never mind. Unfair question. Well, hang in there. The law will keep you fed, till you move on to something else."

"Something else?"

"Hell, yes. Surely you don't want to be trudging through courtrooms forever."

"Well—"

"There's no future in that. You know where the future is?"

"Uh, plastics?"

"No. Turkish mutual funds."

"I beg your pardon?"

"You heard it. I'm not going to say it again. Now that we've declawed the Russian bear, some of those third-world countries are making money for the first time, and they don't know what to do with it. A smart man playing some smart investments could make a killing. And that's what it's all about, right?"

"Well . . ."

"You don't want to be chasing child-custody payments for the rest of your life, do you?"

"Well . . ."

"Look, Kincaid, I get more cases these days than I can possibly handle. I refer out as many as I take. I'll keep you in mind. If I get some small-potatoes stuff I don't want to screw with, I'll send it your way."

"Well, gee whiz. Thanks very much."

"No problem." He looked at Ben pointedly. "I can be a help to people I consider my friends. If you get my drift."

Ben had a sneaking suspicion that he did.

To Ben's relief and, truth be told, his mild surprise, they completed the nine holes. There was a brief discussion of making it eighteen, but Ben pleaded work and begged off. Pearson and Bentley followed his lead, while Crenshaw, tired as he was, or seemed to be, proceeded to the tenth tee. Ben watched Crenshaw recede into the distance. " 'S wonderful . . . 'S marvelous . . ."

Ben and Captain Pearson left the course and headed back to the main club building. Pearson gave Ben his personal short course on how to improve his golf game. Ben listened politely as Pearson babbled on about Pings and torque and swinging the club like you're serving a tray.

As they passed Pearson's office, Ben noticed three black teenagers sitting inside. And one of them was distinctly familiar.

It was Booker—Joni's boyfriend. And, according to Ernie Hayes, a member of a major Tulsa street gang.

The one he said was always hanging around the country club.

Ben was about to ask Pearson about that when the office's mahogany door abruptly closed, with Pearson on the other side.

Well, Ben thought, you can't get rid of me that easily.

Checking both ways down the corridor and finding it momentarily uninhabited, he pressed his ear against the door.

It wasn't that hard to hear, as Pearson was screaming. "What in God's name are you doing? Coming here in broad daylight!"

The restaurant maître d' suddenly appeared in the corridor. Ben moved away from the door and tried to act as if he had lost his balance. With the huge golf bag on his shoulder, his performance wasn't altogether unbelievable.

He hustled back to the pro shop and turned in his gear. It had been a miserable afternoon, but he was glad he'd done it. He'd picked up some fascinating tidbits about the board members. Problem was, the tidbits didn't add up to a murderer. He was going to have to keep on probing.

Starting with the man on the other side of that mahogany door.

As soon as Kincaid was out of sight, Chris Bentley quietly stepped through the patio doors and ducked down the secluded staircase that led to the private locker room.

Bentley slid into what was called the Golden Room by those in the know. An exclusive hideaway for the board members and a few of the staff. A quick look around told him no one else was here at the moment.

Good. Now, which one was it? Twenty-two, twenty-four . . . Yes, that was it. He loved these new computerized digital locks. He had arranged for their installation himself. All the boys on the board had a great feeling of security knowing their locker could be penetrated only by entering a four-digit code chosen by and known only to the owner of the locker. Truth to tell, though, Bentley knew the universal access code that would open all of them. But there was no need for anyone else to know about that.

Quietly, with studied stealth, Bentley opened the locker.

There it was. A bright red baseball cap. Boy's size.

Bentley grabbed the cap and shoved it under his shirt. Christ. Imagine if Kincaid had found this! That would've been the end of the world, as he knew it, anyway.

He closed the locker and tiptoed up the stairs. He'd shove it into his golf bag for now, then get it off the grounds. No one need be the wiser.

Back outside, Bentley headed back toward the clubhouse. The sun felt warm and refreshing, and he basked in it, with the happy inner glow of a man who has only narrowly missed being found out.

* 30 *

Loving checked the address again: 6826 South Sandusky.

He checked the number on the curb. Sure enough. This was the place.

He'd had a hell of a time finding it. Jones identified Carlee Toller on the list he'd compiled of people who worked at the Utica Greens Country Club ten years ago, but the Tulsa Metro residential records showed no trace of any such person. Searching the court records, Loving eventually discovered that Carlee Toller had become Carlee Crane about a year after the murder. And Carlee Crane *was* listed in the residential records. She co-owned a house with her husband, David Elroy Crane.

And here it was. Nothing fancy, but a decent spread with a nice view. A lot better than Loving got out the one window of his fleabag apartment on Sixty-first. Seemed like all the lowlifes in Tulsa hung out there. Of course, as far as Loving was concerned, that was part of its appeal.

He approached the door and knocked. A few moments later a young woman with long blonde hair answered the door.

"Yes?"

"Afternoon, ma'am." Loving squared his shoulders and tried to look reasonably respectable. "I'm a private investigator. I'm workin' for a lawyer, Ben Kincaid."

Her eyes darted, just for a fleeting instant. A telltale sign, Loving thought. She recognized the name. "May I ask why you're here?"

"You worked at the Utica Greens Country Club ten years ago, didn't you, ma'am?"

"Well . . . yes." The woman licked her lips. "That was a long time ago, though. I quit after just a few months."

"I know. But you were there at the time Maria Alvarez was murdered, weren't you?"

She made several false starts before answering. "Maria . . . Alvarez? I don't think I know her."

"Did more than one woman get murdered at the country club that year?" Pull back, Loving, he told himself. It's too soon to get tough with her. "You must remember when this happened."

The woman's voice seemed to come from far away. "I do recall . . . something along those lines. Not much."

"You don't remember a murder that happened where you worked? I woulda thought that was all people talked about for days."

"But—I mean—you have to understand—it's been so long—"

Loving frowned. Something about this woman's answers made him very suspicious. They just didn't ring true. He'd had innumerable interviewees lie to him over the years, and he thought he knew what it sounded like.

"Ma'am, Mr. Kincaid represents Leeman Hayes, a nice young guy who's been accused of murderin' this woman. Hayes goes on trial soon. If you know anything about this, you need to tell me."

"I don't know anything about it. How could I? I didn't see it, did I?"

Loving wasn't sure if she was asking the question of him or herself.

"I'm sorry I can't be of more help." She began to close the door.

Loving jammed his foot in the path. "Ma'am, I'll do whatever I can to protect you. If you're worried about the newshounds hasslin' you or the killer comin' after you or somethin', don't. I'll be your personal bodyguard." He flexed his impressive biceps. "And I'm pretty good at it."

"That isn't it. I just don't know anything, that's all." She tried again to close the door. "If you don't move your foot, I'll have to call the police."

"At least take Mr. Kincaid's card," Loving said, pressing it through the doorway. "If you think of anything that might be helpful, call. Please. A man's life is at stake. You may be his only hope."

The woman took the card, then slammed the door shut.

With someone else, Loving might've been tempted to get tough and play the bullyboy, but he had a hunch he wouldn't get anywhere that way with this woman. No amount of badgering was going to change her mind.

He would just have to wait and hope she changed it herself.

* 31 *

After dinner that night, Joey emphatically reminded Ben and his mother that he had not eaten for at least three hours. Mrs. Kincaid prepared a bottle of formula and administered it to her grandson. Against his mother's protestations, Ben prepared a sleeping bag for himself in the living room, as he had the night before, so his mother could take the bed.

Once Joey finished the bottle, Mrs. Kincaid tried to rock him to sleep. While she did, she sang to him. Ben was surprised; he didn't recall ever hearing her sing before, except maybe in church. She had a charming, melodic voice.

"He doesn't seem to be dropping off," Mrs. Kincaid whispered. "Maybe you could play something on the piano."

"You're doing just fine," Ben said. "I bombed out with lullabies last night."

Mrs. Kincaid tried a few more tunes. Ben leaned against the sofa and savored her soothing recital. After several choruses of "Twinkle, Twinkle, Little Star," however, he was astonished to hear her break into a slow rendition of . . .

"Flintstones . . . meet the Flintstones . . . they're the modern Stone Age fa-mi-lyyy. . . ."

Ben listened in amazement. By the final note, Joey's eyelids were closed. Mrs. Kincaid rocked him a bit longer, then lowered him into his makeshift crib.

"This has to be the most astonishing coincidence of all time," Ben said when she returned. "The first night I had Joey, I was having trouble getting him to sleep, and he wasn't responding to any of my lullabies, so I started singing the

Flintstones song. I don't know why I thought of that; it just popped into my head."

Mrs. Kincaid smiled.

"I can't believe we both thought of the same song," Ben continued. "In fact, I can't believe you even know the Flint-stones song."

Mrs. Kincaid began thumbing through a decorating magazine she had brought with her. "It's not a coincidence."

"What do you mean?"

"Don't you remember anything? I used to sing that song to you when you were just a babe."

Ben didn't bother protesting. Even if he didn't remember, it had to be true. Some neural synapse in the inner catacombs of his subconscious classified this unlikely song as a lullaby. "Why on earth would you sing—"

"You were a horrible baby to put to sleep. Not that you were a horrible baby. On the contrary, everyone adored you. So bright, so funny. But you never wanted to sleep. After all, if you went to sleep, you might miss out on something. You couldn't imagine the tricks I used to get your little eyes closed."

"But—why the Flintstones?"

"I don't even remember. Probably just something I resorted to in desperation one night that worked. Of course, anything that worked I would never forget. Remember, this was back in the early Sixties. The Flintstones were all the rage. Your father and I used to watch it every Friday night."

"My father! *The Flintstones!*"

"Oh, he loved that show. Especially the pet—what was his name? Dino. Dino would run in and tackle Fred and your father would just become hysterical. And he loved the song. Sang it all the time."

"My father—sang?"

"Oh yes. And I believed he played it on the piano."

Ben stared at her. "My father played the piano?"

"Of course he did. Played a little guitar, too. He was never as accomplished as you—never had the time. But he loved it. Why do you think we had that lovely grand piano?"

"This can't be true."

Mrs. Kincaid rolled her eyes. It was an expression that really annoyed Ben, principally because he recognized it as an expression he frequently used himself. "I know. I'm just a coldhearted society matron who only cares about appearances. And your father was just a hard-hearted right-brained arch-conservative who only cared about his pocketbook. Well, Benjamin, we all have to grow up sometime."

This was the third time Ben had been told that in as many days, and he didn't like it any more now than he had before. "I don't recall my father ever showing the remotest interest in music."

"Your father loved music. But he had a keen sense of responsibility, too. After all, he had a wife and two children who depended on him. Not to mention parents who had rather demanding expectations."

Ben didn't recall his grandparents, either. They were all dead before he turned ten. "The way I remember it, every time I sat down to listen to a record or play the piano, my father gave me some stupid chore so I wouldn't be 'wasting my time.' And he just about blew a gasket when I told him I was going to be a music major."

"He was afraid that you wouldn't be able to make a living. That you'd never accomplish anything and boomerang back to us every time we turned around. You certainly wouldn't be the first rich kid who didn't turn out well."

"So all those angry lectures and slaps up the side of the head were for my own good, is that it?"

"As a matter of fact, yes." She paused thoughtfully. "You have to understand, Benjamin—your gifts were so great, your father couldn't stand to see them go to waste. You know, your father had quite a struggle to become a success in his medical practice. Just between you and me, he wasn't half as smart as you are, but he made up for it with hard work. He wanted to make sure you didn't fail to realize your potential because you never learned how to work, never learned how to accomplish anything. And he wanted to make sure you'd be able to support yourself. He wanted to make sure you wouldn't be left wanting."

"That's pretty ironic," Ben said bitterly. "Given what he did in his will."

Mrs. Kincaid's back stiffened. "That, of course, resulted from an entirely unrelated matter. As well you know."

Ben's face tightened. "My father couldn't abide my decision to pursue law instead of medicine. He couldn't abide my not following in his exalted footsteps."

"That's so foolish. Your bitterness is blinding you."

"It's true, and you know it."

"It's true that your father wasn't pleased with your career choice. He didn't consider law a particularly honorable profession. But that played no part in his decision to change his will."

"I don't want to talk about it." Ben pushed himself to his feet. "I can't believe my father played the piano. And I never even knew."

"You knew once. You used to sit on his lap and sing songs with him. Don't you remember? What were your favorites? 'This Old Man.' 'Three Blind Mice.' 'Pease Porridge Hot.' I can't remember them all." Her eyes closed, and a warm smile emerged. "You were the happiest little boy in the world when your father sang and played with you."

"I don't recall him ever playing—*anything*—with me."

She shook her head. "More's the pity. That's when you fell in love with music, Benjamin. It was a gift your father gave you."

Ben didn't know what to say. This didn't accord with his memory at all. But he knew his mother wouldn't lie to him. "For instance . . . what else did we sing?"

"Oh, you name it. Hundreds of songs. Nursery rhymes. And your father loved all the old standards."

Ben felt his chest tighten, like fingers clutching at his heart. Or was it his memory? "What was his favorite?"

Mrs. Kincaid looked at him with genuine surprise. "Don't you remember? It's such a silly song. 'Polka Dots and Moonbeams.' "

* 32 *

"And you didn't even ask him?"

"Well, we were getting along so well, I didn't want to spoil everything. . . ."

"So you just let it go."

"For the time being . . ."

Rachel Rutherford leaned sideways against the wet bar, a Bloody Mary crooked in her hand. "So let me get this straight. You saw a strange man talking to Abie on the street corner, apparently offering him a ride . . . and you didn't even ask Abie who it was? What kind of miserable father *are* you?" She hurled her drink across the room; it shattered against a full-length mirror.

"I was trying to be a good father," Hal Rutherford said defensively. What a crappy way to start the day this was. Barely out of their separate beds and already fighting. "That's why I didn't say anything. We were having a good time. Abie seemed to be responding to me. I didn't want to spoil everything by turning the ball game into the Spanish Inquisition."

"And what if this man shows up again, huh? What then?"

"Keep it down," Rutherford said, waving his hands. "Abie's probably awake. He might hear."

Abie was, in fact, hearing every word. He had learned long ago that they didn't realize how loud their voices were. And when he hunkered down next to the air vent in his bathroom, he could hear every word they said downstairs.

"I'm not going to let something horrible happen to my son, Hal. We went through too much hell to get him. I won't let it all be for nothing."

211

"Rachel, you're exaggerating this situation wildly out of proportion."

"How do you know?" She stood so close to him he could feel the alcoholic spray on his face. "Answer me that, Mr. Know-It-Fucking-All. How do you know?"

"If it will make you happy, I'll go talk to Abie." Rutherford sighed. He really hated to do it. They had actually had a pleasant time together, first at the ball game, then afterward at Baskin-Robbins. For the first time in months he felt like his family was on the road to recovery. Unless, of course, his wife destroyed all the goodwill he had created.

"Does it have to be now? This instant?"

She glared at her husband. "What are you waiting for? Until it's too late?"

"Fine. I'll do it now. Bitch." He trudged unhappily up the long winding staircase.

Abie, of course, heard him coming. He scrambled away from the vent and pretended to be emerging from the bathroom.

He met his father in the hall. "Hi, Dad. Wanna shoot some baskets?"

"Uh, no, son. Not right now. I need to . . . ask you some questions, okay?"

Abie tried to walk past him. "I'm not in the mood right now."

Rutherford placed his hands firmly on his son's shoulders. "I'm sorry, son. We can't put this off any longer. Who was that man I saw you talking to when I drove up in your mother's car?"

"What man?" Abie wasn't exactly sure why, but for some reason, he didn't want to tell his father about Sam. For one thing, Sam had asked him not to. Even beyond that, though . . . it seemed wrong, somehow. Besides, he was certain his father wouldn't understand, and would probably make a big deal out of it. "I don't know who you're talking about."

"Now, Abie, don't be contrary. I saw you talking to him. Who was he?"

Abie twisted underneath his father's grasp. "He's just a friend, okay? So leave me alone."

His father did not release him. "How did you meet this friend?"

"He helped me out one day, all right?" Abie shouted. "He saved me from two moron bullies from school."

"Bullies? I didn't hear anything about this. When was this?"

"What difference does it make? Sam was there when I needed him. Unlike you!"

Abie squirmed out from under his father's hands and started to run, but his father grabbed his arm and jerked him back.

"Now look here, son. You may not like it, but I'm your father, and when I ask you a question, I expect an answer."

"Let me *go*!"

"Not until you tell me everything about this . . . Sam."

"I won't! I won't tell you anything. I hate you!"

Like the first bolt from a gathering storm, a sudden rage swept through Rutherford's body. It was everything working at once—Abie, Rachel, the booze—

He wasn't sure what caused it, but suddenly he was consumed with an anger he could not contain. He reared his hand back and slapped Abie with all his might.

Abie's head jerked backward. His head ached; he felt as if it might snap off his neck. It was a long moment before he felt sufficiently oriented to talk.

"I hate you!" he shouted, when he could. "I hate you and I always will." With the same fury Rutherford had shown a moment before, Abie bent down and bit his father's hand. His father cried out. Without wasting a second, Abie tore away from him and raced down the stairs.

He passed his mother as he bolted through the living room, but he didn't stop to talk. He didn't look back; he knew his father would be close behind him. He had seen the expression on his father's face when he bit him. Abie knew that if his father got a hold of him now, something terrible would happen.

Abie raced out of the house and across the wide, well-trimmed front lawn. Just as he passed the tall hedge that lined the perimeter of their property, a familiar face emerged.

"Sam!" Abie shouted. He was so overwhelmed with relief and joy he could have cried. He ran up to the man and hugged his legs. "What are you doing here?"

"I was bringing you this." He held up the boy's blue book bag. "You left it in my car yesterday." He crouched down to Abie's level. "You look scared. Is something wrong?"

"It's my dad. He already hit me once, and he's trying to do it again. He's gonna kill me!"

"Not if I can help it," Sam said resolutely. "Come with me."

Abie glanced over his shoulder. His father hadn't come out of the house yet. Maybe Mom slowed him down. Still, there was no time to waste.

Abie eagerly took Sam's hand. "Where are we going?"

"My car is parked just down the street. I'll get you out of here."

Together, they jogged down the street. "I sure am glad you were here," Abie said breathlessly, once he was in the car. "You saved me from the bullies before. I should've known you'd save me again."

The man smiled. "Just relax. I won't let your father hurt you."

Abie believed him. Hadn't Sam always been there when he needed a friend? Unlike his father. "You're the greatest."

"Thanks. So are you." The tall man snapped his fingers. "Hey. I know a really fun place we could go. What do you say?"

"Whatever you want," Abie answered. "I'll do whatever you want."

"That's good to hear," the man said, his eyes twinkling. "That's very good indeed."

* 33 *

First thing in the morning, Ben stopped by his office to check on what progress, if any, his associates were making. Christina was hard at work preparing exhibits and witness examinations for the trial. He hadn't actually asked her to do that, but he was relieved to see it was getting done. He had been concerned that he would never be ready when the trial started, especially since he was spending most of his time investigating, but seeing the amount of quality work she already had managed to generate gave him a glimmer of hope.

Jones had prepared a report summarizing all the information about the murder he could glean from newspapers and other written records, which he presented to Ben in a spiffy plastic folder with a spiral binder. If they were in high school, Jones would definitely get an A. The contents of the report were excellent, too. Jones even found some video footage in the local TV news morgues. He also prepared a streamlined statement of facts and chronology.

Ben took out his pencil and made a few crucial additions to the chronology based on the information he had gathered during the past few days. It raised many questions, but provided very few answers.

On his way out, Ben bumped into Loving. "How's the investigation going?"

"Not so well, Skipper. I've been interviewing all the potential witnesses Jones and Christina came up with. Or trying, anyway. They're not very cooperative."

"Anyone know anything?"

"Not so far. Well, one gal I thought knew something, but she refused to talk to me."

"Keep working on her. And all the others."

Loving pounded his meaty fists together. "You want I should bust some heads?"

"Uh, no. Not at the moment. But I would appreciate it if you could do some checking on a guy named Ronald Pearson." Ben quickly outlined what he knew about Pearson. "I thought maybe you could talk to some of your buddies who are engaged from time to time in, um, less-than-legal occupations."

"You mean crooks."

"Well, yes. See if any of them know anything about drug running from Peru. And see if anyone knows what Pearson might be doing with members of a North Side street gang."

Loving's eyes moved closer together. "Them gangs are bad news, Skipper. If you're messin' with them, I better stick close to ya. I wouldn't want nothin' to happen."

Ben smiled. Everyone should have a two-hundred-and-fifty-pounder who idolized him. "I'll be all right, Loving. See what you can find out. If you turn up anything, I want to know immediately."

Ben found Mike at his desk at Central Division headquarters. He was hunched over a tall stack of reports, a toothpick jutting out of his mouth, a hand pressed against his forehead, and the other fist crumpling an unwanted piece of information.

"How goes it?" Ben ventured.

"Like hell," Mike said. "I got so many—" He stopped abruptly. "Where have you been?"

"I beg your pardon?"

"Your face is red."

"I don't quite follow."

"You've been out in the sun!"

"Oh, right. Got some exercise yesterday."

"*You?* I thought the only exercise you got was walking up the stairs to your apartment."

"I'm broadening my horizons."

"Uh-huh." Mike leaned back in his chair. "What did you do, play a fever-pitched round of croquet?"

"Golf, actually."

Mike looked astonished. *"You? Golf?"*

"It's not that demanding a sport. . . ."

"Yes, but it requires you to be outside. To get hot. Sweaty even."

"For your information, I happen to like the outdoors."

Mike chuckled. "I remember Julia telling me about how when you were a little kid your parents had to lock you out of the house to get you to play outside. And even then you'd just stand by the door wailing to be let back in."

"That was a long time ago. I'm not quite the wimp you make me out to be."

Mike continued strolling down Memory Lane. "And I remember hearing about that time Julia put fake vomit on one of your comic books. Said you cried for hours. Even after she showed you it was fake."

Ben coughed. "I've always taken good care of my books. . . ."

"And the time she showed you a squished pearl tomato and told you it was the neighbor's dog's eyeball."

"I still don't find that remotely humorous—"

Mike slapped his knee. "And the time she told you the scratches would come off your records if you baked them in the oven—"

"Look, could we talk about the case?"

Mike grinned. "Whatever you say, *kemo sabe.*"

"Thanks loads. Have you heard anything new about the Leeman Hayes prosecution?"

"Well, of course, I'm not officially involved in that case. But it's just possible I accidentally overheard Bullock talking too loudly for his own good while we were in the cafeteria line."

"Accidentally overheard what?"

"Bullock bragging that he took over the case and was calling in all his markers to win it."

"Great. Just what I wanted to hear."

"You'd better look out for him, Ben. He's got a lot of markers to call, and he knows how to make them count, too."

"I'll stay on my toes. Anything more specific?"

"Heard he's planning a surprise witness."

"That would explain why he's delaying giving me a witness list. Any idea who the witness is?"

" 'Fraid not."

"Or what the witness will say?"

"Not really. But I did see a form in the main office that indicated Bullock was pulling a lot of old police reports. Does your man have a record?"

"I don't think so." With a sudden frisson of horror, Ben realized he hadn't thought to check. "I'll make sure."

"Do that."

"Anything else?"

"Sorry. The cafeteria line moves pretty fast."

Ben nodded. "Oh well. Appreciate the help. Still looking for that child molester?"

"When I can. According to Chief Blackwell, now I'm also supposed to be investigating the youth-gang problem."

Ben's ears tingled. "Youth gangs? You?"

"What, did you think I just push paper all day long?"

"No, but I thought you occasionally investigated homicides. . . ."

"Unfortunately, there have been several gang-related homicides. And now that I'm division supervisor, the whole mess gets laid at my feet. Blackwell says we have to make a concerted effort to confront these threats to the family unit. God knows there's never been a worse time in history to try to raise a family than now."

Ben decided he could spare a few more minutes for this chat. He pulled a chair up to Mike's desk. "How did this youth-gang business get started, anyway?"

"You mean historically? Adult gangs have been around since the dawn of civilization. And they still are. What's the mob, after all, but a great big gang for grown-ups? People learned long ago that there's strength in numbers. And the people most likely to learn that lesson are the people who have no power individually. The poor. Ethnic minorities."

"And children."

"Too true. It wasn't until after World War Two, though, that the current gang movement began. Gangs formed mostly along ethnic and racial lines, though not always. It wasn't a bad idea in the abstract—it gave young people a sense of identity. A sense of power. Unfortunately, somewhere along the way some of them decided to try to better their situation via crime. And violence."

"This is fascinating, Mike, but what I really meant was how did it get started in Tulsa?"

"Well, we're not the worst off by a long shot, but we've got 'em. You know, in Chicago there are forty known street gangs with over twenty-eight thousand members. I know of four gangs in Tulsa, with a couple hundred members. Still, it's not anything to laugh about."

"Who runs these gangs?"

"Usually some older, more experienced man acts as the fearless leader and provides direction. Provides arms. Organizes their activities."

"A member of the same ethnic minority?"

"Not necessarily. It's not unknown for a white man to run a black gang, or a black man to run a Hispanic gang. If they can earn the gang members' trust and provide them a means of scoring some big bucks—hey, why not?"

"Any special qualifications for the job?"

"The main thing the leader needs is the cash to get the operation, whatever it is, running."

"So we're looking for a wealthy man," Ben said.

"That's often the case. Got anyone in mind?"

A wealthy man with known connections to youth gangs, Ben thought. A man who might have a need for many hands reaching into the poorest parts of the city.

Hands to distribute foreign-import drugs.

"I might," Ben answered. "Let me do some more checking."

"If you say so. I'd like to put one of these ganglord sons of bitches behind bars."

Ben took his legal pad out of his briefcase and quickly sketched a design. "I saw a kid the other day in what looked like a red-and-black jacket. Emblem was a swastika inside a heart."

"Fifteenth Street Demons," Mike explained. "Did he have a weird circular pattern on the front of his jacket? And a big capital D?"

"Yeah."

"Definitely a Demon. They're the worst in the city. By far."

And one of them was dating Joni. "What have they been up to?"

"You remember all those drive-by shootings last month?"

Ben nodded.

"We think they were behind it. We can't prove it, but that's what we think. We've also linked them to burglaries and drug pushing at city schools. Even grade schools."

"Foreign drugs?"

"Mostly, yeah. Except for the pot—Oklahoma's number-one cash crop. Problem is, their ace rivals, the Cobras, have traditionally controlled the North Side drug traffic, and they're not too keen on competition. If we don't cut off the Demons' supply soon, there's gonna be a hit. And some kids are gonna die."

"How old are these gang members?"

"It varies. Sixteen to twenty, typically. But I've seen them as young as ten."

"Ten! You must be joking."

"Nope. Gangs actively seek out and recruit kids at ten and eleven. They perform an important function."

"I hate to ask, but—what is it?"

"You're the amateur sleuth, Ben. Can't you figure it out? If the ten-year-olds get caught, they'll be treated less severely by the cops and the courts than teenagers would be, and much less severely than adults would be. When the gangs go out on raids or whatever, they often give the drugs or the guns to the ten-year-olds, to protect the leaders and the older guys from arrest."

"So the kid gets picked up on a serious felony charge when

he's ten. What a swell way to start your life. That's really disgusting."

"You don't have to tell me, pal. I've been tearing my hair out over this for weeks, since that big rumble on Brady left three teenagers dead on the pavement."

The phone rang. Mike stepped away and took the call. There was a long silence.

"Damn." More time passed. Mike scribbled an address on his notepad. "Damn, damn, damn."

After he hung up the phone, Ben asked, "Who was that?"

"Switchboard. A little kid's been grabbed by some unidentified man. Spotted driving away in a gray sedan, couldn't get the license-plate number. I'm out of here." He grabbed his overcoat.

"Is this related to the other child-molestation cases?" Ben asked.

"Possibly. All I know for now is that some superrich kid has been nabbed. Utica Hills type. Name's Rutherford."

Ben's eyes widened. "Abie Rutherford? Parents named Harold and Rachel?"

Mike checked his notes. "That's right. You know them?"

Ben grabbed his briefcase. "I'm coming with you."

✳ 34 ✳

The Drillers weren't playing today, so the man in the red wig was forced to come up with a different diversion to win over Abie. It was too soon to take the boy directly to his apartment. Abie liked him, and trusted him, but perhaps not well enough for what he had in mind, what he wanted, what he desired.

Not quite yet.

Celebration Station had been Abie's idea. It was a mini–amusement park, one of a chain, near Fifty-first and Yale. Miniature golf, bumper boats, arcade games, pizza—enough to divert the attention of a ten-year-old for a few hours. The only problem, at least from the man in the wig's standpoint, was that it was very popular. And very public.

"Can we really go to Celebration Station, Sam?" Abie had asked with obvious excitement. "That'd be great!"

"Have you ever been before?"

"Nah. My dad wouldn't take me. He took me to Bell's once and hated it. He said, 'Never again.' "

"Really? I love Bell's. I'd go all the time if I had a special friend to take with me. Maybe you'd like to be my special friend."

Abie beamed.

"Your father must not know how to have a good time."

"You can say that again."

"Well, today we do Celebration Station. Next time we'll catch Bell's."

Reluctantly, Sam headed toward Fifty-first and Yale. Well, he reasoned, in large public places like that, no one really notices anyone else. And if they did, so what? He and Abie would look like a father and son on a day's outing. On the remote chance that someone was able to detect something amiss, they would never be able to identify him. No, they would give the police a description of some foolish-looking man with fuzzy red hair and owlish glasses. He was safe.

"Can we ride the bumper boats?" Abie asked. The man could smell the closeness of the boy, the sweet aroma of his skin, his body. His heart beat wildly out of control with anticipation.

They did, and the bumper cars as well, and the go-carts. All contraptions from which thrill and pleasure were derived from knocking the occupants around as harshly as possible. Sam grinned and bore it. With each ride, Abie became more consumed with pleasure, more enamored of his new companion.

After his turn on the go-carts, Abie ran to a water fountain for a drink. The heat was beating down on all of them; the physical activity had sent their perspiration glands into overdrive.

While Abie drank, the tall man reached down and placed his hand under the boy's armpit, then tasted his sweat.

Oh God— He felt a sudden urgent throbbing in his groin. He knew he couldn't wait much longer. It would have to be today. And soon.

The sooner the better.

By the time they had ridden all the rides twice, the man in the red wig knew all inhibitions Abie might have once had about talking to strangers were gone. Why should they apply to him, anyway? He wasn't a stranger. He was Abie's best friend.

"Want a Sno-Kone?"

Abie responded with his usual enthusiasm. As they walked to the Sno-Kone cart near the front parking lot, Abie reached out and took Sam's hand.

That was when he knew. The boy was ready.

A grizzled old man sitting inside the Sno-Kone cart peered down at them, one eye open, one eye closed. "How can I help you fellas?"

"Two Sno-Kones."

The old man seemed to be eyeing both him and the boy carefully. Too carefully for his comfort. "What flavor?"

"Oh, I don't know. What do you recommend?"

"What's the boy's favorite?"

"I—Abie, what flavor do you like?"

"Cherry!"

"Cherry it is. Two cherries."

The old man whirled around on his stool, scooped up the crushed ice in conical paper cups, and applied the artificial cherry flavoring.

Sam took the two cones and surreptitiously crumpled a white powder palmed in his right hand into one of them.

"How much do I owe you?" he asked.

"Well . . ." The old man scratched the side of his face, then nodded toward Abie. "Is he a Leo?"

"Is he—what?"

"A Leo. Born this month. If he is, he gets his free."

The man frowned, glanced down at Abie. Abie shook his head.

"Sorry. I'll just pay for it."

After paying, he passed Abie the doctored Sno-Kone. Together, they walked back to the car.

"Did you have a good time, Abie?"

"Did I? Wow! That was so much fun. Thanks." He hesitated for a moment. "It's been great, but—I wonder if I should maybe call my parents."

Experienced as he was, the man had anticipated this development and prepared for it. "Do you want to call them?"

"Not really. But I don't want them to worry. 'Specially Mom."

"Then relax. I called them."

Abie appeared both astounded and relieved. "You did?"

"Yes. While you rode the bumper boats the second time. Talked to your mother. We both agreed it might be best if you spent the day with me. It will give your father some time to cool off."

"And Mom said it was okay?"

"Oh yes. She was all for it."

"Great!" He took the man's hand again. "Where can we go now? Bell's?"

"Actually," the man said as he unlocked the car, "I know a place that would be even more fun than that. A private place."

"Will there be anything for me to do there?"

"Oh yes," the man said with vigor. "It's all for you. We can play games. Very special, wonderful games. We'll have a chance to do things you've never done before."

"Will it be fun?"

The man closed his eyes. "Heavenly."

"All right! Let's do it!"

"Off we go," the man said. He pulled out of the parking lot with a heart so happy he thought it might burst clean apart.

* 35 *

Ben gripped the dashboard of Mike's Trans Am. "Would you slow down already?"

Mike stared straight ahead at the road before him, hands clenching the steering wheel. "No," he said politely.

"Look, I know you're a macho cop. I've known for years. You're two-fisted, hard drinking, and tough as nails. You don't have to prove it to me by driving fast enough to break the sound barrier!"

"I'm in a hurry," Mike muttered.

He jerked the wheel to take a sharp left curve. The wheels screeched; Ben thought he felt the two right tires lift off the pavement.

"I'm serious! Slow down!" He would've complained more, but as far as he could tell, his protestations were making no impact whatsoever. "What's your big hurry, anyway?"

"A little boy has been kidnapped. Isn't that reason enough?"

It was a dire situation, to be sure, but it didn't explain this burst of reckless driving, even by Mike's standards, or the gloomy mood that had descended on Mike since he took that phone call. "You think that same creep has struck again, don't you? The chickenhawk. The one who killed those little boys."

Mike's chin rose slightly. "I never hypothesize in advance of the facts."

"But that's your gut feeling?"

"One of the witnesses saw a gray sedan speed away from the scene after the last boy was hit by the car on Memorial. And this Rutherford man saw a gray sedan carry away his little boy."

"Could just be a coincidence."

Although his speed did not decrease in the least, Mike's head turned slowly to face Ben. His eyes burned holes into Ben's forehead. Then he returned his attention to the road.

"What's the status on the boy who was hit by the car, anyway?"

"About five-thirty this morning he died. He never regained consciousness." Mike's voice remained perfectly flat, but Ben wasn't fooled. "His parents waited by his bedside for days, but they never got a chance to talk to him. Never got to say goodbye."

Ben was silent for a long moment. "Did the boy . . . suffer?"

"You mean after he was hit?" Mike twisted his shoulders and shifted into the fast lane, accelerating faster than Ben would've thought possible. "Hard to say. No one really understands how much pain people feel when they're in a comatose state. But before . . ." Mike took a deep breath. "Before he was hit by the car, he was violated. Molested. Anally. And this chickenhawk did . . . other things to him, too. Just tortured the poor kid."

Ben drew in his breath. Words left him.

"The medical examiner says it went on for hours. Maybe days. Till finally the boy managed to escape. And as a reward for his efforts, he got smacked by a car.

"The sooner I talk to Rutherford's parents, the sooner I can get on this bastard's trail," Mike continued. "And the hotter the trail, the better the chance of success." He glared at Ben. "Understand now?"

Ben nodded quietly. "Floor it."

Abie watched as Sam inserted his key and opened the door. He tried to pay attention, to be aware of where he was and what they were doing, but it was so hard. He felt sleepy, so sleepy he could barely keep his eyes open. He couldn't seem to focus; everything was a hazy blur, like when he put on his father's bifocals.

Sam pulled him through the door. "Wait here while I get a few things. I'll be right back. Then we'll go somewhere else and do something really special. I promise. You're going to love this. Okay?"

"Okay, Sam." Abie slumped down in a white recliner and flopped his book bag into his lap. His body felt heavy, tired. He didn't know what he had done to so exhaust himself.

He heard a rustling in the back room. Sam was searching for something in a closet. Whatever. Abie leaned back his head and closed his eyes. The clattering continued. What was all that noise, anyway? Never mind; he was too tired to care.

His mind drifted back in time. How had he gotten so worn-out? He had gone to bed at the usual time, didn't do anything out of the ordinary. It hadn't been that tiring, riding bumper boats and go-carts. But he felt utterly exhausted now. In fact, he'd been feeling strung out ever since—

His eyes opened.

Since he ate that Sno-Kone.

Was it possible . . . ? He'd heard of stuff like that, on television and in movies. Drugs. Stuff that made you sleep. But nobody did that in real life.

Did they?

Abie felt a nervous shiver run through his body. It seemed to energize him, though, to shake his body out of its stupor.

What did he know about Sam, anyway? Was it possible Sam . . . wasn't the friend he acted like he was? Was it possible . . . ?

Abie pushed himself to his feet. He staggered across the living room of the apartment, weaving back and forth like a drunk. Where was Sam? He wanted to ask him a question or two. . . .

Somehow, Abie managed to find his way to a door and opened it. Oops—wrong room. Sam wasn't in here. He had almost closed the door again when he noticed something strange about the opposite wall. It was colored and—was it just weird wallpaper, or what? It was so hard to tell; he could barely see it.

He entered the room and approached the wall. They were pictures. Photographs, cut out and taped to the wall.

And all the pictures were of little boys.

Some of them looked like they'd been cut out of magazines, but most of them were actual photographs. School pictures, or posed family shots with the rest of the family cut out. He recognized some of the other boys as kids whose parents were members of the country club. Abie wondered how Sam got access to all these shots.

Then he noticed something about the boys in the pictures.

All of the boys were about Abie's age. All of them had dark complexions, like Abie. All of them had brown eyes, like Abie. All of them had dark hair.

Like Abie.

The last detail he noticed about the picture wall was the worst of all. One of the photos, the one in the dead center of the wall, was very familiar.

It *was* Abie.

Abie stepped away from the wall. It was the picture that had been taken at the country club just a few weeks before. His parents hadn't bought any; how did Sam get them?

Another thought occurred to Abie, a thought that rang crystal clear in his dazed mind.

When they first met, Sam had acted like he didn't know who Abie was. But now Abie knew that wasn't true. Sam had Abie's picture on his wall.

Sam must've been looking for him.

Forcing his feet to move, Abie backed out of the room. He was moving quickly, gaining speed, and then—

He hit something solid.

Abie whirled around and saw, to his horror, that he had bumped into Sam.

Sam was standing right behind him. For how long?

"What the hell are you doing in here?"

Abie shrank away from him. Sam had never used that tone with him before. And there was something in his eyes, too, something Abie had never noticed before.

Something terrifying.

"I told you to wait outside!"

"I—I—" Abie stuttered helplessly. What could he say? What could he do? "I got confused."

"Confused? About what?"

Some voice inside Abie told him that he didn't need to tell Sam everything he had figured out. "I—I was looking for the bathroom. I'm sorry. I can't think so good. I feel tired."

Abie detected a tiny smile on Sam's lips. "Is that right? Well, let's move on to our next destination. There's a mattress there. We'll both have a nice lie-down."

"Mister, I—"

"Sam." He firmly clasped Abie's shoulders. "Call me Sam."

Abie squirmed under his grip. "I don't think I wanna go nowhere else with you."

"Oh?" A deep furrow appeared on his forehead. "Why is that?"

"I—I dunno. I just—I feel real tired. And I bet my parents are waiting for me."

"What's the matter, Abie? Don't you like me anymore?"

"No, I do! I really do. It's just—I dunno. My mom gets so worried sometimes. . . ."

"It'll be all right. This is play day, Abie." He moved toward the front door, pulling Abie behind him. "We're going to go somewhere now and play."

Abie wanted to resist, but he didn't have the strength. He wanted to yell, to scream out, but he couldn't do it. And he was afraid of what Sam might do to him if he did. He grabbed his book bag and allowed himself to be dragged through the door.

He had no choice. He didn't even know if he could stay awake; he was certain he couldn't fight Sam.

He was helpless.

36

The Rutherford mansion was one of Utica's premiere show-places. It was not far from Philbrook, and as far as Ben could tell, it was every bit as magnificent, perhaps more so. Like Philbrook, it was designed as a Renaissance villa, exquisite in its stone- and brickwork, stately and impressive.

The front lawn was planned, organized, and sculpted in precise detail. Long rows of tall hedges stretched from the street to the front porch. The flower beds were filled with azaleas, bright-colored rosebushes, and flowers systematically and scientifically clustered according to color and family. Ben spotted two gardeners at work; he suspected there were probably more.

All in all, Ben was glad he was arriving with a police officer. If he'd come alone, he'd probably have been chased away or shown the servants' entrance. Or shot.

The front door was opened, predictably enough, by a servant, a black woman in her late fifties. She was even wearing a uniform, a black blouse and skirt with a white frilled apron.

"I'm Lieutenant Morelli," Mike explained. "I'm here to see Mr. and Mrs. Rutherford."

Mike offered her a card, but she didn't take it. "Follow me."

She pivoted with an air of weary but formal detachment. The inside of the mansion was decorated with subdued colors, warm lights, and many mirrors. Ben's mother's home in Nichols Hills was stunning, but it looked like the Hayes residence compared with this place. This was the kind of mansion that could result from nothing less than vast quantities of money and the carefree ability to spend it.

"They're waiting for you in the living room," the maid said, pointing toward an interior passage. She detoured in the other direction and pushed through a swinging door. The kitchen, Ben thought, or perhaps the butler's pantry. Ben saw the woman sit down on a stool in front of a small black-and-white television playing one of those televangelists—Ben couldn't keep them straight.

The living room, as the maid had so quaintly put it, was astounding. Normal houses had living rooms; only palaces had rooms like this. The walls were floor-to-ceiling mahogany, except on one wall, where a huge bookshelf covered the same immense space. Light poured down from two rows of small high windows, casting crisscrossing light beams in either direction. Stuffed heads adorned the wall above and beside the fireplace mantel, as did several framed works of modern art that Ben didn't doubt were originals.

"You must be Mr. Rutherford," Ben heard Mike say, shaking him out of his architectural reverie. Rutherford was standing by the fireplace. Rachel was in a chair just beside him. Her face was streaked with tears.

As Rutherford shook Mike's hand Rachel noticed Ben. "I wasn't aware Mr. Kincaid was associated with the police," she said, brushing away her tears. "Aren't you required to disclose such details when you interrogate people?"

"I'm not with the police," Ben said hastily. "I just happened to be in Lieutenant Morelli's office when the call came in about your son. I recognized the name, so I came along to, uh, see if I could help."

Harold Rutherford scrutinized Ben carefully. Ben had the distinct feeling Rutherford didn't like having Ben here. But why?

"Can you tell me what happened?" Mike said abruptly. "The sooner we get through the preliminaries and get to work, the better the chances for your son."

"The—chances?" Rutherford's voice sounded hoarse. "I—I don't know what happened exactly. I was having a discussion with Abie. An argument, I suppose. There was nothing extraordinary about it; it happens quite frequently. Then, all of a sudden, he dashed out the door. Stupidly, I paused to talk to"—

he looked down at his grief-stricken wife—"Rachel. Just for a few minutes. Seconds, really. Then I ran out into the front yard, just in time to see Abie ride away with a stranger."

"Did Abie have anything with him?" Mike asked.

"Just the clothes on his back."

"Did you get the make of the car? Model? License plate?"

"I'm afraid not. I was too far away."

"What shade of gray?"

Rutherford appeared baffled. "Are there shades of gray?"

"Yeah. Silver. Metallic. Gunmetal."

"Ah—I don't know. A dark gray. Closer to black than white."

Mike began making entries on his notepad. "That narrows it down to probably a couple hundred thousand cars. Can you tell me anything else about this man?"

"All I saw was the back of his head."

"Are you sure it was a man?"

"Well—I assumed—"

"Don't." Mike scribbled a few more notes. "What color hair?"

Ben could see Rutherford was becoming flustered under Mike's barrage of questions. "I—I'm not sure exactly. Bright red, I think. It was curly and"—he waved his hands around his head—"bushy."

"Like an Afro?"

"Why, yes, exactly." His face suddenly became alarmed. "You don't suppose Abie was taken by a—a—colored person."

"With a bright red 'fro? I kinda doubt it."

Rutherford released his breath. "Well, that's a relief."

Ben could see Mike's teeth gnashing. "Have you ever seen this man before?"

"The man with the red bushy hair?"

Mike shrugged. "Perhaps. That was probably a disguise. Ever notice anyone who fit his general description? Ever notice anyone hanging around the neighborhood who didn't belong? Or maybe lurking about Abie's school?"

Rutherford seemed disturbed by the prospect. "Of course

not. Wait"—he snapped his fingers—"of course! The man Abie was talking to yesterday. His car. It was also gray."

Mike flipped a page in his notepad. "Care to tell me what you're talking about?"

"I was picking up Abie to take him to a baseball game. I was late. Car trouble."

Mike looked up. "What kind of car trouble?"

Rutherford frowned. "Well, I hardly see how that matters—"

"If it didn't matter, I wouldn't have asked."

Rutherford drew in his breath, obviously annoyed. "A fan belt snapped."

"Could it have been cut?"

Rutherford seemed genuinely taken aback. "I—suppose it could have been. My man was quite surprised. He said the belt was just replaced a few months ago."

Mike nodded thoughtfully.

"Anyway, I had to borrow Rachel's car, so I was late. When I arrived, Abie was talking to someone in a gray car. After I pulled in behind, the gray car drove away."

"Was it a sedan?"

"Uh—I'm not sure."

"Did Abie actually get in the car?"

"No. But he did throw his book bag in the backseat."

"Book bag?"

"Right. From school. It's navy blue. About so big."

Mike frowned. "Who was in this car?"

"I don't know. That's what Abie and I were fighting about this morning. I asked him who it was. He refused to tell me."

"That fits," Mike said grimly. "The first thing they do is extract an oath of secrecy. To protect themselves."

"What are you talking about?"

"Sir, I don't want to worry you unnecessarily, but I don't think your son was taken by accident. I think he was chosen. I think this man sabotaged your car and would've taken Abie yesterday if you hadn't shown up at the last moment. He's been stalking your boy."

"You think he wants . . . ransom?"

Mike looked down at his notepad. "I hope so."

"You hope so? What on earth are you talking about?"

"If this man is the same one I've been hunting . . . he may have other motivations."

"But—how can you know who he is?"

"I've been working on a series of child abduction cases for several weeks now. And this case fits the pattern."

"Oh, my God. And were these other children ransomed?"

"No," Mike said. "They were molested. Then killed."

Rutherford looked at his wife, then turned away as her eyes flooded with tears.

"I'm sorry, Mr. Rutherford, but you deserve to know the truth. Have you and your son been getting along?"

"I—I don't know what you mean."

"I think you do."

Rutherford glanced back at his wife again, but her face was buried in her hands. "To be perfectly honest, Lieutenant, Abie and I have . . . not been on good terms lately. Perhaps it's my fault, I don't know. He's been quite hostile toward me. Going through a phase, I suppose."

"Perfect."

Rutherford started. "I beg your pardon?"

"That's perfect for someone who wants to insinuate himself into your son's affections. The perfect opening. He'll try to be the daddy Abie isn't getting at home."

"Look here. Rachel and I have always done our best to provide—"

"Don't take it the wrong way, sir. Kids go through all kinds of fits and starts and crazy ideas as they grow up. A certain amount of unhappiness and dissatisfaction inevitably sets in, no matter how swell a parent you are. Creeps like the man who nabbed your son exploit it. That's all."

Rachel Rutherford brushed away the hair clinging to her wet face. "Lieutenant, do you think that—that—" Her voice cracked. She pressed her hand against her mouth. A few moments later she managed to continue. "Do you think that this man may have already—already—"

"There's no way I can be certain, Mrs. Rutherford," Mike

said gently. "But I don't think so. Child molesters aren't rapists. They like to take their time. Seduce their victims. But he won't wait forever. That's why it's so important that we move quickly."

The telephone rang. Rutherford and his wife both looked stricken.

"Well, don't just sit there," Mike said. "Maybe I'm wrong. Maybe it is a ransom demand. Someone answer it!"

Rachel extended her trembling hand and picked up the phone.

"Yes?"

A moment later she released her breath. "It's for Gabrielle."

Gabrielle was the maid who had shown Ben and Mike into the house. When called, she entered the room and took the phone. "Yeah? Oh, hello, Corrine."

"What's the meaning of this?" Rutherford demanded. He was talking to his wife, not Gabrielle. "Servants taking personal calls? On our line?"

"Where else would she take a call?" Rachel retorted. "She's here all day long."

"She shouldn't be taking personal calls when she's working. You need to put your foot down, Rachel!"

"Why me? So you can shuffle off to the country club and ignore the needs of your family?"

"I do not ignore the needs of my family!"

Tears once more streamed from Rachel's eyes. *"Tell that to my Abie!"*

Even though he knew he was asking for trouble, Ben stepped forward and placed his hand on Rachel's shoulder. "It's all right," he said quietly. "I know what a strain this must be for you."

"It's just—it's just—" She gasped, struggling to catch her breath. "It took us so long to get a child. We went through such hell. If something happens to Abie—I don't think I could bear it. I don't think I could go on living. I don't think I'd want to live."

Gabrielle interrupted. "Mr. Rutherford?"

Rutherford looked at the maid crossly. "Not now, Gabrielle."

"But, Mr. Rutherford—"

"And for God's sake, get off the phone. We're expecting a very important phone call."

"But, Mr. Rutherford—"

"Gabrielle, I gave you an order and—"

"But, Mr. Rutherford!" she shouted. "It's about Abie!"

The room fell deathly quiet.

"What about Abie?" Mike said quickly.

Gabrielle pointed toward the phone. "This's my good friend Corrine. She's the maid over at the Crenshaws' place. She's got a little boy about Abie's age. He comes over sometimes to play."

Rutherford's eyes widened. "My boy plays with the son of a—"

"Shut up!" Mike commanded. The look in his eyes made clear that he would brook no more interruptions. "What does Corrine say about Abie?"

"Well, I knows it sounds crazy, but she was taking her boy out to that big park this afternoon, you know, that Celebration Station place out at—"

"I know where it is," Mike said. "Go on."

"And she says she saw Abie there. With some man with big red hair." The maid frowned at Rachel. "Do we know anybody that looks like that?"

"How long ago was this?" Mike asked urgently.

"About an hour or so."

Mike grabbed the phone and pumped Corrine for more details, but there were no more to be had. All Corrine knew was that when she left, Abie was still there.

Mike tossed the phone back to Gabrielle. "Thank your friend for me." He started for the door.

"Where do you think you're going?" Rutherford asked.

"Celebration Station, of course. Come on, Ben."

Rutherford stepped in front, blocking the way out. "Wait just a minute. I still want to know—"

Mike shoved Rutherford out of the way. "I don't have time to answer stupid questions."

Rutherford looked as if he had been slapped in the face. He stood frozen in place as Mike and Ben raced from the house. The last thing Ben heard as the front door closed was Rachel's uncontrolled sobbing, the agonized sound of her loss, her pain. And her fear.

Her profound fear that they would be too late.

* 37 *

Abie tried as hard as he could to keep his eyes open as Sam dragged him from the apartment to . . . someplace else. Abie couldn't remember ever being so tired, ever having to fight so hard just to keep his eyelids up. Every so often he would lose the battle. His lids would fall and his body would droop, but a swift jerk on his arm from Sam would urge him onward.

He didn't have any idea where they were. He knew he should try to find out, should try to look for landmarks, but his dazed mind simply wasn't capable of it. Maybe he could run to a phone, he thought fleetingly, or stop someone on the street. But Sam selected their route too carefully, weaving in and out of alleys and crossing through abandoned buildings. They never passed anyone, and they never came near a phone.

A few scattered, blurry images were all Abie could distinguish. He was certain they had left Sam's apartment. As they passed through one building he saw numbers, lots of yellow numbers. No, not yellow numbers—numbers on a yellow background.

They headed toward a dark opening, not a door but . . . a hole. Through the hole . . . it was dark inside. Forbidding. Abie was afraid that once he was in there, he might never come out.

They passed through the opening, and then plunged into the darkness. It became dark, and cold. At times Abie could barely see anything at all. Then they walked through a wall. . . .

His mind rebelled at the thought. Walk through a wall? You can't walk through a wall, unless you're a ghost, and Abie didn't think he was, at least not yet. But that's what they had done.

And there were airplanes. Abie definitely remembered seeing airplanes. Were they up or down or . . . ? He was so confused.

They emerged from the dark building. The glaring light made his eyes water. They walked for a long time—how long he wasn't sure. Minutes? Hours? He still had no coherent sense of time.

Finally, when he thought he couldn't walk any farther, they approached another crumbling ruin of a building. Sam slowed as if they were going inside. Abie eyed Sam carefully. For the moment Sam was intent on his destination, eagerly marching toward the building with Abie firmly in hand. With the least movement possible, Abie quietly dropped his book bag onto the sidewalk. They entered the ruin and walked up an old wooden staircase. The stairs creaked and swayed beneath their feet; Abie felt as if the whole thing might give way at any moment.

They stepped through a door at the top of the stairs. And then . . .

"Here we are," Sam said.

For the first time since they left the apartment, Sam released Abie's arm. Abie moved away from him and concentrated as hard as he could on *seeing*. There was something lying on the ground, something flat and white with brown spots.

A mattress.

And there was something beside the mattress. Something standing on three long spindly legs. It looked to Abie like a monster, a giant spider, or one of the Martians in Abie's illustrated edition of *The War of the Worlds*.

He stepped closer, reached out, touched the long thin legs. No—it wasn't a monster and those weren't legs. It was a tripod. And on top—

A camera.

"I'm sorry for the delay," Sam said, smiling. "I know that was a long walk. I'm afraid I wasn't as prepared as I should have been. I had to stop by my place to get some film."

But you already have my picture, Abie thought. Something inside told him to keep the thought to himself.

"All right," Sam said, placing both hands firmly on Abie's shoulders, "now we're going to play a little game. I think you're going to like it. I know I will."

Back in the Trans Am, Ben said, "You know, Mike, as soon as Rutherford gets his head together, he's going to start calling your superiors. He probably knows Chief Blackwell personally. Probably plays golf with him."

"Screw it," Mike said as the car careened onto Harvard. "I'm not going to sacrifice that little boy just because his dad is a major asshole."

Mike slapped the flashing red light on top of his car and kicked into high gear. A few minutes later they were in the Celebration Station parking lot.

"We haven't got time to waste," Mike said curtly. "The more we mess around, the colder the trail gets. I'll hit all the food-and-game employees inside the main building. You quiz everyone outside running the rides."

Ben nodded. He had often admired Mike's facility for taking charge of a dire situation. It was a facility Ben knew he lacked. When the going got tough, his brain turned to mush.

Ben systematically worked his way through the outside amusements—the go-carts, the miniature golf course, the train, the bumper boats. The questioning was problematic, to put it mildly. The number of kids and adults passing through every day made recollections of particular individuals almost impossible. Moreover, virtually all of the employees were teenagers—those least likely to notice unusual pairings, or to remember them even if they did.

The young man running the bumper-boat concession was the best contact Ben made.

"I do kinda remember a dark-haired little boy with a tall man with red fuzzy hair. I thought that was such a weird contrast— fair dad, dark kid. And there was something weird about that hair. Something weird about that guy, too."

"Weird in what way?" Ben asked.

The boy frowned. "I'm not sure I can put my finger on it.

Just didn't seem right. The kid loved being here at the park, but the dude seemed kinda uncomfortable."

"Did you notice anything else about the man?"

"Nothing comes to mind."

"Please try. It's very important."

The young man's forehead wrinkled. "He was wearing a light sport coat—blue, I think. Yeah, blue, and a T-shirt beneath it."

"Do you remember anything about the T-shirt?"

"Well, it had this funny black face with a green helmet. . . ." He snapped his fingers suddenly. "Marvin the Martian."

"Who?"

"Marvin the Martian. You know, the cartoon character. The dude was wearing a Marvin the Martian T-shirt."

Now that was something that might help them make an ID, if they could ever find the man. "Do you remember when you saw them?"

"Not exactly. But it's been at least an hour."

"Any idea where they went?"

"Sorry. I was running my ride. I just saw them pass through the line several times, that's all."

Ben took down the boy's name and address and thanked him for his assistance. He finished interviewing everyone else working outside, but he didn't get any more information of value.

Ben met Mike inside the main building, where pizza was served to a host of kiddies watching Audio-Animatronic animals sing and joke onstage. "Any luck?"

Mike shook his head. "A few people kinda sorta vaguely remember seeing someone like that, but no one knows who they were or where they went. Nothing useful."

"Why on earth would a child molester bring a kid to such a public place?" Ben asked as they returned to Mike's car.

"It's part of the seduction," Mike answered. "He's trying to become Abie's friend, to make what lies ahead all the easier. He's courting Abie."

Ben felt a wave of revulsion rush over him. Of all the disgusting things he'd come into contact with over the years, this had to be the worst. The absolute worst.

"Excuse me. Are you gentlemen with the police?"

Ben looked up. Someone was calling to them from inside a Sno-Kone cart. As they approached, Ben saw that it was an older man, in his sixties at least, in a green camouflage jacket and khaki slacks.

"I'm with the police," Mike said. "Why do you ask?"

"I saw you askin' a lotta questions to everybody and their dog inside. Thought eventually you'd get around to askin' some to me."

"We're trying to gather information about a young boy who was here earlier with a red-haired man wearing a blue sports coat and a T-shirt," Mike explained. "Did you see them by any chance?"

"I sure as the world did," the old man said. "They bought two Sno-Kones from me. Cherry. That's the most popular flavor, you know. Some days grape will have a nice run, but cherry is—"

"Excuse me for interrupting," Mike said, "but I need to know about this red-haired man. As quickly as possible."

" 'Cept he weren't red-haired," the old man replied. "Least not really. He was wearing a wig."

Mike leaned forward. "Are you certain?"

"Shucks, yeah. I wasn't born yesterday. I know a natural-born redhead when I see one. It's more than just the hair, you know. Their whole complexions are different. He weren't no more a redhead than you or me. And then there was the resemblance between the man and the boy."

"What about it?"

"There weren't none. Not in the least. And the man didn't know what flavor Sno-Kone the boy liked. Didn't even know when his birthday was. Mighty suspicious."

"You're awfully observant. . . ."

"For a Sno-Kone vendor?" The old man chuckled. "Let me tell you something, sonny. I been driving this cart for fourteen years, since I hit retirement. I've worked LaFortune Park, the River Parks, the Fair. I know when things look right and I know when things look wrong. And when a man wearing a disguise shows up with a little boy who don't favor him in the least, that's when things look wrong."

Ben nodded. He was convinced. "Can you tell us anything else about the boy?"

"Yeah. The man called him Abie."

Bingo. "This is very important," Mike said. "Do you have any idea where they went after they left here?"

" 'Fraid not. They didn't say. I don't think the man took much of a cotton to me. He took his Kones and moved off in a pretty big hurry."

Ben was disappointed. For the briefest moment it had sounded as if they might have a lead that would help them find Abie.

"I did take a precaution, though," the man continued, "just in case it turned out the police were lookin' for Mr. Fake-Red-Hair. Which, it turns out, you were."

He opened the drawer of his cash register and withdrew a scrap of paper. "As the man drove off I took down his license-plate number. Here."

Mike snatched the paper from him. "I can't thank you enough."

"Always happy to oblige," the man said, pleased. "Now, can I sell you two fellers a Sno-Kone?"

"Sorry. We've got to run. But if this lead pays out, I'll come back and buy your whole damn cart. Come on, Ben. Let's move."

* 38 *

"But why do you wanna take my picture?"

Abie tried not to slur his words, but he was finding it as hard to talk as it was to stay awake, or to resist—to do anything other than follow Sam's lead.

"So I can see you when I'm not with you," Sam replied, smiling calmly. "We're friends, aren't we?"

Abie still thought it smarter not to tell Sam about his doubts. But he had to slow Sam down somehow. "Don't you already have a picture of me?"

A tiny bit of the placid smile disappeared from Sam's face. "What are you talking about?"

"I saw it. In your apartment. You had my picture on your wall."

"Ye-es," Sam said slowly. "I got that from, um, an acquaintance at the country club. I like to have pictures of all my friends."

"Then you don't need any more."

Sam rubbed his hands down Abie's shoulders and firmly clasped his wrists. "But that was such an . . . impersonal picture, Abie. You're my special friend, and I want a special picture of you. A personal picture. One that's just between you and me."

"Don't—wanna!" Abie tried to twist away from him, but he didn't have nearly enough strength.

"Abie. This is very unfriendlike. Didn't we have fun at Celebration Station? Didn't I buy you a Sno-Kone?"

"That—doesn't—"

"Come on, Abie. Be a grown-up. Grown-ups don't mind doing favors for one another."

Abie's eyes dropped down to the floor. "What kind of favors?"

"Like letting me take pictures of you."

"What kinda pictures?"

"Well . . . like these." Sam released the boy's arms and walked back to the camera equipment. He began rummaging about in a black bag.

Abie glanced at the door they had come in through. He wanted to run, to get away from Sam and go home to his parents. But could he make it to that door without being caught? And that staircase outside—it was so old and dangerous; Abie wasn't sure he could get down by himself.

And if he didn't get away, if Sam caught him, what would Sam do to him? It was too risky. Too impossible. He wasn't even sure he could find the door—his eyesight was so blurry.

"Here we are," Sam said triumphantly.

The loud voice startled Abie out of his reverie. The opportunity was lost.

Sam handed Abie a magazine. "See? That's what I had in mind. Just silly little pictures. Harmless."

Abie thumbed through the magazine. It wasn't a nice magazine with slick paper, like the ones his mother got in the mail. The paper was rough and coarse.

Abie glanced at the pictures. All of them were of little boys about his age. But they weren't wearing any clothes, or at least not many. Some of them were posed in strange positions or with chains and black leather stuff Abie didn't recognize. In some of the pictures, a little boy was posed with a grown-up man. They looked like they were doing really weird gross things to one another. Why would anyone want to do stuff like that?

Abie closed the magazines. The pictures were making him sick. He didn't even know why. They just did.

"Doesn't that look fun, Abie? Wouldn't you like us to have some fun like the people in the magazine?"

Abie didn't answer. He didn't want to say yes, but he

couldn't think of any answer that wouldn't infuriate Sam. It was so hard to *think*.

"Answer me, Abie. Wouldn't you like to take some pictures like that?"

There was something new in Sam's eyes, something that frightened Abie. If he could run through that door now, he would, no matter what the chances. But Sam had clamped his hands down on his shoulders again. Abie couldn't move.

"Answer me, damn it!" Sam literally picked Abie up off the ground and shook him violently back and forth. "Don't you want to pose for the goddamn pictures!"

Abie felt tears welling up in his eyes. He didn't want to cry; his dad had told him that only babies cry. But he couldn't help himself. He was so scared. So so scared.

"You're being a bad boy, Abie!" Sam was screaming now. He shook Abie again and again, harder and harder. "You shouldn't be a bad boy. Bad boys have to be punished! Don't you understand?"

"S-sure," Abie said, voice cracking. "What—whatever you want."

Sam took a deep breath, then released it. The color returned to his face.

"Well, good," Sam said finally when he had sufficiently recovered himself. "That's very good indeed. Let's take some pictures, then. Now, do you want to take your clothes off yourself"—he leaned forward and pressed his face into the boy's hair, drinking in his scent—"or should I take them off for you?"

Mike drove Ben up and down the streets of the abandoned Richfield section of north Tulsa. Ben scanned the streets on both sides of the car. It was all unfamiliar to him. Richfield was a district Ben had never had any occasion to visit. As far as he knew, no one ever came here.

Most of the buildings had been razed. The few that were still standing were gutted or boarded up. Rubble was strewn throughout the streets and alleys. A few years back a wealthy real-estate developer had proposed developing this part of town into an upper-class preserve, a yuppie enclave. Gilcrease, only nicer. He bought up and tore down most of the residences and street-front stores, but before he got to the renovation part of the plan, the oil bust hit, followed by the long-lingering recession. The project was abandoned. And Richfield was left in shambles, even worse off than it had been before.

"Are you sure this is where the creep lives?" Ben asked as he stared at the urban oblivion.

"I'm sure this is the address the DMV gave me for his license-plate number."

"Are we sure it belongs to the man we're looking for?"

"The car registered is a gray Ford sedan. Unless he stole the car, this is the right address."

Ben peered through the passenger window at the vast wasteland. "But no one could live out here."

Mike nodded grimly. "I think we have to face reality. The man we're after is smart. And careful. And he didn't start this sick business yesterday, either. He prepared."

"How do you mean?"

"I mean, for instance, he registered his car and license under a fake address. It's not that hard to do. No one really checks; most of the time the officials will blindly accept anything you write on the form."

"That's disappointing."

"Very. After all, if the address is fake, it's a safe bet the name is fake, too."

"But why here? Why this address?"

"Beats me. Probably it's the first address that came to his mind. Maybe he'd been out here for some other reason and knew no one lived here. After all, the only way he could be caught would be if he gave an address already claimed by someone else. The computer would catch that. So he probably—"

Without warning, Mike slammed down on the brakes. Since he had been traveling at a considerable speed, the sudden stop threw Ben forward against the dash.

"What are you doing?" Ben screamed. "There's not another

car in sight! Only you could nearly kill us when you're the only car on the road."

Mike didn't say anything. He was staring out the window on his side of the car.

"What's the matter? What are you looking at?"

"I'm not entirely sure. But I think it's . . . *yes!*" Mike popped open the door and sprang out of the car. "Blue!"

"Blue?"

"Right. I'll go in the front. You drive around the block and watch the rear exit. And call for backup. We may need it. Don't let him get away!"

"Blue?" Ben wanted to ask several more detailed questions, but it was too late. Mike was already barreling across the street, his trench coat flapping in the breeze.

What was it Mike saw? Ben squinted into the blazing sun and peered at the building Mike was making a beeline for. It looked like all the rest of them to Ben. Empty, hollowed out. Ruined. Graffiti on the walls. Nothing out of the ordinary. Except—

Wait a minute. He was looking too high. There was something on the ground, something on the sidewalk in front of the building.

Something blue.

Ben crawled into the driver's seat and threw the car into drive while fumbling with the handset.

It was a blue book bag.

* 39 *

"That's it, Abie. Now just a few more."

Abie stared into the camera lens and tried his best not to cry. He was so scared of Sam. The look in his eyes terrified him; he was certain the man would hurt him if he got mad again. If Abie didn't do everything Sam wanted him to do.

Abie had stripped down to his underwear, no further. Sam had grinned, said something about taking it one step at a time, and began clicking the camera. He kept moving Abie around, repositioning him, telling him to act happy or sad or other words Abie didn't even understand. Abie hated this, he felt . . . he didn't know. Gross. Dirty. It made him sick, and it made him sad.

It made him want to be home with his mommy.

And dad.

Sam stepped away from the camera. "All right, then. Let's try another pose."

"Don't wanna," Abie whispered, backing away.

"Tired of posing? Well, I guess that's fair. You've been working hard. Maybe we should take a break." He reached out and grabbed Abie's hand. "Maybe we should do something else. We could play a game. You and me, together. A real fun game. Would you like to do that?"

"No," Abie said, lower lip protruding. "Don't wanna play a game. I wanna go home."

"All in good time, Abie. All in good time." He held fast to Abie's hand. "Do you like to be touched, Abie?"

Abie tried to twist away. "No!"

"What about when your mother pats you on the back to help you fall asleep? I bet you like that, don't you, Abie?"

Abie continued to squirm. "So?"

"Well, that's okay for little babies, Abie, but grown-ups have other ways of touching. Better ways. Would you like to learn about those?"

Abie was so scared he didn't know what to do. Tears tumbled out of his eyes. He yanked as hard as he could, but he couldn't get away.

"I said, would you like to learn what grown-ups do?"

Abie continued to struggle.

"Answer me, Abie." The man pulled the boy close to him. His hands slowly moved around Abie. "Do you want to do something wonderful?" He stroked Abie's chin. "Do you?"

"No!" Abie took Sam's hand inside his mouth and bit down on it as hard as he could.

Sam shrieked.

Abie tried to break away, but Sam still held his arm firmly.

"You ungrateful brat!" Sam slapped Abie, hard, right across the face. Abie tumbled backward, falling onto the exposed concrete floor.

"I didn't want to do that," Sam said quickly. His breathing was becoming fast and irregular. "You made me do that. You're a dirty boy, and you had to be punished. Now let's see if we can do better—"

Abie pushed himself to his feet. Something about the slap had worked wonders, had shaken him out of his lethargic, dazed state. He felt a surge of energy charging through his body. He was free of Sam for the moment. He was going to make the most of it.

Abie ran behind the camera. "Stay away from me!"

"But Abie. We're friends."

"We're not friends! You're not my friend. You're—I don't know what you are. But I don't like you anymore."

A dark cloud seemed to cover Sam's eyes. "Don't be this way, Abie." He stepped slowly toward the boy.

"Stay away from me!" Abie reached into the equipment bag, pulled out the Polaroid camera, and threw it at Sam.

Sam dodged the camera, but it fell with a crash onto the concrete floor, shattering into pieces.

"Now look what you've done," Sam snarled. "You've ruined the camera." He continued advancing toward Abie. "I don't allow my little boys to hurt my belongings."

Abie grabbed the black bag and hurled it at Sam. Sam caught it, but the impact knocked him backward.

"All right, Abie. Now I'm mad." His jaw was tightly clenched. "And you don't have anything left to throw, do you?"

Abie ran to the back of the room. He slammed against the door and turned the knob—

It was locked.

"How stupid do you think I am, Abie? Of course I locked the door. We wouldn't want anyone walking in on us, would we?"

Abie kicked and pounded on the door, all to no avail.

"It's pointless, Abie. It's a very strong lock. I put it in myself."

Turning, Abie saw Sam hovering over him, his face burning with anger. Abie pressed back against the door, more scared than he had ever been in his life. There was nothing else for him to do, nowhere else for him to go. He was trapped.

"Now I've got you, you dirty, weak little boy. And now you're going to be punished. Over and over again. Until you're clean."

Abie screamed, but even as he did he knew that he was far, far away from anyone who could help him.

* 40 *

Why did it always happen like this? Sam thought. Why were the little boys always so mean, so unappreciative in the end? Didn't they know he loved them? Didn't they know all he wanted was to take care of them, to share something wonderful with them? Couldn't they see that?

He pinned Abie against the door. He pressed his hand firmly against Abie's chest, then leaned forward and immersed his face in Abie's hair. *Oh God!* He smelled so delicious! So intoxicating! He loved this boy so much.

"I'll give you one last chance to be good, Abie. Won't you play with me?"

"No!" Abie screamed, tears in his eyes. "I don't want anything to do with you. I want to go home!"

Sam reared back his hand and slapped the boy across the face, even harder than before. He grabbed Abie and pounded him against the door. "I was so good to you. I gave you everything you wanted. And how do you repay me? *How?*" He squeezed Abie so tightly his fingers left impressions on the boy's skin, then pounded him against the door again and again.

"You're hurtin' me!" Abie cried.

"I'll do worse than that." He took his free hand and clamped it around the little boy's throat. Abie gasped, but too late. He couldn't get any air.

"I don't want to do this, Abie. I truly don't," Sam said as he squeezed even tighter. "But you've left me no choice. You're no use to me when you act like this. No use at all." He pressed his thumb down against Abie's larynx while tightening his chokehold.

Why did it always have to end this way? It could have been beautiful. They could have trusted one another—

But no. Abie had proven he couldn't be trusted, just like the boy in the park, and the boy at the mall, and all the others. He couldn't take the chance of their escaping once they made it clear they would talk.

They had to die.

Gritting his teeth, he squeezed even harder. Abie's face was turning blue, and he no longer appeared to be breathing. It would be only a few more seconds now. . . .

* 41 *

Just as Sam tightened his chokehold he heard a tremendous booming noise, and the wall behind Abie seemed to lurch forward. Distracted, the man eased his grip on Abie's throat. What in the hell . . . ?

Wait a minute. It wasn't the wall moving. It was the door.

Someone was trying to break down the door. Someone was trying to get into his secret place.

Before he could react, the door bowed forward again, and a few seconds after that it burst open, knocking Abie several feet into the room. Abie fell face forward on the concrete floor, motionless.

Sam jerked his head around and saw a bulky man with dark wavy hair and—despite the fact that it was probably a hundred degrees outside—a tan trench coat. He was holding a gun.

"Freeze, you son of a bitch," the newcomer said. "You're under arrest."

Mike tried to absorb the scene as quickly as possible. The man crouched in front of him had to be the pervert. He was tall and he was wearing a Marvin the Martian T-shirt and a red wig that had fallen forward on one side.

A few feet into the room, Mike saw a small boy lying on the cold floor. He wasn't wearing anything except his jockey shorts. He didn't move.

Mike would've liked nothing more than to grab the sex offender and pound his face against the wall a few thousand times, but he somehow managed to restrain himself. "Get down on the floor," he barked. "Hands behind your back."

Mike pulled his cuffs out of his back pocket, then was startled by a muffled gasping sound from the boy. A trickle of blood dripped down the side of his face; he seemed to be having trouble breathing. He might need CPR. As in immediately. *Damn.*

"Don't try anything," Mike ordered. He quickly slid the cuffs over the man's wrists, then stepped over him to get to the boy. "Don't try to get away," he warned, then he crouched down beside Abie's body.

"Are you all right?" He touched the side of the boy's face. No reaction.

He turned Abie's head around, placed two fingers against the neck, and searched for a pulse. "Goddamn you," Mike murmured. "If you've killed another one—"

The man on the floor was smiling at him. Grinning.

Mike gripped the boy by the shoulders. "Come on, Abie. Don't give up. Come back to us."

Still no response.

Mike held his hand over the boy's mouth. He didn't feel anything.

Damn, damn, damn. He would have to try CPR. Maybe if he just got the boy breathing again, he'd come back.

Mike cleared the boy's mouth with his finger and tilted back his head. As a police officer, he'd been trained in all forms of CPR. The techniques were slightly different for small children, but damned if he could remember exactly how. He'd just have to plunge in and hope for the best.

He started CPR, watching to see if the boy's chest rose.

No luck.

Come on, Abie! He crouched down again and blew air into the child's lungs. Don't give up on us, Abie. Don't give up!

The man in the wig hit Mike in the gut, knocking him onto his back. A follow-up kick to Mike's hand sent his gun skidding across the room. Mike pushed himself back up on all fours, but before he could do anything, the man hit him again, this time with a foot pounding into the small of his back.

Mike fell down onto the concrete. His face hit the floor, momentarily scrambling his brains. Stupid fool. He'd gotten so concerned about reviving Abie he'd forgotten to keep his eye on the goddamn pervert. He shook his head forcefully, trying to clear away the cobwebs.

He heard the man coming at him again. Grunting, Mike rolled over onto his back. The man was almost directly over him. Straining with all his might, Mike raised his feet and kicked the front of the man's kneecaps.

The attack took the man completely by surprise. He cried out, then crumbled to the floor. Mike saw his opportunity. While the man struggled to pull himself together Mike gave him his best roundhouse punch to the stomach.

The man screamed. Mike followed insult with injury—he caught the man between the legs with a swift kick to the groin. Mike's instructor at the academy had been right—trite though it may be, it was the most decisive way to stop an attack. The man doubled up and went reeling across the room.

He fell back onto a mattress in the center of the room beside a camera. Just looking at the scenario made Mike feel ill. It didn't take much imagination to figure out what this was about. And when the lab boys developed the film, as they would be required to do, he would have to look at the pictures. . . .

Mike blocked it out of his mind. First things first. Apparently he hadn't done as good a job on the sicko's knees as he had hoped. The man was getting himself up and his legs seemed to be supporting him. He was desperately trying to pull himself together, gasping for air, leaning on the tripod.

"Stay down, you sick piece of scum," Mike said, lumbering toward the camera. He was breathing rather heavily himself. And where the hell was his gun? "Don't give me an excuse to shove you out a window. I'd enjoy it too much, and that's—"

The flash went off directly into Mike's eyes. He was standing barely a half a foot from the camera and looking straight at the bulb; the sudden illumination blinded him.

He reached out for the creep, but he was already gone. Mike could hear the footsteps of the man scrambling away.

Mike blinked rapidly, trying to clear his vision. Still blind as a bat, he stumbled toward the door. He couldn't see anything, but he remembered generally where the door was. He made it to the top of the stairs, but remembered how dangerous and unstable they had been. He had almost killed himself coming up. And back then he could see where he was going.

He could barely hear the man's footsteps now; they were far ahead of him.

Damn safety anyway! It was now or never. Mike extended one foot and lowered himself onto the first step. So far so good. He took another step, then another. If he just took it easy, didn't rush, didn't take any chances, he should be—

Suddenly the ground went out from under him. His feet sank through the stairs, plummeting him downward. He extended his hands to break his fall, and just in time. He narrowly missed falling all the way through.

"Ben!" he shouted. There was no response. Naturally. Ben would be on the other side of the building watching the rear exit. And he wouldn't see the perp because, thanks to Mike's own stupidity, he was escaping through the front door.

He had to face facts. The son of a bitch had gotten away. The best thing Mike could do now was get back to that little boy and get him medical attention as soon as possible.

If it wasn't too late.

The white light obscuring Mike's vision gradually dissipated. He managed to extract his legs from the hole in the steps and to crawl back up. He ran into the room and knelt over Abie's body.

The boy still had not moved.

This was the worst of all, the most crushing failure. Not only did the pervert escape, but the little boy—

Wait a minute. Did he imagine that, or did the boy . . . ?

Yes! He moved. Praise God Almighty—*he moved!*

"Abie, can you hear me? How do you feel? Can you breathe? Does your head hurt?"

Abie blinked rapidly several times, then peered out through clouded, watery eyes. "Who . . . ?"

"I'm a policeman," Mike said, his heart nearly beating out of his chest. "I'm—I'm here to help you."

Abie's breathing slowly became more regular. His lips

trembled, and all at once he began to cry. "Will you please take me home?"

"Of course I will." Mike scooped the boy up and cradled him protectively in his arms. "Don't worry about a thing," he whispered. "Everything's going to be all right now. Everything's going to be fine."

THREE

*   *

The Hands of Justice

* 42 *

Ben pushed his way through the crowd to the front of the seventh-floor courtroom. People were squabbling over seats and shoving one another out of the pews. "I was here first!" he heard, and "No fair saving seats!" and other cries he would've expected on a playground perhaps, but not in a state courthouse.

Seats were at a premium; the courtroom wasn't that large and there was a long line of would-be spectators outside. Everyone seemed interested in this case, not just in Oklahoma but throughout the country. Several network news reporters were present, as well as a few representatives from major newspapers. Court TV had even asked for permission to broadcast portions of the trial, but Ben had refused to consent.

Ben couldn't believe so many people were galvanized by this murder trial. He wasn't sure who or what to blame. Maybe it was the heat—everyone was looking for a diversion from this oppressive humidity. Maybe it was the media. They'd been playing the hell out of the story. The ten-year-old "impalement from the past" gave them abundant grist for the evening-news mill, usually playing up the gruesome details of the murder itself. The line separating tabloid TV and legitimate journalism seemed to be getting thinner every day.

Or maybe the appeal was the implied class struggle—a poor developmentally disabled black man accused of committing a violent crime in a citadel of opulent wealth. Or maybe it was just the ever-present interest some people have in other people's business. Courtrooms provided a justifiable opportunity to pry into the affairs of others.

Ben finally made it to the defendant's table. Leeman wasn't there. Christina wasn't either, but she had clearly been there earlier; all Ben's notebooks and exhibits and other trial paraphernalia were lined up and organized.

"How about a few words on the trial, Mr. Kincaid? Do you expect to win?"

Ben turned and saw a man on the other side of the railing extending a microphone as close to Ben's face as possible. The first two rows on the right side of the gallery had been roped off for the press. A badge on the man's lapel identified him as a reporter for Channel 2.

"Sorry," Ben answered. "In my experience, television coverage of legal matters is somewhat less than accurate."

"Come on," the reporter said. "All I need is ten seconds."

"I know," Ben replied. "That's the problem."

Ben scanned the two full rows of coiffed heads jockeying for position behind the man from Channel 2. They probably wanted to be on the scene so they could do a live remote from the courthouse. Beth Rengel and Clayton Vaughn, the Channel 6 anchorpersons, were both there. As was Karen Keith, interviewer and all-around smart lady. Leslie Turnbull and Rick Wells. And Ben's personal favorite, Karen Larsen. He might consider giving her an interview. If she promised to give him more than ten seconds.

"Starting to feel the heat, Ben?"

Jack Bullock was hovering over Ben's table.

"It's always tense just before a trial begins. There's nothing unusual about that."

"I guess you still think you can pull a rabbit out of your hat and get your boy free so he can skewer some more women, huh?"

"Jack, you know I have an obligation to represent my client to the best of my ability. I have no choice—"

"You took this case voluntarily, Ben. No one forced it on you."

"I took this case because I think Leeman Hayes is innocent. Why are you taking this so personally?"

"Because it is personal to me. I care about people, Ben. I

care about this city. I'm not in this for the big bucks and the swimming pools and the million-dollar homes. I want to make the world a better place. And I don't like people like you getting in my way."

"Jack . . ." Ben shook his head sadly. What was there to say? And what was the point? "I'd like to go over my notes. If you'll excuse me."

"Whatever you say." Bullock drew himself up, then added quietly, "I've got a surprise for you."

Alarm bells rang out in Ben's brain. "What are you talking about?"

Bullock strolled back to his own table. "Have fun reviewing your notes."

"In case you haven't heard, Bullock, trial by ambush is history. My client has a constitutional right to know the accusations that will be made against him at trial."

"Wah, wah, wah," Bullock mock-cried. He began whispering to his second chair, Myrna Adams.

Great. Kincaid glanced over his shoulder and noticed the reporters were scribbling away. They had probably caught most of that dramatic little exchange. The press seemed to love it when lawyers started bickering. He could see it now—a murder trial billed as the grudge match of the century.

Bullock still had not even acknowledged the possibility of a plea bargain. Normally, given the difficulties inherent in trying a ten-year-old crime, Ben would've expected a deal proposal to be the first words out of the prosecutor's mouth. But not this time. Bullock seemed determined to make this charge stick.

The buzz in the courtroom suddenly diminished. It wasn't the judge; he was still in chambers. All the heads in the gallery were facing the rear.

Leeman Hayes was being escorted into the courtroom.

Despite the ban on cameras in the courtroom, Ben saw several flashes go off and heard the soft whir of minicam motors. Two men from the sheriff's office escorted Leeman to the front of the courtroom. Ben smiled and offered Leeman the chair beside him. Leeman returned a small smile, but it was clear to Ben that he was terrified. Ben wondered—not for the first time—just how much of this Leeman really understood. He could imagine the questions racing through his mind. What are we doing? Why are all these people here? Why are they staring at me?

Ben patted Leeman on the shoulder and gently turned him away from the gallery. "It's all right. Just forget they're here. The only part of this room you need to be concerned with is up front."

Leeman leaned forward pensively, his chin resting on his hands.

Ben had visited Leeman several times since their first meeting. Although he hadn't obtained any new information, he thought Leeman had come to know him a little better, and had perhaps even come to trust him. According to Vera, Leeman had only two visitors: Ernie and Ben.

With each visit, Ben had become more and more convinced that Leeman was not competent to stand trial, no matter what the state's shrink decreed. Judge Hawkins, however, had denied all Ben's motions to revisit the issue. Hawkins insisted that this trial had been delayed long enough. It was time to see justice done.

Justice. What a concept.

Leeman's head cocked at that odd angle. "Papa . . . ?"

"Sure. He's here. He's in one of the back rows. See?" Ben pointed him out. Ernie saw them looking and waved.

"Don't . . ." Leeman's neck extended and twisted. He turned his shoulders awkwardly.

Don't . . . wanna be here? Ben guessed. "I understand, Leeman. No one wants to be here. But we have to clear this up once and for all."

Leeman shook his head vigorously. "Don't . . . go back."

It was the most words Ben had ever heard Leeman speak at once. Don't . . . go back? To the hospital, Ben realized. Don't wanna go back to the many many hospitals.

"Home," Leeman whispered softly.

Ben laid his hand on Leeman's. "I'll do my best," he said. He tried to sound confident.

Leeman lifted his chin tentatively. "Later . . . ?"

"Later?"

Leeman struggled to finish the thought. "Beet-hooven."

Ben smiled. "It's a date."

Ben heard the sound of shuffling feet coming from the front of the courtroom. The chamber door opened, and Hawkins's bailiff stepped out. "All rise."

The crowd hushed and rose to their feet. Judge Hawkins emerged from chambers, draped in his black robe, and moved somberly to his chair at the head of the courtroom.

"All right, then," Hawkins said briskly. "Let's not waste any time. Call the case."

The bailiff did so. When Leeman heard his name, he started to rise. Ben gently tugged him back down into his seat.

"Very well," Hawkins said. "The court has determined that the defendant is competent to stand trial. Let all those with business before this court now come forward."

The judge paused a millisecond, then continued. "Gentlemen," he said, gazing down at Ben and Bullock, "let's get this show on the road."

* 43 *

"First off," Judge Hawkins announced, "we need to pick a jury. Bailiff, call the first twenty-four veniremen."

The bailiff pulled out a large bingo hopper filled with names written on slips of paper. The names of the potential jurors were taken at random from driver's-license rolls and copied into the hopper. The names of those who had managed to get themselves excused were removed. As Ben knew all too well, that often left only the names of those too bored or too stupid to figure a way out of jury duty.

Twenty-four potential jurors filled the jury box. Ben wrote down each of the names as it was called. The really slick courtroom attorneys memorized them so they could impress the jurors by addressing them by name. Ben's memory wasn't half that good. Still, if he could remember a few of the names, maybe he could drop them at judicious moments, then glance back at his chart as necessary.

Now began what Ben considered the greatest guessing game ever devised by man. Based upon a host of indirect questions and stereotypical juror profiles, he had to determine who would be good jurors for his client. Did he want men or women, rich or poor, young or old, white or black? It was worse than being in Vegas; the game was just as unreliable, but the stakes were much higher.

The initial panel was over two-thirds male—not what Ben had wanted. He needed sympathetic souls, and sympathy was a characteristic more commonly attributed to women than men. Ben also saw an unusually high number of ties and jackets—apparel that denoted professionals, individuals with money. Rich people were generally assumed to be conservatives; conservatives tended to convict. Poor people were considered more likely to empathize with the plights of other poor people, although sometimes they could be harder on their own than anyone else.

And then there was the race issue. Ben would normally assume that the more black jurors he had, the better. This jury panel had two, for the moment, anyway. The United States Supreme Court had ruled that jurors could not be removed on the basis of their race alone; counsel were required to present an articulable reason for any minority removal—hardly a difficulty for an experienced trial attorney. Bullock would undoubtedly remove them both; he would simply come up with some nonracial excuse for doing it. How could Ben contest it? How could anyone claim to know what goes on in the murky mind of a lawyer?

Ben glanced over his shoulder and, to his relief, saw that Christina had returned. She was sitting in the back of the courtroom in the area reserved for counsel's staff. Thank goodness. Her instincts were far better than his. Jury selection was the province of someone who understood people; people mystified Ben.

The judge instructed the jurors to give their names, addresses, occupations, and the occupations of their spouses, if any. In a few instances, the judge asked for some additional clarifications. Not often. That completed, Hawkins waved the prosecution into action.

As the prosecutor, Bullock got the first shot at the jury. He made some introductory remarks and told a few little jokes. As anticipated, he called the jurors by name. Show-off. Although Bullock knew Hawkins wouldn't let him try his case during voir dire, he gave enough hints about the subject matter of the case to whet the jury's appetite so they would be primed and ready by the time they got to his opening statement. In solemn tones, he let them know that this case involved "shameless, cold-blooded murder."

Ben could see the jurors' eyes brighten. Murder sounded so exciting, so glamorous. Up until that point, for all they knew, they might be hearing a traffic case. Now they knew they were in for something considerably more interesting. The Big Time.

"Ladies and gentlemen," Bullock continued, "it is a sad reality of life that all men are not created equal. Some men are born with birth defects, learning disabilities, special problems. We are, of course, sympathetic to them."

Juror heads nodded. A few of them glanced at Leeman. In Ben's experience, jurors were quite adept at putting two and two together.

"There is a point, however, at which sympathy can be taken too far. Some would say that a learning disability, for instance, is no excuse for antisocial behavior. And nothing can justify murder."

Ben knew how this game was played. While Bullock delivered this little heartfelt oration, he was scanning the jury for facial expressions indicating disagreement.

"What about you, Mr. Smithson?" Bullock nodded toward an elderly man in the back row. "Do you think there is any excuse for murder?"

"Well," Mr. Smithson said, clearing his throat, " 'course I think a man's entitled to act in self-defense. To protect himself. Or his property."

"Certainly," Bullock said, nodding vigorously. "There are legal defenses. But do you think a man has carte blanche to commit murder just because, say, he's not quite as bright as me and you?"

"No, of course not."

"And would your opinion change if this hypothetical person had a learning disability? Not insane, mind you, but just a little slower than the norm."

Mr. Smithson shook his head. "Don't s'pose it would."

Bullock quizzed three more of the jurors along these lines. Very smart, Ben had to acknowledge. Bullock instinctively understood what the hardest part of his case was—he was trying to convict a mentally retarded man. Bullock was confronting the problem head-on, rooting out any natural sympathies that might prevent the jury from convicting even if the evidence indicated that they should.

Bullock asked these and other related questions for close to an hour. Finally, he moved on to the next major voir dire issue.

The death penalty. The Supreme Court had laid down the law on this matter, too, in the famed Witherspoon decision. Prosecutors had considerable leeway to ensure that their juries were *death-qualified*, that is, capable of delivering the death penalty if they believed the facts justified the sentence.

"Mrs. Skaggs," Bullock said, addressing the middle-aged woman in the far right corner of the box, "do you believe in the death penalty?"

"Yes," the woman replied emphatically. "I certainly do. An eye for an eye. That's what the Good Book says."

Bullock nodded. "Would everyone else agree with that? Let's have a show of hands. Who believes in the death penalty?"

The hands rose sporadically, but eventually, twenty hands were in the air. Without saying another word, Bullock turned to face the judge. Hawkins coughed, as if breaking out of a reverie, and glanced at his jury chart. He then dismissed the four jurors who did not believe in the death penalty and called four more to take their places.

Smoothly done. Bullock had, of course, demanded their removal, but in a subtle way that didn't make him look like a villain in front of the jury. Ben didn't bother objecting. The law on the issue was clear. The jury was supposed to apply the law, not debate policy. If a juror wasn't willing to apply the death penalty—the law of the state—given the proper proof of guilt, he or she must be excused.

"Mrs. Skaggs," Bullock continued, "a lot of people believe in the death penalty in principle, but when they're sitting on a jury, they find they cannot personally give the death sentence to anyone."

Mrs. Skaggs nodded silently.

"Ma'am, assume that I proved this young man's guilt beyond any question. Would you be able to give him the death penalty?"

She hesitated. "I—I believe that I—yes, I think that I could do that."

"Are you sure? You must understand that if you deliver a sentence of death, there will be no possibility of probation or parole, and you must assume there will be no appeal. If you vote for death, execution will follow. The defendant will be killed by lethal injection."

Bullock took a deep breath and paused to let the words sink in. "No matter what you may have heard or read, you must assume that your sentence of death will be carried out. Given that assumption, would you still be able to deliver a death verdict?"

Mrs. Skaggs swallowed. "I—I'm just not sure."

"I see." Bullock's years of experience were paying off. He was consistently finding the doubters, the weak links that might prevent a guilty verdict, and exposing them. "What do you mean when you say you're not sure?"

"I mean—" Stress lines crisscrossed the woman's forehead. "I want to do the right thing. I want to do my duty. But when you put it like that—well, it's almost like I'd be killing the man myself."

Bullock did not contradict her. "And would you be able to do that, ma'am?" He was being gentle about it, but he was definitely pushing. He needed an unequivocal *I couldn't do it* to get her dismissed for cause. Otherwise, he would have to use one of his limited peremptory challenges. "I'm not saying it would be easy. But could you do it?"

"I—I'd try to be fair."

"Mrs. Skaggs, you're not answering my question." He gestured back toward Leeman. "Could you look this man in the eye and say, 'Sir, you must die for what you did'?" His voice swelled in volume. "Could you do that?"

Mrs. Skaggs stared helplessly at Bullock, then looked up at the judge. Hawkins turned away. No succor there.

"I—I guess I'd just have to wait and see."

"I'm sorry, Mrs. Skaggs. That's unacceptable." He was really leaning on her now. "I need an answer from you. Could you condemn this man to death?"

"But—" The poor woman was beginning to sound desperate. "I haven't even heard the evidence yet."

"Mrs. Skaggs, we're not asking you to determine if he is in fact guilty. But assuming that the evidence later proves that the defendant is guilty, could you render the death penalty? Could you sentence this man to death as required by the laws of this state?"

Mrs. Skaggs's lips twitched, her eyes flickered. She didn't respond.

"The juror will answer the question," Judge Hawkins intoned.

"I—I—" Mrs. Skaggs lowered her face. "I don't think I could. No."

"Thank you very much for your candor," Bullock said. He was being very warm now, very friendly. And why not? He had what he needed.

Judge Hawkins excused Mrs. Skaggs and called another juror to take her place.

Ben cast a reassuring smile in Leeman's direction, leaned back in his chair, and tried to make himself comfortable. If the first hour was any indication, they were going to be here for a good long while.

* 44 *

Bullock continued his exacting line of death-penalty questioning with each and every member of the jury panel. The Supreme Court said he had a right to a panel of twelve jurors who were willing to deliver the death verdict, and he wasn't going to sit down till he had one. Of course, this made it all the more likely that the jury would be predisposed to render the death penalty, but there was nothing Ben could do about that. That was the law.

Bullock's questioning went on for hours. Ultimately, he removed five more jurors, who were immediately replaced. About one-thirty in the afternoon, Bullock called it quits. It had been a long haul, although pitifully short compared with other death-penalty jury selections, which sometimes went on for weeks.

Judge Hawkins motioned for Ben to begin his questioning.

"Your honor, I wonder if it might not be best if we took a lunch break now. The jury's been sitting for over four hours. They must be starving." Always be the jurors' friend, Ben reminded himself. Can't hurt.

Hawkins glanced at his watch. "No, let's proceed. We'll break after your questioning."

Ben frowned. "Your honor, I think the jurors' attention will be—"

"I said proceed, counsel."

"But your honor—"

"I said, proceed. If you're so concerned about the jurors' well-being, don't waste a lot of time."

So that was it. The judge was going to hold lunch in limbo

as long as Ben asked questions. Every minute Ben went on, the jurors would be reminded that they were hungry, and restless, and it was all Ben's fault. It seemed the hanging judge was already doing his bit to squelch the defense.

Ben squared his shoulders and approached the jury box. He started with Mr. Franklin, a gruff, sturdy-looking man in his mid-forties. Ben suspected that Franklin was an ultraconservative, lock-'em-up-and-throw-away-the-key type, but jurors rarely admitted that on direct questioning. There were other ways, however.

"Mr. Franklin, I recall you said earlier that you were, to use your own words, a strong lifelong believer in the death penalty. Correct?"

Franklin ran a finger under the waist of his blue jeans. "You got that right."

"Is that an opinion you share with any of your friends?"

Franklin eyed him suspiciously. "Which friends?"

"Well . . . are you a member of any organizations?"

"I go to church every Sunday, if that's what you mean."

It wasn't, but it was interesting just the same. "Are you by any chance a member of the ACLU?"

Franklin snorted. "You gotta be kiddin'."

"How about the NRA?"

"Since I got my very first gun."

"I see. And when was that?"

"My daddy gave it to me the day I turned fourteen. A real pretty little Winchester."

Ben nodded. "And can you explain why you believe the death penalty is a good idea?"

"Objection," Bullock said. "This is not relevant. Mr. Kincaid is inquiring into the man's personal political beliefs."

"On the contrary," Ben said, "I'm inquiring into the man's beliefs about the death penalty—the same thing Mr. Bullock has questioned them about for the better part of the day."

Judge Hawkins waved his hand with a distracted air. "I'll allow it." It was the easiest alternative.

"Well," Mr. Franklin answered, "I always thought the

general idea behind capital punishment was to set an example. You know, scare them straight."

"You understand that would be an improper reason to render a death sentence, don't you?"

Franklin frowned. "I . . . don't quite follow."

"Your decision has to be based on the evidence. The facts of this case. The deterrent effect your verdict might have on third parties is irrelevant."

"Well, I don't think it is."

"That's the law."

"Well, then it's a stupid law." A few of the other jurors joined him in a chuckle.

Ben tried to smile. Didn't want the jury to think he was a stiff. But he had to keep working on Franklin, too. He had to get him off the jury before he convicted Leeman just to "send a message" to criminals everywhere. "Mr. Franklin, can you assure me that you'll render your verdict solely on the basis of the evidence presented in this courtroom?"

"I'll do my best."

"But can you guarantee that you won't be influenced by your desire to deter future murderers?"

"Well, I can't be altogether sure—"

"You have to be sure, sir. Can you reach a verdict without giving any thought to the effect the verdict might have on persons other than the defendant?"

There was a long pause, but eventually he answered. "Well, if that's what the law says I have to do, that's what I'll do."

Needless to say, this was not the answer Ben wanted to hear. He didn't believe for a moment that Franklin could decide the case without prejudice. He did believe that the man wanted to stay on the jury—probably so he could send the defendant up the river.

Ben gave it one more try. "Are you saying that you're sure you can decide this case solely on the basis of the evidence presented in this courtroom?"

"If that's what the judge tells me to do, then that's what I'll do."

That was it, then. Franklin gave him no concrete grounds for removal for cause. If Ben wanted to get rid of him, he'd have to use one of his precious peremptories.

Ben proceeded to question each member of the panel. In addition to following up on the death-penalty issue, he tried as gently as possible to expose any possible bigotry or prejudice that might come Leeman's way because he was black. It was an almost impossible mission. He couldn't ask the tough questions without risking offending some of the jurors, and he absolutely positively could not risk offending some of the jurors.

The last man Ben questioned was Harvey Prescott, an accountant, the youngest man on the jury. He was even younger than Ben, about twenty-eight.

"Mr. Prescott, you also indicated that you believed in the death penalty, is that correct?"

"It is."

There was the tiniest hesitation in his voice, just as there had been when Bullock questioned him on the same subject. There was something he hadn't said yet; some detail they hadn't yet uncovered.

"You seem unsure."

"No—I'm sure. The death penalty is a good thing. A necessary evil."

"And you believe you could hear the evidence with an open mind and be fair about your deliberations?"

"Oh yes. Yes, definitely."

Hmmm. Ben gave it another try. "You don't think you would be hesitant to condemn a man to death by lethal injection?"

"No, not at all. I consider that the most humane way to execute a convicted murderer."

Keep digging, Ben told himself. "And you believe that executions are necessary?"

"Oh, yes." Prescott hesitated a moment, then added, "And they save the taxpayers a lot of money."

Aha! "Can you explain what you mean by that, Mr. Prescott?"

"Isn't it obvious? When I worked for the government, I

frequently examined the state's books. Incarcerating a man for life costs the taxpayer a fortune. Execution saves a lot of bucks."

"Actually," Ben said, "studies have shown that because of appeals and all the related legal activity, incarceration is significantly cheaper than death sentences."

"Objection!" Bullock said instantly, as Ben had known he would. The judge sustained, but it was too late—the information was already out.

"I'll rephrase my question," Ben said. "Mr. Prescott, I'm sure you realize that any sentence must be based on the evidence presented, not a desire to make the state more fiscally sound."

"Well, I like to keep an eye on the dollars and cents—"

"Mr. Prescott, can you assure me that you'll make your determination solely on the basis of the evidence presented in the courtroom?"

Prescott folded his arms across his chest. He was practically sulking. "If I have to."

Ben turned slowly. "Your honor—"

"He answered in the affirmative," Hawkins said, cutting Ben off. In other words, I'm not doing you any favors, counsel for the defense. "Anything else, Mr. Kincaid?"

"Yes." Ben asked a series of questions designed to subtly expose any racial bias. As he soon learned, no one was a member of the NAACP, but no one was a member of the KKK either. No one had a SAY NO TO HATE bumper sticker. None of them had seen *Malcolm X*. One woman had seen *Boyz N the Hood*, but only because her girlfriend told her she thought it was a musical. Several of them had read Ellison's *Invisible Man* in school, since it was written by an Oklahoma author, but most felt it was no longer relevant to today's society. Ben nodded his head politely. If only it were true.

Ben questioned extensively, but obtained no obvious expressions of racial prejudice. All he got were suspicions, specters. He ran over a few more key points and dropped several reminders that the defendant was innocent until proven guilty beyond a reasonable doubt. There was no point in pushing it any further. He had already learned everything he was ever going to know about these people.

Now the guessing game began. Armed with nothing but stereotypes, answers to indirect questions, and superficial impressions, Ben had to make several potentially life-and-death determinations.

Such was the science of jury selection.

Judge Hawkins called a short recess. After consulting with Christina, Ben went back into the judge's chamber with Bullock. As predicted, Bullock removed both black jurors, claiming that their lower-income status might prejudice them in favor of the defendant. Yeah, right. Ben had little choice but to remove Mr. Franklin and Mr. Prescott. On Christina's recommendation, he also removed a handyman who sat to the right of Franklin. Ben would normally be inclined to retain a blue-collar, hardworking man, but Christina said he gave her "bad vibes." She also thought the man had laughed a bit too heartily at Franklin's little joke.

Good enough for Ben. He took the man off the jury.

Ben had more peremptories, but had no real grounds for exercising them. Five removals left a jury of twelve, plus several alternates.

Hawkins brought counsel and the jury, what was left of it, back into the courtroom and reconvened the proceedings.

"Very well," Hawkins said, again glancing at his watch. "We'll take a lunch break"—at least he didn't add *finally*— "and we'll reconvene in one hour for opening statements. And counsel, please be brief. No longer than half an hour, or the bailiff will ask you to step down. After all, it's been a long day."

* 45 *

When the court reconvened after lunch, Bullock jumped to his feet and strode confidently to the jury box, like Babe Ruth approaching the plate. Strong, commanding, self-assured. He leaned across the railing that separated the attorneys from the jury, getting closer to them than Ben would've thought possible, much less desirable.

Bullock made eye contact with each of the jurors in turn. His head was nodding subtly, and his smile bore the mark of one who knew the truth and was confident they would believe him. In his own way, Bullock was enlisting their support, engaging their confidence, before he had spoken a word.

"No tricks," Bullock said, and then nothing. He let his words resonate and linger till the courtroom was once again awash in silence. A skillful ploy. In a matter of moments the stultifying banality of jury selection was washed away. They were mesmerized, eagerly anticipating his next word.

"No tricks," Bullock repeated. "Well, not from me, anyway. I don't need them, and I wouldn't use them if I did. Now the gentleman on the other side"—he jerked his head in Ben's direction—"that's another matter. I've seen him resort to all sorts of shenanigans. He'll make you laugh, he'll make you cry. He'll play on your emotions, your sympathy. He'll break the rules. He'll do whatever it takes to accomplish his goal. Which is to thwart justice, and put his man back on the streets."

"Objection!" With great trepidation, Ben violated one of the traditional courtesies of trial practice: no objections during opening statement. But this was too much—this wasn't a preview of the evidence; it was a personal attack.

"Your honor, this is not relevant, and furthermore, it's grossly prejudicial."

The judge nodded. "Sustained."

Bullock smiled. He leaned even closer to the jury and whispered. "See?"

That underhanded son of a— In a matter of moments, Bullock had set the stage, casting Ben as the shyster trickster, someone who obviously was trying to hide the truth—because he objected to Bullock's improper tactics. This put Ben in an impossible position. If he made future objections, the jury would suspect he was trying to pull some underhanded trick. If he didn't object, Bullock would walk all over him. And Leeman.

"Here's what happened," Bullock continued. "No embroidering, no huffing or puffing, no dramatic flourishes. Just the facts." He paused again, then lowered his voice. "Ten years ago, on a hot August night, a female immigrant named Maria Alvarez was killed in the caddyshack at the Utica Greens Country Club. 'How was she killed?' you may ask. With a golf club. And how could a golf club become a deadly weapon?"

Bullock held them in suspense for a protracted moment. "Someone brought it down on her head, at least once, maybe several times. The last blow broke the club in two. Then the assailant took the broken shaft"—he leaned in closer, acting it out—"and rammed it through her throat."

He pivoted and walked away from the jury while continuing to talk. "Shoved it clean through her neck. Came out the other side. Pinned her against the wall." He rubbed his hands together as if washing them clean. "Needless to say, she died."

He placed one hand on the defendant's table and leaned in to face Leeman Hayes. He was forcing the jury to look at the defendant as they listened to the description of this grisly event. Forcing them to make a connection between the defendant and the crime.

"There's no dispute about anything you've heard so far. They're all facts, all a matter of record. There's actually only one question remaining unanswered: Who killed her?"

He walked around the far end of the defendant's table, doing a little dance around Leeman. "The prosecution has a good deal of evidence that will help you answer that question. Frankly, I've been prosecuting for years, and this is the strongest case I've ever seen."

"Obj—" No. Ben clamped his lips together and sat back down. This personal testimonial about the weight of the evidence was grossly improper, but he feared the prejudice created by another objection would be the greater evil.

"A police officer found Leeman Hayes, the defendant, at the scene of the crime, not long after the woman was killed. The defendant was a caddy at the country club. You might think it perfectly natural for a caddy to be at the caddyshack—until I tell you that the murder took place after midnight on a Tuesday morning. None of the other caddies were there at that time of night. Only the defendant."

An ironic half smile played upon his lips. "You know, normally when I talk about the defendant having blood on his hands, I'm speaking metaphorically. Not this time. This time it's the literal truth. When Leeman Hayes was apprehended, he had blood on his hands. Caked under his fingernails. Smeared on his face. And the forensic testimony in this courtroom will verify that it was the blood of Maria Alvarez.

" 'What other evidence is there?' you might ask, as if any more was really required. Well, the golf bag from which the murder weapon was taken was found in the defendant's locker; it had been stolen that day from the club pro shop. In that locker we also found jewelry belonging to the murdered woman. But the best evidence of all, I would have to say"—he held them near breathless in anticipation—"is the defendant's confession."

Several of the jurors' heads rose. They looked back at Leeman, and this time their expressions were more exacting, more suspicious. A confession, after all, changed everything.

"Objection!" Ben rose to his feet. He couldn't let this one go by, no matter what prejudice might arise. "I object to counsel's characterization of the wordless videotape reenactment as a confession. That is a question of fact to be determined by the jury—"

"The prosecutor is permitted to describe the evidence he will present, isn't he?" Judge Hawkins frowned. "They haven't changed the rules while I was eating lunch, have they?"

The jury tittered.

"Your honor, opening statement is not supposed to be argumentative. He's prejudicing the jury's interpretation of the evidence before they've even had an opportunity to see it!"

"Objection is overruled. Please continue, Mr. Prosecutor. And I instruct the bailiff to add five minutes to the prosecutor's time to compensate for this outburst."

Gritting his teeth, Ben retook his seat.

"Now, as some of you may have guessed from the questions I asked earlier," Bullock continued, "Leeman Hayes is considered to suffer from some mental retardation." He jerked his thumb back at Ben. "At least, that's what the defense's paid witnesses will say. Our docs say he's capable of distinguishing right from wrong. It is true that his language skills are not very advanced. But as you will see, he confessed nonetheless, and his confession was recorded on videotape."

Bullock waved his hands. "I'm sure defense counsel will try everything he can think of to keep you from seeing the tape, or he'll try to suggest that the confession isn't what any fool can see it is. Don't be tricked. You're smart people. You can see the truth for yourselves. And once you witness the defendant's confession, how can there be any doubt about what happened that hot August night?"

Slowly, Bullock returned to the jury box. "I wish I could tell you why Leeman Hayes murdered that woman, but I can't. Not with certainty. Maybe it was robbery—he did take her jewelry. Maybe it was a sudden fit of frenzy. Or maybe it was something . . . sexual. . . ." He pronounced the word as if it had eight syllables. "We've all heard . . . stories about men with Leeman's condition and their . . . appetites. . . ."

Ben was clenching his fists so tightly he almost drew blood. This was beyond the pale.

"But the truth is, I don't really know. I do know that for whatever reason, Leeman Hayes did kill her. Fortunately, the state does not require you to determine a motive. It's nice, it makes for a good story, but it's not required. All you have to determine is whether the defendant killed the woman."

Bullock leaned over the rail. "And I'm confident that by the end of this trial you will be convinced, as I am, that he did kill Maria Alvarez. In cold blood. In the most grisly fashion imaginable."

Bullock slowly drew away from the jury box. "I have every confidence that you will do the right thing, that you will find Leeman Hayes guilty as charged, and assess the maximum sentence for this heinous deed. Thank you."

The judge waited until Bullock was seated, giving him a nice dramatic close to his oration. "Mr. Kincaid, would you care to—"

"Yes." Ben walked around the table and approached the jury. He wanted to get at them while Bullock's words were still ringing in their ears.

"Actually, ladies and gentlemen of the jury, trying to determine what you personally think occurred ten years ago in the Utica Greens caddyshack is not, as Mr. Bullock says, 'all you have to do.' As the judge will later instruct you, forming a mere opinion as to guilt or innocence is not your job. Your job is infinitely more difficult. You must determine whether the prosecution has proven beyond a reasonable doubt that the defendant is guilty of murder. The burden of proof is entirely on them. If they do not prove his guilt beyond a reasonable doubt, you have no choice. Regardless of what your personal suspicions may be, if the prosecution does not meet this high standard, you must find Leeman Hayes not guilty."

Ben took a deep breath. He hoped it sank in, and that when they heard it later from the judge, they would understand what it meant.

"There are two kinds of evidence," Ben continued. "There's what we call real evidence, and there's circumstantial evidence. All of the evidence the prosecution will present today is circumstantial evidence. No one saw Leeman do it, no one heard him do it. They're all guessing, just guessing, based upon alleged evidence discovered after the fact.

"Moreover, none of this evidence excludes other suspects.

In other words, the prosecution's evidence, at best, shows that Leeman Hayes *could* have killed Maria Alvarez. It does not prove that he did. Remember, in order to convict this man, the prosecution must prove that he did in fact commit the murder. Beyond a reasonable doubt. No lingering suspicions, no nagging questions. Nothing. No reasonable doubt."

No objection? Ben wondered. To his detailed, not to mention argumentative, elucidation of the phrase *beyond a reasonable doubt*? Bullock must've decided he wasn't going to make any objections for a while, to prove to the jury that Ben was the only one trying to hide anything from them.

"After the prosecution completes its evidence, assuming the judge doesn't throw the case out of court"—Ben almost laughed himself; wishful thinking—"then we will have a chance to put on our evidence. Let me assure you we don't plan any tricks or shenanigans. We're just going to help you understand what transpired that night ten years ago."

Ben wished he could be more specific about the evidence they would put on, but the truth of the matter was, he still didn't know. So far, they had no strong affirmative defense. All he could do was impeach the prosecution's evidence, and hope that Loving came up with a witness or Jones discovered something of value in the Peruvian records.

"It's true, as the evidence will show, that Leeman has been repeatedly diagnosed, since birth, as mentally retarded. It is also true that it is very difficult for him to communicate. He will not take the stand in this trial, not because he has anything to hide, but because it would simply be impossible for him to answer the questions. Imagine, if you will, how vulnerable that makes him. Imagine how easily he could be manipulated by policemen, lawyers. Imagine how difficult it would be to defend himself against those determined to see him pay for a crime he didn't commit."

"Objection," Bullock said. "This is argumentative."

"Sustained. Be careful, counsel."

Believe me, Ben thought, I was. I carefully made sure Bullock would have to object so the jury could see I'm not the only trickster in the courtroom.

"All I ask is that you be fair. It's true, my client Leeman has some special problems. He has lived with those all his life. But we're not asking for sympathy, and we're not asking for any special favors. All we're asking is that you be fair. To everyone. And that you remember those all-important words—*beyond a reasonable doubt.* Thank you very much."

Ben took his seat. He glanced at Leeman. His eyes were focused on Ben, watching, considering.

"Well, it's late," the judge said. "Let's call it a day. We'll start tomorrow at nine with the prosecution's first witness. The jury is cautioned not to discuss the case with anyone"—he glanced out into the gallery—"including the press. Court is adjourned."

The sheriff's men escorted Leeman back into custody. Even before the judge was out of the courtroom, Ben found minicams and microphones shoved in his face.

"Mr. Kincaid, what's your reaction to the prosecution's claim that they have a videotaped confession?"

"It isn't true," Ben replied.

"And what about the blood on his hands?"

"That's not conclusive—"

"And the jewelry? What about the jewel—"

Ben pushed the reporters out of his face. "Look, let's let the case be tried in the courtroom, and you guys figure out some other way to beat *Wheel of Fortune* in the ratings, okay?"

Idiot, he muttered to himself as he plowed through the mob. Now he would undoubtedly be painted as the obstructionist in the evening-news reports. Ben wanted to kick himself. Reporters could be so annoying, it was easy to forget how easily they could manipulate public opinion.

Ben saw Christina waving to him from the back. She had a getaway car waiting, thank goodness. The sooner they were out of this madhouse, the better.

* 46 *

From the courthouse, Ben sprinted over to police headquarters, Central Division. After asking a few questions at the front desk, he learned that Mike was on the third floor. In the interrogation chambers. Still.

Since the witness was a friendly one, Ben wondered why Mike was using the formal interrogation room. He soon had his answer.

Abie's parents were in the observation room, watching everything through an acrylic one-way mirror. Mike had undoubtedly insisted on isolating the boy from his parents during the questioning, and the Rutherfords undoubtedly insisted on not letting the boy out of their sight. And this was undoubtedly the compromise.

"How's it going?" Ben asked Rutherford as he entered the observation room.

Rutherford nodded a polite greeting. Ben could tell he was torn. He didn't like Ben, and he didn't want him to be here, but it was difficult to be too rude to one of the men who had just rescued your son.

Rachel Rutherford was standing close to the mirror, her hands pressed against the acrylic. She was as close to her son as the room would permit.

"Any luck?" Ben asked her.

Rachel shook her head. "Very little. But I don't think Abie's holding anything back."

"I'm sure he wouldn't intentionally prevaricate," Ben said, "but after such a traumatic experience, witnesses typically have a hard time recalling details. That's with adults. With a child, separated from his parents and scared to death, the psychological prohibitions multiply. Has Mike suggested hypnosis?"

"He did," Rutherford said. "We forbade it."

No great surprise there. According to Mike, Rutherford had been nothing but an obstacle since they recovered Abie. Rutherford was guilt-ridden, afraid that his own inattentiveness and insensitivity had driven his son into the arms of a child molester. Now he was overcompensating, becoming so protective that he interfered with the police's efforts to track the maniac down.

Ben turned back toward Rachel. "Has the sketch artist been in?"

"Oh . . . yes . . ." She gestured unhappily toward a charcoal sketch on the conference table in the center of the room.

Ben picked up the sketch and scrutinized it. The only salient features that emerged were a full and flowing head of red hair, which was almost certainly a wig, and thick black glasses, which were also probably part of the disguise. The rest of the sketch was utterly undistinguished. It could be anyone. It was useless.

"What about the car?" Ben asked.

"Registered under a false name. Seems he renewed the driver's license of a teenage boy who died six years ago. There's nothing to trace."

Another dead end. The pervert seemed to have thought of everything.

Ben watched as Mike asked a few more questions. Abie seemed distant, unfocused, tired. He wasn't saying much.

Mike called a break. Abie tried to leave the room with him, but Mike ordered him to stay put. Abie reluctantly agreed.

Mike stepped outside. Ben entered the hallway and met him.

"How's the kid holding up?" Ben asked.

"The kid is fine," Mike said, rubbing his hands together. "I, on the other hand, am a nervous wreck."

"Been with him all day?"

"Off and on. When the shrinks didn't have him."

"What's their verdict?"

"They think he's doing remarkably well. They want him to remain under observation and in therapy for a while, but he seems amazingly resilient. No incurable traumatization."

"So what's the problem?"

"The problem is that Abie's just a boy. Kids don't really notice what grown-ups look like. After all, adult faces are two or three feet away, up in the sky. Add the fact that this creep was wearing a disguise, and you have a witness who will never give us a definitive ID. We're going to have to find him on our own."

"What about that hellhole we found with the mattress and the camera?"

"We've torn the place apart, examined everything. The mattress, the camera equipment, every scrap of paper, and every piece of lint. Nothing we can trace."

"Did the creep take the kid anywhere else?"

"That's where Abie's testimony gets really hairy. I think he did, but I can't get anything concrete out of the kid's descriptions. He had already been drugged by the time they left Celebration Station. He was weaving in and out of a thick fog the rest of the day. And needless to say, the creep didn't leave a trail of bread crumbs for us. We're damn lucky Abie thought to drop that blue book bag."

"Abie's damn lucky you saw it. And came to his rescue."

"And what a two-edged sword that's turned out to be!" Mike suddenly exclaimed.

"How do you mean?"

"I mean, the kid's been hanging all over me. Keeps talking about how I'm his hero, and I'm such a great guy, and when he grows up he wants to be just like me!"

"You don't like being promoted to local hero?"

"Not when it means I have a ten-year-old for a groupie! It's embarrassing!"

"Doesn't fit the tough-guy image, huh?"

"I can't get away from him for five minutes! He says he doesn't feel safe without me. He says he wants me with him all day long."

"Surely he'll get police protection until this sicko is caught."

"Natch. But get this—Rutherford pulled a few strings with a country-club buddy. Chief of Police Blackwell, to be specific."

Ben nodded. He'd had the pleasure of meeting Chief Blackwell. Except it was no pleasure.

"Blackwell has assigned me to be the kid's bodyguard! Can you imagine? *Me!* An experienced professional homicide detective! Reduced to being some kid's baby-sitter."

"A fate worse than death," Ben said sympathetically. "Sounds like you better catch this perp."

"Believe me, I'm trying."

"How are the kid's parents?"

"A royal pain in the buttinsky, that's how."

"Care to be more specific?"

Mike shrugged. "It's always this way with these rich types. They don't want anything to do with the police. Our work is dirty. It's beneath them. They treat us like servants, like the people they pay to take out the trash. And they're scared to death of bad publicity. They'd rather let a pervert roam the streets indefinitely than risk getting their name in the paper." Mike glanced at his watch. "I'd better go back in. If I'm separated from the kid much longer, he'll come out and attach himself to my sleeve."

Ben returned to the observation room. He saw Mike reenter the interrogation room where Abie was waiting patiently.

"Lieutenant Morelli!" Abie cried, in his high-pitched chirp. He threw his arms around Mike and hugged him like a long-lost brother. Mike looked as if he were going to die.

"Looks like Abie has really taken a shine to Lieutenant Morelli," Ben commented.

"Yes, hasn't he?" Rutherford said dryly. "He never greets me like that."

"Perhaps that's because Lieutenant Morelli didn't wait until he'd completed another nine holes before coming to his rescue," Rachel said icily.

Rutherford glared at her, fuming.

Ben turned toward the mirror and pretended he hadn't heard.

"All right," Mike said to Abie. "Tell me again about the walk from Sam's apartment to the mattress room."

"I don't 'member much," Abie said unhappily. It was apparent that he wanted nothing more than to please his hero by providing useful answers. He simply had none to give.

"Can you describe the building the apartment was in?"

"I think it was white. Or sort of grayish."

"Made of?"

"Brick. Oh, wait. Maybe wood."

"Was it an apartment complex or a boardinghouse?"

"I think it was—oh—jeez, Lieutenant. I dunno."

Mike cast his eyes heavenward. This was getting them nowhere. "Can you tell me anything about the building?"

Abie thought hard. "There were some little men outside."

Mike blinked. "Little men?"

"Uh-huh."

"You mean, children?"

"No, little *men*."

"Midgets?"

Abie squirmed. "More like trolls."

"Trolls?"

"Yeah." Abie leaned forward. "I got this book at home by Maurice Sendak, and it has the coolest-looking trolls."

"And these . . . trolls . . . they were outside the building?"

"Right. In the garden, I think."

"The garden? What kind of garden?"

"Oh, I don't know. I just saw the trolls."

Right. Trolls. Mike made a notation in his notebook. "Describe the route you took when you left the apartment."

Abie shrugged. "It's real hard to remember. He was like dragging me the whole time, and I couldn't see much. Everything was kinda fuzzy, you know?"

"Do the best you can."

"Well, first he dragged me past the trolls. . . ."

Mike gritted his teeth. "Yes, yes. Something other than the trolls, please."

"Well, I remember I looked at the ground for a long time, 'cause I was afraid if he saw my face he might—I don't know—he might do something to me. Then we walked into this real dark narrow place. And then I saw all the yellow numbers."

"Yellow numbers?"

"Yeah. Well, doors with numbers on yellow . . ."

Mike's mouth hung open for several moments. "Yellow—what?"

The strain showed in Abie's face. "I don't know. I was so afraid, and I was trying not to look up—"

"It's okay, Abie. It's okay." Mike patted the boy on the back. "Tell me what else you recall."

"Well, we walked by all the numbers and then we walked through a wall."

"Wait a minute. Walked through a *wall*?"

Abie looked as if he might burst out crying at any moment. "Uh-huh," he whispered.

"Okay, okay. And what did you see when you walked through the wall?"

"Airplanes."

"Airplanes? Toy airplanes? Radio-controlled airplanes?"

"No. Real airplanes."

"What were they doing?"

Abie looked at Mike as if he had suddenly dropped about five hundred IQ points in the boy's estimation. "They were flying, of course."

Mike pressed his hand against his forehead and paced around the perimeter of the small room. Ben knew what he must be thinking. The drug in Abie's system had had a more profound effect than they realized. His descriptions just didn't make sense.

"Do you remember anything else?" Mike asked.

"We walked for a long time after that."

"What direction?"

"Uh . . . I'm not sure."

"Was the sun in front of you or behind you?"

Abie thought for a moment. "I don't remember."

"Okay. How long did you walk?"

"Gosh, I dunno. A long time."

"Half an hour?"

"Yeah, maybe."

"More? Less?"

Abie bit down on his lower lip. "About half an hour, I think."

Well, that's something useful, Ben thought. Maybe. He knew that the time estimates of adults separated from their wristwatches were often wildly inaccurate. An estimate made by a kid in a high-stress situation after being drugged was even more suspect.

"What's the next thing you remember seeing, Abie?"

"We went inside another building and walked up those rickety stairs. Then we came to the room where he kept the mattress and the camera." Abie smiled proudly. "Boy, I really smashed up one of his cameras but good, didn't I?"

"Yeah, kid. You did a real number on it." Mike put on a brave smile, but Ben found it patently unconvincing. Truth was, it would be virtually impossible to find the apartment where the creep first took Abie based on this information.

And there was another truth, one even more unsettling and inescapable. In this pervert's long and checkered history, none of his victims had ever gotten away before. Abie was the only person alive who could possibly identify him. He hadn't—but the creep didn't know that.

They could hope that he would forget about Abie, would consider him too high a risk to approach now. But no one really believed that. It didn't fit the profile. Child molesters were obsessive to the extreme. Once they fixed on a particular child, they stayed fixed.

As long as Sam was a free man, Abie wasn't safe. Sam would be doing everything he could to find Abie.

And kill him.

* 47 *

When Ben returned to his boardinghouse that evening, he scurried past Mrs. Marmelstein's room at the foot of the stairs. Fond of her as he was, he had no time for a discussion of who turned off the water or why the electric company expected to be paid on time. He was beat, and he needed to spend at least four or five hours preparing for the next day's trial.

Joni was sitting in her usual spot in the middle of the stairs playing an incomprehensible card game. Jacks went atop kings, hearts went atop diamonds. He couldn't detect any pattern at all.

"What is this game you're playing, anyway?" Ben asked.

She continued to lay down the cards. "It's called E.R.S."

"Does that stand for something?"

"What a profound insight."

"What does it stand for?"

She placed the queen of hearts on the four of clubs. "Not telling."

"Can I guess?"

"I suppose," she said, terribly bored.

"Equal Rights Solitaire."

"*Hard*-ly."

"Emergency Room Standoff."

"Oh, Ben, you're so pedestrian. Like Ward Cleaver or something."

"I give up. What does it stand for?"

She lifted her hand as if to brush her hair back, then stopped, remembering that her hair no longer reached her shoulders. "I think it's best that you don't know."

Ben sat down on the stairs beside her. "Mind if we talk about your boyfriend for a moment?"

She blanched. "You didn't tell my parents . . . !"

"No, no. But I need to talk to him. Do you think you could arrange it?"

"Whaddaya wanna talk with him for?"

"Well . . . I think he's connected with some gentlemen I saw at the country club the other day."

Joni laughed. "My Booker's never been inside a country club in his life."

"I didn't say he was. But I did see some of his, uh, clubmates there."

Joni's face darkened. "What are you talking about?"

"I'm talking about his gang. The Demons."

Joni scooped up her cards. "You don't know what you're talking about."

Ben took her arm. "I think I do. I saw him a few days ago at the home of my client. And he was wearing a black jacket embroidered with the gang emblem. A swastika with a heart around it. My cop friend tells me that identifies him as a member of the Demons gang, a hot number on the North Side."

Joni folded her arms across her chest, but remained sullenly silent.

"My friend believes the Demons are breaking into drug peddling, challenging the Cobras' turf. He thinks they're selling the hard stuff, the junk that comes in from across the border."

Joni glared at him. "All this time Jami has said, 'Don't be telling your secrets to our Benjamin. He's just a cop, basically.' And I always say, 'It ain't so. Ben is good people.' " Joni's lips pursed. "But I guess Jami was right."

"Look, Joni, I'm not trying to get you or Booker into any trouble. He did that for himself when he joined the gang. But if you'll let me talk to him, I may be able to help him before he spends the next ten years making license plates at McAlester."

Joni eyed him suspiciously. "And what's in it for you?"

"He may have some information that could help my client. Like I said, I just want to talk to him. You pick the place."

"How do I know I can trust you?"

"Come on, you know me better than that. Have I ever lied to you? Have I told anyone about you and Booker? Have I told Jami you wore her Paloma Picasso earrings to the Blue Rose and lost them?"

"How did you—?"

"I'm very observant. Come on, Joni. What do you say?"

Joni stared at him for a good long time, then slid her playing cards back into the box. "No promises." She stood, then climbed up the stairs to her apartment.

When Ben walked through the door of his apartment, the first thing he saw was Christina sitting in an armchair rocking Joey. Joey's tiny eyelids were closed. He appeared to be fast asleep.

"Ssshh," Christina whispered. "He's sleeping."

"Ah. Thanks for the tip." Ben gently dropped his briefcase and sat on the floor beside Christina. "This is a surprise. I didn't expect to find you here."

Christina placed her finger under the collar of Joey's bright green pajamas and unfolded a crease. "Oh well . . . I thought you might need help preparing for court tomorrow."

Ben nodded. "Which doesn't really explain why you're looking after the baby. Something that, as I recall, you complained mightily about when I asked you to do it."

"Well, your mother wanted to fix you a nice dinner—"

"My mom is cooking? Again?"

"—and someone had to look after the kid, so . . ." She shrugged. "It's a burden, but I'm bearing it bravely."

Ben glanced at the contented baby in her arms. "You're hiding your misery admirably."

"Well . . . he's been pretty good tonight. I think we're coming to understand one another."

"Splendid." Ben pushed himself to his feet.

"Ben?"

He turned. "Yes?"

"What are you going to do about your mother?"

Ben frowned. "What do you mean?"

"I mean you have to decide what you're going to do. She can't live here in your apartment forever."

"I rather assumed she would be heading home soon. . . ."

"With the baby, right?"

"Well . . ." Ben squirmed.

"I thought so. That's exactly what you're hoping she'll do."

"It shouldn't be for very long. Jones is still searching for Julia. For all we know, she could come back for Joey tomorrow."

"Ben, you're not being realistic. Julia has no intention of returning anytime soon. If she did, she wouldn't have left him in the first place."

"Well, what do you want me to do about it?" Ben threw his hands into the air. "Christina, I can't raise a baby! I don't know the first thing about it."

"You're just making excuses."

"My mother is infinitely better qualified to raise children than I am."

"Julia left him with you, not your mother."

"Only because she wasn't home."

"You don't know that for a fact."

"It makes more sense for Mother to do it. She's had experience."

Christina's eyes seemed to catch fire. "Ben, your mother is sixty-six years old."

"So?"

"So that's no time to be taking on a major responsibility like a baby. She should be relaxing, taking life easy."

"She'll hire help."

"Oh, that's a great attitude. Let the servants do it." She muttered under her breath. "You're no better than those country-club slobs you keep putting down."

"That's hardly fair."

"That's the truth."

"Christina, you're being irrational."

"Ben, when are you going to stop avoiding every family obligation? Are you planning to go through your whole life without being responsible for anyone?"

Ben tried to answer, but he was too slow. Christina took the still-sleeping baby and marched out of the room.

Reluctantly, Ben entered the kitchen. He found his mother facing the stove, poking a wooden fork into a frying pan. She was wearing an elegant pleated skirt, a silk blouse, and an Oriental jacket. And over it, she had draped Ben's apron, which announced in big black letters LAWYERS DO IT IN THEIR BRIEFS.

"It was a gift from Christina," he blurted out.

Mrs. Kincaid turned and stared at him oddly. "This fork?"

"No, the—never mind. What are you doing?"

She smiled. "Fixing your dinner."

"Again? What is it?"

"Well . . . I'm not entirely sure yet. Chicken and something. I'm a bit rusty on my recipes, you know."

"I still can't believe you can cook!"

Mrs. Kincaid breathed heavily. "I always told your father we should take more pictures. Maybe even movies. 'Little boys don't remember,' I told him. But he said, 'Nonsense. A boy always remembers his mommy and daddy.' " She shook her head sadly. "I was right."

She fumbled for a moment in the pocket of the apron. "I've been carrying a picture around in my purse. I thought you might be interested."

Ben took the small black-and-white photo from her. The man in the forefront was Ben's father, although he was much younger than Ben ever recalled seeing him before. He was leaning over a little boy, tickling him.

A little boy with light brown hair and a thinnish face.

The boy was laughing hysterically, and gazing up at the man with loving eyes.

Ben's eyes.

Ben shoved the picture in his pocket. "You didn't need to cook dinner—"

"I wanted to do it. I used to be a wonderful cook. People raved about my food. Why do you think the relatives always came to our house on Thanksgiving?"

"I rather suspected they hoped to be included in the will. . . ."

Mrs. Kincaid ignored him. "We didn't hire Rhiana until you were almost eight, when we needed more help, mostly with you, because you kept sneaking out of the house and going to the library or whatever when you were supposed to be doing your chores. But Rhiana was a splendid cook and it was easier to just let her do it."

She smiled, then returned her attention to the frying pan. "That's why I'm enjoying my stay at your place so much. I have to admit, I was planning to just take the baby and leave, but I'm having such a good time I've decided to stay."

"Do tell," Ben murmured.

"It's just like life was for your father and me, back before he'd had a lick of success. Very primitive. And very fun."

Ben stared blankly at her, trying to reorder reality in his brain. "Well, I need to prepare for trial. . . ."

"Of course."

"I probably won't eat much."

"Of course."

"Actually, I may play the piano a little while, just to—"

"To help you focus. Of course."

Ben drew in his breath. "Mother, why do you keep saying *of course*? Am I so predictable?"

She smiled again, and patted his cheek. "You're not predictable, Benjamin. But you're just like your daddy."

Ben's face twisted up in a knot. "You must be kidding! Me? Like my *father*?"

"He would work all night sometimes when he was preparing for a test or, later, a big operation or a new procedure. He wouldn't eat much, because his mind was focused on his work. He'd listen to Herb Alpert albums to block out distractions and help him concentrate. Personally, I hated that insipid trumpet music, but it seemed to make him happy."

"But—I'm not anything like my father!" Ben protested. "I—I hate trumpet music."

"Whatever you say, dear." She resumed her tossing and stirring.

Ben left the kitchen. Christina wasn't in the living room; just as well, probably. He sat down at the piano and picked out the first few notes of "Venus Kissed the Moon," one of his favorite Christine Lavin songs. It was a beautiful tune, but he was tired, and there were too many random thoughts vying for his attention. He grabbed his briefcase and headed toward his bedroom.

He entered the darkened room and flipped on the overhead light. He started to fling himself onto the bed—then screamed.

Christina rushed into the room. "What? What happened?"

"On the bed." Ben pointed, grimacing. "A dead animal!"

"What, someone put a horse's head in your bed? This case is nastier than I realized." Together, they gazed down at the covers. And saw the tiny carcass of a dead mouse.

"Oh, yuck," Christina said succinctly.

"Double yuck," Ben echoed.

"Giselle?"

"Well, I hardly think it was my mother!"

Christina backed out of the doorway. "What are you going to do with it?"

"I suppose I'll clean it up." He sighed. "What a shock. Now I'll probably never get to sleep."

Christina patted him on the shoulder. "There, there, Ben. Just get rid of the carcass. Then I'll come sing you the Flintstones song and rock you to sleep."

Ben did not smile.

* 48 *

Carlee Crane sat upright in bed eating Blue Bell Rocky Road ice cream. She was making a mess of it, getting it on her hands and the sheets. She didn't care. She wanted ice cream. She needed ice cream. That's what she kept telling herself, anyway.

As she ate, her husband Dave entered their bedroom. She watched him undress for his shower. The camping trip had done him good; he'd picked up some sun, and he looked as if he'd dropped a few pounds. Not that he needed to.

She watched silently as he dried himself off, then put on the blue pajamas he almost never wore and crawled into bed beside her.

They had not spoken all evening.

There had been no fight, nor any need for one. Ever since the camping trip, something had been . . . different. Their relationship was strained in a way it never had been before.

It wasn't that Dave resented what had happened to her, or what she was going through. He didn't know what to do; he didn't know how to respond. He was lost. She was certain he still wanted to be a good husband. He just didn't know how.

And so he remained silent. Once or twice she had tried to raise the issue, had tried to get him to talk, but each time he ignored her, or glared at her with that "not in front of the kids" expression of his. Now that the boys were in bed, it seemed too late, too far gone.

Too much damage done.

301

Well, hell. She wasn't giving up that easily. She put away her ice cream. He was facing away from her, curled up in a ball, safely tucked away in his blue pajamas.

"Dave?"

He made a muffled *mmmm* noise.

"That trial began today."

Silence. No *mmmm*, no nothing.

"The trial of that black man. Leeman Hayes. The one who's accused of killing that foreign woman ten years ago."

"I know," he said, without turning around.

"A man who works for the defense attorney came to the house and asked me if I knew anything about the murder. He said they needed witnesses for the trial in the worst way. And now the trial has started and according to the news they still don't have any witnesses."

"You shouldn't watch the TV news," Dave said evenly. His voice seemed distant and muffled. "It just upsets you."

"Dave, I'm almost certain that poor man didn't kill that woman." She paused. "Forget the almost. I know he didn't do it."

"Then who did?"

"I don't know. But I know the killer was taller, and older. And he wasn't black."

"And you acquired this sensational knowledge from a vision you had while we were camping in the mystical Arbuckle Mountains?"

"It wasn't a vision, Dave." She leaned over his shoulder. "It was a memory."

"A memory that you totally forgot about until now."

"I realize that must seem strange to you. It seems strange to me, too. I can't explain it. But that's what happened. I saw what I saw."

"How could you have seen the murder?"

"You know I used to work at that country club. I must've been working late one night . . . yes, I'm sure that's it. I was working late. I was working overtime, cleaning the kitchen after it closed down at eleven. My creepo boss kept saying he'd promote me to waitress if I put in enough overtime. I was so poor back then, I would've done almost anything for a little extra cash. I walked home from work, because I didn't have a car. I was crossing the grounds on my way home that night, and I heard this scream and I ran to the window and . . . and . . . that's when I saw it."

"What did you do afterward?"

"I—I just don't know." She shook her head violently, as if trying to dislodge the memory trapped up there somewhere. "That's still a total blank. I remember thinking I had to tell someone, I had to report this. . . ."

"But you didn't. Right?"

"I'm . . . not sure."

"Did you talk to the police?"

Carlee's head tilted slightly. "I . . . don't think so."

"Great." Dave pounded his fist into the pillow. "What's the first thing you do recall?"

She shook her head. "I recall being at home afterward. I guess I went on as if nothing had ever happened. I—I didn't remember it."

"Carlee . . . that's ridiculous."

"It is not."

"It is. Think about what you're saying. 'I saw a murder but it slipped my mind.' That's absurd."

"Dave . . ." Her eyes turned away. "I think I should contact that attorney. I think I should offer to testify."

"No."

Carlee leaned away, literally taken aback. Dave was a peacemaker, a compromiser. She didn't recall a flat-out *no* from him in their entire married lives. Until now.

"Dave, I think I have an obligation."

"To do what?" He rolled over and grabbed her wrist. "To make a fool of yourself? To turn this family into a laughingstock?"

"Dave—"

"And what about the children? Have you thought about them?"

"I don't see how this affects—"

"Children talk, Carlee. If you testify, especially if you testify that you saw a murder but then forgot, you're going to be all over the papers. All over the TV. And everyone's going to be laughing at you. The kids at school will pick it up. You know how cruel children can be. 'My mother says your mother is nuts.' 'My daddy says they should lock your mama up and throw away the key.' 'Where's your dad, Gavin? Maybe your mom killed him and forgot about it.' "

"Dave, our boys are strong and smart. They can handle a little—"

"And what about me, Carlee?"

"I—don't—"

"What about *me*? Will you think about that for just one minute? What's this going to look like at the office? Is Hannigan going to continue to let me work with his star clients after you've been ridiculed on the evening news?"

Carlee didn't know what to say. This was a reaction she hadn't anticipated, would never have dreamed possible. . . .

"Dave," she said finally, "I can't just button my lip and let them give that man the death penalty if I can help him."

"I agree. But believe me, your testimony isn't going to help him. In fact, it might hurt. They'll think his lawyer put you up to it. They'll think he's so desperate he'll try anything."

Carlee held her tongue. That was a possibility she hadn't considered.

"Believe me, you'll do more good for that man if you just stay quiet. And I know it will be better for your family." He reached out and turned out the lamp.

Their bedroom went dark. Carlee sat up for a long time, long after they were both quiet, long after she heard the soft, steady snoring of her husband.

All she wanted to do was what was right. But what was right? It was so hard to know anymore. What was right? What was real? What was true?

What should she do?

Eventually she laid her head upon her pillow and prayed for

sleep. She prayed that dreams would come and take her away from all this confusion, all this uncertainty, all this indecision brought on by the curse of memory.

But that night her prayers were not answered.

* 49 *

On his way to the back of the house, Royce spotted two little statues embedded in the garden. He'd never noticed them before.

He crouched down and took a closer look. They were dwarfs, cute little guys with picks and shovels, like in that movie he saw when he was a kid. Which ones were they? Dopey? Sneezy? Sleazy?

He laughed. If these guys were perched outside this place, he was betting on Sleazy.

Royce's friend was waiting for him when he arrived.

"Where have you been? I told you I wanted you back before dark. Have you been to the police?"

"Relax, already. I'm your friend, remember? Didn't I get you out of those cuffs?"

Yes, his friend thought. And I probably should've wrapped them around your worthless throat right then and there. "What did you learn?" he asked, eyes narrowed. Without the fake glasses, the natural coal gray of his eyes shone through with even greater penetration.

"You're safe," Royce said calmly. "At least for now."

"And the boy?"

"Well, that's another matter. He's under police protection. He's got a bodyguard assigned to him day and night. You're not going to be able to get anywhere near him."

The other man paced slowly around the sofa. "For how long?"

Royce glanced up from the magazine. "I don't get ya."

"How long will he be under police protection? They can't baby-sit the little bastard forever."

"Huh. That I don't know."

"How much did he talk?"

"From what I gathered, he said pretty much everything he knew. Fortunately, that was practically zippo. Like I said, you're safe."

"They can't identify me?"

"If they could, do you think I'd be at your place having this conversation?"

"What will the police do now?"

Royce's expression became a bit more somber. "Well, my buddy on the force isn't privy to all the top-level discussions. But my general impression is that they've got a lot of man-power searching for this apartment."

"Damn!" The man pounded his fist down on the glass table-top. The glass bowed and shuddered but, to Royce's relief, did not quite break. Control, he told himself. Control. "You will check in with your police contact every day, understand?"

"Sure."

"I want to know everything. Absolutely everything. At the least sign of danger, I want to be informed immediately."

"Sure, sure, sure. But I don't see what you're getting so upset about. So what if they do find your apartment? They can't prove it was you."

"You idiot!" Again the fist went down on the glass. "They have the boy."

"So?"

"The boy can identify me. That's what they're counting on. He may not be able to find me, but once they do, they can use the boy to lock me away for a good long time. Maybe forever."

"Huh. I guess I hadn't thought about it like that."

The man approached Royce, laying his hand gently on Royce's head. "And you don't want that to happen, do you, Royce?"

"Of course not."

"You know, if the police arrest me, they're going to ask how

I became so attached to little Abie. I might have to tell them about you."

"Hey, now wait a minute. I didn't tell you what to do."

"They won't see it that way. They'll see you as an accomplice. A pimp."

Royce frowned. "Fine. What do you want me to do?"

The man's hand suddenly closed into a fist, tightly clenching a handful of Royce's hair. "Find me a way to get to the boy."

"Oww! You're hurting me!"

Royce's friend smiled, effecting a frightening change in his demeanor. Temper, temper, he scolded himself. He released Royce's hair and walked back around the sofa to the table. "I've never let one of my little friends escape before. Not for long, anyway. I don't like it."

"But I thought they were your little buddies. They wouldn't hurt you. . . ."

"Not intentionally, no. But Abie is so sweet, so eager to please. He might talk to them without realizing that he was betraying me." His forearms trembled. "I don't like being . . . vulnerable."

"I don't think you have much to worry about—"

"I don't want to worry at all!" His fist came down like a hammer. This time it happened. The glass tabletop shattered under the impact, splintering the glass, cutting his hand.

Please don't do it again, Daddy. Please! It hurts, Daddy. It hurts!

The man clenched his eyes shut and slowly withdrew his blood-streaked hand.

"Don't make me punish you, too, Royce," the man continued, in an eerie, flat voice. "Get me that boy."

"I—I'll do my best."

He grabbed Royce by the throat. "Don't give me stupid platitudes. Do it!"

"All right, all right." Royce broke away, rubbing his sore throat. "Why do I always have to do the hard work?"

"The hard work?" The other man began to chuckle. "But, Royce, all you have to do is find him." His coal-gray eyes became small and black. "I'm the one who has to kill him."

* 50 *

If possible, the courtroom was even more crowded than it had been the day before. Word had gotten out; Courtroom Three was Tulsa's hottest ticket. Ben had expected the media to be there in full force; he wasn't expecting the horde of non-professionals: the retirees, the street people, the bored house spouses. The spectacle of seventy-year-old grandmothers squabbling for seats in the gallery was pretty sickening.

As Ben scanned the gallery he saw several familiar faces. Almost all his acquaintances from the country club were there; Crenshaw and Bentley were sitting together near the jury box. Their clothes alone were sufficient to cause them to stand out from the rest of the crowd. The Rutherfords were there also, but they were not sitting together. Harold was near the front; Rachel was in the rear, pressed into a corner. Ben couldn't help but suspect that this separation was significant.

The back doors opened, and Mitch escorted Captain Pearson to a seat. Apparently, Mitch wasn't staying. Poor chump; he probably had to chauffeur Pearson over.

Ben waved to get Mitch's attention. "Baby-sitting Cap'n Ron?" Ben asked.

"No comment," Mitch replied.

"I have a question. Suppose I wanted to learn who on the Utica Greens board was communicating with person or persons unknown in Peru. How would I go about it?"

Mitch thought for a moment. "Well, if they were communicating from someplace other than the club, I wouldn't have any idea. But all of the board members have offices at the club. Deliveries and faxes are always logged in by the desk secretary. I could check for FedEx packages or certified letters from Peru. I could check the guest register for Spanish-sounding names. And I could check the phone bills for long-distance calls."

"That would be great," Ben said. "When can you start?"

"Now, wait a minute. . . ." Mitch looked nervously toward the back of the courtroom. "I'll have to get approval from Pearson."

"No. You can't tell him you're doing it."

"Why not?"

"Well, principally because he'll tell you not to."

"Then I don't think—"

Ben laid his hand on Mitch's shoulder. "Look, Mitch, I don't want you to lose your job. But if I don't get this information, and as soon as possible, my client could end up convicted for a crime he didn't commit."

"But still—"

"C'mon, Mitch. I can tell you're a good guy. You're not like these country-club clowns you work for who don't care about anything but their own comfort. You care about other people."

"Laying it on a bit thick, aren't you?"

Ben shrugged his shoulders. "I'm desperate."

Mitch frowned. "I'll have to do it at night. When no one else is around."

"Excellent."

"It'll take several days. I have other duties."

"Understood. But tell me what you've found as soon as possible."

Mitch nodded. "I'll stay in touch."

"Thanks."

Leeman was already at the defendant's table. His eyes had pronounced circles; his expression was long and drawn. He looked tired.

And scared.

Ben was startled by a sudden thud. "Whaa . . . ?"

"Morning, Kincaid." It was Bullock. He had dropped a huge banker's box of documents on the table.

"What's this mess?" Ben asked.

"New exhibits," Bullock replied succinctly. "We've added a few witnesses. But as you've pointed out before, trial by ambush is history. So here are the files. You're on notice."

"How nice," Ben said. "And a full two minutes before the trial begins, too."

"I always play by the rules. I'm required to give you notice. I just did."

"By the way, I didn't think very much of your opening statement."

Bullock cocked his head to one side. "The truth hurts, doesn't it?"

"Your opening had nothing to do with the truth. It had to do with prejudicing the jury by focusing their attention on the attorneys instead of the evidence."

"Is that against the rules?"

"Maybe not, but—"

"When the evidence shows the defendant is guilty, like in this case, for instance, then I prosecute him. That's my job. That's what I believe in. Your problem is that you don't have any convictions. How could you? I know I'm performing a service. I'm acting for the greater good. That's why I don't mind pushing. I won't violate the rules, but I have no problem doing anything within the rules that will help make my case. Consider yourself warned." He marched to the prosecution table without a backward glance.

A few minutes later Judge Hawkins stomped into the courtroom. After letting the bailiff do his bit and giving the jury their daily instructions, Hawkins invited Bullock to call his first witness.

"The State calls Dr. Hikaru Koregai to the stand."

Ben almost smiled. He felt like he and Dr. Koregai were old friends. Koregai had been a medical examiner for over twenty-five years; he'd worked on every homicide Ben had been involved with since he moved to Tulsa. He was well-known for his expertise in forensic medicine, his ability to stay cool under cross-examination, and his in-your-face "why the hell should I help you?" manner. The coroner with an attitude.

After establishing Koregai's expertise and credentials,

Bullock took him back to the night of the murder. Koregai was called to the scene of the crime by a Sergeant Tompkins shortly after the body was discovered.

"What condition was Maria Alvarez in when you arrived?"

"She was dead."

"Did you confirm this opinion?"

Koregai arched an eyebrow. He didn't like being doubted, not even by friendly interrogators. "Yes. I searched for vital signs. There were none. She was dead."

"Do you have an opinion as to the cause of her death?"

"Technically, she died of cranial cerorexia—the loss of oxygen to her brain. The more immediate cause of death was the loss of blood and the collapse of her respiratory system."

"And what caused that?"

"The shaft of a golf club had been forced through her neck. The wound was fatal."

"Would death have been immediate?"

"Possibly."

"But not certainly?"

"The wound was fatal," Koregai continued, "but not necessarily immediately so. She may have died quickly. Or she may have been pinned to the wall, in excruciating pain, for some time."

"I see," Bullock said somberly. He shook his head sadly from side to side, then cast a firm glance at Leeman. The jury did the same.

"Dr. Koregai," Bullock continued, "I have some pictures I'd like you to identify."

"Wait a minute," Ben said. "I object. Mr. Bullock has made this discussion grisly enough. We don't need to see photos."

Counsel approached the bench. Bullock gave the photos to the judge, who passed them to Ben.

Every one was a grotesque, full-color, blood-splattered picture of the victim pinioned to the wall. Bullock was obviously trying to turn the jury against Leeman by emphasizing the grotesque nature of the crime.

"I repeat my objection," Ben whispered to the judge, out of the jury's hearing. "These pictures contribute nothing that hasn't already come out through Dr. Koregai's testimony. They have no probative value, and they could greatly prejudice the jury. Their verdict should be rendered based upon the facts, not passion stirred up by inflammatory nonevidence."

"Your honor," Bullock said innocently, "the law requires me to positively identify the victim."

Judge Hawkins gazed at the photos. These were so hideous even he didn't want to look at them. "Don't you have any other photos of the victim? Perhaps one that doesn't show blood gushing from her neck?"

"Your honor, this was the condition of the corpse when Dr. Koregai arrived. He can only identify what he saw." Bullock leveled his eyes. "If I can't use these photos, my case will be greatly prejudiced. I might even have to dismiss."

Hawkins grimaced. "Oh, very well. Objection overruled."

"Judge, I protest!" Ben said.

"Your objection is already on the record," Hawkins said huffily. "Let's get on with this."

Ben ground his teeth together and returned to his table. If he had any doubts about his standing in this trial before, they were all gone now. Hawkins was a prosecution man through and through. He was going to be no help to Ben at all.

Koregai identified the pictures, and the bailiff duly presented them to the jury. Each juror studied them for a few painful moments, then wordlessly passed them down the row.

Ben didn't have to read minds to know what they were thinking. They were thinking that this murder was more than a murder. It was an abomination, a sacrilege. They wanted to convict the person who did this.

And without exception, each juror, after he or she examined the pictures thoroughly and passed them on to the next juror, looked across the courtroom at Leeman Hayes.

* 51 *

After lunch, Bullock called his next witness. With the medical testimony out of the way, Ben expected Bullock to take them directly to the night of the murder. To his surprise, Bullock instead called someone he'd never heard of before.

"The State calls Ramona de Vries."

Who? Ben whirled around and made eye contact with Christina, who was rapidly rummaging in the files. She shrugged; she was as much in the dark as he was.

While the woman walked to the witness stand Ben searched through his notes and outlines for some mention of a Ramona de Vries. His eyes fell on the large cardboard box Bullock had dropped on his table that morning.

There she was—right on the top. A file folder labeled RAMONA DE VRIES. Ben had noticed it earlier, but the name didn't mean anything to him and he hadn't had time to browse.

Bullock had stung him again. If Ben objected because Bullock had called an unendorsed witness, Bullock would rebut that he had provided the defense with advance notice and full disclosure. And no protest was made—not on the record, anyway. And as long as the record was clear and there was no risk of appeal error, Hawkins would have no problem letting Bullock get away with anything.

And Ben was the one who kept getting called a shyster trickster.

Ramona De Vries was a well-kept woman in her mid-forties, with strong features, a firm chin, and hair the color of steel. She didn't look as if she wanted to be here. But then, who did?

While Bullock introduced the witness, Ben scanned the file and tried to figure out who she was and what connection she had to the case. Ramona de Vries was a wealthy society woman. Married, rich beyond measure—and she spent most of her time at the Utica Greens Country Club. Even after listening to the first several minutes of her testimony, though, Ben still couldn't fathom why she had been called.

Until Bullock took her to the day of the murder.

"Ms. de Vries," Bullock asked, "were you at the Utica Greens Country Club on the afternoon of August twenty-fifth that year?"

"Goodness, it's been so long ago." She waved her hand wearily. "I believe I was."

"What were you doing about two in the afternoon?"

"I was sunbathing near the pool."

"Were you alone?"

"I didn't have anyone with me. There was someone else sunbathing. A blonde woman, as I recall. Maybe a few others. I'm not sure."

Bullock approached the witness. "Ms. de Vries, I'm going to hand you a picture of a woman I will represent to you was named Maria Alvarez." Bullock showed what looked like a passport photo to the judge, then to Ben.

"Thought you didn't have any pictures of the victim that weren't splattered with blood," Ben whispered to Bullock.

"Guess I forgot about this one," Bullock whispered back. He passed the photo to the witness. "Have you ever seen this woman before?"

"Why, yes. I saw her that day at the club."

"Really," Bullock said, feigning surprise. "And what was she doing at the club?"

"I can't imagine," de Vries replied, one eyebrow arched slightly. "I mean, she obviously shouldn't have been there. She couldn't have been a member. I don't know how she made it through the gate."

"What was she doing when you saw her?"

"She was talking to some of the other members—or trying to, anyway. No one wanted anything to do with her. Rather understandable, if you know what I mean."

"Did you know what she wanted?"

"Not then, but she eventually approached me. I was sunbathing by the pool, and she just walked up and started babbling at me. I mean, can you imagine? I was appalled. I pulled my sun hat down over my eyes and tried to ignore her, hoping she would go away. But she didn't. I mean, really!"

"What did she ask you, Ms. de Vries?"

"Well, that's just it. Who could tell? She was rattling on in some foreign language. Spanish, I suppose. I couldn't make heads or tails out of it. I mean, if those people insist on coming to our country, they could at least have the decency to learn the language."

"Could you . . . tell what she wanted?" Bullock was obviously pushing for something in particular. He wasn't quite leading, but he was getting pretty close.

"I might have been mistaken, but at the time I thought she was looking for someone. I couldn't tell who. I mean, I couldn't imagine that she would know anyone who was a member, and if it wasn't a member, why was she looking for them there? Maybe she was after one of the staff, I don't know. I couldn't understand it."

Bullock took a step closer to the witness stand. "What happened when you told her you couldn't help her?"

"Well, you just wouldn't believe it. She started to screech and wail and moan. She actually cried, tears streaming down her face. It was disgraceful. Finally, she wandered off, probably so she could accost some other poor defenseless member. She was a menace, running around the club, bothering everyone like that. I mean, who knew what she might do?" She folded her arms across her chest. "I almost called security. I really did."

"Did you notice what Ms. Alvarez did after she left you?"

"How could I help it?"

"Were you the only person watching her?"

"Oh no. Someone else was watching her very carefully."

"And who would that be?" Bullock asked, as if he didn't already know.

"Him," she answered, pointing at the defendant's table. "The caddy."

"Let the record reflect that the witness has identified the defendant," Bullock said. The judge nodded. "How do you know he was watching, Ms. de Vries?"

"Well, I saw him, of course. I could hardly miss it."

"Was he near you?"

"Constantly. He was always loitering near the pool. Anytime he wasn't on the golf course where he belonged, he was at the pool."

"Did this make you uncomfortable?"

"Of course it did. Why do you think people join country clubs? It's to get away from—" She cut herself off. Even Ramona de Vries seemed to realize that this was going too far. "I mean, that's why we built the caddyshack, for God's sake. To give them someplace to stay. He should've stayed in it."

"And why was Leeman watching her?"

"Objection!" Ben said. "Calls for speculation."

Judge Hawkins shrugged. "I'll allow it. Please answer."

"Well . . ." Ramona's lips thinned. "I think he . . . liked her."

"Liked her?"

"Yeah. Very much. His eyes never left her body. And the expression on his face." She arched an eyebrow. "Like a dog eyeing a piece of meat."

"Objection!" Ben cried.

Hawkins gazed down at him. "On what grounds, Mr. Kincaid?"

Ben sputtered for a moment. Improper use of metaphor? In fact, he didn't really have any grounds, but he couldn't tolerate just sitting there while Bullock used Ramona to develop his sex-pervert theory.

"Well, your honor . . . it's just . . . it's . . . not right."

Hawkins pressed two fingers against his brow. "I don't think I'm familiar with the *not right* provision of the Evidence Code, counselor. Overruled. Proceed, Mr. Bullock."

Bullock nodded. "When did you last see the defendant that day?"

"When he left the pool area."

"And why did he leave?"

"He was following the woman."

"Do you know why?"

"Well, you know . . . they like the dark ones. . . ."

"Objection!" Ben repeated, then hastily added: "Speculation. Lack of personal knowledge."

The judge nodded. "So you have read the Evidence Code after all. I'm so pleased. Objection sustained."

"That's all," Bullock said, retaking his seat. He'd made his point clear to the jury.

"Cross-examination?" the judge asked.

"No kidding." Ben positioned himself squarely in front of the witness. He was going to have to be forceful with her. She had tried to paint Leeman as a deviant; Bullock would use that in closing argument to create a motive for murder. He had to rehabilitate Leeman's reputation.

"Isn't it quite a coincidence that Leeman happened to be loitering by the pool at the exact moment this unknown woman came by?"

De Vries seemed unperturbed. "Not really. As I said, he came there all the time."

"Was he permitted to swim?"

An involuntary shudder passed through her body. "No, of course not."

"Then why would Leeman come to the pool?"

"Well, do I have to spell everything out? All the women at the pool would be wearing bathing suits. I myself was wearing a skimpy little two-piece number. I had anticipated being able to sunbathe with a certain amount of privacy. I could go to a public pool if I wanted to be leered at."

"What makes you think Leeman was looking at you?"

"A woman knows these things." To his horror, out of the corner of his eye, Ben saw one of the female jurors nod her head. "After all, everyone knows what they're like. They have these . . . urges. . . ."

"They?" Ben pounced on the word. "And when you say *they*, are you slandering blacks or the mentally retarded?"

"Objection," Bullock said.

"Sustained," Hawkins said quickly.

Ben leaped right back into the fray. "Did you ever report the woman to security, ma'am?"

"No. Well, before I had a chance, he killed her."

"Your honor!"

The judge nodded. "The witness will refrain from speculating. The jury is instructed to disregard."

"How did you find out the woman was dead?"

"My masseuse told me when I arrived at the club the next day."

"Were you upset?"

"Well, of course I was upset. I mean, it happened right there at the club!" She paused for a moment. "Although, really, in a way, I suppose I felt a certain amount of relief. If she hadn't been there, he undoubtedly would've gotten someone else."

Forget about trying to rehabilitate Leeman's reputation; Ben had to get this dangerous witness off the stand. "Nothing more."

"Redirect?" the judge asked.

"Can't say as I see any reason for it," Bullock said confidently. In other words, since Ben hadn't laid a glove on Ramona during cross, he was going to leave well enough alone.

Ben couldn't blame him for that. Truth of the matter was, so far, Ben hadn't put the least little dent in Bullock's case. If things didn't take a turn for the better soon, Leeman didn't have a prayer.

* 52 *

"The State calls Sergeant Wilford Tompkins."

Tompkins approached the stand in full uniform, naturally. Juries liked uniforms; they made witnesses seem so official and important. He was a tall man, boyishly attractive, clean cut with a face that dripped of honesty. Bullock couldn't have gotten a better witness from Central Casting.

Bullock raced the witness through his background and credentials. He was a family man with twelve years on the force, two at the time of the murder. He was on duty the night Maria Alvarez was killed.

"Who called the police and notified them that a murder had occurred?" Bullock asked.

"We still don't know," Tompkins replied, in a typical police-witness matter-of-fact manner. "The call came from the vicinity of the country club, but the caller didn't leave a name."

"Didn't the police dispatcher record all incoming calls?"

"Yes, but the tape is staticky and indistinct. You can't even tell if it's a man or a woman."

"Okay. What happened?"

"Upon arrival, I immediately made my way to the caddyshack. The light inside the building was on. I entered and found . . . the remains."

Bullock insisted that Tompkins identify the body he found as Maria Alvarez. It gave him a splendid opportunity to drag out those full-color photos again.

Tompkins described the state of the corpse when he arrived. His testimony didn't differ from that already introduced by Dr. Koregai.

320

"Was anyone else in the shack when you arrived?"

"Yes. The defendant. Leeman Hayes."

Ben glanced at Leeman. He was sitting at the defendant's table with the same ambiguous expression on his face.

"What did Mr. Hayes do?"

"As soon as I entered the building, he began to run. I commanded him to stop, but he continued to flee."

"What happened next?"

"Following standard procedure in such situations, I gave pursuit. Fortunately, he wasn't a fast runner, and I was able to apprehend him without drawing my weapon."

"Did he resist arrest?"

"Very much so. He struggled and fought. He even bit my arm. And he made a strange wailing sound. Like a sick dog."

"Did you attempt to question him?"

"I did attempt it, but he was unresponsive. Therefore, I cuffed him to the door. I secured the crime scene, radioed for backup, contacted Homicide, and proceeded with a preliminary investigation."

"Why did you call Homicide?"

"That's standard procedure. And frankly . . . I wasn't sure what to do next."

"Had you ever handled a homicide before?"

"Oh, sure. But never one like this. This was . . . different. Worse."

"In what way?"

"Well . . . for instance . . . it's standard procedure to leave everything just as you find it when you arrive at a homicide scene. But I wasn't certain whether it was . . . right to leave that woman's body just . . . hanging there like that. Staked against the wall. It seemed . . . inhuman."

"I'm sure the jury appreciates that it was a difficult decision for you. Did you investigate the scene?"

"Yes. I had pretty much covered the entire caddyshack by the time the homicide investigators arrived and relieved me."

"Did you discover anything noteworthy?"

"Yes. I found a row of lockers where personal belongings were kept by the individual caddies."

"What did you find?"

"In the defendant's locker, I found a small six-club golf bag. It had five clubs inside."

"Only five?"

"Yes." He took a deep breath. "The sixth club was the murder weapon. It was a matched set."

An electric ripple passed through the jury box. This was probably the most damning piece of evidence yet.

"Did any of the other lockers have clubs?"

"Oh, yes. Most of them, in fact. I suppose most caddies are budding golfers. But only the defendant's contained the clubs in question. It's a very distinctive set."

"Do you know where this set of clubs came from?"

"I learned later. It had been stolen from the pro shop."

"Anything else in the locker?" Bullock asked.

"Yes. A necklace."

Bullock held up a necklace in a clear sealed bag. "Is this the necklace?"

Tompkins examined it. "Yes. I initialed the bag after sealing the necklace inside at the crime scene."

Bullock had it admitted into evidence. "Do you know to whom the necklace belonged?"

"We believe it belonged to the murder victim, Maria Alvarez. It matches a bracelet she wore."

"I'm surprised you didn't find the bracelet in Mr. Hayes's locker as well."

"It was hidden by the victim's dress. The necklace would have been exposed, however."

Bullock gave the necklace to the bailiff, who in turn passed it to the jury. "I notice that the necklace is broken. Any idea how that occurred?"

"Yes. The necklace was broken by the murder weapon."

"Can you explain?"

"When the shaft of the golf club impaled her, it must have severed the necklace. Not to mention the woman's neck."

"Thank you," Bullock said solemnly. "No more questions."

"You may inquire, Mr. Kincaid," the judge said, nodding in Ben's direction.

Ben walked directly to the stand, silently plotting his strategy. There was no point in coming on too strong. The jury seemed to like the witness—they usually trusted police officers—and probably thought he was telling the truth. For that matter, so did Ben. What he had to demonstrate was that Tompkins's evidence didn't prove as much as Bullock suggested.

"Let's make one thing clear right off the bat, Sergeant," Ben began. "You didn't see Leeman Hayes kill Maria Alvarez, did you?"

"Well, no . . ."

"And you didn't discover any eyewitnesses to the crime, did you?"

"No."

"And you never heard Leeman confess to the crime, did you?"

"No. He wouldn't talk to me at all."

"Wouldn't? Or couldn't?"

"I beg your pardon?"

"You're assuming a lack of cooperation, Sergeant. All you actually know is that he didn't answer your questions, right?"

Tompkins squirmed slightly. "I suppose that's true."

"Thank you. Now, did you ever determine why Leeman was at the caddyshack so late at night?"

"Well, I assumed he was after that woman—"

"Come now, Sergeant. If you were going to kill someone, would you do it at the Utica Greens caddyshack?"

Tompkins hesitated. "Well . . . I would never kill anyone."

"No, I'm sure you wouldn't. But it's not an ideal place for a murder, is it? Bound to be discovered. Quickly."

Tompkins cast a sideways look at the jury box. "I never claimed the defendant was very smart."

A few chuckles from the jury box. Ben plowed ahead. "Did you ever consider any other reasons why Leeman Hayes might've been at the caddyshack that night?"

"Such as?"

Ben glanced back at Ernie Hayes in the gallery. "Well, did you notice whether Leeman had a pillow there?"

Tompkins squirmed a bit more this time. "Well . . . I didn't find one in his locker."

"No, that wouldn't be a very comfortable place to sleep, would it?" This time the chuckles were with Ben, not against him. "And did you notice whether Leeman had a sleeping bag in the shack?"

Tompkins frowned. "I reviewed the inventory list before I came to court today, and it did show that we found one blue sleeping bag."

Ben spread his arms wide. "Would it surprise you, then, to learn that Leeman slept at the caddyshack?"

Tompkins was surprised. "No one ever said anything about that. . . ."

"So he would've been there even if he had nothing to do with the murder, right?"

Officer Tompkins cocked his head. "Or that might explain why he chose to commit the murder there."

"What?"

"Maybe he brought the woman back to his, er, sleeping bag, and when she wouldn't cooperate—"

"Just answer the questions." Ben riffled through the other cross-ex questions he had jotted down beforehand on index cards. When would he learn? Just ask the yes or no questions and don't give the witness a chance to get creative. "Sergeant Tompkins, you're aware that Leeman is developmentally disabled, aren't you?"

"I didn't know it that night, but I've learned since."

"Now you've told the jury that he struggled and resisted arrest. Do you suppose it's possible that he just didn't understand who you were and what you were doing?"

"I plainly identified myself as a police—"

"Plainly for you and me, maybe, but what about a young man barely capable of speech? You burst into his bedroom, tackled him, cuffed him, and started shouting questions. Would he know what was happening? Wouldn't he be scared to death?"

"Objection," Bullock said. "Who's asking the witness to speculate now?"

"Sustained," Judge Hawkins ruled.

"Sergeant, you testified that you found some golf clubs in Leeman's locker, correct?"

"That's correct."

"But isn't it also true that Leeman didn't have a lock on his locker?"

A wrinkle creased Tompkins's brow. "None of the lockers had locks."

"Did you ever see Leeman open the locker?"

Tompkins thought for a moment. "No, I don't suppose I did."

"Did you ever see Leeman put anything into it?"

"No."

"And you weren't in the shack before the murder occurred."

"Right."

"So anyone could've put that golf bag in there, right?"

"I suppose that's technically correct."

"In truth, Officer, you have no physical link between the items found in that locker and Leeman Hayes."

"It was his locker."

"Answer the question, sir."

"That's true," he said reluctantly.

"And you have no personal knowledge about how those goods got into the locker."

"I didn't see it myself, no."

"And in truth, you don't really know why Leeman was at the caddyshack that night."

"Right."

Ben leaned in close. "The only reason you arrested him is . . . he was the only person there, right?"

"Well, he was the only living person there."

"What was your probable cause for the arrest, Officer?"

Bullock leaped to his feet. "What's this, Kincaid? More tricks?"

Ben glared back at him. "Your honor, may we approach the bench?"

"Approach."

They did so.

"Your honor," Ben whispered, "I think we have a serious evidentiary problem here. If the arrest was unconstitutional, then all the evidence obtained subsequent to the arrest, including the videotaped interrogation, is inadmissible."

"So that's your game," Bullock snarled. "Judge, you see how he's trying to thwart justice."

"The officer didn't have probable cause!" Ben insisted. "You can't arrest someone just because they're available!"

"What about the clubs and the jewelry in the locker?"

"Tompkins discovered that *after* he arrested Leeman."

"What about the attempted escape?"

"Escape? He wasn't in custody. He was free to go wherever he pleased."

"Your honor, this is totally frivolous," Bullock protested. "Mr. Kincaid will do anything to keep his client from being tried on the evidence."

"This is a serious matter," Ben insisted, "particularly when you're dealing with a developmentally disabled person such as my client. He's a prime example of why our Constitution guarantees certain rights. Such as the right not to be arrested just because you happen to be sleeping at the scene of a murder."

Bullock drew himself up defiantly. "Give me a chance to redirect. I'll establish cause for the arrest."

"Fair enough," the judge said.

"If he doesn't," Ben insisted, "I'll renew my motion."

"I don't doubt that for a moment," the judge said wearily. "Proceed, Mr. Prosecutor."

Bullock stood beside the jury box and faced the witness. "Sergeant Tompkins, a question has arisen as to whether you had sufficient grounds to make an arrest. Now, in addition to being at the scene of the crime—the only person at the scene of the crime—do you recall any other details that indicated that the defendant committed the crime?"

A cold chill shot down Ben's spine. He realized now where Bullock was going.

"Objection," Ben said. "He's trying to introduce new evidence on redirect."

Hawkins flung his pen down on his desk. "What is it with

you, Kincaid? You're not happy when he doesn't put on the evidence, and you're not happy when he does."

"Your honor, he can't raise new matters on redirect—"

"He's responding to your objection, counselor."

"Fine. Let him. But that's no excuse to violate the—"

"Mr. Kincaid, I have already ruled." Hawkins's cheeks were turning crimson and puffy. "Now sit down."

Ben slunk back into his seat.

"As I was asking," Bullock continued, "do you recall any other factors, Sergeant?"

"Just one," Tompkins said. He paused. The jurors leaned forward ever so slightly.

"And what would that be?" Bullock asked.

"He had blood all over his hands."

Ben checked Mrs. Alexander, on the front row of the jury box. Her lips parted; her eyes widened.

Damn. This was a setup.

"On his hands?"

"Yes. On his hands, and up and down his arms. It was all over him."

"That was the defendant?"

"Yes. Him." Tompkins pointed at Leeman. "He had the victim's blood all over him."

Suddenly Leeman bolted upright in his chair. He stared at Tompkins, his eyes wide, his face terrified. And then, to Ben's horror, he held out his hands and began rubbing them furiously, fast and desperately. Like a pathetic Lady Macbeth, he couldn't get the blood off his hands.

Ben pushed Leeman back into his seat and shoved his hands under the table, but it was too late. The jury had seen all.

Once the unexpected performance was over, Bullock lowered his head gravely. "And after you noticed that the defendant literally had the victim's blood on his hands, you arrested him?"

"Of course. Wouldn't you?"

"Indeed I would," Bullock replied. "No more questions, your honor."

"Anything else from the defense?" Hawkins asked.

Better to leave bad enough alone. "No," Ben said.

"Then I will recess this court for the day. We'll resume tomorrow morning at nine. Dismissed."

The judge exited and the courtroom exploded into pandemonium. The whir of mechanical flashes and the drone of shouted questions echoed between the walls.

Ben ignored them. He glanced at Leeman, and saw to his dismay that Leeman was still wringing his hands under the table. Pontius Pilate gone mad.

The first day of testimony was over, and Ben didn't need to consult with Christina to know how it had gone. Bullock had taken every hill, had won every important point.

The reality of the situation was perfectly clear to Ben now. The truth was of no importance. Bullock was going to win, not because Leeman was guilty, but because Bullock understood how the justice system worked, what judges liked, what jurors thought. He had twenty years in the trenches, twenty years hard-won trial experience on Ben.

Ben had heard it since he was One-L at OU, but he'd never really believed it until now.

Facts didn't win trials. Evidence didn't win trials. Lawyers won trials.

Bullock was going to win this trial, not because he represented the truth, but because he was a better lawyer than Ben was.

A few more days in court like this one, and the truth wouldn't matter anymore. The jury would be convinced of Leeman's guilt. Leeman would be doomed.

Before he had ever had a chance to live.

* 53 *

"Got it!" he exclaimed.

Royce looked away from his new camera. He'd had to buy a new one, since his good buddy left his old one in that deserted building with the kid. He'd spent the past hour trying to figure out how it worked. Seemed like the high-end cameras got more complicated every year. Soon only computer programmers would be able to operate them. "Got what?"

The man's dark eyes glistened. "A plan."

"For what?"

"To get the kid."

Of course, Royce thought. What else? Ever since his friend's narrow escape from the law, he'd been obsessed with getting to that boy. His desperation grew more intense every minute. Royce hated to think about what was likely to happen to that kid if he ever got his hands on him.

"Look," Royce said, "the police haven't come anywhere near you. Don't you think the safest thing would be to just leave him alone?"

"No, imbecile. Don't you know every stupid cop in this city is looking for me?"

"But they haven't found you, have they?"

"They will. I have to make sure that when they do, they don't have a witness to identify me."

Royce felt a sudden chill. He didn't at all care for the look in the man's eyes or the expression in his voice. "If you're so sure the cops are on your ass, why don't you just move?"

"And live in fear? Always looking over my shoulder?

Always worrying that my life might be ended by some stupid, naughty boy? *Never!*"

This guy was over the edge, Royce realized. Around the bend. Totally and dangerously nuts.

"Have you been following the Leeman Hayes trial, Royce?"

"I hear what they say on the evening news."

"Well, it's in the state courthouse, Fifth and Denver, sixth floor."

"Why are you telling me?"

"Because I want you to be there tomorrow."

"Tomorrow? I'm supposed to be taking pictures down at Monte Cassino—"

"Cancel."

"I can't cancel—"

"Those miserable school brats will still have their fake smiles a week from now. *I* need you at the courthouse."

Royce's shoulders sagged. "What is it you want me to do?"

"Just be there. I'll be there, too, but I want you to act as if you don't know who I am."

"Then what's the point of—"

"Just be there. I'll give you further instructions when you arrive."

"But how—"

"*Just be there!*" His face burned red; his head trembled.

Royce sat down quietly and placed his hands in his lap. "Okay. Whatever you want."

"Good." He walked across the room and stared into an ornate hanging mirror. "It isn't fair, you know. I was so nice. All I wanted was to love him, to cherish him. And how does he reward me?"

With a sudden burst of rage, he jerked the mirror off the wall and threw it across the room. Royce ducked just before the mirror smashed against the wall with a tremendous crescendo of glass and metal.

Royce crawled out from behind the sofa. Next time he was in this apartment alone, he was definitely removing all the glass objects.

His associate collapsed into a chair. "He hurts me, that's

how. He threatens me. Well, no more. It's into the closet for you, Abie Rutherford. Into the closet, and you won't come out until you've been punished. *Punished!*"

To Royce's astonishment, his friend began to cry. "That's right," he said softly. "Punished till he hurts. Punished till he cries for mercy. But there will be no mercy."

He lowered his head, tears streaming down his face. "It's only fair," he gasped. "It's only fair."

Royce edged quietly toward the door.

"But who will punish me? Who will punish *me*?" The man stared down at his own hands.

The last thing Royce heard as he slipped out the door was the sound of his friend shouting at top volume and crying with the same breath. "Mommy? Daddy? Tell me what to do! *Who will punish me?*"

* 54 *

After he got out of the courthouse, Ben stopped by his office. To his dismay, yet another stranger bearing a briefcase was pacing around in the lobby.

"Let me guess," Ben said. "You're from the air-conditioner company."

"As a matter of fact, yes," the young man said, after a moment's hesitation. "And I'm not leaving until you've paid your bill in full."

"I hope you're wearing comfortable shoes," Ben muttered. He approached Jones's desk. "Got a minute?"

Jones appeared to be buried. He had a telephone receiver on each ear, a word-processing screen beeping at him, and a printer spewing out paper. "Take a number."

Jones shouted a few words into the receiver on the left, then slammed it back down into the cradle. "I hate reporters!"

"Calm down," Ben said. "They're just doing their job."

"Well, at the moment their job appears to be prying into the private affairs of lesser human beings."

"Who called?"

"You name it. Everyone in town wants to talk to you. Everyone in the state, actually. Channel Six wants to do a live remote with you on the ten o'clock newscast."

"Tell them no."

"Are you sure, Boss? Bullock's going to be on."

"That figures. He's pulling out all the stops to win this one."

"Aren't the jurors told not to read or watch any reports about the case?"

"That's what they're told. But there's no way of knowing what they do in the privacy of their homes, is there?"

"If you don't show up, Bullock'll have the stage to himself."

Ben picked up a stack of mail and thumbed through it. "Judges don't appreciate lawyers who try to curry favor for their clients in the media. The Rules of Professional Conduct aren't that keen on it either."

"Look, Boss, if you don't want to talk about the facts of the case, that's fine. But this would be a great opportunity to ask potential witnesses to come forward."

Ben considered. "That's hardly standard procedure."

"This is hardly a standard case. You haven't had nearly enough time to prepare, and finding witnesses to events that took place ten years ago is practically impossible."

"You have a point there." Ben glanced up from the mail. "Who's doing the interview? Clayton Vaughn?"

"No, the good-looking one. Beth Something-or-other."

"Oh." Ben tilted his head to one side. "What about Karen Larsen? Did she call?"

"She's on Channel Eight."

"I know. I watch her Saturday mornings sometimes while Giselle and I have our breakfast."

"Me, too," Jones admitted. "She's a babe."

"Jones, you sexist pig. She's a journalist. First-rate. Very classy."

"A bit defensive, aren't we? What's the matter, Boss? You got a crush on her?" Jones grinned from ear to ear. "Look at your face turning red! Boss, I do believe you're sweet on her."

"Don't be ridiculous."

"What a surprise! The Boss has a crush on a morning-show hostess."

"I most certainly do not." Ben averted his eyes. "So . . . did she call?"

" 'Fraid not, Boss. You want me to call her? See if she's free for dinner?"

"Don't be stupid."

Jones continued grinning. "What else is there about you I

don't know? Do you have secret fantasies about Connie Chung?"

Ben threw the mail in Jones's face. "I'm going home now to prepare for tomorrow's trial."

"How's it going?"

"Don't ask. If anything turns up, contact me immediately."

"Will do. And here's the number of the television station. You need to call and tell them yea or nay."

"All right. Let me think about it some more."

"And, Boss—"

"Yes?"

"Really, don't be embarrassed. When I was a kid, I had a huge thing for Marcia. You know, on *The Brady Bunch*."

"Goodbye, Jones. Have a nice day."

* 55 *

Carlee Crane sat in bed chowing down a jumbo-size bag of powdered doughnuts. She was watching the ten o'clock news. She never used to. She never used to be interested. But now she was.

Dave didn't want her to watch the news. He said it would upset her.

He was right.

The Leeman Hayes trial had begun. Without her. She had not volunteered her testimony. Dave had gotten his way on that dispute. And he had never mentioned it since. He knew better than to press his luck. Once the victory was won, the smart man kept his mouth shut about it.

The silver-haired anchorman summarized the day's events. According to him, the prosecution was assembling a "seemingly airtight case." The defense hadn't had a chance to put on any evidence, but it was questionable whether anything could dislodge the clear inference of guilt the prosecution was establishing.

He cut to his female co-anchor, who was conducting an interview by live remote with the two attorneys handling the case. The man from the district attorney's office opened by reassuring the audience that he would stop at nothing to ensure that the citizens of Tulsa could sleep safely at night, and that he would make every effort to see that justice was done.

While the prosecutor talked, Dave entered the bedroom. Must've finally gotten Ethan and Gavin to bed. He was frowning, and Carlee knew why. There she was, watching the news, just as he had asked her not to do. She didn't mean to make him mad; she just couldn't help herself. She had to know what was happening.

At last, the anchorwoman pried the DA away from the microphone and introduced the attorney representing the defendant. Carlee recognized him from the newspaper. He was much younger than Bullock—early thirties, tops. He seemed less assured and less accustomed to speaking on television; in fact, he stammered and looked downright nervous.

"Mr. Kincaid, do you agree with the statements Mr. Bullock has just made?" the woman asked.

"No, I don't," he said emphatically.

"Why not?"

"I'm not going to go into an argumentative evaluation of the facts. That's for the courtroom, not the evening news."

"He won't talk," Bullock interjected, "because he has nothing to say. He has no defense."

"That's about as true as most of what the prosecutor has said so far," Kincaid replied.

"Well, if you won't talk about the case, why are you here?" the interviewer asked.

"To make a plea." The defense attorney turned and stared directly into the camera. Carlee had the eerie feeling he was looking at her. "My main difficulty in preparing this case has been that the crime occurred so long ago. I know there must be people out there with knowledge about this case, but how do you find them after so many years?"

"I can see where that would present a difficulty," the reporter commented.

The attorney continued. "If there is anyone out there who knows anything about this crime, and I mean *anything*, please come forward. You can call me at my office; it's listed in the phone book. If you know anything at all, please contact me. An innocent man's life depends on you."

The anchorwoman asked another question, but Carlee didn't hear it. Dave had moved in front of the television. He was staring down at her.

"You're going to testify, aren't you?"

Carlee looked away. "Didn't you hear what he said?"

"But, honey—people will laugh at you! Your story is incredible. It's worse than incredible. It's ridiculous."

"I can't hold back just because I'm afraid someone might laugh at me."

"What about the kids?"

"They're tough. They'll survive."

"What about my job?"

"I can't believe you'd lose your job over this."

"Why take the risk? Remember what happened when Craig Banner's wife filed that sexual-harassment suit against her boss? She was splashed all over the news for weeks. People were calling her names, laughing at her. And two weeks later Craig lost his job."

"I think that's a risk we have to take."

"Even if it tears our family apart?"

Carlee wrung her hands around the doughnut bag. "Even if it tears our family apart."

Dave stared at her for a long time. Then, to Carlee's surprise, he snuggled beside her and wrapped his arms around her. "You're right, of course. Good for you."

"What? You're not upset?"

Dave smiled. "Well, I'm not happy about it. But I care more about you than my job, or my house, or anything else, for that matter. I know this has been tearing you up. I know you haven't been sleeping at night, or functioning during the day. You've been eating junk food like it was going out of style."

"I'm afraid I may have gained a few pounds. . . ."

"Forget it. You've been stressed out. I should never have tried to keep you from coming forward. I forgot one important fact."

"What's that?"

He squeezed her tightly. "I forgot what a good-hearted, good-natured, all-around *good* person you are. You can't stand by quietly if there's any chance you might be able to help an innocent man. You just can't do it. It's not in you. Whatever it costs, you're going to do what you have to do." He kissed her lightly on the neck. "That's what I forgot."

"I'll go see that attorney tomorrow, then." Carlee pressed

closer to him, then rolled over onto the bed, tugging him down with her. "Dave, I love you so much."

He grinned at her and began unfastening the buttons on her nightie. "Ditto."

* 56 *

Ben parked his car just behind his mother's Mercedes. Hard to miss; it stood out like a diamond in the dirt. Miracle she still had her hubcaps. Statistically, Tulsa was the car-theft capital of the nation; most people in this neighborhood either parked in garages or made do with worthless wrecks like Ben's Honda.

Ben approached his boardinghouse cautiously. This was not a good neighborhood, especially so late at night. He normally tried to be home before dark, but trials made that impossible. Especially when you're doing interviews on the ten o'clock news.

As expected, Bullock had used the forum to grandstand and try to influence the outcome of the case. Ben couldn't believe some of what Bullock said. It was as if he were willing to do or say anything to—

"Pssst."

Ben froze. He looked all around him, but saw nothing. He had almost made it to the front porch of the house. Where . . . ?

"Pssst."

Ben looked around the corner of the house. It was pitch-black. He couldn't see a thing.

Cautiously, Ben stepped around the side of the building. There were no streetlights, or any other lights, that reached back here.

He followed the wall to the back of the brownstone. He knew from prior visits that the would-be backyard was a small rectangular area overgrown with grass and weeds. For a while Ben had parked his Honda back here, till someone had the bad taste to put a dead body in it. After that mess was finally cleared up, Ben decided it would be best just to leave his car on the street. Really, what could anyone do to it that hadn't already been done?

Ben squinted, trying to detect some reflection or movement somewhere in the darkness. He couldn't find any. He kept walking, slowly, one step at a time, feeling his way along the back wall.

Ben heard a sudden crash. He literally leaped up into the air. He felt as if his heart was going to pound its way out of his body.

Trash bins. He had walked into the Dumpsters and knocked the lids down. Swell. If there was anyone back here, he wouldn't be taking him by surprise.

Two hands slapped down on Ben's shoulders from behind. Ben whirled around, his heart racing.

The figure before him was visible only as a shadow, an immense shadow, outlined against the dark sky.

"You wanted to see me?" His voice was deep and menacing.

"D-did I? I'm Ben Kincaid. I'm an attorney—"

"I know who you are. Did you have some bizness wi' me?"

Something about his voice, his size, and his diction triggered a lightbulb in Ben's brain. This was Joni's boyfriend. Booker. She *had* arranged a meeting.

"If you wants to talk, talk," the deep voice commanded. "I ain't s'posed to be here. If certain people knew, they'd cut my eyeballs out. Yours, too."

"Then why did you come?"

" 'Cause my Joni asked me to. I do it for her. Not you."

Ben plunged in. Time was probably of the essence. "You know who Leeman Hayes is, right?"

"I saw you there at his papa's house, and you saw me."

"Right. Do you realize I'm defending Leeman on a murder charge?"

"Didn't Leeman kill no one. No way, no how. He wouldn't do that."

"I agree," Ben said. "Unfortunately, I have to prove it. That's why I wanted to talk to you."

"I don't know nothin' about no murder."

"Probably not," Ben agreed. "But I think you do know something about the Utica Greens Country Club."

"What makes you so certain?"

"I saw you and your gang buddies in Captain Pearson's office."

"We ain't no gang."

"Fine. Your youth group. Your poor boys' Rotary Club. Whatever you want to call it. I've seen you in uniform, so don't bother lying. You're a Demon." Ben knew he was taking a major risk, talking tough with a guy like this. Somehow, though, he thought he would get farther if he could earn his respect.

"So what's your point?"

"I want to know what the connection is between the gang and the country club."

Booker drew himself up. "You know what would happen if my friends knew I was talkin' wi' you?"

"Yeah. The eyeballs thing. So answer my question already. What's the connection?"

"We . . . do some bizness together."

"What kind of business?"

Booker folded his arms across his chest. "I ain't sayin'."

"Booker, this could make the difference between life and death for Leeman. Think about it. Does Leeman Hayes deserve to die? Or be imprisoned for life? For a crime he didn't commit? While some other SOB who really did it goes free?"

There was no answer.

"How would you feel if Leeman was a member of your gang? How would you feel if he was your brother? Would you let him die for nothing?"

Booker hesitated a few seconds longer. "We run pickups and deliveries for Pearson."

"Deliveries of what?"

"Valuable goods."

"And by goods, you mean drugs."

The shadow that was Booker nodded slowly.

"Cocaine, right?"

"Among others."

"Who gets the stuff?"

"Don't know. We pick it up for Pearson so he doesn't have to risk gettin' his pretty white neck thrown in jail, and he pays us for it. Part in cash, part in kind. What he does with his cut I don't know."

"And where do the Demons get the stuff?"

"Comes in from Peru," Booker replied. "Pearson arranges it. He knows lots of people down there."

"How long has this gone on?"

"Don't know. Since I been with the Demons."

"When did you join?"

" 'Bout three months ago."

"Are the Demons planning a hit on the Cobras? Or vice versa?"

"What's that gotta do with Leeman?"

"Probably nothing. But it could make this a pretty unpleasant time to be a Demon."

The big youth moved closer to Ben. Ben couldn't actually see the approach; he saw only the widening of the black shadow that blotted out the sky; he felt only the heat radiating from the boy's huge frame.

"Joni tell me that if I help you, you won't tell her parents about us."

"I never made that promise."

The two huge hands descended once again on Ben's shoulders. "Then you promise me."

Ben tried to look him square in the eye, which was difficult, since he couldn't even see his face. "Look, I'm not planning to tell anyone anything. But you can't keep this romance a secret forever. Eventually someone's going to find out. You're going to have to face up to her parents."

"Joni don't want that to happen now. When the time come, I'll face it."

"Tell you what. You promise me you'll get out of the Demons, and I'll keep my mouth shut."

"You don't know what you're askin'."

"I know the Demons are heading toward some serious trouble. And I don't want you and Joni to get tangled up in it."

"You don't care about me."

"I care about Joni. And I don't think it would make her very happy if she could only see her boyfriend twice a month on visiting day. Believe me, Booker, you don't need the gang. You can make it without them."

"The Demons cared about me when no one else did."

"Maybe so, but Joni cares about you now. Whaddaya say?"

Booker slowly removed his hands from Ben's shoulders. "You just don't know what you're askin'."

"As a matter of fact, I do. I know how hard it is to get out of a gang. But you need to do it anyway. Quickly."

The shadow took a step back. "I'll give it some thought."

"Good." Ben started to leave, then stopped. "And by the way. I wouldn't wait until Joni's parents find out about you by accident, or hear it from Mrs. Marmelstein or something. I'd tell them myself. They might not like it, but they'll appreciate your honesty."

The shadow nodded.

"Thanks again. And good luck."

Ben tiptoed upstairs and quietly turned the key in the door. He hoped his mother wasn't too upset or worried or whatever it was mothers did.

As if he didn't have enough problems already, now he had his mother questioning and frowning and suggesting in her subtle way that everything about his life was second-rate. Pressure like this he didn't need. He had assumed she would leave after a few days; now she seemed to be treating this like an extended holiday.

Ben tiptoed into the main living room. To his surprise, he found his mother sound asleep on the sofa. Joey was cradled in her lap, equally asleep.

He tiptoed closer. There was a soft whistle of air flowing in and out of her teeth, a rhythmic singsong. In sleep, her usual steely facade was gone. She seemed so vulnerable, sitting there, eyes closed. So old. So fragile.

There was a plate of food on the dining table. More chicken something-or-other. He took a bite. Not bad, even cold. Not bad at all. He wolfed down the entire plate. Mother was definitely recovering her culinary talents.

He tiptoed back into the living room. He thought about waking her, but she seemed so relaxed he didn't have the heart. He lifted Joey out of her arms and carefully laid him down in his makeshift bed. Then Ben returned to the living room and put a blanket over his mother.

It was then that the memory hit him. He was three, maybe four, and they were back at their house, not the palatial one in Nichols Hills, but someplace they had lived before, someplace smaller, someplace . . . closer. He was playing in bed—no, he was sick. He had a high fever, a virus or something, and he was stuck in bed but he couldn't sleep, and his mother was reading to him, keeping him company. She was sitting in the chair beside his bed, but she fell asleep.

Ben saw it all with crystal clarity, even though he hadn't remembered the incident for years. Little Ben pulled a heavy blanket off his bed and wrapped it around his mother. He remembered it all so vividly, it was as if he were doing it right now, this instant, feeling just as he did then.

He remembered why he did it, too. It wasn't because he felt guilty. It wasn't because he was afraid she would be mad at him, or disappointed.

It was because he loved her.

Gently, he kissed his mother on the cheek and tiptoed out of the room.

Maybe it wouldn't be such a horrible development if she stayed a bit longer. After all, she was helpful with Joey. And she made a dynamite chicken something-or-other.

He was definitely going to have to get her Mercedes off the street, though.

* 57 *

It was like waking up in the middle of a Rube Goldberg nightmare machine. The shrill ringing of the phone blasted Ben out of a deep slumber. Groping in the darkness, he knocked the phone off the end table. The phone fell on his cat; his cat leaped into the air and landed on Ben's face. Startled, Ben cried out, if only for a brief instant.

But a brief instant was long enough. A few seconds later Ben heard the muffled sound of Joey crying in the next room.

He grabbed the phone receiver, silencing the offending ringing. "Just a minute," he whispered.

He heard the shuffling slippered footsteps of his mother trudging toward the baby. What a trouper.

Well, he thought, I'll relieve her as soon as I get this thoughtless heathen off the phone.

"Who the hell is this?" Ben barked.

"My God, you sure are grumpy. What, did I interrupt a sexy dream?"

"Mike? Is this you?" It was. "What's going on in that febrile brain of yours? Don't you know it's"—he glanced at the digital clock—"three-twenty in the A.M.?"

"I know the time. Have you got the temperature?"

"Look, just because you stay up all night reading Shakespeare aloud to yourself doesn't mean—"

"I'm at a crime scene, Ben."

That slowed him down. "A—you mean a—"

"Yeah. The kind with dead bodies in them."

"Does this relate to the Abie Rutherford abduction?"

"So it seems. And it relates to your murder trial as well."

345

"It does?" Ben tried to clear the cobwebs out of his head. "In what way?"

"Well, I think you can now safely eliminate one of your suspects."

"Really? Why?"

Mike paused a good long while before answering. "Because he's dead."

By the time Ben arrived at the spacious Utica Hills mansion, the corpse had already been removed. Ben was not disappointed.

He thumbed through the crime-scene Polaroids Mike had given him. "I don't believe it," Ben said over and over.

"Believe it. This is one weird world we live in."

"This is beyond weird. This is . . . grotesque." He held the first photo out at arm's length. It revealed the clear image of a blond man in his early forties. He was naked, except that he was wearing women's stockings and a garter belt and had a plastic bag over his head and an apple in his mouth. "What on earth was he doing?"

"I believe this is what the experts refer to as autoerotic asphyxiation," Mike explained.

"What?"

"People who are into this stuff have known for some time that orgasm seems more intense when you're on the brink of asphyxiation. The lack of oxygen induces light-headedness, which reduces inhibitions and, um, enhances the sexual experience. And the appeal to those with masochistic tendencies is obvious. This clown was apparently trying to induce this heightened super-sexual state while engaging in a, um, solitary sexual practice."

"And?"

"And he got a little too excited and went a little too far and choked to death. It only takes seven pounds of pressure to collapse the carotid artery, and—*boom!* You're unconscious within seconds." Mike shrugged. "That's why they call it dangerous sex."

Ben dropped the photos. "What'll they think of next?"

"Oh, this is nothing new. It's been around for centuries, probably since someone first noticed that hanged men often got an erection while in the noose. De Sade described it in detail in *Justine*. It's in Beckett's *Waiting for Godot*, too. Experts attribute about fifty deaths a year to this."

Ben stared at his friend. "Mike—why do you *know* these things?"

"All in a cop's job description."

"Right. Even if some wackos really do this—why would Chris Bentley? It doesn't make any sense."

"Oh, I don't know. Didn't you tell me he had a reputation for being a sexual adventurer?"

"Well, yes. But with women."

"And didn't he tell you he was having trouble finding his next conquest?"

"Well, yes, but—"

"Put it together, Ben."

"But—Bentley is handsome. Good-looking. Rich."

"And only ugly poor people engage in deviant sex practices? Welcome to the real world, Ben. The rich dudes are in there pitching, too. They have time on their hands and the money to get what they want."

"And you guys think Bentley was the child pervert."

"That's the official word from Chief Blackwell. We found this." Mike picked up a paper evidence bag and, using his gloved hand, withdrew a red baseball cap.

"And that cap belonged to the little boy who was hit by the car?"

"Yes. The boy's parents have definitely ID'd it. The kid's name is written under the brim."

"Any other evidence?"

"Not that I know of. Let me check. *Hubbell!*"

Within seconds, a uniformed police officer was standing at attention. "Yes, sir!"

"Tell me what you've found," Mike growled. "Other than the cap. And the corpse."

"So far, sir, we haven't discovered anything noteworthy."

"What!" Mike's eyes widened explosively; his fists

clenched. "Do you mean to tell me you've been searching for over two hours and haven't found a damn thing?"

"I—I—" Hubbell swallowed. "We've been very thorough, sir. My men have searched the entire house. It's a very large house—"

"Then you'll search it again," Mike commanded. "And again and again, if necessary. And then start on the grounds." Mike stepped right into his face. "And I hope you find something of interest this time. For your sake!"

Mike stepped back, leaving poor Hubbell dangling in the breeze.

"Dismissed!" Mike barked. Hubbell scrambled away as quickly as possible.

Mike's face and demeanor gradually returned to their prior states. "Sorry you had to see that, Ben."

"Not at all. I love to watch you go into your tough-cop routine. You ought to be nominated for an Emmy."

"I don't know what you're talking about." Mike switched the toothpick he was chewing to the other side of his mouth. "But I know that if there are any more clues around here, Hubbell's gonna find 'em."

"But what if they don't find anything else? After all, they haven't so far."

Mike stepped out of the light cast by the lamp on the marble table. "That's what troubles me."

"How do you mean?"

Mike's voice slowed. He seemed to be choosing his words carefully. "Chief Blackwell's treating this child-molestation case like a done deal. Solved. He's pulling my men off the case. Told me to terminate the watch on Abie Rutherford in twenty-four hours."

"And that bothers you?"

"Yeah. That bothers me a lot."

"You think Blackwell is wrong?"

"Blackwell is a politician. He has to answer to the press. If you give him a likely suspect in a high-profile case, he's going to take it." Mike's head slowly turned to face Ben. "But what if he's wrong?"

"How can he be wrong?" Ben asked. "If Bentley isn't the one, how did he get that cap?"

"I don't know," Mike murmured. "But somehow, the whole thing doesn't seem right. It's too easy. Too convenient."

"I don't follow."

"Look, I've been chasing this man for months. I've studied all the profiles. Bentley doesn't fit."

"You've said yourself that offender profiles are unreliable."

"Yeah, but not this unreliable. You have to understand. These pedophiles—they become consumed with this sexual need. This desire. It controls their whole life. Where is the evidence that child molestation played *any* part in Chris Bentley's life? Where are the dirty magazines? The pictures of little boys? The naughty toys?"

"Maybe he kept them somewhere else to be safe. Just as he took Abie to that North Side ruin with the mattress. It would be stupid to keep anything in his own home."

"Maybe," Mike said, stroking his toothpick. "Maybe."

"And look at these pictures, Mike. You have to admit this guy is some kind of pervert."

"Yeah—*some* kind of pervert, but not the *right* kind of pervert. Everyone indulging in deviant sexual practices is not a pedophile."

Ben laid a hand on Mike's shoulder. "Are you sure you're not upset just because . . . you didn't catch him? I know you've put a lot of time in on this case."

"Maybe you're right. Maybe I need time for it all to sink in." He half smiled. "My father always used to say, 'Mike, the only thing you hate more than doing work is having someone else do it for you.' "

Ben grinned. If only half of Mike's stories about his father were true, he'd been a hell of a character. "Mike . . . did you like your dad?"

Mike's eyebrows rose. "My dad? Hell, yeah. He was great."

"Really?"

"Oh yeah. We used to play basketball out on the driveway, wrestle. We fished, we camped. It wasn't all just jock-macho stuff, either. He was the one who first turned me on to

Shakespeare. And the greatest thing about him was, no matter how busy he got, and he was pretty busy sometimes, he always made sure he saved time for me."

"Sounds like a pretty spectacular dad."

"He was. He was my hero, all through my childhood. Hell, all through my life. He was a model father. He's the reason I always wanted . . . I mean . . . you know, when I was married to your sister, we always wanted . . ." Mike's voice trailed off. "But we never got any."

"Yeah," Ben said quietly. "I know."

"Hell, my dad was the one who first turned me on to police work. Did you know that? I started showing some interest in crime, reading Sherlock Holmes, and he didn't discourage me like some fathers would. He took me to the police station, introduced me around, helped me learn how to become a cop."

"So he approved of your career choice?"

"Oh yeah. Is that so amazing?"

Probably only to me, Ben thought. "I guess I'm not used to the idea of a father charting the course of his son's life."

"Ah, but they all do." Mike smiled. "One way or the other."

* 58 *

Judge Hawkins surprised everyone by arriving early the next morning. Ben was running late; he'd overslept (a nasty consequence of visiting crime scenes in the middle of the night) and he'd barely had time to grab all his files and scramble to the courthouse. Fortunately, he'd done his preparation the night before.

"Let's get this show on the road," Judge Hawkins said. He appeared a bit grumpier than usual today. "And counsel," Hawkins added, looking only at Ben, "some of the examinations yesterday were, in my humble opinion, somewhat over-leisurely. Let's see if we can pick up the pace, shall we?"

Ben didn't smile. They had made it through three witnesses yesterday, for Pete's sake. Hawkins was trying to intimidate him into going easy on the cross-ex of the prosecution's witnesses. Ben wasn't about to shortchange Leeman's defense just to keep the judge from getting antsy.

"The State calls Dr. Martin Paglino to the stand."

Another expert? Ben was surprised; he thought the State had completed the forensic aspect of its case. The jury was ready to get on with the nitty-gritty. Including the much-anticipated confession.

Paglino was a short man of slight build with an academic bent. Turned out he worked the night shift in the forensics lab at Central Division, and consequently he was assigned the chore of analyzing the physical evidence collected at the Alvarez crime scene.

"Dr. Paglino," Bullock asked, after the preliminaries were

completed, "did you have a chance to examine the blood splatters that were scraped off the defendant?"

"I did."

"And what did you find?"

"I found that the blood came from the victim, Maria Alvarez. It matched both in type and in rtDNA structure."

"How reliable is rtDNA blood comparison, doctor?"

"In my opinion? One hundred percent."

Bullock strolled past the jury box, allowing the jury time to absorb the import of that statement. "And did you find any of the defendant's own blood on the surface of his skin?"

"No."

"Was there any indication that he was harmed in any way?"

"Not that I saw."

"So there was no evidence of self-defense. Or even a struggle."

"No."

A bold conclusion, but as an expert, Paglino could get away with it. There was no point in objecting and creating an issue where none existed. Truth to tell, there *was* no evidence of a struggle.

Bullock continued. "Did you search the crime scene for fingerprints?"

"I personally did not," the doctor said hastily, as if somewhat taken aback by the suggestion that he might actually perform physical labor. "I have people who do that for me."

"Of course. Did you examine the prints they collected?"

"I did."

"Did you find any prints that belonged to the defendant?"

"Oh yes. All over the crime scene."

"Objection!" Ben said. "Of course his prints were all over the place. He worked there. He slept there!"

Hawkins peered down from the bench. "I fail to see what evidentiary objection that statement conveys."

Ben didn't either, but it was a fact he definitely wanted to bring to the jury's attention. "Sorry, your honor."

Bullock proceeded. "Exactly where did you find the defendant's prints?"

"On his locker."

"What about the golf bag that was found inside the locker?"

"His prints were all over it."

"Of course, he was a caddy."

"True. But that particular set of clubs was new. None of the caddies' prints were on them."

A soft muttering was audible from the jury box.

"Did you find the defendant's prints anyplace else?"

"Yes." There was an extended pause. Ben had come to recognize this as a sign that Bullock's witness was about to unload a biggie. "His fingerprints were found in numerous locations on the victim's clothing."

"His prints were on Maria Alvarez?"

"Yes."

"What part of her body?"

"Mostly her upper body. Waist, neck, torso."

"Near the point where the murder weapon entered her body."

Dr. Paglino looked at the jury. "Exactly."

Bullock pivoted on one heel and returned to his table. "No more questions."

Ben was up before Judge Hawkins had a chance to invite him. "First of all, Dr. Paglino, let's talk about what you didn't say. Then we'll get to what you did say."

The doctor bowed his head. "As you wish."

"For instance, you didn't mention the necklace that was purportedly found in Leeman's locker. Did you find Leeman's prints on that?"

"By its nature, a linked chain of gemstones makes a poor surface for body-oil deposits—"

"Answer the question, Doctor."

"I'm trying to explain that this doesn't necessarily mean—"

"Leave the arguing to the lawyers, doc. Did you find his fingerprints on the necklace?"

The doctor exhaled. "No."

"And you looked, didn't you?"

"Of course I did."

"Probably looked as hard as it was possible to look. Mr. Bullock probably ordered you to look eight or ten times. But you didn't find anything, did you?"

"As I said, no."

Ben realized he should move on. He was just so elated to have finally scored a point, no matter how small, that he wanted to savor the moment as long as possible. "What about the golf club? The murder weapon."

"What about it?"

"I'll bet you checked it for prints, too."

The good doctor was becoming visibly perturbed. "You're right."

"Did you find Leeman's fingerprints on it?"

"Oh yes."

"Where were the prints?"

"Where would you expect? On the grip. The handle."

"So," Ben said, "the prints were consistent with the possibility that Leeman tried to remove the club after she had been murdered."

"Objection!" Bullock said. "Calls for speculation."

"No I didn't," Ben said quickly, before Hawkins could rule against him. He'd seen this coming and chosen his words carefully. "I asked if the evidence was consistent with a particular hypothetical scenario. That's a permissible line of inquiry with an expert witness."

Hawkins grudgingly overruled the objection. "The witness will answer."

"I'll repeat," Ben said. "Is the fingerprint evidence consistent with the possibility that Leeman tried to remove the club from the woman's neck?"

"The evidence is consistent," Paglino said, "with the theory that the defendant held the club by the grip when he rammed it through the victim's throat."

"That wasn't my question," Ben said calmly. "Stop trying to ram the prosecution's conjectures down the jury's throat. Just tell them what the evidence is."

"We found distinct fingerprints on the club grip. The defendant clearly held it tightly."

"But there's no way you can tell from the prints *why* he held it."

"That's true."

"Thank you, Doctor. Now, you said you found Leeman's prints all over the victim's upper body."

"That's true. It would be difficult to thrust in the club without impacting to some degree on the body."

"Doctor, wouldn't these prints also be consistent with a simple hug?"

Paglino paused. "Did you see any of the pictures taken of that woman at the crime scene?" he asked.

"Yes," Ben replied. "We all did."

Paglino nodded. "I wouldn't have hugged a body in that condition. I don't think anyone would."

"Maybe the hug occurred before the murder," Ben suggested.

"Maybe it did," Paglino replied. "Maybe she didn't like it. Maybe he wouldn't stop. Maybe that's why he killed her."

Damn. Just when he seemed to be on the verge of making a dent in their case, he played right into Bullock's sex pervert theory. "You don't know for a fact that that's what happened, do you, Doctor?"

"No, of course not."

"Then why do you keep suggesting events to the jury that are not supported by your evidence?"

"I'm just answering your questions."

"You're just saying exactly what your boss told you to say. Right, Doctor?"

"Objection!" Bullock shouted. "This is grossly offensive!"

"I agree," Judge Hawkins said. "Consider yourself warned, counsel. Another outburst like that and you'll be in contempt. Do you have any more questions of this witness?"

"No," Ben said quietly. Threaten me all you like, Hawkins. I made my point. And some of the jurors may have been listening. "That's all."

"Anything more from the prosecution?" the judge asked.

"Just one more witness," Bullock answered. "The witness we've all been waiting for. The State calls Detective Theodore Bickley to the stand. And," he added, "we instruct the witness to bring his videotape with him."

* 59 *

While the witness moved to the front of the courtroom, the bailiff set up the television and VCR and positioned them so the jury could watch.

Lieutenant Bickley could've been Paglino's brother—the one who couldn't get into medical school. He was short, compact, wiry, aggressive. Overcompensating, according to Mike. Mike rarely spoke ill of another police officer, and this was no exception, but Ben still had the distinct impression Bickley was not one of Mike's favorites.

After the witness's background and credentials were established, Bullock asked Bickley to recall the night of the murder ten years before.

"Why were you at the crime scene, Detective?"

"When Sergeant Tompkins radioed in, he indicated that he had discovered a homicide. I was the homicide detective on call that night."

"What did you do when you arrived?"

"First, I conferred with the officers on the scene—Tompkins, Sandstrom, and Morelli. Then I inspected the crime scene. I carefully completed a search of the building and the surrounding grounds."

"Did you interrogate Leeman Hayes?"

"I tried. He was cuffed to the door when I arrived. I read him his rights again, then asked him what happened. He didn't respond."

"What did you do?"

"Well, I realized this case was going to require special attention, so I finished the physical investigation and postponed the questioning for a more formal environment, after I'd had a chance to consult with specialists in . . . difficult witnesses."

"When did you resume the questioning?"

"The next day. About twelve hours later."

"Is there a record of this interrogation?"

"Yes. A videotape."

"Was it common procedure to tape interrogations ten years ago?"

"No. Matter of fact, we had only obtained the video equipment a few weeks before. The reason I thought to use it in this case was, well, the defendant was not answering our questions verbally, but in some instances, he seemed to be . . . acting out his answers."

"You mean, in sign language."

"No. I don't think he knew sign language. It was more like . . . pantomime."

"You're saying the defendant was . . . a mime?"

Ben frowned. Cheap shot, Bullock.

"It's hard to explain," Bickley said. "I can probably explain it better if I can show the tape."

"The tape would assist you in delivering your testimony to the jury?"

"Definitely."

Bullock had Bickley identify the tape and establish the chain of custody. Then he offered the tape into evidence. Ben renewed his prior objections to the use of the tape, but they were overruled. Bullock requested that the jury be permitted to view the tape. Judge Hawkins consented.

Although Ben wasn't able to keep the tape from being used at trial, he successfully insisted that the entire tape be shown. No edited versions, no cutting to the good parts. Ben wanted the jury to understand that the pantomime in question wasn't something Leeman blurted out suddenly; it came only as the product of long, high-pressure, intensive questioning.

Ben had another reason as well, although he would never have admitted it to the judge. The tape showed almost half an hour of fruitless questioning before the critical performance.

Ben hoped that by the time the jury got there, they would be too brain-dead to be horrified.

Unfortunately, this was not to be. From start to finish, the jury seemed fascinated by the tape. Ben supposed it was like being invited backstage—getting to see how confessions are extracted. The climax to the drama came in the form of Leeman reenacting the murder of Maria Alvarez. Although Ben had seen it many times before, it was no less chilling seeing it again.

Through Leeman's eyes, the jury witnessed the whole terrible crime. They saw Leeman run up to Maria and shove her back against the wall; they saw Maria scream in terror. They saw the club plummet down on Maria's head, then saw the broken shaft pierce her throat. Worst of all, they saw Leeman's rage, the expression on his face that seemed to say he was capable of doing anything to anyone.

In the midst of all that, Ben wondered if anyone had noticed the quick quiet moment when Leeman held his palm flat over his eyes. *See?*

He doubted it. He hadn't noticed it himself the first two times he viewed the tape.

After the tape was shown, Bullock concluded his examination. Ben raced to the podium.

"Detective Bickley, how long did you question Leeman before you began videotaping?"

"I'm not sure," Bickley answered.

"Can you give me an estimate?"

"More than two hours."

"So by the time we get to what you called the pantomime, Leeman had been subject to questioning for almost three hours."

"I suppose that's right."

"And this wasn't the first time you questioned him, was it?"

"No. This was the afternoon session. We had interrogated him unsuccessfully for about two and a half hours that morning as well."

"That would be an extremely stressful way to spend the day, don't you agree?"

"All the proper procedures were followed. He exercised his right to have an attorney present. He even had his father there."

"And none of that changes in the least the fact that you pounded him with questions for over five hours. Won't you agree that would be rather stressful?"

"For him or for me? I was doing all the work. He never said a word."

Ben walked back toward the defendant's table where Leeman sat. For once, Ben wanted the jury to notice Leeman.

"Detective, you're aware that Leeman suffers from special learning difficulties, aren't you?"

"That's what I've been told."

"Do you have any reason to doubt it?"

"I'm always suspicious when attorneys start making excuses for defendants." He winked at the jury. "Most of these guys only turn out to be nuts after the lawyers get their hands on them."

"Are you a psychiatrist, Detective?"

"No."

"Are you a specialist in learning disabilities?"

"No."

"Are you any kind of medical doctor?"

"Obviously not."

"Then I'll ask you to keep your uninformed opinions to yourself." Sometimes, a sharp word was better than an objection. "Did you consider having a therapist present at the questioning?"

"I don't recall that we did."

"Did you consider consulting a specialist in learning disabilities or special education?"

"Look, our budget is extremely limited—"

"Don't make excuses, Detective. Did you?"

"No. Look"—Bickley leaned forward, pressing against the outer perimeter of the witness box—"our job isn't to make the witness as cozy and relaxed as possible, okay? Our job is to get him to talk. And to accomplish that goal, we do what it takes." He glanced hastily up at the judge. "Within the boundaries of the law, of course."

"So in other words, you had no intention of giving Leeman a fair shake."

"My intention was to follow the law to the letter. Which I did. End of story."

Ben walked to the VCR, grabbed the remote, and ran the tape back to just before Leeman began his protracted reenactment, when he briefly put his hand over his eyes. *See?*

Ben replayed the snippet three times, until he was certain everyone had observed the action. "Detective, what is the significance of that gesture made by Leeman Hayes before he began the pantomime?"

"The significance? I suppose the sun got in his eyes."

"The sun? You appear to me to be indoors. In a room with no windows."

"Okay, the overhead lights then. So?"

"Your testimony is that the overhead lights shone in his eyes for two seconds just before he began the reenactment—and never before or after. Give the jury some credit, Detective."

"Objection," Bullock said angrily. "This is argumentative."

"Agreed," Hawkins said. "The objection will be sustained. I remind counsel of my previous warning. I meant it."

Ben decided to take another tack. "Detective, you've acknowledged that Leeman was trying to communicate through pantomime, correct?"

"I guess that's so."

"And your testimony is based upon your interpretation of some of his gestures, right?"

"Right."

"To be fair, then, shouldn't we try to interpret *all* of his gestures? Not just the ones you find useful."

"I think I already said—"

"Shouldn't we be trying to determine what he meant when he put his hand over his eyes?"

Bickley smirked. "I'm more interested in the gestures that came later. Like when he beat the woman over the head with the golf club."

"That's your interpretation," Ben said evenly. "But it's a pretty selective one, isn't it? Interpreting the action to which I directed your attention spoils your entire confession theory, doesn't it?"

"I don't know what you mean," Bickley said, but as Ben gazed into the man's eyes he was certain that he did. He had undoubtedly told Bullock, too. They knew. They both knew. They had known all along.

"When you put your hand over your eyes in that manner," Ben continued, "you're communicating that you're *looking. Seeing.* Wasn't Leeman trying to say that this was all something that he *saw*?"

"I wouldn't say so, no."

"Is that because you didn't take that meaning, or because you don't want to spoil Mr. Bullock's case?"

"Objection!" Bullock shouted. He was getting angry, or at least putting on a good show of it.

"Sustained. Counsel, the only reason you're not in jail right now is that I don't want to prejudice your client's rights in the middle of a trial."

The hell you don't, Ben thought.

"*After* the trial, I may not be so generous. If you can't control yourself, I'll terminate this examination."

Ben continued to stare down the witness. Hawkins wouldn't be jumping all over him if he weren't close to something. He couldn't let up now. "Isn't that what Leeman was trying to say? Isn't that what he meant? That he was going to reenact for you something that he *saw*?"

Bickley began to squirm uncomfortably. "How should I know what he was trying to say?"

"Perhaps if you had bothered to consult some people who were trained in this area, you would've known."

"Objection!" Bullock repeated.

Ben ignored him. "Isn't it true that you didn't have anyone there for the same reason you didn't ask anyone about it later. Because you didn't want an unfavorable interpretation to screw up your airtight case!"

"That's a crock of—"

"Objection!" Bullock insisted.

The judge leaned forward. "Counsel—"

Ben plowed on ahead. "Isn't that true, Detective?"

"That's preposterous. I don't—"

"Isn't it true?"

"Look," Bickley said, almost shouting, "we all saw what we saw! The tape speaks for itself."

"No it doesn't!" Ben shouted back. "It doesn't speak for itself because Leeman can't speak for himself. He can't defend himself against people like you who are more interested in getting convictions than getting the truth!"

Judge Hawkins pounded his gavel. "Counsel, I want you to sit down! Now! This examination is over!"

"This is a gross injustice, your honor! They stacked the deck against Leeman ten years ago and they're still stacking it today."

The judge continued to pound. "I am commanding you to sit down!"

"But this isn't a search for the truth! This is a travesty!"

The judge motioned for the sergeant at arms.

"All right, all right," Ben said, brushing him away. "I'm sitting already."

The judge relaxed a bit, then drew himself up and spoke to the jury in his most authoritative tone. "You will disregard every word of counsel's outbursts. In fact, you will disregard his entire cross-examination. I order it stricken from the record. And Mr. Kincaid, we will be discussing disciplinary action at the conclusion of this trial. That's a promise."

Ben didn't doubt it. He didn't look forward to that, but he had to break through the stone wall Bullock and Hawkins were erecting around his client and try to make the jury see the truth. He probably hadn't accomplished a damn thing, but it was just possible someone in the jury box heard what he was trying to say. At the least, Ben had forced the jury to focus on the central ambiguity of the tape. With any luck, perhaps he slowed down the Bullock juggernaut. A little bit, anyway.

"Mr. Bullock, any redirect?"

"Yes." Bullock rose to his feet slowly. Ben had the impression he hadn't actually prepared anything; he just didn't want the jury to go home with Ben's impassioned speech ringing in their heads.

"What happened," Bullock said finally, "after the defendant finished his reenactment of the murder?"

Bickley twisted his neck and adjusted his tie. "You saw it for yourself. He ran away. Ran into the corner and folded up into a ball."

"Did you ask any further questions?"

"No. I didn't see much point."

"Did you hear anything the defendant said?"

"I don't think he said anything. But I saw him. I saw the look in his eyes."

Ben raised his head. This sounded like it was coming dangerously close to opinion testimony rather than fact, but given Ben's performance a few moments before, he didn't think the jury would be impressed by any great show of outrage.

"How would you describe his expression? Was he scared?"

"Scared? No, that wasn't it. Let me tell you, I've been on the force for eighteen years, and I know that expression. It isn't fear. It's shame."

"Nothing more," Bullock said quickly, and sat down.

Hawkins pointedly did not ask Ben if he had any recross. "The witness will step down. Anything further from the prosecution?"

"No, your honor. The prosecution rests."

"Very well, then we'll retire for the day. Court will resume at nine o'clock in the morning with the defendant's first witness. If you gentlemen have any motions you'd like to raise before then, see me in chambers."

Ben did, of course. He would make the traditional motion for a directed verdict, but it would do no good. Hawkins was a prosecution judge, and even if he wasn't, the prosecution had met its burden. They proved that a murder had occurred, and gave more than adequate reason to believe Leeman Hayes was the murderer. What's more, the jury believed it; Ben could see it in their eyes. If Ben was going to turn the jury around, he was going to have to give them some evidence that made them question what they already believed, something that created a reasonable doubt that had not previously cluttered their thoughts.

Ben saw Bullock moving toward the back of the courtroom, where a group of reporters was waiting for him.

"Not yet," Ben told him. "I've got motions to make."

"Myrna can handle that, I'm sure," Bullock said, grinning, barely looking back.

The message was clear. Bullock believed he was winning by such a gigantic margin that he could leave his junior assistant to handle Ben's fruitless motions while he schmoozed the press. In other words, he had nothing to worry about. He thought he had the trial in the bag.

And the terrible thing was, he was right.

FOUR

* *

Time for Your Punishment

* 60 *

Ben returned to his office, pushed his way past the air-conditioner bill collector, and tried to firm up his defense plans. Unfortunately, he really didn't have any. He hadn't uncovered any compelling exculpatory evidence, certainly nothing sufficient to offset the powerful case Bullock had made for the prosecution.

He'd been through the materials Jones had prepared several times. Jones did good work; unfortunately, the evidence just wasn't there. Leeman had had little on his side ten years ago; that was undoubtedly one reason his former attorney pushed for an incompetency ruling. And gathering evidence now, ten years after the fact, was nearly impossible. Who remembered that far back? Who stayed in one place that long? If any helpful witnesses had ever existed, they were almost surely gone now.

Christina entered his inner office. She was wearing a pink chiffon skirt, purple sweater, and penny loafers.

"Nice outfit," Ben commented.

"Well, thanks," she replied. "I like to dress up for court dates. Don't you think I look divine?"

"I think you look like Annette Funicello," Ben replied. "I thought you were going clothes shopping with my mother."

"I want to. But I've been somewhat busy with this trial thing, you know?"

"Sorry to inconvenience you."

"That's all right. I'm used to it."

Ben pushed away from his desk. "So how's the trial look from the gallery?"

Christina averted her eyes. "Well . . . you haven't put on

your case yet. I'm sure it will look better once you get a chance to strut your stuff. You didn't have many facts on your side, but your crosses showed great élan. You're really becoming good in the courtroom, you know it?"

"Compared to what?"

"Well . . ." A sly grin crossed her face. "Compared to when you started."

It was always dangerous to have someone around who knew you before you knew what you were doing. "Are you saying I was incompetent when I started?"

"Not incompetent. Naïve, perhaps. Inexperienced. Pathetic, at times. But not incompetent."

"Glad to hear I've improved."

"Well, so are your clients."

Ben pushed around the quagmire of trial-related papers on his desk. "But it doesn't change the fact that I don't have a defense for Leeman Hayes. He deserves better than me."

"You'll think of something. I know you will. You always do." She bent down and kissed him on the top of the head, then left his office.

Ben tried to return to his work, but less than a minute later Jones popped through the door. "Got some more info for you, Boss."

"About what?"

"About Peru."

Ben raised an eyebrow. "Anything helpful?"

"Maybe. I started with the police records, but I couldn't turn up anything on Maria Alvarez. Apparently she was never in trouble with the law. I tried the Central Registry. They had a birth certificate, but that didn't get me anywhere. Then I thought to try hospitals. Hospitals usually keep very detailed records. Two days later I had her."

"She'd been in a hospital?"

"Oh yeah." Jones grinned. "Before she came to the States. Isn't that great?"

"I don't know. Why do I care whether she went to a hospital or not?"

Jones began to pout. "Gee, Boss, I'm just trying to help. . . ."

"You mean you've been researching all this time, and all you've learned is that Maria Alvarez once went to a hospital?"

"Boss, you just don't get it. This is the key to the whole case."

"Excuse me." To Ben's surprise, Christina was standing in the doorway again. "There's a woman here who would like to talk to you, Ben."

"Tell her to make an appointment."

"She wants to talk to you now."

"I'm trying to prepare for this trial!"

"That's just it, Ben. She says she has information that can help Leeman Hayes. She heard you on the newscast yesterday asking for witnesses, so she came to see you."

That got Ben's attention. "Well, ask her to wait a minute. Now, Jones, what did you mean—"

"She can't wait," Christina insisted. "She says she has to pick up her kids at Riverfield Country Day School. She says if she's late, they'll charge her a dollar a minute."

"Jones, can I put you on hold for a moment?"

"Sure, Boss," he said, still pouting. "Whatever makes you happy. I'm not important."

"Thanks. Maybe we can go for an ice cream later. Show this woman in."

She was a young woman, in her late twenties probably. She had shoulder-length blonde hair and vibrant blue eyes. She was wearing blue jeans and a short-sleeve blouse. She introduced herself as Carlee Crane.

"Thank you for seeing me," Carlee said. "I know you must be busy."

"My legal assistant says you know something about the Maria Alvarez murder."

"That's true. . . ."

"Great." Ben leaned forward in his chair. "What do you know?"

"Well, you see . . ." She swallowed, then fidgeted with her purse. "I know this is going to sound strange, but—I saw it."

Ben's eyes ballooned. "You saw the murder?"

"That's right. I was an eyewitness. I was working in the

kitchen in the dining room at the country club late that night, trying to build up some overtime. They kept promising they'd promote me to waitress, but the maître d' was hitting on me, and I wouldn't play along, so I stayed in the kitchen. It was a crummy job, but I was very poor, and I was trying to save up for a car. . . ."

Ben tried to restrain himself. "Pardon me, but could we talk about the murder? I want to make sure I understand this. You actually saw the murder? Like, with your own eyes?"

"R-right."

"Why on earth haven't you mentioned this before now? Like ten years before now?"

"Well, this is the really strange, embarrassing part, Mr. Kincaid. To tell you the truth—I forgot about it."

"You *forgot*?"

"I know that sounds impossible, but it's true." She walked across the tiny office to the window. "It was such a shock, such a horrible, horrible thing. I must have just—blocked it out of my mind somehow."

"But how could you—"

"I can't possibly explain it in any way that makes sense. I just know I didn't remember. My memory was unreliable. It was playing tricks on me. Can you imagine?"

Without thinking, Ben withdrew a photograph from his pocket. It was the photo of him, at age three, and his father, tickling him, both of them laughing hysterically, having a wonderful time.

"I'll do my best," Ben said quietly. "Now sit down and tell me the whole story. From the beginning."

* 61 *

Mike tried to look tough as he swaggered down the dark city streets of Tulsa's North Side. He walked with his hips first, his trench coat flapping, a bounce in his step and a toothpick between his lips. Don't mess with me, he told the denizens of the night (and they were out there; he knew they were). I'm bad. Very bad. Bad for your health.

Okay, so maybe the toothpick didn't add that much, but he had gone almost two weeks without lighting that damn pipe and he wasn't going to stop now. Personally, he had always thought his pipe smoking inoffensive, even charming, debonair, but it was clear to him that the rest of the world no longer shared his sentiment. He was tired of standing by himself at parties. And it had been months since he'd been out on a date. . . .

Months? Truth to tell, he hadn't been on a date since he saw Julia the last time, and he wasn't sure that could be classified as a date. After all, she was his ex-wife. And there was the minor detail that she was still married to another man at the time.

At the time. No longer. If he lived to be a hundred, he would never understand that woman. Which would be okay, if he could just forget. But memories were funny things. Some of them were gone the next day. And some of them lingered like an albatross, haunting the shadowy recesses of your brain, refusing to set you free.

Just like Julia herself.

He had perfected this macho strut (so he hoped) during the time he had spent doing undercover work in many of these same North Side neighborhoods. Then, it hadn't been just an affectation. It was a survival technique.

Speaking of survival, if Chief Blackwell found out what Mike was doing, his would be at an end. Blackwell had been giving press conferences all morning announcing that the child molester was dead. All the news shows carried the story. How could they resist? A handsome, wealthy, charity-working socialite turns out to be a pedophile who accidentally kills himself while indulging in deviant dangerous solo sex. A journalist's dream.

So now the city of Tulsa assumed the pedophile's reign of terror was over. Parents breathed a sigh of relief. Mike had already been replaced as Abie's personal bodyguard, and the watch on Abie was to be terminated, effective nine o'clock tomorrow morning. It was all over. But . . .

But what if they were wrong?

The question continued to haunt Mike.

There was only one way to know for sure, and that was to find the apartment, the place where the pervert took Abie. If Bentley hadn't planned to die, he wouldn't have removed all his pedophilic paraphernalia. There had to be evidence there that would tell them for certain who the man was.

The only trouble was finding it.

Mike could probably spend his nights, maybe even his days, looking for this place, but he also wanted someone to watch Abie after the police watch terminated. He couldn't do both. Especially without tipping off Blackwell. Which meant he couldn't use any of the other men on the force.

Well, he had until nine before he had to worry about Abie. For now, he was going to try to find the damn apartment.

Airplanes, Abie had said. I saw airplanes in the sky. Real airplanes. Overhead.

Assuming that he wasn't hallucinating, which was possible, since he had been drugged, Abie must've been somewhere near the airport, Tulsa International, on the North Side between Sheridan and Memorial. Problem was, the airport was surrounded on all sides by residential and commercial properties of all shapes and sizes. Abie's description eliminated nothing.

Well, if police work were easy, then everyone would be doing it, right? Mike had taken a map of Tulsa and drawn a series of concentric circles around the airport, ever widening. He walked the lines systematically, moving outward from the airport. Eventually, he would have to come across the place where the maniac took Abie.

He just hoped he knew it when he saw it.

He turned a corner and was immediately approached by an emaciated young woman in a green halter top, short-shorts, and a white billowy scarf. Granted, it was hot, even at night, but her attire was a bit scanty even for August.

"Wanna have a party?" she asked, stepping closer to Mike than would normally be deemed appropriate in polite society.

"I don't think so."

"I'll make it worth your while."

"I don't doubt it."

"I'll show you a good time."

"Thanks, but I'm really not interested."

"Bet I could make you interested." She wrapped her scarf around his neck and pulled him closer to her. "What do you say, you handsome devil, you?"

Of course, Mike thought, the easiest way out of this would be to simply utter three words: I'm a cop. But that would undoubtedly throw her into a panic, and maybe her pimp, too, wherever he was lurking. Vice squads always worked in pairs, and for good reason. Plus, if he identified himself, he had an obligation to haul her in. He didn't want the word to get around that the cops were soft on hookers. But he didn't want to mess with an arrest right now; he had more urgent concerns.

"Look, lady, I'm sure it would be heaven on earth, but I just don't have time right now." He gently pushed her away. "I'll take a rain check, okay?"

"You're making a big mistake."

"I know. By the way, do you work this area often?"

"Every night, lover boy."

"I don't suppose . . . you wouldn't've happened to have seen . . ."

"Spit it out, handsome."

"Have you ever noticed any trolls in the area?"

The young woman gave him a long look. "Trolls?"

Mike felt his face flushing. "Yes, trolls. You know, cute short little guys . . ."

"My man Eduardo is barely five foot. We call him the Stump. That isn't why, though."

"No, I mean real trolls. Like from a fairy tale or something."

"You believe in fairy tales, handsome?"

"Maybe a picture of trolls? A poster? A sign?"

"Sorry. Doesn't ring any bells." She smiled at him again. "You sure you wouldn't like a quickie? I think you could use some peace of mind."

"No, thanks." He walked past her and continued in the same direction. Poor kid—she was probably a runaway, probably a junkie. A while back he and Ben had had some close dealings with teenage prostitutes. Closer than he ever wanted to have again. It wasn't a pretty picture.

He tried to clear his mind. He couldn't afford to be distracted. He was going to keep at it, until he was done, until he found what he was looking for.

Until he knew Abie was safe.

It was tough being someone's hero. They expected you to do things right.

* 62 *

It was dark by the time Ben got home that evening, but it didn't matter. He could have closed his eyes and still found his way to his room. All he had to do was follow his nose.

"What is this?" Ben asked as his mother slid the plate in front of him.

"A spinach soufflé, of course."

"Is this another of my childhood favorites?"

Mrs. Kincaid took her place at the other end of the table with a much smaller portion of the same. "I'm afraid not. We could never get you to eat any green vegetables. Actually, we could never get you to eat anything green, period. I had hoped you'd improved your eating habits since then."

Ben stared at his plate. "Well . . ."

"Don't bother lying. I've been through your kitchen cabinets."

"You looked through—"

"Don't protest. It's a mother's prerogative."

Ben took a bite of the soufflé. It was actually quite tasty. Barely tasted of spinach at all.

"Something seems different," Ben commented.

"About the soufflé?"

"No. About my apartment."

Mrs. Kincaid looked back at him innocently. "Such as what?"

"I'm not sure. Can't quite put my finger on it."

Mrs. Kincaid shrugged, then changed the subject. "How is the trial going?"

Ben shook his head. "You don't want to know."

"Benjamin, if I didn't want to know, I wouldn't have asked."

Ben drew in his breath. Mothers. "I start putting on defense witnesses tomorrow morning."

"Who are your witnesses?"

"Well, I've got a new eyewitness who forgot that she was an eyewitness for about ten years. Her testimony could be critical, but to make it credible, I'm going to need an expert on memory loss who can explain this phenomenon to the jury. Jones is currently scouring the countryside for such an expert. And if that doesn't work, I may call some of the country-club board members, none of whom are going to want to tell me anything."

Mrs. Kincaid took a tiny bite of her soufflé, chewed it thoroughly, then swallowed. "Perhaps I can help."

Ben smiled politely. "I hardly think so."

"Why not? I've been dealing with wealthy, high-society sorts for half my life. What kind of men are they?"

"I didn't know there were different kinds."

"Of course there are. They can be divided into two main categories: those who worked hard and earned their money, and those who inherited it. Which are these?"

"The latter I think, with one partial exception, and he's dead. What difference does it make?"

"It makes all the difference in the world, if your plan is to trick them into saying something they don't want to say. That's what lawyers do, isn't it?"

"Well . . . I wouldn't put it quite like that. . . ."

"These men are probably well educated, right?"

"Undoubtedly."

"So you're not going to outthink them. Nothing personal, Benjamin." She batted a finger against her lips. "You need to make them *want* to talk to you."

"And how do I do that?"

"What you have to understand is that men who inherit money have enormous insecurity complexes. If you've earned a tub of money, that's one thing. You can feel good about that. You can have a feeling of personal accomplishment. But a man who has just been given everything, through no virtue of his own, even though he never accomplished anything of value in his whole life, is going to feel terribly inadequate. He will worry about what other people think of him." She paused. "He thirsts for the opportunity to brag about himself."

"And how am I going to use that in court?"

"Think about it, Benjamin. If your man sees an opportunity to strut, he's much more likely to say something a cooler head would realize shouldn't be said. Don't you see that?"

Ben tapped his fork on the rim of his plate. "That's not bad. I'll give it some thought."

Mrs. Kincaid beamed. "What do you know? Perhaps your old mother isn't as out of touch as you thought."

Perhaps not. "I still think there's something odd about my apartment."

"I'd say there are many odd things about it," Mrs. Kincaid replied dryly.

"No, I mean—" He snapped his fingers. "I'm not sweating!"

"I'm so pleased, Benjamin."

"No, I mean—that's it! For the first time in weeks I'm not sweating."

Mrs. Kincaid began to look somewhat uncomfortable. "Oh, really . . ."

"I know the temperature hasn't dropped. . . ." Ben walked into the living room. The answer was perched in the window. "There's an air-conditioning unit! Someone put a new air conditioner in my window."

"Indeed?" Mrs. Kincaid said absently. "My goodness . . ."

"You did this." Ben stomped back into the kitchen. "You had an air conditioner installed."

"Well, it has been terribly hot. . . ."

"How dare you!"

"Benjamin, it was miserable in here! Think of the baby—"

"If you needed an air conditioner, you should've told me. I would've bought one."

"Well, Benjamin, I know you've been financially strapped. . . ."

"That's beside the point."

"But I have more money than I—"

"I've told you repeatedly that I don't want any of my father's money!"

"It's *my* money—"

"It's *his* money!" Ben pulled the snapshot out of his pocket and threw it on the table. "His! And if he had wanted me to have it, his will would've read quite a bit differently."

"All the will said was—"

"I don't want to rehash it!" Ben realized he was shouting, and realized that he had no business shouting at his mother, but he couldn't stop himself.

"Benjamin, you're being irrational. It's just an air conditioner."

"This is not about an air conditioner. This is about whether I'm going to be in charge of my own life!"

"Oh, Benjamin—" Her voice cracked. "That's so . . . stupid!"

"Right. Now you're going to make me feel guilty, like you and my father have all my life."

Mrs. Kincaid drew her head erect and threw her shoulders back. "I'll have the air conditioner removed."

"Good."

"While I'm at it, I'll remove myself also."

Ben hesitated only a moment. "Well . . ."

Too late. She marched out of the kitchen.

"Mo-*ther*—" But she was gone.

Ben slumped down in his chair. He hadn't meant to yell at her. He really hadn't. She was right. He *was* being stupid. Irrational. But he just couldn't help himself. Somehow, for some reason—

Damn.

He picked up his fork and took another bite of the soufflé, but the taste had gone out of it.

* 63 *

Early the next morning, with Joey bundled in his arms, Ben stopped by his office to see if Christina and Jones had accomplished their missions. Unfortunately, on his way in, he nearly tripped over the man from the air-conditioning company.

"Are you still here?" Ben said. "Get a life already!"

"I told you, I'm not leaving till this bill is paid. I'm on permanent assignment."

"What is it with you? I've admitted that I owe you money. I've told you I'll pay it as soon as I can. What more do you want? Just repossess the damn thing and get it over with. Or file a lawsuit, like everybody else in the country."

"A fine attitude for you to take. I'm not the deadbeat who missed a payment. If you'll just pay me what you owe, I'll be gone."

"Look, I'm in the middle of a murder trial, and what's worse, I'm losing. I need an expert witness that I haven't got, my mother is mad at me, I'm stuck with my sister's baby, and my cat keeps dropping dead animals in my bed. I didn't get a lick of sleep last night, and frankly, I don't have time for this. So get out of my face!"

Unfortunately, Ben's diatribe woke the baby. Joey's tiny eyelids opened, and he began to sob.

Christina emerged from the back room and took the baby from him. "Now look what you've done."

"He was sound asleep a moment ago."

"Right. Till you started in with the air-conditioner man." Christina waved him toward a chair. "Sit down and collect yourself."

"I do not need to collect myself!"

"Right."

Ben allowed himself to be dragged to a chair. Christina got the formula out of the diaper bag, poured it, and plopped a bottle in Joey's mouth. The caterwauling subsided.

"Do you need a massage?" Christina asked.

"Is this one of those deals where you draw concentric circles around my temples and mutter the secrets of the cosmos into my ear? No, that's not what I need."

"True. What you need is a major sedative, but all I can offer is the massage." Ignoring him, she began massaging his scalp with her free hand. "What are you doing with Joey? You're due in the courtroom in less than an hour."

"Mother left."

"Where did she go?"

"I don't know. When I got up, she was gone."

"I can't believe she would leave you with the baby when you're in the middle of a trial—" Christina stopped, then her eyes narrowed. "Ben, did you do something crazy?"

"I most certainly did not."

"She just decided to pack her bags and say *au revoir*, with no provocation."

"Well, I didn't say—"

"Ben, how *could* you?"

"How could I what?"

"How could you be mean to your mother? I mean, she's your *mother*!"

"I didn't do anything that—"

"I bet you did. You yelled at her, didn't you, and said something awful?"

"Well . . ."

"I knew it. Did she tell you she was leaving?"

"Well, yes, but I assumed she was taking the baby with her."

Christina stopped massaging. "Ben, when are you going to figure it out?"

"Figure what out?"

"This is your blind spot. Deep down, I know you're a sweetheart. But when it comes to your family, you go off the deep end."

"I don't think that's—"

"And the worst of it is, I never got to go clothes shopping with her!"

On this point, Ben joined in her grieving. "Look, Christina, I hate to lay this on you, but you're going to have to look after Joey while I'm in court."

"No way!"

"I'm sorry, but what else can I do?"

"Let me see. Day care. Mother's Day Out. A Skinner box. There are many possibilities."

"Be serious. I don't have time to arrange for child care. You said you and he were getting along—"

"Ben, you need to stop relying on other people to do all the hard stuff and start acting like a responsible parent."

"But I'm not a responsible parent—"

"Exactly my point."

"I'm not any kind of parent. This is just a temporary situation."

"Yeah, right." Christina repositioned the bottle in Joey's mouth, then passed him back to Ben. "Fine. I'll baby-sit." She rummaged through the diaper bag. "I can't believe I'm doing this. Again. During a major trial. I'm a trained professional. I have a certificate from TJC!"

"Why don't you take him back to my apartment? He seems comfortable there. And . . . um . . . I just had a new air-conditioning unit installed. And if Mother happens to come back, you can give her the kid and head for the courtroom."

"I suppose—"

"Pardon me."

Both Ben and Christina turned. A middle-aged man in a herringbone jacket was poking his head through the front door. "Are you Ben Kincaid?"

"Yes. Can I help you?"

The man stammered awkwardly. "Well . . . I was told I could help you."

"Help me—how?"

"I'm a doctor. Oh, how stupid of me." He patted his jacket and searched through his pockets frenetically, removing tissues, eyeglasses, and a pocket watch. "Here's my card. Dr. Emil Allyn."

"And how can you . . ."

"I guess I haven't made myself clear. I'm a psychiatrist."

Ben's brow protruded. "Christina, if this is your idea of a joke . . ."

"No, no, no," Allyn insisted. "When I say *help*, I mean . . . well, I'm a specialist in traumatic memory suppression."

Ben stepped forward and clasped the man's shoulder. "Jones came through! You're my expert witness!"

Allyn looked faintly embarrassed. "I guess so. If you wish me to be."

"I do! Believe me I do!"

"Well, uh, fine then. By the way . . ." He pointed. "You're getting formula on my suit."

* 64 *

As Ben pushed his way forward he could feel the heat radiating from all points in the courtroom. The place was packed. Not only was every seat in the gallery filled, but to make matters worse, there were two rows of standing-room observers on three sides. It was like trying a case in a sardine can.

Everyone Ben had noticed in the gallery on previous days was there again today. Ernest Hayes was back, of course, with several of his children. He kept glancing back at two black youths standing in the rear. They weren't wearing their matching jackets, but Ben was almost certain they were Demons.

The coterie from the country club was all there, including Harold and Rachel Rutherford. Today, they were sitting together. Though the physical space between them had closed, Ben had a feeling the emotional space between them was as great as ever.

To Ben's surprise, he saw Mike enter the courtroom, with Abie clinging tightly to his pant leg.

As they walked down the nave of the courtroom, Harold Rutherford stopped them. "Abie!" he said to his son. "I wasn't expecting to see you here!"

Abie did not answer.

"I don't think Abie should be here," Rutherford told Mike.

"Just a brief stop," Mike answered. "I need to speak with one of the attorneys. Then we'll be leaving."

"They say the trial will probably end today," Rutherford said. "Abie, would you like to do something afterward?"

Abie took an extended interest in the parquet floor.

"Maybe we could go to Bell's, if you wanted." He glanced at his wife. "Or we could just go to the mall and . . . hang out. Whatever . . ."

Abie squeezed Mike's hand and tried to pull him away.

"I'll bring him back to the house this afternoon," Mike said. "Maybe you can work something out then."

Rutherford nodded politely, then let them pass.

Mike struggled through the crowd and made his way to the defense table, boy in tow.

"What a cute pair you two make," Ben said, punching his pal on the shoulder.

"We do not," Mike said, bristling. "I've never been cute in my entire life."

"You are now. You really seem like a natural for this sort of work. Kind of like Mary Poppins."

"Ha-ha."

"Maybe you should give up law enforcement and open a day-care center."

Mike laid a finger firmly on Ben's chest. "That's enough."

Ben laughed. "Sorry. Didn't mean to suggest that you had a sensitive side." He leaned into Mike's ear and whispered, "Why do you still have the kid? I thought Blackwell called the protection off."

"He did. But the Rutherfords don't know that. I'm not letting the kid roam unprotected till I'm absolutely positive it's safe."

"I see." Ben leaned back and spoke normally. "What brings you to court?"

Mike glanced down at Abie. He was fascinated by the courtroom and the crowd and didn't appear to be paying any attention to Ben and Mike. "I need a favor. Will you help me?"

"If I can. What do you need?"

"This is a problem that should be very familiar to you by now. I need a baby-sitter."

"Mike—"

"Look, I can't ask any of the boys on the force. I'm not even supposed to be doing this. If Blackwell found out I wasn't treating this case as closed, he'd be royally pissed."

"Mike . . . maybe you should just give this a rest. After all, they found the baseball cap. . . ."

"Look." Mike stepped closer to Ben and dropped his voice to a whisper. "The last few nights, while I was off duty, I did some footwork in the area where I think the creep took Abie. Covered almost half of it myself, block by block."

"Have you slept?"

"Not in three days, but that's beside the point."

"Mike, you can't—"

"Just listen. I think I'm close, Ben. I really do. I can't explain why, but I think I'm closing in. I know I am. If I can find the creep's lair, then I'm certain I'll find something that will tell us for sure who he is. Or was. If it was Bentley, fine. We can all rest easy. But if it wasn't . . ." He glanced down at the boy. "Then Abie is still in danger. I want to finish my search today, without delay, before Blackwell finds out what I'm doing. And I can't do it with—" He jerked his head violently in Abie's direction.

"But Mike—I'm in the middle of a trial!"

"Well, what about Christina?"

"She's at my place looking after Joey."

"Perfect!" he exclaimed. "If she's already stuck baby-sitting, she won't mind taking one more."

"Well . . . I suppose you can ask."

"Great. I'll drive over now. By the way—" His voice dropped again to a whisper. "Word at the station is that Bullock has plotted a nasty surprise for you. I mean something even worse than what he's done already. Stay on your toes."

Swell. "I'll do my best."

"I know you will." He slapped Ben on the back. "Personally, I hope you kick Bullock's butt, but I never said that."

"Of course you didn't."

"Break a leg."

A few minutes after Mike left, Leeman Hayes was escorted into the courtroom. Ben heard some footsteps in chambers, and the bailiff announced the judge's entrance.

"I'm glad to see everyone made it back to the courtroom

today," Judge Hawkins said. "Mr. Kincaid, I guess it's your turn at the tee. What have you got for us?"

Ben pushed himself slowly to his feet. "The defense calls Ms. Carlee Crane."

* 65 *

As Carlee walked to the witness stand Ben scrutinized the faces in the courtroom, including the jurors. Everyone looked puzzled. Who on earth could this woman be? they undoubtedly wondered. Bullock seemed equally perplexed, probably marveling at how Ben had kept the identity of one of his witnesses secret so long. That, of course, is easy, if you don't find her until the day before.

Carlee settled into her chair and glanced uneasily at the jurors. She looked nervous. But, of course, every witness was nervous; Ben knew nervousness was not exclusive to the dishonest. He hoped the jury knew, too.

Ben ran through the preliminary foundational questions, then proceeded to the night of the murder.

"Carlee, what were you doing on August twenty-fifth, ten years ago?"

Carlee stared out into the gallery, probably looking to her husband for moral support. "I was working at the Utica Greens Country Club."

"And what were you doing there?"

"I was working in the kitchen."

"As a cook?"

"More like a scullery maid. Any kind of grunge work that needed to be done, I did it."

"Do you remember what you were doing the night of August twenty-fifth?"

"Yes, I believe I do. The kitchen closed at eleven o'clock, but I agreed to do the cleanup afterward, which usually took at least an hour. I didn't like it, but I needed the money. Plus, my boss, Mr. Franklin, kept saying that if I accumulated a hundred hours of overtime, he would make me a waitress, which paid better and didn't require you to stay up all night scraping dried goo off plates. Except when I finally had enough hours, Mr. Franklin asked if I liked Mantovani and would I like to see his collection of erotic videos and what color underwear did I wear anyway—"

"If we can get back to the country club," Ben said.

"Yes." Carlee folded her hands in her lap. "So I was working late that night."

"When did you finish in the kitchen?"

"About midnight."

"Then what did you do?"

"I left the main building, where the dining room and kitchens are, and started for home. I didn't have a car, so I had to walk, even if it was late at night. I had found that the quickest way home was to take a shortcut across the golf course between the first and eighth tees."

"Did that route take you anywhere near the caddyshack?"

"Pretty close, yeah. Normally I never noticed, but on this night, as I passed by, I heard some loud voices coming from inside."

"Did you investigate?"

"Oh, yeah. I mean, I'm not normally nosy, but that was so strange. I didn't think anyone would be in there at that time of night."

"What did you do?"

Carlee looked down at her hands. Her voice began to show signs of hesitation. "I approached the side of the building closest to me—the north side—and looked in through a window. It was open."

"What did you see?"

Carlee licked her lips, then gathered her thoughts. "I saw—" She inhaled deeply. "I saw a dark-haired woman pressed into the corner of the room."

Ben held up the previously identified picture of Maria Alvarez. "Was this the woman?"

Carlee glanced at the picture. "Yes, that was her."

"Are you sure?"

"I'm positive."

"Why was she in the corner?"

Carlee looked anxiously at the jury. "She was being forced back . . . by a man."

"Was the man holding any kind of weapon?" Ben asked.

"Yes. A golf club."

"What did he do with it?"

Carlee closed her eyes, focusing on the flickering memory. "They talked for a few moments . . . I couldn't hear what they said. Then the man raised the club over his head. The woman's eyes widened in terror and she screamed."

"And then?"

"And—and then the man brought the club down on her head. He raised it again, and this time brought it down on her shoulder. She screamed, but she stayed on her feet."

"How many times did he hit her?"

"I'm—I'm not sure. Two or three. Then the club broke. That made the man mad. He picked up the broken shaft and"—she looked away suddenly—"pierced the woman's throat."

Ben allowed her a moment before proceeding. "How could you tell what he did?"

"I . . . saw it. With my own eyes. The woman was scream-ing, but when the shaft went through her throat . . . it was as if her voice disappeared. Instantly. That was even more fright-ening. Then the blood spurted everywhere, out of her neck and her veins, and . . . and . . . the smell engulfed the room. That sickly sweet smell of blood . . ." She began to sob. "You can't imagine how . . . horrible it was . . . I was only seventeen at the time. I had never seen anything like that before. . . ."

Ben passed up a tissue by way of the bailiff and gave Carlee a few moments to collect herself. "What did you do next?"

Carlee wiped the tears from her eyes. "I don't know. I was in such shock. The next thing I remember, I was home in bed."

"I understand. Now, Carlee, this is a very important ques-tion." Ben could see the jurors leaning slightly forward with anticipation. They knew what the question was going to be. "Who was the man you saw in the caddyshack?"

"But that's just it—I don't know. He was facing away from me."

Ben knew he had to follow up quickly, before the jurors' interest became irritation. "Could you describe him?"

"He seemed tall. At least six feet, or close. Medium build." She took another deep breath. "And he was white."

Hallelujah. "Are you sure about that, Carlee?"

"Oh yes. He was only about ten feet away from me."

"Is it possible there was a trick of the light that distorted his skin color?"

"No. He was a white man."

"Thank you." The good stuff was over, but Ben knew what this witness's principal weakness was. Trial Tactics 101 told him it would be smarter to expose it himself than to let Bullock make a fuss about it during cross-ex.

"Carlee, since you were an actual eyewitness to this murder, why haven't you come forth before now?"

Carlee turned to the jury and offered them her most sincere expression. "Well, until recently . . . I didn't remember."

"You didn't remember? You forgot?"

"I don't think it was that I forgot so much as that"—she struggled for the right words—". . . I blocked it out."

Ben checked the jury. A few expressions of skepticism, but no out-and-out disbelief. So far, so good. "What caused you to remember?"

"Well, that's difficult to explain. I was on a camping trip with my family—my husband and my two boys. I heard a radio report about this case . . . then later, my husband hurt himself while he was showing the boys how to use a knife properly. It was a small cut, but it bled like crazy. The blood got all over him, and the smell permeated the air, and—"

She looked down suddenly, as if trying to drag the memory out of some cerebral cellar. "And then I remembered. Just for an instant. I flashed on that poor woman, screaming, blood spurting all over her. It was like I was back there, if only for an instant."

"And you realized you were seeing a memory you had suppressed?"

"Not at first. But the next day I saw my husband chopping firewood. From behind, he resembled the man in the caddyshack. He raised his weapon over his head and brought it down hard, and—" She looked up suddenly. "That's when I knew. I saw the whole thing again, front to back, like a movie played out before my eyes. Except this was real. It happened. I was there."

Good enough. That should give the jurors something to think about and, with any luck, would provide the first kernel of a reasonable doubt. "Thank you, Ms. Crane. No more questions at this time."

All eyes in the courtroom passed to Bullock, who sat at his table stroking his chin. For a man who had just heard a surprise eyewitness testify, he seemed singularly undisturbed.

Bullock rose to his feet. "No questions, your honor."

Judge Hawkins himself was caught short this time. "No questions? You mean—you're not going to ask her anything?"

"No, your honor." Bullock lowered himself to his seat. "The defense may call its next witness."

What in the . . . ? Ben stared at his opposite number, utterly flabbergasted. What did he think he was doing? Not crossing an eyewitness? It was crazy! Was he throwing in the towel?

Ben knew better. Bullock would never give up. The only reason he would pass on cross-examination was . . . if he didn't think it was necessary.

Now that was a disturbing thought. Unfortunately, Ben didn't have time to dwell on it.

"Call your next witness," the judge ordered.

"Very well," Ben said. He helped Carlee down from the stand and asked her to wait in the gallery in case he needed her later. "The defense calls Dr. Emil Allyn."

* 66 *

As with any expert witness, the first twenty or thirty minutes of Dr. Allyn's testimony were spent establishing his credentials and getting him qualified as an expert. Ben probably drew it out longer than necessary, but he was taking no chances: He had barely had time to provide the doctor with a rough outline of the subjects they would cover; there was no time to polish.

To Ben's happy surprise, Dr. Allyn performed sensationally. His demeanor was superb and his answers were lucid and concise. He came across as authoritative, but not overbearing; confident, but not egomaniacal. And his professional qualifications and publications on the subject of repressed memory were so extensive they couldn't be seriously challenged. Even by Bullock.

Once Dr. Allyn's expertise was established, Ben launched into the heart of the matter—giving Carlee's testimony the strength of scientific credibility. "Dr. Allyn, can you explain to the jury what is meant by psychogenic amnesia?"

The doctor shifted his gaze to the jury box. "Psychogenic amnesia occurs when a person participates in or witnesses an event so frightening or threatening or guilt provoking that the individual blocks it out of his or her memory to avoid reliving that terrible moment."

"What kind of events could cause this reaction?"

"Any shocking, horrible occurrence. One common cause is child abuse, physical or sexual. Evidence is mounting that such abuse is far more common than we in the psychiatric community realized, because many of the victims subsequently shut the horror out of their minds."

"What if a seventeen-year-old girl witnessed a gruesome, violent murder? Would that be sufficient to induce psychogenic amnesia?"

"Given the right circumstances, it could well be."

"Psychiatrically speaking, how would such an event occur?"

"First, you should understand that traumatic memories form in an altered state of consciousness in which the laws of ordinary memory do not apply. A blanket of amnesia can cloak memories of these intense, violent experiences, particularly when they occur while the person is still a minor. The memory remains suppressed until an adult experience pierces the veil."

"Would that adult experience be something equally intense?"

"Usually not. No, in most cases, the event is something perfectly ordinary that nonetheless jogs the memory and unlocks the closed door."

"For instance, seeing something visually similar to the crime?"

"Correct, but this recovery phenomenon isn't limited to visual input. We have five senses, after all. As you may know, our sense of smell is the most acute of the five, and it is also the sense most closely linked to memory. A familiar smell can recall a past event more readily than any of the other senses."

The foundation was laid. "Dr. Allyn, do you know a woman named Carlee Crane?"

"Yes. I had a private consultation with her earlier today. And of course I heard her testify."

"As you know, she testified that she witnessed a murder, repressed it, and was then reminded of it by several events that occurred while she was camping with her family. Doctor, I know you weren't at the caddyshack the night of the murder, and you can't possibly say with certainty what Carlee saw. But let me ask you this. Is what she described to the jury possible?"

"Her tale of repressed memory is in complete conformity with the current research on this subject."

"So her teenage mind might have repressed that bloody murder?"

"That is consistent with psychiatric opinions on this subject."

"And the incident at Turner Falls, where she saw her husband hurt himself, might have reawakened the memory?"

"Even more than seeing—smelling. Remember, she testified that she detected the sickly sweet smell of blood. That's an unusual, pungent odor—and one she might reasonably not have experienced during the intervening ten years. That may have been enough to bring the memories back."

Despite the relative lack of preparation, this testimony was proceeding even better than Ben had hoped. "To your knowledge, doctor, has the legal community addressed this issue?"

"Oh yes. Since 1988, courts and legislatures in more than twenty-three states have made it possible to bring civil or criminal actions based upon recovered memories."

"And have people done so?"

"I know of over three hundred lawsuits pending at this time involving repressed memories."

Ben whistled. "I guess this isn't all that uncommon, then." He flipped to the next page of his outline, hoping the jury was getting the message.

"Well, it doesn't happen every day, but evidence is mounting that it is far more frequent than we realize."

"And when these people do finally remember what happened, do they typically try to . . . resuppress the memories?"

"That does sometimes happen, but that's not the typical case. It is far better for the person to come forward with what they know. To cleanse themselves of it, so to speak. Only after the patient has retrieved the memory and integrated it in their conscious mind can the healing begin. Only then can the process of getting on with life become possible."

"Thank you, Doctor. Nothing more at this time."

Ben felt a wave of relief as he sat down. That had gone without a hitch. He had not only gotten his eyewitness to tell her story, he'd gotten a psychiatric expert to make it seem credible.

He patted Leeman on the shoulder. Things were looking up.

"Well, then, Mr. Kincaid," Judge Hawkins said. "Call your next—"

"Excuse me." It was Bullock, rising to his feet. "If I may ask just a few questions."

"Oh—of course." Hawkins seemed faintly embarrassed. He had assumed—much like Ben—that if the man hadn't crossed the eyewitness, he wasn't going to cross her expert either. It appeared they were both wrong.

"I don't think this will take long," Bullock said. He walked casually to the stand and positioned himself beside Dr. Allyn. "Doctor, you testified that a growing number of psychiatrists have come to believe that memories may be suppressed over long periods of time."

"That is correct."

"Is this . . . the only viewpoint on the subject?"

The doctor shook his head. "Far from it. Many of my colleagues believe this whole idea of psychogenic amnesia is the biggest scientific blunder since Piltdown Man."

"Really," Bullock said, with what sounded to Ben suspiciously like feigned surprise. "Why would they say that?"

Dr. Allyn removed his glasses. "The problem is that no experiment has ever demonstrated empirically that this syndrome is real. Therefore, it cannot be proved. It is just a theory, not a fact. All the evidence is anecdotal, and it mostly comes from psychologists who have already presumed that the phenomenon exists."

"Why would they do that?"

"Well, it's a natural belief for a Freudian psychiatrist. It arises from the Freudian model of *hysteria*—which includes *repression*, the theory that we suppress what we cannot face. Unfortunately, over time, we have learned that Dr. Freud, brilliant though he was, had an extremely skewed scientific method. Very few of his findings are believed to be literally true today."

"You mean, not every guy wants to sleep with his mother?" Bullock cast an ironic smile toward the predominantly male jury.

"Something like that, yes."

"If this repression concept doesn't really exist, how can you explain all these people who claim to have repressed memories?"

"If the theory is false, then these must be false memories."

"Meaning . . . lies?"

"Not necessarily. Fantasies. Or hallucinations. Wish fulfillment."

"But not reality?"

The doctor cleared his throat and looked directly at the jury. "No. Not reality."

Ben rose an inch out of his chair. What the hell was going on here? Whose expert was he, anyway? Bullock was leading Allyn down the primrose path, and the learned doctor was following him blindly. In fact, he seemed to be going . . . willingly.

Bullock continued. "Surely a trained psychotherapist can distinguish a true memory from a false one."

"That's not as easy as you might think. You have to realize that even with true memories, remembering is not an act of reproduction. It is an act of reconstruction. As a person remembers, gaps and details are naturally filled in. Sometimes this accretion process occurs accurately. But sometimes not. Experiences can be altered as they're hauled out of that gigantic file cabinet we call our brain."

"Could those gaps in a person's memory be filled in by the suggestions of other people?"

"Oh yes. Happens all the time."

"So if a person with . . . let's say . . . an erratic memory came to someone else"—Bullock glanced at Ben— "and that someone gave her all the details of a certain event the way he wanted people to believe it happened, she might well start *remembering* that what she saw occurred as he described it."

Bullock had crossed the line from hypothetical to the present case. But that didn't slow Allyn's answer in the least. "That is correct."

Bullock stepped away from the witness. "Dr. Allyn, you told the jury that you examined Carlee Crane, correct?"

"I interviewed her about this incident, yes."

"Well . . . what did you think of her?"

Ben felt a sudden, painful pounding in his chest.

"I thought she was young. Good-natured. Sincere . . ."

Ben released his breath.

". . . but misguided."

Ben's lips parted. His pulse raced.

"Misguided?" Bullock leaped on the word like a mongoose on the attack. "Does that mean she's not telling the truth?"

"Oh no. I don't think so."

The spectators in the gallery began to stir.

"No," Dr. Allyn continued, "she believes what she says, but that doesn't mean it truly happened."

Something was wrong here. Something was very wrong. No expert witness would do this. No paid professional witness would be such a shameless turncoat. No one would be so cooperative on cross-examination. Unless . . .

Unless that was what he had planned to do all along.

"As I said," Allyn continued, "Ms. Crane is a very good-natured, nurturing, maternal person. She told me she read a newspaper account about this trial, and later saw something on television about it. I believe that when she was exposed to these media influences, she felt a natural empathy for the defendant. She wanted to help him, but she had no means of doing so. And so her subconscious mind created a memory."

"A memory that would get him off the hook."

"That's correct."

"Even though she never saw the murder."

"That's what I believe. She fabricated the entire incident."

Ben turned and saw Carlee in the gallery, her hands pressed against her face. Her husband was trying to comfort her, without much success. The look on her face was heart-breaking. She was being humiliated in public, just as she had feared. Carlee stood and ran out of the courtroom. Her husband rose to follow.

His glaring eyes met Ben's. The message was clear.

You should've prevented this.

This is your fault.

"Would Ms. Crane be the first person who ever fabricated a memory?" Bullock asked.

"Oh, far from it. I've been called in on several cases of purported juvenile sexual abuse, only to later find that the child wasn't even living with the accused parent at the time the event supposedly occurred. In my office last week, a lady told me she woke up one morning and remembered that she had been abducted by a UFO and impregnated by aliens."

Bullock slowly returned to his table. "Dr. Allyn, do you believe Carlee Crane was an eyewitness to the murder of Maria Alvarez?"

"No, I don't. I'm sure she means well, but I don't believe it"—he chuckled—"any more than I believed last week's patient was carrying a Martian baby."

The jury smiled.

"Thank you. No more questions."

The judge looked up from the bench. "Redirect?"

Ben knew his expert had switched alliances in midtrial. A redirect would just be asking for trouble.

But what the hell. He had to try. For Leeman's sake. And Carlee's.

"Dr. Allyn, have you ever spoken to the prosecutor, Mr. Bullock, before today?"

The doctor paused before answering. "No. Why?"

Ben's mind raced. Either he was lying, or this betrayal had been arranged through a third party. It was impossible to know. Ben hated cross-exing in the dark.

"Have you spoken to anyone about your testimony?"

"Mr. Kincaid, as you know, until this morning, I didn't even know I would be testifying."

"Have you made a deal with the prosecutor?"

"A deal? What are you babbling about?"

"Why have you changed your testimony?"

"Changed? Changed from what? This is the first time I've given it."

It was useless. Ben knew he had been stung, but he simply didn't have enough information to prove it. "No more questions."

As he returned to his table Ben checked the faces in the jury box. No doubt about it. The effect of Bullock's cross had been total and devastating. Carlee Crane would be written off as a well-meaning crackpot.

Leeman Hayes was back to square one. With no defense.

How could Bullock have known what was coming? How could he be so confident the expert would cave in during cross?

As the doctor passed out of the courtroom Ben saw Bullock wink at a man in the back row. The man looked familiar.

Ben craned his neck for a better view. It took him a minute to place the man. Then the light dawned.

The air-conditioning company bill collector. The new one. The one who wouldn't take "get lost" for an answer.

The man who had staked out Ben's office for the past few days.

Ben turned toward Bullock, who was grinning broadly.

Their eyes met. And it all became clear.

The bill collector was a spy. Bullock's spy. That's how the prosecution knew Ben had a repressed-memory witness. They probably fed Jones the expert—an expert already prepped to shaft the defense during cross.

No wonder Bullock hadn't crossed Carlee. He knew he didn't need to.

The judge was pounding his gavel and shouting, trying to get Ben's attention. "Any further witnesses, Mr. Kincaid, or does the defense rest?"

God, no. Not now. Even if he had nothing more to say, he couldn't leave the jury on this note. "We will proceed, your honor."

"Fine. Call your next witness."

"The defense calls—"

Ben had to think on the spot. Where did he go now? Who was left? What else did he have?

His eyes inadvertently returned to Bullock. He was leaning back in his chair, his arms folded, his legs comfortably crossed. He was so smug it was unbearable.

Ben couldn't leave it like this. No way in hell.

He inhaled deeply and pulled himself back together. "The defense calls Ronald Pearson to the stand." He paused. "Captain Pearson, that is."

* 67 *

Lieutenant Mike Morelli plodded down the pavement of Third and Nowheresville. He was following the route outlined on his map, following a trail of ever-widening concentric circles radiating from Tulsa International. He was hot and sweaty, his feet hurt, and he had blisters on both big toes. He told himself to ignore his discomfort. He wasn't going to stop until he found what he was looking for.

Mike might have been more willing to rest if a superior had imposed this impossible mission upon him, but since he'd thrust it upon himself, and since he knew it was only a matter of time until Blackwell brought it to an end, he couldn't give up. He did feel bad about dumping Abie on Christina, especially when she already had Julia and what's-his-face's baby to worry about. Abie was pretty cute, even if he was a kid. It was hard to get too grumpy with someone who worshiped everything about you, including the rumpled coat you normally hid deep inside of.

He had an obligation to give Abie some hope of long-term safety. And that hope could come about only if the man who had kidnapped him was caught. Or dead.

Mike thought he was getting closer. He couldn't explain why, but that didn't particularly trouble him. The longer he served on the force, the more he realized that data was not as important to a police officer as instinct. Maybe he was deluding himself; maybe he subconsciously assumed he must be getting close because his feet felt as if he had crisscrossed the whole city three times over. Then again, maybe his subconscious was zeroing in on something his conscious mind hadn't discovered yet. Whatever. He thought he was getting close.

Mike turned a corner too quickly and brushed shoulders with a burly teenage boy in a jeans jacket with the sleeves cut out. He was holding a can of spray paint.

"Excuse me," Mike said.

The boy whipped around, then growled in a low voice. Yes, growled.

Mike checked the emblem sewn on the back of his jacket. A snake curled around a handgun. He was a Cobra.

Mike hated the Cobras. They pushed drugs. And they killed kids.

And now this punk had the gall to growl at him. It would have given Mike great pleasure to call that an assault and give the clown a swift punch in the chops (in self-defense, of course), but for once, better judgment prevailed. Business before pleasure. Child molesters first; thugs second.

He let the Cobra pass.

Mike resumed walking. A few seconds later he turned the corner and noticed the stop sign:

Obviously Cobra handwork. Now Mike wished he had stopped the creep; he was marking his territory and declaring his deadly intentions. Mike had learned that gang graffiti was neither random nor meaningless. You just had to know how to read it. The big letters at the top, the *placa*, was the territorial marker. The CB was the Cobra's marker. KING was the kid's gang name; DK meant *Demons Killer*. BOBA was undoubtedly the name of the poor Demon who had been targeted. And for what?

No question. 187 was the penal-code number for homicide.

After the hit, King would draw a cloud around Boba's name, or perhaps add the letters R.I.P.

Mike had been right. The Cobras were on the move, planning hits to undermine the Demons' rival drug-distributing network. If something didn't happen soon, it would be too late for Boba. And a lot of other kids as well.

Mike punched the LED button on his digital watch and checked the time. He'd been walking for over six hours. Add that to the seven hours he'd been clocking each night for the last three nights and . . . well, it was probably best not to dwell on it. He'd been at it for a while. And so far all he had was . . . sore feet and two major blisters on his toes.

And a chance to get reacquainted with some of the worst parts of north Tulsa. What a panoramic display, Mike thought, scanning the streets surrounding him. Urban blight. Poverty. Crime. Human misery. All his favorite scenery. After all, why go to the beach when you can go to—oh, say, Dino's Hubcap Emporium, or the Wizard's Smoke Shop, or the crumbling remains of the ABC Taxicab Company, or—

Wait a minute. Some half-remembered detail was nagging at him. *What?*

The taxicab company. That was it.

Without looking, Mike plunged off the sidewalk and crossed the street. The front of the stone building was crumbling; the faded paint lettering identifying it as the ABC Taxicab Company was barely visible. The door was bolted and the windows were blocked. It didn't look as if ABC had been in business for years.

Mike peered down an alley beside the building. It was dark, even though the sun was blazing overhead. The alley was littered with trash and debris. Mike found a huge pile of broken booze bottles stacked against one wall, along with spoiled food and human waste.

He spotted a burlap bag that looked as if it were someone's bedtime blanket. A homeless person must be using the alley for shelter.

Holding his breath, Mike trudged onward. About halfway down the side of the building, he found the hole. A large hole, as big as a door, in the side wall.

And then we walked through the wall.

Mike looked inside.

There was no movement, no sign of life. Of course there wasn't, he told himself. What were you expecting? Shake out of it. He was not in danger here. He was just poking around.

Mike stepped through the hole. There were no signs of life, true enough, but there were many taxicabs. Old yellow cabs, most on blocks, the tires having long since been lifted.

Mike looked under one of the hoods. Nothing. Anything of value must've long since been removed. Still, there was something about this place. . . .

Mike snapped his fingers. He was looking at this all wrong. He was thinking like an adult, viewing it as an adult would. Abie was only ten; he had an entirely different perspective on the world.

Mike crouched down and surveyed the room from a height of, oh, say, four feet. The view was very different. You didn't focus on the cars, because you weren't looking down on them. All you saw were the doors.

Yellow doors. With numbers.

Mike raced through the building: 54-28X. 54-76X. 64-99C. The numbers flew past.

Abie had been here.

Mike checked the opposite wall. Sure enough, there was a hole in it, too, even larger than the other one. They must've passed through this building as a shortcut.

Mike ran through the second hole. His excitement was mounting. If there had been any doubt before, it was gone now. He *was* close.

The hole led to the back end of the block. On the opposite side, Mike spotted a row of low-income houses.

Mike tried to concentrate. Why would it make sense to go through that building?

He checked his map. The deserted building in Rockville where he found Abie was due north from his current position. Someone could stay away from the major streets and still get there from here in half an hour easily. But they wouldn't cut through this building unless they were coming from . . .

Directly south, Mike spotted the backyard of a white plasterboard home. The yard was barely big enough for the clothesline strung across it. Extending out from the house on the upper level, though, Mike saw some sort of . . . attic? No.

Extra room. With a separate set of stairs.

That was it. That's why the police weren't finding him. They were looking for apartments. There was probably no way to tell from the front of that house that it had an extra room. The police wouldn't even stop.

Mike jumped over the chain-link fence. He was happy to find there was no dog. The staircase allowed the tenant to come and go without communicating with the people who lived in the main house. Perfect for a kiddie pervert. He could go about his business . . . well, unmolested.

Complications would arise only when he was bringing a boy home and thought there was a possibility of some . . . noise. That was undoubtedly when he used the abandoned building in Rockville. He would walk there to prevent anyone from spotting his car. And once inside, the boy could scream and cry as loud as he was able. . . .

No one would hear him.

Mike checked the garden by the staircase. *Eureka!*

Statues of two dwarfs. Or trolls, if you prefer.

Mike ran up the stairs to the private room. He pressed his ear against the door. At first, he didn't hear anything. Then he did. Someone was talking in a low voice, barely audible.

Mike reached inside his coat and withdrew his Bren Ten automatic. By all rights, he should get a search warrant, then come back and knock politely. . . .

Aw, screw it. For all he knew, there was another exit. The pervert could get away, and he would never come back.

Sorry, no warning today. Mike knew he was violating about thirteen different judicial decisions, but this time he just wasn't taking any chances. What had the Supreme Court done for him lately, anyway?

Mike took a running leap and threw himself against the door. It splintered like dried twigs. He crashed down inside the room, then rolled. He sprang to his feet, gun clutched in both hands.

"Freeze!"

He looked left, then right. He whirled around.

Nothing.

There was another room. A kitchenette. Slowly, gun still poised, Mike stepped through the passageway. . . .

Still nothing. There was no one else here. There was no other way out, either. But he was sure he had heard voices. Was he totally hallucinating?

When Mike returned to the front room, he saw it. The radio. The son of a bitch had left the radio on.

Mike checked it out. It was an alarm radio. The alarm probably started while the boarder wasn't here to turn it off.

Where was he?

Mike fumbled with the radio, trying to shut off the noise. He punched all the buttons. Nothing worked. Finally, in frustration, Mike picked it up and threw it across the room.

That worked. And now, in addition to breaking and entering, he could add property damage to his list of crimes.

Mike took a long slow breath. He really needed to get a grip. He was letting this search get to him, letting this case get to him. It was just so horrible. Little boys. Total innocents. They don't know what's going on. They can't protect themselves. They're helpless. And alone. How did that line by Olive Schreiner go? "The barb in the arrow of childhood suffering is this: its intense loneliness, its intense ignorance."

He searched the outer room and the bathroom, but found nothing of interest. Then he tried the bedroom.

The room was dark. The curtains were drawn, and the overhead light didn't work. Consequently, he almost missed it at first. Then, when his eyes made contact, he gasped.

He had read about this, of course. He had read that pedophiles loved to look at pictures. That they kept souvenirs. Abie had even mentioned that the creep had pictures. But Mike had no idea.

Wallpaper could not have covered the wall more efficiently. From floor to ceiling, the wall was layered with pictures of little boys.

They didn't vary much. All were in the eight-to-ten range. All were dark-haired, dark-eyed, pretty. Some of the pictures had obviously been torn out of catalogs—underwear ads and such.

But most of them were photographs. Slick, professional work. Big smiles, cheesy grins. Bland backdrops.

They were school photos, most of them, anyway. Did the creep know the photographer—or was he the photographer?

Mike had to find out. He began jerking drawers out of the desk in the bedroom. When he drew open the fourth drawer, photos slid out from the back.

Mike picked them up, then suddenly felt as if someone had squeezed his heart in their fist. It was not until some minutes later that he realized he was weeping.

Mike recognized the boys at once. They were the victims. Andy Harden. Jimmy Whalen. The Connell boy.

These were Polaroids, and they had been taken at that goddamned building in Rockville where the pervert kept his mattress. The boys were naked, or stripped down to their underwear. They had been arranged in a variety of sickeningly obscene poses. But that wasn't the worst of it.

All the photos except Mickey Connell's were smeared with blood. Mike knew with instant certainty that the blood was the blood of each child. Smeared on by his killer.

That was why the Connell boy's didn't have any. The car had gotten him before the killer could.

Mike reached back into the drawer. Pieces of a photo were strewn about. Someone had ripped a picture into shreds.

Mike didn't have to reassemble the pieces to identify the subject. It was Abie.

Mike slammed the drawer shut and began tearing the room apart. He had to find something. Something, *anything*, damn it! There was no way in hell that Chris Bentley lived in this dive. It was someone else. Someone *else*!

He wiped his eyes and tried to think clearly. He had to *focus*. This man was out there, damn it! And his plan of action was clear; the torn photo left no doubt about that. Mike had to figure out who this sick bastard was before he got to Abie.

Like he had the others. The little boys in the Polaroid parade. Smeared with blood.

Mike spent the next half hour searching every nook and cranny. While groping about in the bedroom closet, he accidentally dislodged a shoe box. When it tumbled to the floor, the lid fell off and out spilled two pairs of socks, two rolls of pennies, and two keys on a chain.

Mike clutched the keys in his hands. A piece of tape on one key read: C-D-Y-S-K.

The key chain bore a regal lion pennant. And the lettering read: UTICA GREENS COUNTRY CLUB.

There *was* a connection.

Mike shoved the keys into his pocket and raced out the door. Even if his big toes protested, he would run all the way back to his car. From there, he could call Tomlinson and tell him to get a warrant. With a warrant, Tomlinson could cover up Mike's illegal search and bring in a proper crime-scene team. Surely they could find more identifying clues.

If not, they could just wait till the chickenhawk came home. But it was always possible he wouldn't. It was possible he would realize his lair had been discovered.

It was possible he already had.

In the meantime Mike was heading to the county courthouse. He remembered Ben saying something about the importance of the caddyshack keys, but he couldn't recall the details. Ben would know what it meant. Who it was.

That was what Mike wanted to know, what he had to know.

Who it was they were looking for. He had to know that, before it was too late.

Before Abie became just another bloody photograph.

* 68 *

Captain Pearson looked as if he had been knocked in the face. Ben's announcement of his next witness seemed to come as a surprise to everyone, including, to be truthful, Ben. He wasn't entirely sure why he had decided on Pearson. The deed was done now, though. He would have to make the best of it.

Pearson was on his feet in the gallery, but he wasn't moving. "Do I have to do this?" he asked the judge.

Judge Hawkins appeared confused. "Didn't counsel discuss your testimony with you in advance?"

"Hell, no."

Hawkins gave Ben a long look. "Is this true?"

"Yes, your honor."

"You gave him no advance warning?"

"He isn't a friendly witness." Ben glanced at the jury, making sure they got that. "But he possesses critical information."

"Very well," the judge said, scowling. "But I'll be watching you carefully. Behave yourself. I won't have you harassing someone who didn't even know he was going to testify."

"No, your honor. Of course not." Like hell!

Judge Hawkins motioned, and Pearson strode unhappily to the witness stand.

"Good afternoon," Ben said.

Pearson grunted in reply.

"Shall I call you Mr. Pearson or Captain Pearson?"

"Mr. Pearson will be fine."

Ben established the essential background details: that Pearson was the self-styled captain of the country-club board of directors, that he had been for years, and that he had general supervisory authority over the country club's affairs.

"Mr. Pearson, you held the same position ten years ago, when Maria Alvarez was killed, right?"

"What are you implying? That *I* killed that woman? This is outrageous!"

"Please answer the question," Judge Hawkins said firmly.

"Yes," Pearson spat out. "I was in charge ten years ago. But I had nothing to do with this mess."

"Were you at the club the night the murder occurred?"

"I most certainly was not!"

"What were you doing?"

"I was at home, sound asleep, with my wife."

"Your honor, I object," Bullock said. "This isn't going anywhere. This is a pure and unadulterated fishing expedition."

Ben racked his brain for a response. It was hard to come up with a good one when Bullock was basically right.

"Are we going to sit here while Mr. Kincaid calls every member of the club to the stand and tries to get them to confess?"

Hawkins leaned over the bench. "It would help if you got to the point, Mr. Kincaid. If you have one."

Ben nodded. Time for a bold initiative. "Mr. Pearson, isn't it true that you've been supplying illegal narcotics to country-club patrons for years?"

The uproar in the courtroom astounded even Ben. People rose to their feet; reporters sent messengers running toward the back door. Judge Hawkins pounded his gavel, trying to quiet everyone.

"That's a serious accusation, your honor," Bullock shouted over the hubbub. "Mr. Kincaid better have some proof."

"I'm inclined to agree," Hawkins said. He was mad now, no doubt about it. "Mr. Kincaid?"

"I'm waiting for the witness to answer my question."

"No!" Pearson shouted. "It's a lie!"

"Permission to treat the witness as hostile," Ben said.

"Under the circumstances," Hawkins said, "we can hardly claim that he's your bosom buddy, can we? Granted."

"Captain Pearson, isn't it true that your fellow board member Dick Crenshaw has a major cocaine problem?"

Pearson's eyes darted toward the gallery. Crenshaw was there, watching him very closely. "I don't pry into other people's problems. . . ."

"The day we all played golf together, he was on a coke high. Till it ran dry. Then he was on a coke low. Right? You were there."

"That doesn't mean he got the stuff at the country club!"

Ben saw heads nod in the jury box. They had picked up on the implied admission. "Where else would he get it?"

"How would I know? Look, if you have questions about Crenshaw, ask Crenshaw. I don't know where he gets it."

"I think you do. I think you've been supplying it to him for years. You put that monkey on his back." Ben paused. "I wonder if he won't admit it when I call him to the stand, since you've all but admitted he's an addict."

Pearson hovered over the edge of the witness box. "I will not sit here and let you call me a . . . a drug pusher!"

Again, Ben checked the faces in the jury box. On this issue, they appeared undecided. But they were definitely interested.

"And what you can't distribute at the club," Ben continued, "you distribute throughout Tulsa via paid accomplices. The same people you use to collect the junk from Peruvian smugglers and run all the other risks. The Demons."

"The *what*?"

"Don't bother acting like you don't know who they are. I saw them in your office."

"You're lying!"

"No, I'm not. Captain Pearson, isn't it true that after we finished playing golf last week, we walked back to your office?"

"Yes, but—"

"In your office I saw four black teenagers wearing jackets bearing the emblem of the largest North Side youth gang, the Demons."

"That's not—"

"I wasn't the only person there that day. Should I call some of your employees to the stand?"

Pearson folded his arms across his chest. "I was interviewing those young men for jobs in the dining room. I believe I mentioned to you that I was hiring. You came in one day while I was talking to an employment agency." He smiled thinly. "Those young gentlemen were part of my new affirmative-action program."

"I don't think so." Ben hated this. It was more like being in the boxing ring than putting on a defense. But he had to keep it up until he got what he needed. "You would never allow those boys to work in your dining room. You're a deeply prejudiced person."

"Another lie!"

"You have no minority employees working in the main club building, right?"

"We had some black caddies."

"And that was darned big of you, but I'm asking about the real employees. The full-timers. No minorities, right?"

He sank back in his chair. "Well, that's why I started my affirmative-action program."

"Wrong. I heard your phone conversation when you were talking to the employment agency. You told them you weren't interested in any non-Caucasians."

"I said no such thing."

"Not in so many words, maybe, but you communicated the message, just the same. I was suspicious at the time, so I made notes and later consulted a friend of mine at the EEOC. Turns out code phrases like yours are commonly used to communicate illegal hiring preferences."

Pearson's eyes broke contact. "I don't know what you're talking about."

Ben glanced at his notes. "For instance, you said, 'Let me talk to Mary. No, not Maria. Not Rochelle.' That meant you wanted to hire Caucasian women, no Hispanics, no blacks. Then you said, 'Let me have suites fifteen through twenty-five.' That meant you wanted young women, ages fifteen through twenty-five."

"The guys in the clubhouse like to look at the pretty young things, okay? After a hard day's work at the . . ."

"Nineteenth tee?" Ben suggested.

Pearson pulled himself up, jaw tightly clenched. "There's nothing wrong with hiring attractive young women to be waitresses. Everyone does it."

"And excluding minorities?"

"Look, it's a private club. We can do whatever the hell we want."

"Maybe so, but the point is, there's not a snowball's chance that you were going to hire a bunch of big tough black gang members as waiters. They were there to deliver or pick up drugs."

"You'll never prove that!" Pearson's defiant voice echoed through the courtroom.

Maybe not, Ben thought, but the jury was listening, just the same. He decided it was time to switch subjects. "You do a lot of traveling to Peru, don't you?"

Pearson's head twitched, startled by the sudden switch in topics. "I suppose."

"I understand a lot of illegal drugs come from Peru."

"Oh, well then, I guess that proves I'm a drug lord."

"Wasn't Maria Alvarez also from Peru?"

"I—think I might have heard that. So what?"

So what indeed? Ben wasn't sure, but it was a hell of a coincidence.

"Did you know her?"

"No, not at all."

"Never?"

"I never laid eyes on her till the police brought around pictures of her corpse."

This was getting Ben nowhere. He rethought his approach. What was it his mother had told him? Give the man something to brag about, that was it. Hmmm.

"What sort of business do you do in Peru?"

"All kinds of things."

"You must be a very enterprising individual, to build a successful business enterprise in a third-world nation."

Pearson seemed to relax a bit. "I've done all right, yeah."

"From what I've seen, you've done extremely well. What

inspired you to instigate operations in Peru? Most people would never have thought of that."

Pearson leaned back in his chair. "Well, the advantages aren't obvious, but after a lot of hard work and bare-knuckles research, I realized there was some serious money to be made. Labor down there is cheap, and the government tends to stay out of your way, unlike here."

"I see. Could you briefly describe the scope of your business empire?"

Pearson turned to the jury and shrugged his shoulders. Now that he was on a subject he loved, he actually seemed to be enjoying himself. "Most of my work is energy-related. I've invested in oil wells. Bought some oil fields. Operated a gas processing plant for a while."

"Anything else?"

"Oh, hell. I've bought and sold small businesses. Bought some polo ponies. Real estate. I've made investments for myself, and I've acted as a broker for others."

It was the word that triggered Ben's memory. The same word Rachel Rutherford had used when she referred to the unnamed lover who had assisted her in her time of need.

"What kind of broker?"

"Oh, hell. I don't know. Land. Leasehold interests. Stocks. Bonds."

"What about babies?"

Pearson's sudden silence resounded through the courtroom. The air seemed suspended, as if time had decided to stand still.

"Don't bother lying," Ben said, bluffing his way through. He was putting all his chips on one roll of the dice now. "She told me all about it."

"I did that on one occasion," Pearson said quietly.

It *was* him. "How did you get into the baby business?"

"I was requested to . . . by a close personal friend."

"A lover?"

Pearson looked back at him blank-faced. "I don't see what that has to do with anything."

Ben decided to leave well enough alone. "Why were you looking for babies in Peru?"

"You probably know how hard it can be for certain people to adopt in America," Pearson explained. "Birthrates are down. Abortion is up. No one seems to care if a kid is illegitimate anymore. For every American baby put up for adoption, there are four couples waiting in line. Obviously, a lot of those people are going to be disappointed."

"So you looked overseas?"

"Exactly. Ten years ago the foreign market for babies was just opening up. Today, it's a steady supply source. I've been told that, on average, twenty American couples adopt overseas babies every day."

"How did you go about this . . . brokering?"

"I contacted an outfit in Houston called the Santa Clara International Adoption Agency. I filled out the forms, ran through all the hoops. Eventually they turned down the couple I represented for the same reason the American agencies had. The father was too old, too inexperienced. But I got friendly with one of the men who worked there, spilled a little cash, bought him a few shots of tequila, and got some information."

"About what?"

Pearson breathed heavily, as if resigned to telling his story but not at all happy about it. "La Flavita."

"And what is that?"

"That's a hotel in one of the scuzziest parts of Peru. A neighborhood I would've never dreamed of visiting otherwise."

"And what was at the hotel?"

"A baby farm."

"Your honor." Bullock rose to his feet. "This story is appropriately lurid and distracting—Mr. Kincaid's specialties—but it has nothing to do with this case. The court has been very patient, but enough is enough."

"Judge," Ben said, "I promise this will connect up."

Hawkins squinted. "I don't see how."

"Your honor, my client is on trial for his life. I ask for the widest possible latitude."

Hawkins glanced at all the reporters in the gallery, then sank back into his seat. "Proceed."

Ben stood directly before Pearson. "Did you go to this . . . baby farm?"

"Of course. It was a pathetic sight, believe me. Not just Peruvian kids. They had castaways and bastards from all over the world. Kids no one wanted. The dust of life."

"Did you have to fill out forms?"

"Nope. All I had to do was open my wallet."

"Did you obtain parental consent?"

"I was told they had done so. Of course, you have to realize this is a third-world country. Parental consent is a whole different animal there. Some poor schmo who has six kids he can't feed might well give consent to sell his seventh, if it enables him to feed the rest of the brood for a few weeks. He might not like it, but he'll do it."

"Because he has no choice."

Pearson nodded slowly. "That's basically correct. Look, I didn't make this world—"

Ben cut him off. "And so—you bought a baby?"

"Eventually. We did quite a bit of bickering over the price. They're tough, and they have an advantage because they're used to dealing with people who are desperate and emotionally involved." Pearson leaned back on one elbow. "But I'm a pretty damn good horse trader myself. We struck a deal, and I brought home a beautiful baby boy."

"Who were the baby's birth parents?"

"I had no idea. I didn't want to know."

"Did you ever hear from . . . La Flavita again?"

"Yes. About six months later. There was some trouble."

"What kind of trouble?"

"With the mother. Claimed she hadn't given her consent, or had done so while under anesthetic, or some such sorry thing. I don't recall the details. Anyway, they were trying to track the kid down."

"So how did you respond?"

"I asked my client what she wanted me to do."

"And what did you do?"

Pearson hedged. "What she told me to do."

"And what was that?"

"I—" Pearson gazed out into the gallery. "I threw the telegram away. I contacted the sender and informed them that the persons in question had moved to another state and I didn't know how to contact them. Didn't even know their names. Couldn't be traced."

"Did you ever hear from La Flavita again?"

Pearson looked down at his shoes. "No."

Ben took a deep breath. "Mr. Pearson, who was your client?"

Pearson gazed out into the gallery.

"Mr. Pearson? I'd appreciate an answer."

"I really don't see how that's relevant."

"Unfortunately, sir, you are not the judge. Please answer."

Pearson gazed up at the judge. Ben had a sneaking suspicion that if Hawkins renewed his application for country-club membership at that moment, it might be accepted. "The witness will answer the question," the judge said solemnly.

"It's confidential," Pearson said. "I made a professional promise I can't violate."

"Yes you can," Ben said. "Answer the question."

"I object," Bullock said. "We can't ask the man to violate a confidential relationship."

"Why not?" Ben asked.

"Well . . . it's a privileged matter. It's like the attorney-client privilege, only—"

"Only for baby brokers?" Ben said. "I don't think so."

"Overruled," Hawkins said unhappily. He turned to face Pearson. "Now answer the question!"

Pearson's shoulders rose and fell heavily. "Rachel Rutherford."

* 69 *

Ben spoke over the buzz that swelled through the court-room. "Nothing more for Mr. Pearson, your honor."

"Cross?"

Bullock rose slowly to his feet. "No, your honor. Mr. Pearson told some interesting stories, but as far as I can tell, they don't have a blessed thing to do with this case."

"I share your mystification," Judge Hawkins said. "But I'm sure Mr. Kincaid will clear it up soon." He glanced at his watch, then Ben. "I'll give you ten minutes."

The judge instructed the witness to step down. Pearson crawled out of his seat, glaring at Ben the whole time.

Ben saw Rachel moving toward the back door. He had to speak quickly. "The defense calls Rachel Rutherford."

She froze in her tracks. She looked back over her shoulder, as if wondering if anyone had spotted her. Then, suddenly, she started moving again.

Ben alerted the court. "Your honor, that's her."

The judge gestured to the sergeant at arms, who sidestepped in front of the door. Rachel froze again, then turned about, a look of utter resignation on her face.

"Let me guess," the judge said. "You've had no advance warning that you would be called to testify. That seems to be one of Mr. Kincaid's trademarks." He sighed. "Please come to the front to be sworn."

Rachel hesitated, then grudgingly faced the inevitable. She stepped slowly to the front of the courtroom.

Ben watched her every movement. He had admired her figure before, back at the spa. Tall, broad-shouldered, statuesque. With short hair. A person looking at her from behind could be fooled into believing she was a man.

"Pssst!"

Ben turned back toward the gallery. Mitch Dryer was leaning over the rail, trying to get his attention.

"I got the papers you wanted," Mitch hissed.

"What? What papers?"

"What papers? The country-club records reflecting contacts between the board members and foreign countries, remember? It was your idea! I've been staying up all night working on it. You wouldn't believe how many there are."

"Great," Ben said. "That may be just what I need. But I can't look at it now. Could you wait until the judge calls a recess?"

"Do you know how much stuff I have here? It isn't going to do you a bit of good till you've gone through it and organized it."

"Damn! I can't possibly do that now. Look, I hate to impose, but would you mind delivering this to my legal assistant?"

"Is she here?"

"No. She's at my place taking care of a baby and a young boy. She'll probably be grateful for the distraction. If she finds anything useful, she can prepare exhibits for trial."

"Okay. Where is she?"

Ben gave Mitch his address. "Tell her to get on it right away."

"If you say so. She's not going to be mad at me, is she?"

"Nah. But she may try to get you to sing the Flintstones song."

Mitch looked at Ben strangely, then picked up the document box and left the courtroom.

By this time Rachel had been sworn and had settled into the witness box. "Would you state your name, please?" Ben asked.

"Rachel Rutherford." The surprise of being dragged to the stand was deeply affecting her. She seemed unnerved.

Ben established that she was married to Harold Rutherford, a member of the Utica Greens board of directors, and that she often went to the club herself.

"You have one son, isn't that right?"

"You know it is," she said softly.

"What's his name?"

"Abraham Martin. We call him Abie."

"Could you describe Abie?"

"Describe him?"

Ben nodded. He was doing his best to be gentle. If he pushed too hard, he knew she'd crumble. "If you wouldn't mind."

Rachel shrugged. "Well, he's ... around four feet tall. Maybe a little more ... I don't know. ..."

"Dark black hair, right?"

She ran her fingers through her own sunny blond hair. "Right."

"Dark complexion?"

"True."

"Prominent nose."

"Y-es."

"Your honor," Bullock protested. "What could possibly be the point of this?"

"Let me ask one more question," Ben said, and he didn't wait for a response from the bench. "Abie doesn't look much like you, does he?"

Rachel's lips drew together. "No."

"And he doesn't look much like your husband, does he?"

"If you're trying to prove that he was adopted, let me make it easier for you. He was. I've already told you that."

"That wasn't actually my point, ma'am. My point is that his features could be considered somewhat ... South American."

A flicker of light shone in her eyes. It wasn't much, but it was enough to tell Ben he was right.

"Ms. Rutherford, is Captain Pearson the ... *broker* ... who arranged the adoption of Abie?"

No answer.

"Please, Ms. Rutherford. I need an answer. Is your Abie the boy he bought at that baby farm in Peru?"

All at once her carefully composed veneer dissolved. She pressed her hand against her face. Tears spilled out between the fingers.

"You have to—" Her voice broke. More tears fell. "You

have to understand." Her voice was barely more than a whisper.

"Understand what, Ms. Rutherford?"

"How—desperate we were. How desperate I was. I wanted a baby so much. My body ached for one, can you understand that? I *ached*. And yet, a baby was the one thing my body denied me. We tried everything. Fertility treatments. Drugs. Counseling. You name it. None of it helped."

"So you decided to adopt?"

"Yes."

Slowly, haltingly, Rachel took the jury through the five years of pain she had endured as she and her husband undertook the adoption process. All the American agencies that rejected them because her husband was too old. The con-man lawyer who repeatedly took their money promising them a baby, but delivering nothing. She told them about her suicide attempts.

"That's when you turned to Ronald Pearson, isn't it?" Ben asked.

"I—I didn't know what else to do. Ronnie always seemed so . . . capable, so efficient. Like he could accomplish anything. So I asked him to do this for me. And he did."

"Why would he go to so much trouble for you?"

Rachel glanced down at her hands. "I rather like to think it's because he loved me."

Ben nodded. "How much did you know about how Mr. Pearson got the baby?"

"Until today, next to nothing. I knew some money changed hands. I knew he was using his South American connections. You have to understand—when I went to Ronnie—I didn't want to live anymore. I had tried to kill myself twice and I knew I would try again. I didn't know he *bought* the baby exactly, but—"

She lowered her head, and her next words were even softer than before. "But I wouldn't have cared."

Ben gazed across the courtroom at the poor, tormented woman. "You wanted a baby that much."

"I did. I had to have a baby. If I didn't—I would've died. I know it."

"And after you got him?"

Her head rose slowly. "I would've done anything to keep him. Anything at all."

* 70 *

Bullock took a shot at breaking the jury's rapt attention. "Your honor, I reurge my objection. This testimony is not relevant."

"I think the connections are emerging," Ben replied.

"What connections?" Bullock insisted. "What is Kincaid trying to prove? That this woman murdered Maria Alvarez? Even his own alleged eyewitness said the murderer was a man!"

"Your honor, if you'll just allow me a few more questions . . ."

"That's what he said the last time," Bullock urged. "Judge, this has gone on long enough!"

Hawkins shook his head. "Overruled. You may continue, counsel."

Ben approached the witness stand and gently laid his hand on the edge of the box. "Ms. Rutherford, you're the blonde sunbather Ramona de Vries remembered seeing by the pool, aren't you? When Maria Alvarez was at the country club."

Her nod was barely perceptible.

"Would you tell the jury what Mrs. Alvarez said to you?"

"If I knew, I would. But she was babbling in Spanish. I had Spanish in high school, but it's been so long, I couldn't follow her. She was so distraught, so excited. All I picked up was, 'niño, niño'—baby, baby." Rachel paused. "And that was enough to terrify me."

"What did you tell her?"

Seconds seemed to drag out like days. Rachel appeared

trapped—trapped by an answer she didn't want to give, but knew she couldn't avoid.

"All I did," Rachel said finally, "was tell her to talk to my husband."

"Your honor," Ben said, without missing a beat, "if the prosecutor will waive cross-examination, I will call Harold Rutherford to the stand."

"Counsel?"

Bullock waved his acquiescence. He seemed to realize this trial was spiraling out of his control.

The judge called Harold Rutherford to the front. He met his wife at the gate separating the gallery from the main courtroom. They looked at one another and exchanged a deep, penetrating gaze. Ben would've given a great deal to know what mutually understood information was being conveyed in their eyes.

The sergeant at arms led Rutherford to the front of the courtroom where he was sworn. Rutherford settled into the witness chair and stared ahead at Ben, his face a stony mask.

After establishing Rutherford's identity and background, Ben said, "Mr. Rutherford, there's one issue everyone in this courtroom is wondering about, so if you'll excuse me, I'll cut to the chase."

"As you wish."

"Isn't it true that Maria Alvarez was your adopted son Abie's natural mother?"

"No. That's not true. I mean—" His voice betrayed the barest hint of a tremor. "How would I know? I know nothing about the woman."

"Mr. Rutherford, one of my assistants has been scrutinizing Peruvian data banks for days, including birth records. And hospital records. He learned that shortly before Maria Alvarez applied for a visa to come to this country, she was in a hospital having a baby. A baby boy."

His lips tightened. "So you say."

"Would you like to see the birth certificate?" Ben held out the papers. "Or the hospital records?"

Rutherford waved them away. "What difference would it

make? I was the adoptive parent. They never tell us who the natural parents are. I have no way of knowing."

"Didn't Maria Alvarez tell you she was Abie's mother when she came to the country club?"

Rutherford hesitated. He couldn't deny talking to Maria without calling his wife a liar. "I vaguely recall trying to talk to the woman," he said at last. "But I don't recall what was said. It certainly had nothing to do with my son. She probably wanted a job. Or a handout."

Ben stepped closer. "Mr. Rutherford, isn't it true Maria Alvarez told you she was Abie's mother?"

"No."

"Didn't you ask her to meet you later that night? At the caddyshack?"

"Absolutely not."

Ben addressed the court. "Your honor, I request that Carlee Crane be brought back into the courtroom."

The judge nodded at the bailiff.

"And don't tell her anything before she gets here," Ben added.

The courtroom waited in suspended animation while the bailiff stepped out. Rutherford's face remained impassive.

When the bailiff returned, the courtroom was so quiet the creaking of the doors sounded like thunder. Behind the bailiff followed Carlee Crane.

Ben gestured for her to come forward, but she stopped halfway down the nave.

"My God!" She whispered, but the whisper was audible in every cranny of the still courtroom. Her face shifted from astonishment, to disbelief, to fear.

One by one, the spectators followed Carlee's line of vision to the front of the courtroom—and the witness stand. Rutherford stared back at her, his eyes cold and hostile.

Carlee held out a shaking arm and pointed. "It's him. He's the man I saw in the caddyshack!"

"Your honor, I protest!" Bullock said angrily. "This is grossly improper!"

Hawkins banged his gavel. "I admit I didn't realize Mr. Kincaid intended to—"

"This is outrageous!" Bullock continued. "And the jury has been hopelessly tainted by this improper identification. I move for a mistrial."

"A mistrial!" Ben said. "Are you kidding? On what basis?"

"That woman trying to testify is not on the witness stand."

"Fine," Ben said. "I'll excuse Mr. Rutherford, recall Carlee, and have her repeat what everyone in the courtroom has already heard."

"I'll object to that," Bullock said. "She's already testified, and she couldn't identify the killer. She can't change her story now."

"What are you trying to do? She saw him! Why do you want to suppress her testimony?" Ben walked right up to Bullock. "Unless you care more about winning than you do about seeing justice done."

Bullock glared back at him silently.

"The motion is overruled," Hawkins said angrily. "Please continue with the direct examination of this witness."

Ben stepped forward until he was practically hovering over Rutherford. "You can save everyone a lot of trouble by just telling us the truth now."

Rutherford's eyes darted from Carlee, to Ben, to the jury. "I don't know what you're talking about."

Again, Carlee broke the silence. "My God, didn't anyone hear me? He did it! He killed her! I *saw* it!"

"Your honor, I want that woman out of here!" Bullock shouted.

The judge nodded and instructed the bailiff to remove her. The jurors' eyes were moving like Ping-Pong balls, back and forth, from Carlee to Rutherford.

"Is it true?" Ben asked.

"Of course not," Rutherford feinted.

"There's no point in lying anymore. Isn't it true you told Maria Alvarez to meet you late that night in the caddyshack?"

"No."

"Isn't it true you wanted to meet there because you thought you'd be alone?"

"I said no!"

"Isn't it true you grabbed a golf club, swung it over your head, and killed her?"

"No, no, *no!*"

"But he's *lying!*" Carlee was halfway out the door, struggling with the bailiff. "Don't you understand? I *saw* him!"

Rutherford jumped out of his seat. "Would you *shut*—" He froze, hands clutching the rail.

"Mr. Rutherford, surely you realize that if you don't confess, the most likely suspect will be your wife."

A tiny turn of the head.

"Is that what you want—your wife in prison? After all you've done to protect her?"

Rutherford gripped the railing so tightly Ben was afraid it would snap.

"It's over, Mr. Rutherford," Ben said quietly. "Why don't you just tell us what happened?"

Rutherford's large chest heaved. The trembling spread from his arms and rippled through his entire body. Finally, all the wind seemed to blow out of him, like the final gust of a hurricane. He collapsed back into his chair.

"You have to understand," Rutherford said, in a voice so dispirited that it seemed to come from an entirely different person. "You just . . . have to understand."

"Understand what?" Ben asked.

Rutherford cradled his face in his large hands. "How much Rachel wanted children. And how much I wanted to make her . . . happy." He paused. "We needed a baby."

"She told us that was all she lived for."

"She didn't exaggerate. Rachel is not a . . . strong woman. She's a good woman. A loving woman. But not strong. When she discovered she couldn't have children . . . it was like she had lost a limb."

He inhaled, searching for words. "She couldn't function. Couldn't live. Tried to kill herself. Twice. Almost succeeded. She cut her own flesh. Can you imagine?" He looked down at his hands. "But even when she was alive . . . she wasn't really alive. She told you everything we tried. Nothing worked. And worst of all, she had to suffer through all those cruel deceptions, all those painful near misses. Thinking she had a baby, then having it snatched away from her. She couldn't survive that again. I knew it as certainly as I knew anything. She just would not have survived."

Ben spoke softly. "Maria Alvarez wanted her baby back, didn't she?"

Rutherford nodded. Tears crept out of the corners of his eyes. "My Spanish isn't perfect, but it's good enough to understand what she wanted. She'd changed her mind. Wanted Abie back. I'm not sure she ever really consented to the adoption, at least not when she was in full possession of her senses. As soon as she got out of the hospital, she started trying to get him back. But by then, Abie had already been snatched by the merchants at La Flavita. By the time she tracked them down, he had already been sold to Pearson and taken to the United States. So she came to the United States to get her son back." He paused again. "Our son."

Rutherford lifted his head. "And she could've gotten him, too. The manner in which Ron handled the adoption was, well, less than legal. If she had raised a stink, made a complaint at the embassy or filed a lawsuit or something, she'd have gotten her baby back. Courts always favor the natural mother. I knew that." He gazed at his wife, now seated in the third row of the gallery. "I also knew what that would do to my Rachel."

"So you asked Maria to meet you at the caddyshack. Late at night."

He nodded. "I had the keys to that place. All of us on the board did back then. I thought it would be deserted. Safe." He leaned forward suddenly. "I didn't go there to kill her. I want you to understand that. I tried to reason with her. I told her how attached Abie and Rachel had become. It didn't matter to her. I tried to give her money. That mattered even less."

"And then what happened?"

"She began to get loud, violent. She threatened to report us, to tell everyone we had stolen her son. She said she was going to our house right that minute to take her baby back!"

He covered his watery eyes with his hands. "Don't you see? It would have killed Rachel! Literally killed her! It was self-defense, for Chrissake! I was protecting my wife!"

"By killing Maria Alvarez."

Rutherford shook his head, lost, dazed. "I don't know what came over me. I saw what she was going to do, what it would do to my wife. I couldn't let another baby be snatched out of Rachel's hands. Especially not after she'd spent so much time with him."

He straightened himself and stared at the ceiling. "I just lost control. I grabbed the nearest thing—a club out of a golf bag. I swung it over my head, again and again and—"

He opened his mouth again, but no words emerged. Finally: "I really wasn't conscious of what was happening, what I was doing, until it was all over. Then—I was horrified."

Ben nodded. "And then you tried to cover it up."

"Yes. But before I had a chance, I saw . . . *him*." He shrugged toward Leeman. "He was cowering under one of the cots, watching me the whole time. At least I assumed he was. Maybe he never saw my face; I don't know. I tried to pull him out from under the cot, but he crawled out the other end and ran out of the caddyshack. I ran after him. Ran all over the goddamn golf course, but didn't find him. A few minutes later I came back to the caddyshack."

"And?"

"And, there he was. I don't know where he'd been; must've doubled back on me. He didn't see me come in. I stepped into the shadows and watched as he gazed at the horrible mess in the corner and tried to understand what had happened to the woman. He threw himself on her body. Got blood all over himself. He pulled on the club. I think he was trying to get her down, to put her to rest. But he couldn't do it. Then he ran out of the caddyshack again. That gave me my opportunity."

"To frame him."

Rutherford bit down on his lower lip. "I didn't know that much about the kid, but I knew he was . . . not quite right in the head. I knew he'd have a hard time explaining himself. Figured the courts would go a lot softer on him than they would on me. So I put the golf bag in his locker, with the woman's necklace. I'd lifted the clubs from the pro shop that afternoon—I often did that, to try out new clubs. Leeman caddied for me; that's why his prints were on the bag. I wiped my prints off everything and left. I lived in fear the next few days, thinking that kid might be able to identify me . . . but he never did."

"He couldn't," Ben said. "I don't know if he saw your face. But even if he had, he wouldn't have known how to communicate the information."

"I felt horrible when he was arrested. I really did. But I always thought . . . since he was, you know, that he wouldn't be tried. He would just get sent to some home where he'd probably be better off anyway. I had no idea that—ten years later—this mess would come back to haunt us both."

"And your wife?"

"Rachel never knew. I swear to you. She may have . . . wondered, but she never knew."

"Your honor," Ben said quietly, "I move that the case against Leeman Hayes be dismissed."

"Counsel, approach." Ben and Bullock walked to the bench. "It certainly seems like an appropriate motion to me, Mr. Prosecutor. Any objections?"

"About a million. For all we know, Kincaid may have paid this man—"

Hawkins cut him off. "Paid a member of the Utica Greens Country Club to confess to murder? Turn on your headlights, Bullock."

"But—" Bullock sputtered pointlessly, but there was really nothing he could say. "No objection," he growled finally.

Judge Hawkins pounded his gavel. "This case is dismissed. Mr. Rutherford, I think the district attorney would appreciate it if you would not leave town anytime soon. And Mr. Hayes—" Hawkins made eye contact with Leeman. "There is nothing I can say or do to compensate you for the time—the years you have lost. You have my sincerest apologies." He pounded his gavel again. "And now you're free to go."

The courtroom was in an uproar. Ernie Hayes shouted for joy, then raced to the front, the rest of the family close behind him. Ben started to join them when he felt something yank him back.

It was Jack Bullock. "So you did it again, eh, Ben? You must be very proud of yourself."

"Jack . . . Leeman was innocent."

"That doesn't justify all your courtroom chicanery. If you could prove the man was innocent, why didn't you just tell me?"

"Jack, I've been telling you he was innocent since day one. You haven't been listening. I didn't understand the whole story myself until today."

"Sure. How stupid do you think I am?"

"Jack—" Ben reached out to him. "Now that this trial is over . . . I was hoping maybe we could . . . I don't know . . . patch things up. We used to be so . . . close. I mean, you know, we worked together so closely. We could be like that again."

"Impossible. We're on different sides now."

"No," Ben said firmly. "That's where you're wrong. We're both on the same side. We both have the same goal. We just work from different sides of the courtroom."

"I'm sorry, Ben," Jack said briskly. "I hate to say it, but quite frankly, I don't want anything to do with you." He turned on his heel abruptly and returned to his table.

Ben watched him go. You were like a father to me, he thought.

And now I've lost you, too.

Ben tried to get to Leeman, but Ernie Hayes was blocking the way, hugging his son with all his might. Leeman's brothers and sisters stood around them, trying to edge their way in. Ernie was pretty choked up; he kept thwopping his son proudly on the back.

They were oblivious to Ben, and Ben wasn't surprised. He'd seen this before. While the trial was on, the lawyer was the star of the show, front and center, the main man. But once it was over, he was superfluous. Family was what it was all about now.

Come to think of it, Ben mused, family was what it had been about all along.

71

Ben was startled to see Mike barreling down the center of the courtroom. He burst through the crowd congregating around the defendant's table and fought his way upstream through the reporters and spectators.

"Is it over?" Mike shouted.

"Yeah. We got the charges dism——"

"I found the apartment."

Ben instantly knew what he was talking about. "That's great. Have you told Chief Blackwell?"

"No. I came to see you first."

"Me? Why me?"

"Because I found this." Mike dangled the Utica Greens key chain in Ben's face. "I found a lot of other crap, too. Really sickening stuff. There's no question about it now. The chicken-hawk is not dead. He's alive and well and he's planning to kill Abie." Mike shoved the key chain back into a paper evidence bag. "One of these keys is labeled C-D-Y-S-K. Didn't you tell me the country-club board members were the only ones who had keys to the caddyshack?"

"No," Ben said. "I told you that's how it was ten years ago. After the murder, they restricted access. Now the only one who has a key is"—a sudden pallor washed across his face—"the grounds manager."

"Who?"

"Mitch. Mitch Dryer."

Mike grabbed Ben's shoulders. "Then he's our man. Do you know where he is?"

Ben tried to answer, but found that his voice had left him.

"Did you hear what I asked? This is important!"

Ben finally managed to choke out the words. "I just gave him my address. So he could drop by my apartment."

"Where Abie is?"

"Where Abie is," Ben echoed. "And Christina. And Joey."

Wonderful. As if she didn't have enough to do. Christina wedged the bottle under her chin and gripped the baby tightly. Abie was in the next room working a puzzle; he would surely be all right for a few more minutes. She pushed off the sofa and opened the door. "Yes?"

"You don't know me," the nice-looking young man on the other side of the door said, "but your friend Ben Kincaid does. My name is Mitch Dryer. And I have something for you. For all of you."

* 72 *

"Come on in," Christina said.

Mitch lifted a large cardboard box filled with paper and entered the room.

"I could use the company of another adult," Christina added. "Do you by any chance know what *seven, eight* is?"

"I . . . beg your pardon?"

"You know. *Five, six, pick up sticks.* But I can't remember what *seven, eight* is."

"Well," Mitch hedged, "it's been a while for me. . . ."

"Yeah. Me, too. Say, don't you work at the country club?"

"That's right," he said. "How did you know?"

"Oh, I remember seeing your name in Ben's notes. What brings you here?"

"Ben asked me to sort through a few million pieces of paper and look for connections between board members and foreign countries, especially Peru. But when I reported back, he said he was too busy and told me to bring the stuff to you."

"That's my Ben all right." She nodded toward the north wall. "Put the box down there. I'll get to it as soon as the baby sleeps. If he sleeps."

"Being difficult, is he? Here, why don't you let me try?"

"Sure."

Christina passed the baby to Mitch. A strange tingling sensation trickled up and down her spine. Now, that's odd, she thought. She watched Mitch gently rock the baby in his arms. He was good with Joey. So why did she feel so uneasy?

She shrugged it off. Probably some weird offshoot of unrequited maternal instincts. She was becoming attached to the

438

baby, so she didn't want anyone else to hold him. "You said you brought something?"

"Oh, right." Still cradling the baby in one arm, he reached into his back pocket. "A new pacifier." The pacifier was shaped like a bushy black mustache, so that when he popped it into the baby's mouth . . .

"Was this Ben's idea, too?" Christina asked.

"Uh, yeah. How'd you know?"

"It's so Ben. Practical jokes at the expense of an infant."

He laughed. "Oh. I have something for Abie, too. Uh, where is he, anyway?"

Christina felt the tingling sensation again. He knew Abie was here? That seemed odd.

"It's a pennant," Mitch said as he pulled it out of the box. "You know, to hang on his wall. I understand he's a major Drillers fan."

The hairs on the back of Christina's neck stood on end. He shouldn't know that.

"I heard he lost his Drillers cap recently, so I thought, what the heck. He might like this."

"I'm sure he would," Christina said, forcing herself to smile. He shouldn't know that, either.

But she knew who would.

"I'm surprised Ben told you Abie was here. We . . . think someone may be looking for him."

"You mean that sick pervert? The child molester? God, I hate him."

"You know him?"

"No, I just mean—I hate the idea. Of taking advantage of children like that. Torturing them. Forcing them to do . . . things they don't want to do."

Christina stole a quick glance at the bedroom door. Abie was not visible in the open passageway. "I understood this man was very nice to his captives."

"Oh sure. Buy them an ice-cream cone. Take them to Celebration Station. Then rip off their clothes and make them wish they'd never been born."

That was it. No one else could have known about

Celebration Station. That detail had been deliberately left out of the papers.

He was the one.

"Here," Christina said, "why don't you let me take Joey off your hands?"

Mitch pulled the baby away. "Oh, he's no trouble."

"No, I insist."

"Really, he's fine."

"No." She laid her hands firmly on the baby. "Look, he's practically asleep. Please." Christina took the pacifier out of Joey's mouth and took him back into her arms. *"Merci."*

"So . . . where is Abie, anyway?"

"You know," she said, trying to keep her voice even, "the funny thing is, Abie isn't even here right now." Please God, let him stay in the bedroom!

"He isn't? But I understood—"

"He was, but—his mother came and got him."

"His mother?" Mitch's head tilted to one side. "I saw his mother in the courtroom."

"Really?" She laughed nervously. "Well, you know how these rich women are. She probably left him with a Swedish au pair."

"That's hard to believe," Mitch said slowly.

"What do you mean? That I'm lying?"

"No, of course not. I just can't believe that even that rich bitch would leave Abie with a stranger when some maniac is looking for him." His lips curled. "Next she'll probably lock him in the closet."

"I—I beg your pardon?"

"She'll lock him in the closet, because he's been bad. Naughty. And he'll scream and cry and beg to be let out. But she won't let him out."

"I don't under—"

"He'll scream, 'Mommy! Please let me out. *Please.*'" Mitch's face was transformed from that of a man to that of a scared little boy. "'I'm sorry I was bad! *I'll do anything to make up for it!*' And then his daddy will say, 'Perhaps, son. But first you must be punished.'"

Christina tried to maintain a poker face. "Well, I'd better put the baby down for his nap. If you'll excuse me—"

"What?" Mitch's face altered again, yanked back to the present. "I'm sorry, I don't know what I was thinking about. I'll go."

Christina smiled, relieved. "I'll be sure to tell Ben you came by. . . ."

And then a small figure appeared in the bedroom doorway.

"Can you help me?" Abie asked, pouting. "I can't figure out where this puzzle piece goes."

Mitch's face contracted slowly. "But . . ."

Abie scanned the room, first Christina, then Mitch. He stared at Mitch so hard, Christina could almost hear his thoughts. Add a fuzzy red wig. A fake pair of glasses. And—

And then Abie screamed.

In a split second Christina raced between Mitch and Abie. She hit the coffee table, knocking it over. The phone hit the floor; the receiver spilled out of the cradle.

Mitch lunged for her, but stumbled over the table. Christina pushed Abie back into the bedroom. She slammed the door behind them—

Too late. Mitch's foot was wedged in the door.

"You lied to me," Mitch said. His voice was dark and heavy. "You bitch. You're just like all the other lying bitches in the world." He threw his shoulder against the door.

Christina held back the door with all her might. But she knew she couldn't hold him off for long. He was far stronger and heavier than she was.

"Don't let him in," Abie said, sobbing. "Don't let him hurt me."

Christina lifted her shoe and brought the heel down hard on Mitch's foot. Mitch screamed, then jerked back his foot. Christina slammed the door the rest of the way shut, then locked it.

An instant later Mitch threw his weight against the other side of the door. The thin worn plywood shuddered and bowed, but held for the moment.

"You think that's going to keep me out? You filthy whore! You're just like all the rest."

She heard him remove something from his coat. An instant later the tip of a steely knife protruded through the door.

"You're going to be punished," Mitch bellowed. "All of you. That bad boy Abie. That boy baby. And you, you stupid bitch, prancing around in your short skirt, showing yourself to him whenever you can."

She heard him panting as he thrust his knife through the door once again. "You're all going to be punished."

* 73 *

"Hurry!" Ben shouted. He was leaning out of the passenger seat, hovering over Mike as he drove. "Can't this thing go any faster?"

"I'm doing the best I can," Mike muttered, clutching the wheel. "Aren't you the one who normally complains that I drive too fast?" He barreled the Trans Am up the entrance ramp and hit I-244 doing eighty. Once he made it into the fast lane, he pulled his flasher out of the seat divider and snapped it onto the roof of his car. A second later the siren was squealing and cars began to clear out of the way.

"I should've seen this coming," Ben muttered. "The clues were right in front of me. Mitch told me he specially requested the assignment to oversee the caddyshack. Natch. Like you told me—perverts always try to finagle jobs that will put them into contact with kids. What's more, he told me he hated Rutherford's guts. That must be at least part of the reason why he's singled out Abie."

"Gimme the handset," Mike commanded. Ben did as he was told.

A few moments later a voice squawked on the other end. "Headquarters."

"Marty? Mike. I want two squad cars immediately. More if you can get them." He gave her Ben's address. "Any idea how long?"

"I'm not sure, Mike. All the rovers in the area are checking out a reported shooting at the Route 66 Café."

"Damn it, this is an emergency!"

He heard the klickety-klack of buttons on the other end. "I'll put out the word."

"But how long?" There was a short pause. "Damn!" Mike threw the handset across the car, narrowly missing Ben's head. "We'll get there before they do."

Ben removed Mike's car phone from the glove box. He had no idea how to work it. "Get me an outside line."

Mike punched in the access codes, then Ben dialed a local number. His number.

"Busy signal." He looked at Mike grimly. "I don't think Christina would be talking. The phone must be off the hook."

Mike's hands tightened on the wheel. Ben felt the car surge even faster.

They sped past Peoria, watching the other cars pull over onto the shoulder. It would still be several more minutes before they arrived. And there was no telling how long Mitch had been there already.

Ben tried another number. After a second he heard: "Hello?"

"This is Ben. Who's this, Jami?"

"Close. Joni. Hey, Booker told me you two talked. Thanks for—"

"I don't have time for this now," Ben said. "Look, Christina's in my apartment."

"I know. You sly fox, you."

"Do you know if she's had any visitors?"

"I was on the stairs playing cards about ten minutes ago when some hunky dude went up to your apartment."

"Tall? Dark hair? Gray eyes?"

"That's the one."

Ben winced. Mitch Dryer was there.

"Hey, is something wrong? Do you want me to go over there?"

"No. Definitely do not go over there. Christina is in great danger. I need to get a message to her." If it's not already too late.

"Just a sec." The line was muffled for a moment. "Booker says he'll go."

"Booker is at your place now? With your parents?"

"Well . . ." She coughed. "The rest of the family is at the movies right at the moment. . . . Anyway, he says he'll go."

"I don't think that's safe."

"Look, she'll be a lot safer with Booker there than she would be alone. What's the message?"

Ben clenched his teeth. He hated to do this, but she was right. Christina alone wouldn't stand a chance. "Just tell her that he's the one. Without tipping the guy off. We don't want him to go ballistic." If he hasn't already. "And tell her to get the kids out of there. And herself."

"Got it."

"Remember, don't tip the man off."

"Don't worry. Booker is a master of subtlety."

"Look, I still don't think—"

It was too late. The line was dead.

"So what's the word?" Mike asked.

Ben stared ahead at the highway. "Drive like hell," he muttered, clutching the dash.

* 74 *

"You're just making it worse for yourselves," Mitch shouted through the closed, locked bedroom door. "If I hurt myself getting in there, it'll be a lot worse for you."

Christina pushed Abie into the far corner, away from the door.

"Did you hear me?" His voice dripped with contempt. "I have a knife! I'm going to cut you open. I'll cut you in the gut and slash you apart, bit by bit, so you'll die slow."

He paused. Christina waited to hear what venomous threats came next.

"Did you hear me? I'm going to punish you! And I'm going to do the kiddies first! I'll make you watch. *Do you hear me?*"

Abie was terrified. His eyes and nose were running, his limbs were shaking. He clutched at Christina's waist, and began to make a low murmuring sound: "No, no, no, no, no . . ." Christina motioned for him to remain quiet.

"Did you hear me? I'm going to rub your nose in their blood, you fucking whore!"

Christina gripped Abie's shoulder.

"Fine. You asked for it. Here I come."

Christina held her breath. She heard Mitch cross the room, then, seconds later, she heard the front door buzzer. After a short pause, the buzzer sounded again, even more insistently than before.

"All right," Mitch whispered through the locked door, "I'm going to see who's at the door. Remember, I still have the knife. If I hear so much as a peep out of you, he'll be . . . a dead ringer!" Mitch laughed hysterically.

Christina bent down and peered through the crack in the door. The gap between the door and the jamb was slightly larger than usual, probably because of the aged and warped wood. She couldn't see the whole living room, but she could get a narrow view of the front door.

Mitch walked to the door and opened it. Christina was surprised to see a large black teenager standing there.

"Yes?" Mitch said.

"I's here for Christina," the boy said. "Where is she?"

Christina held her tongue. She wanted to cry out, but she knew Mitch's knife was only inches from the boy's throat.

"Christina? Oh, she isn't in right now. She went . . . shopping."

The strapping teenager peered down with an icy glare. "My Joni told me she'd be here."

"Your . . . Joni? Oh—she must be the lass I passed on the stairs. I admire your taste. She's quite a looker."

"She's taken," he grunted.

"Oh, well, yes. Of course she is." There was a protracted pause as the two stared down one another. "Well, when Christina returns, I'll tell her you came by—"

"Isn't that her purse?"

Through the door, Christina saw the boy push Mitch back and enter the room, slamming the door behind him.

"Uh, no. Actually, that's . . . my purse."

"Yours?" Booker walked to the center of the room. He saw the overturned table, the spilled diaper bag, the phone off the hook. "What—"

Christina saw Mitch lift his knife high into the air. She screamed. Booker whirled around, just an instant too late. Mitch wrapped his arm around Booker's neck and pulled his head back. The knife plunged into his chest, just beneath the left shoulder. Blood began to ooze out of the wound. A hollow popping noise came out of Booker's mouth.

Mitch removed the knife. Almost instantaneously, Booker's body shuddered as if he were going into shock. He dropped to the floor, eyes closed, blood gurgling out of the wound and drenching the hardwood floor.

Mitch stepped on top of Booker's body. He raised the knife back into the air. . . .

"No!" Christina shouted. "Help! Someone help!"

Mitch looked toward the closed bedroom door. "You stupid cunt. You're peeking." He marched to the locked door. Christina fled to the other side of the room.

"You've put this off long enough," Mitch shouted. "It's time for you to be punished." There was a brief pause, then suddenly, the door bowed forward. The splitting of wood sounded like the crackling of thunder. The door gave, but it did not quite break.

Not yet.

Christina knew the door wouldn't last much longer. She pushed Abie toward the closet.

"We're going to have to split up," she said.

"No!" Abie started to wail. "Don't leave me alone. He'll kill me! He'll—"

"Abie, snap out of it!" She grabbed his shoulders and shook him. "We don't have time for this. I'll keep that man away from you, but you have to take care of the baby."

Abie's eyes were wide. "Me?"

"Yes." She stood on the lower shelf of the closet and knocked open the panel that led to the roof, her meditation retreat and stargazing sanctuary. "Can you climb up there?"

"I—I think so."

They were interrupted by another clap of thunder. Mitch crashed against the door. The door was buckling down the middle.

"I can make it," Abie said. He stepped onto the lower shelf, knocking a pile of books onto the floor.

Christina boosted him as best she could, but she was only five-foot-one herself. Stretching as far as possible, Abie reached into the hole in the roof and pulled himself through.

"Now take Joey." Christina passed the baby up through the passage, but as soon as he left her arms, he began to cry.

She pulled the mustache pacifier out of her pocket. "Here. Shove this in his mouth. And be very quiet!"

As soon as Abie had the pacifier, she closed the panel,

blocking off the passage. She ran back into the bedroom and opened the window.

Not a second too soon. Mitch hit the door running, and this time the aged wood split apart. He pounded the splintered wood a few times with his fist, clearing a passageway.

Christina desperately looked around the room, searching for some kind of weapon. A rattle? A baby-blue blanket? Ben's CDs? It was hopeless.

And much too late.

"Here I am," Mitch said as he stepped through the door, knife at the ready. "As promised."

* 75 *

But where the hell is the boy? Mitch thought as he entered the bedroom. That was the problem with little boys. They were always trying to get away, trying to escape their punishment. But that wasn't right. It wasn't fair.

"Where is he?" Mitch snarled.

That bitch, that whore—Christina, was it?—ran to the opposite side of the bed, her long red hair trailing behind.

Mitch's mother had had red hair. At least he thought she did. Everything was black in the closet.

Please help me, Mommy. Please!

"I said, where is he?" Mitch leaped onto the bed. "Under here?" Mitch jumped up and down like a madman on a trampoline. If Abie had been under the bed, he'd have been crushed.

"What did you do with my boy?" Mitch bellowed.

"He isn't here," Christina said breathlessly. "He's gone."

Mitch slowly walked across the bed. "You're lying again. I saw him. Where could he have gone?"

"Out the window. He climbed down. Just like a little monkey. He's probably a mile away now."

Mitch jumped off the bed and ran to the window. Christina quickly scurried to the opposite corner.

He surveyed the distance to the ground. "Not possible. You're lying."

"No I'm not. He's gone."

"The fall would've killed him."

"He didn't jump. He . . . climbed."

"On what?"

"I . . . lowered him out the window. With a bedsheet."

Mitch paused a moment. "Where's the sheet?"

"He took it with him. He—"

"Shut up, you liar." Mitch brandished the knife again. "I hate liars. Lying is a sin. Liars have to be punished."

"But why—"

"It's not nice to tell lies. It's not nice to tell secrets. You have to keep the family's secrets. Otherwise, you have to be punished."

"I don't know what you're talking about. Look, you're probably not an evil person. You need help. Just put that knife away, and I promise you I'll—"

"There's nothing wrong with me!" Mitch screamed. *"You have to be punished!"*

He dove across the bed toward her, knife extended. Christina jumped to the side, avoiding him by inches. She raced for the door, but he scrambled across the bed and beat her there. He grabbed her arm while running and swung her against the opposite wall.

She hit the wall face-first. Her eyelids fluttered, then she fell to the floor in a heap.

She didn't get up. She didn't move.

Mitch kicked her in the side. She appeared to be unconscious. At least.

She would have to die, but first things first. Where the hell was the boy?

Mitch scanned the room. The window was an impossibility. But if not there . . . ?

He noticed the closet door was open.

The boy was in the closet.

How appropriate.

Mitch ran into the closet and pushed away the hanging clothes. "Got you!"

There was no one there. But how was that possible? Where could Abie be? And what about that baby?

He saw the books in a mess on the floor. That was odd. The rest of the apartment seemed very tidy, as if it had recently been cleaned. What could that mean?

And then he heard it. Crying. A baby's cry.

And it was coming from above him.

On the roof.

Mitch smiled. He stepped onto the lower shelf and knocked the roof panel out of place. "Olly olly oxen free!"

* 76 *

Abie screamed.

"Peek-a-boo!" Mitch thrust his head through the passage. "I see you."

Clutching Joey in his arms, Abie scrambled to the far side of the eave. Unfortunately, it was less than six feet wide; there was almost nowhere to go.

"You've been a bad boy, Abie."

"I have not!" Tears streamed down Abie's face. "You're bad. You told me . . . bad things."

"That's not true, Abie. I loved you."

"You did not."

"All I ever wanted was what's best for you. For us."

"Then get away from me!"

"Abie . . . is that any way to talk? Remember what fun we had at Celebration Station? We could've had fun like that again. But no, you had to be a bad little boy. A weak, nasty bad little boy." His teeth locked together. "I bet you wet your bed, too."

"I do not!"

"And I bet you like to watch your mother when she parades around in her underwear. When she's . . . nice to you. I bet you like to touch yourself when no one else is around."

"Liar!"

"You don't have to be dirty forever, Abie. It's not too late. I can . . . cleanse you."

"Get away from me!" Abie kicked at Mitch's hands gripping the opening. "I don't want anything to do with you.

You—you're sick! That's what my daddy says. You're a pervert."

Mitch's eyes narrowed to two black slits. "Fine. Then we'll just proceed to your punishment. Do you want to give me the baby, or do you want it to die in your arms?"

Abie pressed Joey close to him. "Stay away from us! Help! *Help!*"

"Too late," Mitch murmured. "Here I come."

Mitch pulled his other arm through the opening, pushed himself up—

Then cried out in pain.

"Aaaaah!"

Christina rammed the book into Mitch's crotch again. Not subtle, but it was all she could come up with on the spur of the moment. The discolored lump on her forehead throbbed. She had been groggy, nearly unconscious, but hearing Abie scream brought her back around. She was functioning, though mostly on impulse power, and she doubted her newfound strength would endure.

Mitch peered down into the closet. "What in the—"

She hit him again. He cried out.

"You goddamn fucking little *bitch!*"

All at once Mitch came tumbling down the closet. He fell on top of Christina, pinning her. His knife spun across the floor.

Christina tried to crawl away. He grabbed her hair and jerked her back.

"I don't need that to punish you," he growled.

Christina kicked him in the shin, then reached out with her fingers toward his eyeballs. Mitch jerked his head back, but her nails scratched his cheek. Enraged, he swung his hand around at her head but missed.

"Help!" Christina shouted. *"Someone help—"*

Mitch clapped his hand over her mouth. Christina bit him. Mitch howled; she sank her teeth in all the deeper. He wrapped his free hand around her throat. Together, they collided into the wall.

Mitch jerked his hand free. Pinpricks of blood showed

where Christina's teeth had been. Mitch looked at the wound and his face turned ashen. Reaching out with the speed of a cobra, he grabbed Christina by the back of the neck and slammed her head against the wall.

Christina's resistance faded with the impact. Her legs wobbled. Mitch twisted her hair around his hand to hold her up and slapped her face, hard. She tried to twist away, but he was still clenching her hair.

"Please—" she gasped.

"Shut up." He brought the flat of his hand back and hit her again. "You should've stayed out of my way, you redheaded whore."

"I couldn't let you hurt my babies," Christina whispered, slurring her words. She was barely conscious.

"You're all alike," Mitch spat back. "You pretend you care, but you don't. You let the daddies do whatever they want. You pretend you don't hear when the baby is screaming. You let him be punished. Well, now it's time for you to be punished."

He reared back his hand, this time balled up in a fist. It hit Christina's face with a sickening impact. She fell to the floor with a thud.

"Dirty cunt," Mitch murmured. He saw his knife lying where it had fallen on the floor and picked it up. "Now you're going to wish you hadn't been bad. You're going to wish you hadn't been born." He straddled her body, clutched her neck with his free hand, and raised his knife into the air.

A gunshot whistled through the room. It missed, but it still attracted Mitch's attention. "Wha—"

"Drop the weapon!" the voice from the living room commanded.

"No!" The knife began to plummet.

Another gunshot rang out. This time the bullet caught Mitch in the chest. He fell backward, toppling off Christina and onto the floor.

Mike ran into the room, his gun clutched in both hands. Ben entered just a step behind.

"Christina!" Ben ran to her side. "Oh, my God! Are you . . . ?"

Christina turned her head minutely to one side. "No." Her lower lip was cracked and bleeding. "I'll be all right. Get the kids."

"The kids! Where—"

"Lieutenant Morelli!" Abie came scrambling down from the roof as best he could with the baby carefully clutched in his arms. "I knew you'd come! I knew you'd save us!"

"Abie!"

The boy ran to Mike and almost threw his arms around him, before he remembered the baby. He held Joey up for Mike.

"Oh, gee, I don't—oh, what the hell." Mike took the crying bundle into his arms, and Abie wrapped himself around Mike's legs.

"I knew you'd come," Abie repeated, gasping and sobbing. "I knew you would."

"Well . . ." Mike's expression was torn between embarrassment and relief. "Sorry I didn't make it sooner." He patted the boy on the head, then snuggled Joey close against his face.

Ben gazed at this heartwarming tableau, then exchanged a meaningful look with Christina.

With the two faces pressed together like that, it was impossible to miss the resemblance.

FIVE

*   *

The Father's Face

* 77 *

Ben stared out his bedroom window, gazing at the illuminated Tulsa skyline. In the few years he'd lived here, he'd learned to love this place. What a crazy town. Culture and cowboys, hoedowns and Holy Rollers. He loved it all. Even the North Side. An acquired taste, perhaps. But at the moment he felt so good, he could appreciate anything.

Christina had mended nicely, and Joni's boyfriend, Booker, was recovering. He was going to have a stiff shoulder for a while, but he'd pull through. Best of all, Leeman Hayes was free, truly free, for the first time in ten years.

Ben was straightening the bow tie on his rented tuxedo when his mother poked her head through the still-smashed bedroom door. "I heard a car pull up outside." Joey was cradled in her arms. She had shown up just a few hours after all the excitement. Turned out she hadn't gone home—she'd just gone shopping. Thought she'd teach him a little lesson in mother appreciation, Ben suspected. Just as well she wasn't here, given what had transpired that day.

"It's probably Christina," Mrs. Kincaid said.

Ben groaned.

"Now, Benjamin. That's not very seemly."

"Easy for you to say. You're not going to the annual banquet of the Tulsa Past Lives Society."

"If you didn't want to go, why did you agree?"

"I didn't. Jones was the one she suckered into it."

"So why are you going?"

"Well, when Jones agreed to look after Joey that first day, he said I'd owe him a big favor."

459

"And?"

"This is it."

"Well, I for one am glad you're going out with her."

"Mo-*ther*, I think you've still got the wrong idea."

Mrs. Kincaid strolled back to the living room, smiling all the way.

There was a knock on the front door. To his surprise, Ben found not Christina, but Ernie Hayes. With Leeman.

"I hope we're not botherin' you," Ernie said. "I'da called, only I didn't know your number."

"That's all right," Ben said. "Is anything wrong?"

"Land sakes, no. Everything's fine. Thanks to you. I cain't thank you enough for taking my son's case."

"Well," Ben said, "you had a lot to do with that decision."

A sly grin played on Ernie's face. "Why, Mr. Kincaid. I don't know what you're talkin' about."

"Uh-huh. Can I get you—"

"Oh, no. We jus' come by for a minute. It was all my Leeman's idea." He pushed Leeman forward.

Leeman extended his arms. He was holding a record album. "You," he said.

"Me? You mean . . . *for* me?" Ben took the well-worn album and examined it. Beethoven's Fifth. Hans Schmidt-Isserstedt and the Vienna Philharmonic. 1966.

"Oh, no," Ben said. "I can't accept it."

Leeman pressed the album back into Ben's hands. *"You."*

"But—it's so rare. You'll never be able to replace it. It's a one-of-a-kind."

Leeman smiled, side to side, ear to ear. It was the happiest Ben had ever seen him. "You . . . too," he said.

Ben felt a distinct itching in his eyes. "Well . . . thank you. Thank you very much."

Leeman nodded, then he and his father turned to go.

Ben returned to his bedroom and put away the album. On second thought—why not? He put the album on his turntable. He might squeeze in the first movement before he had to leave.

A few minutes later his mother was back in the doorway.

"Your date is here."

"Mo-*ther*!" He walked into the living room. "I told you already—"

Ben stopped short. And gaped.

Christina was standing in the middle of the room. She was wearing a black strapless gown with a beaded bodice and hem, long white gloves, and a strand of luminous pearls. Her shoes matched, her earrings matched—even her purse matched. Her long hair was elegantly swirled above her head.

"Christina," he said breathlessly. "You're . . . beautiful."

She batted her eyes. "Thought you'd never notice."

"But—your clothes!"

Christina nodded. "Your mother and I finally went shopping." She smoothed a wrinkle in her velvet gown. "She has such *savoir-vivre*. You should let her dress you, Ben. She's the greatest. Did my hair and face, too. Like my makeup?"

Ben scrutinized her radiant face. The bruises were barely visible. "Well, gee." Ben took Christina's arm. "I guess we'll be going, Mother."

"Of course you will." Mrs. Kincaid held the door open for them. "You children have fun. But don't be out late. And don't drink too much. And stay away from strangers."

When Ben returned to his apartment that night, he found his mother packing her suitcase, hanging bag, and makeup kit.

"You're leaving?"

She meticulously folded a dress and laid it in the hanging bag. "I . . . assumed you would want me to."

"Oh."

"During the trial, you needed someone to help. But now I'm sure I'd just be in the way."

"Oh." Ben helped her zip the well-stuffed bag closed.

"Are they going to arrest that man? Rutherford? The father?"

"I'm sure they will. Hard not to, after he confessed on the record."

"What about his country-club friends? They must have known."

"Possibly. Pearson must've suspected. After all, he secured

the adoption and he saw Maria Alvarez at the club. But he kept quiet all those years. And Bentley figured it out. That was why he searched Mitch's locker and took the incriminating red baseball cap. Hell with the victims—he just wanted to protect the club. And its members."

"Oh, yes." Mrs. Kincaid rearranged what looked like an infinite supply of cosmetics. "They always protect their own."

"That's why Mitch was hired in the first place. He told me he got his job as manager shortly after the murder. They needed someone to handle the police and the media. Someone to cover up the dirt."

"And covering up the first crime bred the next."

"True. If it hadn't been for that, Mitch would've never come to the country club and would've never met the Rutherfords."

"People often pay horrible prices for seemingly small mistakes. It isn't fair, but that's the way it works out."

Mrs. Kincaid snapped her other bags closed and set them on the floor. "There. That's done."

"Are you taking Joey with you?" Ben asked.

She offered a weak smile. "I assumed you would want me to. I'll send someone for him." She sighed. "It won't be easy, caring for an infant again after all these years. But someone has to do it." She hesitated a moment. "And I know you've never wanted to have much to do with your family."

True enough, but the words still cut like a knife. She had always had that talent—the ability to utter a seemingly innocent remark that would slice his heart out.

"Do you think your friend Mike knows?" his mother asked.

"No, I'm certain he doesn't. Mike is incredibly bright, but he has a gigantic blind spot when it comes to Julia. I think that extends to the baby."

"Are you going to tell him?"

"Well . . ."

"A man has a right to know he has a son."

"I don't know. Not now. Maybe later. When the time seems right."

Mrs. Kincaid nodded. "It's a serious responsibility, being a father."

That was abundantly clear. What was it about fathers, anyway? Fathers and sons. What made them do the things they did? Ernie Hayes, who would pull any trick to take care of his boy. Harold Rutherford, who wanted to be a good father but couldn't figure out how. And then, of course, there was Mitch, and the permanent horror his father had visited upon him.

And Ben's father. Or fathers, if you counted Jack Bullock. Not that it mattered now.

"I left something for you." His mother walked into the living room and picked up an envelope resting on the piano. "It's that picture of you and your father. You threw it down when . . . well." She held out the photograph. "I thought you might like to have it."

Ben took the snapshot from her shaking hand. He stared at the strong proud father and the little boy who loved him so much. Ben didn't know either of them. They were strangers.

Ben's mother stood awkwardly in the hallway. "Benjamin, I know you won't like this, but . . ." She shifted her weight to the other foot. "I've been living here in this . . ." Her hand waved spasmodically about the room. "Whatever. I think I've been very brave about it, but—enough is enough." She took another envelope out of her purse. "I've written you a check, and I want you to take it."

"No."

"Benjamin, be reasonable!"

"If my father had wanted me to—"

"Ben, you don't know what you're *talking about*!" Her head snapped back suddenly, as if she herself was surprised at the sudden intensity of her voice.

"I'm sorry, Mother." Ben looked down, pushing away the money. "No."

She sighed heavily, and for the first time Ben thought he saw all her sixty-six years etched in her face. "Well, if you won't change your mind, I guess there's nothing more I can do for you."

She lifted her luggage and started to go.

"Wait."

She stopped.

Ben reached out to her. "There is something."

She turned. Her eyes widened. "Really?"

"Yes." Ben put down her bags, took her trembling hand, and guided her to a chair. "Tell me about my father."

Acknowledgments

Once again I have been fortunate to draw on the expertise of others in writing this novel. I want to thank Linda Barry for sharing her wisdom gained from years of experience working with developmentally disabled children; Judge Thomas S. Crewson, for telling me about the real Leeman Hayes; Walter Booker Martin, Jr., Gang Specialist for the Midwest City Police Department, for putting me in the know and in contact with Oklahoma youth gangs; and Arlene Joplin, of the U.S. Attorney's Office, for keeping me straight on criminal procedure.

I want to acknowledge my sources for much of the historical background material in the book: "The Court Martial of Johnson C. Whittaker" and "The Blacks in Oklahoma," both by Burkhard Bilger and both published in the splendid regional magazine *Oklahoma Today*, edited by the incomparable Jeanne Devlin; and *Death in the Promised Land*, by Scott Ellsworth and published by the Louisiana State University Press.

Thanks to Cecil Adams of *The Straight Dope* for bringing autoerotic asphyxiation to my attention. What a sheltered life I've led.

Thanks also to Michael Stipe of R.E.M., who incidentally was born on the same day, same year, that I was. A fateful day in history.

I want to thank Gail Benedict for her help with the manuscript; Kathy Redwood for her nonpareil secretarial skills; and Drew Graham and Esther Perkins for agreeing to read and comment upon an early draft of the manuscript. Finally, I have to thank my family, Kirsten and Harry and Alice, for putting up with the days Daddy spent on the road, the nights Daddy spent staring blankly at a computer screen, the three A.M. feedings during which Daddy held the bottle with one hand and revised his manuscript with the other, and so forth.

Any cyber-savvy readers who would like to drop me a line are encouraged to do so. I'd love to hear from you. My e-mail address is: willbern@mindspring.com.

By the way, Christina really did buy Ben a brick at the zoo. It's by the elephant house. Check it out.

—William Bernhardt

Ben Kincaid was late getting to his office the next morning, not that that was unusual. What was unusual was that his entire office staff—Christina, Jones, and Loving—were standing shoulder to shoulder just inside the front door waiting for him.

"Let me guess," Ben said. "You're on strike. Look, I don't blame you, but until some of our clients pay their bills—"

He stopped. The huge ear-to-ear grins on their faces told him that wasn't it. "Okay, what, then? Is today my birthday or something?"

"Where have you been?" Christina said, wrapping her arm around his shoulder and pulling him into the office.

"At Forestview. I had to take Joey to school, and then there was this big sign-up for the spring bake sale—"

"Never mind that." Christina pushed him into a chair while

the other two huddled around. "We've been trying to get hold of you all morning."

"Why?"

Jones leaned forward. "I got a call the minute I came into the office, Boss."

"And?"

"The mayor wants you!"

Ben fell deep into thought. Was this about that incident with his daughter at Forestview last Friday? It was just a little bump. And she ran into him…

"Can you believe it, Skipper?" Loving grabbed him by the shoulders and shook him. "The mayor wants you!"

"That's nice…I guess."

Christina cut in. "Ben, do you even know what we're talking about?"

"Well, actually…no."

"The biggest cause célèbre to hit Tulsa in years, and you're totally clueless. What were you doing last night?"

"Well, let me see. I had soup for dinner, then I read *Goodnight Moon* to Joey about eight thousand times…"

She slapped her forehead. "I can't believe it. Everyone in the state watched the chase last night. Except, of course, you."

"Chase? What are you talking about?"

"Ben, the mayor has been charged with murder."

"Murder!" The light slowly dawned. "And he wants me to get him off?"

Christina and Jones and Loving all exchanged a glance. "Well," Christina said, "he wants you to represent him, anyway. *Entre nous*, I wouldn't get your hopes up too high on the outcome."

"What do you mean?"

Christina grabbed his arm. "I'll brief you while we drive to the jailhouse."

Because Mayor Barrett had specified that he wanted to see Ben alone, Christina (after considerable protest) agreed to cool her heels outside while Ben went into his cell to talk to him.

"Don't worry about me, Christina," he told her. "I'll be fine."

"I'm not worried about you. I'm worried about us."

"Come again?"

"I'm afraid you'll do something idiotic like not agree to represent him."

"In fact, I do have some reservations..."

"See! It's starting already. You're going to veer off on some wacky ethical tangent, and we're going to go hungry."

"Just let me talk to him. Then we'll see."

She grabbed him by the lapels. "Ben, promise me you'll take this case."

"We'll see."

"Ben!"

"We'll see."

Ben allowed the guard to lead him down the long metallic corridor. Mayor Barrett had the cell at the far end, a private suite, such as it was. A five-by-seven cell, with a bunk bed, a sink, and an open-faced toilet. Not exactly the mayor's mansion.

He was lying on the bottom bunk, his hands covering his face. When he moved them, Ben saw black and red lacerations on his face, and a bandage wrapped around his jaw and the back of his head.

The guard let Ben into the cell, locked the door behind him, then disappeared.

"How do you feel?" Ben asked.

"Better than I have a right to feel."

"My legal assistant told me you were in a traffic accident."

Barrett tried to smile, although between the bruises and the bandages, his face didn't have much give in it. "I crashed into a brick building with four cop cars, two television helicopters, and about half the world watching. Like I said, I'm better off than I have a right to be."

"Jeez. What were you doing?"

"Trying to kill myself," he said, with a matter-of-fact air that caught Ben unaware. "As it was, I didn't even break a bone. Goddamn air bags."

Ben paced nervously around the tiny cell. There was nowhere to sit, so he stood awkwardly by the cell door and contemplated the dominant question.

This was a part of criminal defense work that Ben particularly hated. Most criminal defense lawyers never asked the question. Since defending a client you knew was guilty raised a million ethical difficulties, most lawyers preferred not to inquire.

Ben, however, wanted to know the truth. He wanted to know where he stood. If he was going to put his name and reputation on the line, particularly in what was certain to be a high-profile case, he wanted to know he was doing the right thing. As his old mentor Jack Bullock used to say, he wanted to be on the side of the angels. But with such a horrible, heinous crime, how could he possibly ask?

Barrett sat up suddenly, hands on his knees. "Ben, I want you to know something up front. I didn't do it."

Ben gazed at him, his face, his eyes.

"I did not kill my wife. I did not kill my two precious daughters. How could I?" His eyes began to water, but he fought it back. "I couldn't do anything like that." He stared down at his hands. "I couldn't."

"I've read the preliminary police report. Neighbors say you and your wife had a disagreement yesterday afternoon."

Barrett nodded. "That's right. We did. I'm not going to pretend we didn't." He spread his arms wide. "It was that kind of marriage. We fought sometimes, like cats and dogs. But we still loved each other."

"What was the fight about?"

Barrett shrugged. "I hardly remember."

"The prosecutor will want to know."

"It was something about the kids. She thought I was spoiling them, giving them everything they wanted. Undermining her authority. And not paying enough attention to her. We'd had this argument before."

"How many times?"

He shrugged again. "I don't know. Many."

"Were these fights...violent?"

He twisted his head around. "Violent? You mean, did I hit her? Absolutely not."

"Well, I had to ask."

"Look, I don't know what people are saying about me now, but I would never hurt my wife. Or my girls. They're the most precious things in the world to me." His voice choked. "Were. I couldn't hurt them. Don't you think that if the mayor of the city was a wife beater, it would've come out before now?"

"I suppose." Ben pulled a small notebook out of his jacket pocket and began taking notes. "So you had an argument. Then what?"

"I can barely remember. It's all such a blur. And smashing into a brick wall didn't help."

"Just tell me what you recall. We don't have to get everything today."

"Well, I got mad. That doesn't happen often; most times I can just laugh it off. But this time she really got my goat, suggesting that I was hurting the girls and all. So I stomped out of the house."

"You left?"

"Right. Got in my car and drove away."

"How long were you gone?"

"I don't know exactly. Not long. Maybe an hour. I got a Coke at a Sonic—you can check that if you want—and I started to feel bad. So what if we disagreed on a few minor points. I loved my wife, and I loved my family. I didn't have any business running out like that. A strong man stands up straight and faces the music. So I headed back home."

"What happened when you got there?"

"I was in such a hurry, I left my car on the street and ran into the house. And—"

"Yes?"

He hesitated. "And then...I found...them. What was left of them."

"They were already dead?"

"Oh, yeah." His eyes became wide and fixed. "My wife was spread out like...like some sick human sacrifice. And my little girls..." Tears rushed to his eyes. His hands covered his face.

"I'm sorry," Ben said quietly. "I know this is hard for you."

Barrett continued to cry. His whole upper body trembled.

Ben took a deep breath. He hated this. He felt like a vulture of the worst order, intruding on this man's grief with these incessant questions. Guilty or not, Barrett was clearly grief-stricken.

NAKED JUSTICE
by William Bernhardt
Published by The Ballantine Publishing Group.
Available in bookstores everywhere.